WHAT THEY SAY ABOUT
LIGHTS! CAMERA! DISSATISFACTION...

Kim Cayer is a natural story-teller with a gift for satire and a beautifully-developed sense of humour that beams from every page.

Lights! Camera! Dissatisfaction... follows the adventures and misadventures of Alice Kumplunkem, as she develops from wannabe actress to the beginnings of a new career out of the limelight. Cayer makes excellent use of the first person to keep the narrative both personal and lively.

This wryly funny book, unabashedly Canadian, shines a glaring light on the behind-the-scenes workings of "show biz" in many of its tawdry forms, involving the underpaid extra, barely-paid stage actress, bunny-costumed performer in a children's play, embarrassed swimsuit model, and much more. The writing reveals deftly-drawn characters – from her sceptical mother, to uncaring directors and self-serving agents, right down to her mongrel cat "Lunchpail". The dialogue is pitch-perfect. The style is engaging and refreshingly unpretentious.

The tale ends happily, of course – but we finish it hoping that Alice will have a whole book of future obstacles and successes to tell us about!

John Ambury, Writers and Editors Network

Why couldn't this have been a film script I was asked to read!?

In a straight read-through, I laughed aloud every few minutes. Though not all the book is set in the film business, the portions that are hit right on the mark.

Ridiculous episodes, unusual characters and odd scenarios abound, but as one who has worked on film sets my entire adult life, I'm here to say that this IS the film biz and *Lights! Camera!*

Dissatisfaction... captures it with two thumbs up!
Bruce Pittman, Worthwhile Movies Limited, Award-winning director of films such as Where the Spirit Lives, Kurt Vonnegut's Harrison Bergeron and The La

Lights! Camera! Dissatisfaction... by Kim Cayer is a relentless rollercoaster of a read, where the first person narrative sucks us inexorably into the word of a brash, expletive-spewing, yet oddly endearing character, who – if we but dare to admit it – skates perilously close to our own reality in her daredevil reactions to what life throws at her. Cayer's prose is effortless. This is fiction with the believability of a biography.
Cheryl Antao-Xavier, In Our Own Words Inc., author and publisher

Lights!
Camera!
Dissatisfaction...

Lights!
Camera!
Dissatisfaction...

Kim Cayer

ROUNDFIRE
BOOKS

Winchester, UK
Washington, USA

First published by Roundfire Books, 2014
Roundfire Books is an imprint of John Hunt Publishing Ltd., Laurel House, Station Approach,
Alresford, Hants, SO24 9JH, UK
office1@jhpbooks.net
www.johnhuntpublishing.com
www.roundfire-books.com

For distributor details and how to order please visit the 'Ordering' section on our website.

Text copyright: Kim Cayer 2013

ISBN: 978 1 78279 568 1

All rights reserved. Except for brief quotations in critical articles or reviews, no part of this book may be reproduced in any manner without prior written permission from the publishers.

The rights of Kim Cayer as author have been asserted in accordance with the Copyright, Designs and Patents Act 1988.

A CIP catalogue record for this book is available from the British Library.

Design: Stuart Davies

Printed in the USA by Edwards Brothers Malloy

We operate a distinctive and ethical publishing philosophy in all areas of our business, from our global network of authors to production and worldwide distribution.

CHAPTER ONE

"Look, Paul, I need a line!"

No, I'm not a coke-head. I'm an actor. Name's Alice. I had just come from my latest job as an "extra" in the film business. My stomach was backfiring from too much coffee and edible oil products. Besides that, my hair was breaking off in chunks due to the massive amount of gel, mousse and hairspray I was required to use to maintain the towering bouffant befitting a Bride of Frankenstein. If you ever catch *The Many Brides of Frankenstein*, look for me. I was Bride #18, the last wife he tied the knot with. But no line. Not even the traditional "I do."

I was, to put it elegantly, fed up. Paul tried to appease me. "So this job wasn't the best. But remember March 25th? Doesn't that day make you proud of your profession?"

March 25th? Oh, yes...the day I got meet my idol, Sheila Holt, in person. I should have been just happy seeing her, but no...I had to try and meet her.

When I read in the newspaper that Dame Holt was coming to Toronto to shoot a film, I pestered Paul for weeks to get me a part. Paul is my agent, the owner and manager of "Paul's People". I joined his agency because I knew he didn't have anyone else like me. He mainly handles midgets and magic acts. I'm his only brunette female. And in his way, Paul came through for me. I was hired as an extra in the elevator scene.

There were eight of us crammed into an elevator, but I was in seventh heaven. Sheila Holt stood directly in from of me! Unfortunately, she didn't have any lines. I was dying to hear her speak in that velvety voice I'd heard in so many late-night movies. "Take your hands off me, sailor," she moaned in *Too Many Nights*. "I'm your woman, cowpoke," she'd gushed in *Last Dance*. After a couple of takes, knowing the scene would soon be completed, I got up the nerve to speak to Her Holtness.

"It sure is hot in here. Aren't you hot?" I asked.

Sheila looked at me imperiously, gave a slight nod and looked away.

I pressed on. "I can smell."

Dame Holt swirled her head back in my direction, her eyes blazing. I was mortified. I had meant to say "I can tell," because I could see beads of perspiration on her brow. But the truth was, I could also smell those beads. But I didn't mean to say it! Believe me!

Sheila began shrieking in a most unvelvetine voice. "WHO is this GIRL?? I want her OUT of my sight NOW! NOW, I said!"

One of the assistant directors ran over to me. "What's your name?" he demanded.

"A...Alice Kumplunkem," I stammered.

"I NEVER want to see her on one of MY sets EVER again!" that dame hollered. She was in full swing now. The other extras acted as if they weren't there; eyes staring dead-ahead, bodies motionless. Best acting I'd seen all day, Sheila Holt included.

"I'm afraid you're fired, Miss Kumpluckem," the assistant director officially said.

The elevator suddenly became quite claustrophobic. "'Scuse me, 'scuse me," I mumbled as I squeezed my way past the crew and my fellow extras, who I could tell were grateful I was the one in shit and not them.

I didn't have the heart to tell Paul that I hated Sheila Holt's guts now. Or that I wouldn't be getting paid for that job. "Paul, my best friend's shooting a film in the Bahamas, my boyfriend is in Africa for the next three months, and I get to ride an overcrowded bus forty-five miles out of the city for a four-hour call? Somehow my life doesn't seem as fulfilling as everyone else's."

I was bitter. Bitter, bitter, bitter. But Paul, as usual, didn't seem to take notice. I desperately needed to make him understand that I was unhappy with the direction my career was going.

"Sure, you know best," Paul flippantly tossed off, his mind already moving on to another subject. "You did that western shoot yesterday, didn't you?"

Boy, did I. I played a dead saloon girl, sprawled halfway across the bar and halfway out of my corset, it seemed. My stomach muscles were aching because of the angle in which I'd hung off the bar. And for lunch, I swear that was the worst egg-salad sandwich I've eaten in my life.

I gave Paul a bored nod. "Well," he began, "the word's out that they're in big legal trouble. Film's shut down, no one's getting paid. Seems like quite a few people ended up with food poisoning."

My stomach gave a lurch to remind me I was there. "I had an egg-salad sandwich and some salmon and a bit of some cold macaroni something. Maybe I have poisoning, too." Now I was worried.

"Well, if you're not dead by tomorrow, you'll live," Paul reassured me, before changing the subject again. "Hey, I have some bucks for you. From *Monster Mash*. Shame they had to cut your scene."

They did? Now that made me seethe. The make-up gal dolled me all up to look just like Jamie Lee Curtis. I thought the scene where I got choked with a shower curtain would be my claim to fame. My poor mother, sick with undiagnosable pains and getting gruffer by the minute, had yet to see me in anything. She was suspicious of this "showbiz stuff" and half-suspected I was walking streets for a living. The other half suspected I was dancing in dark smoke-filled taverns. She doesn't even tell her cronies what dear daughter Alice does for a living. Who knows what kind of films the people in Oak Paw, Saskatchewan watch? Not that I do those kind of films, mind you. But Mrs. Kumplunkem will talk endlessly about darling daughter Louise and her five children, and how much they're soaking Welfare for, and the eight puppies Fido had on the couch of their trailer home.

I wanted Mom to be proud of me for SOMETHING, and *Monster Mash* sounded like a film she'd rent for the grandkids. "Paul, I'm getting out of this business. I'm not making it. I made just under ten grand last year. My dental bill alone cost me a thousand bucks. I'm not getting ahead."

Paul gave me a 'how-dare-you-knock-your-dental-bill' look. "That wisdom tooth removal was the best thing that ever happened to your career, I'll have you remember."

He was right. I had just come from the dentist after having my wisdom teeth removed. I crawled into bed and was settling down to cry for a couple days when Paul called. He had an extra job for me. I had to take it. As I said, the dental bill was $1100, rent was due, as was the phone, gas, cable, water, electricity, etc., etc. Paul told me I had to be on set in an hour. What Paul neglected to tell me was what the job entailed.

I was rushed into wardrobe when I arrived and told to put my costume on. Everything was made of wool, including the booties. I wasn't even finished dressing when an assistant director barged in. "You're needed on set NOW," he informed me.

My mouth was aching and I wanted to take one of the painkillers that my doctor had given me. "I'll be right there," I said, amazed at how so few words could feel so painful.

"NOW," the assistant director repeated.

Don't be a druggie, Alice, I thought. *Fight the pain with your mind.* I followed the A.D. onto the set.

The studio was painted to look as if sand dunes went on for miles, and there was enough real stuff on the floor to cover a couple beaches. I looked at all the other hired extras – a regular crowd scene. I couldn't figure out what I was playing. A pioneer? A Depression-era victim? An Oak Paw resident? The sand felt comforting beneath my wool slippers.

"Everyone here?" the director asked. Someone yelled in the affirmative. "Then let's start up the special effects."

An enormous fan slowly started up, sending a gentle breeze my way. A light mist began to fall from a sprinkler system suspended above. *Aahh, that feels so good on my swollen face,* I thought. As soon as I completed the thought though, it began to get rather gusty. I caught a grain of sand in one eye and a huge drop of water in the other.

"I want more!" the director commanded.

"How's this?" the special-effects master shouted back. Suddenly we were enveloped in a combination windstorm/rainstorm. I could barely retain my balance and was buffeting around the other extras.

"Great! Ready to roll?" the director asked.

A man on a scaffold yelled down. "This light has to be readjusted!"

Two young men immediately began climbing the scaffold. I swerved over to where the assistant director was standing. My head was now starting to join my mouth in wedded agony and I decided I wanted my pill after all. Fighting the wind zone was making me dizzy and I almost wiped out when I entered the calm zone. I approached the granter-of-all-wishes. "Please, sir, may I..."

"We're gonna shoot any minute," he prophesized. "Get back on set."

I turned around and got the film crew's point of view. Two hundred extras, all trying to maintain their balance and failing miserably. Pitiful sight. I walked back to the edge of the wind zone and dove in.

Thirty minutes later I risked a quick glance up. Every time I did so, my cheeks were pelted with stinging sand. The electricians were still fixing something. An extra was blown into me. "Watch where you're going!" I snarled. He gave me a surprised look, as I'd blown into him minutes earlier. I knew the pain was making me miserable, not to mention the rain, wind, sand and my wet, itchy clothes. I made another pilgrimage to the edge of the wind. I was about to step into the peaceful world where I could see assorted film crew members sitting on canvas chairs, eating melon, doing crossword puzzles.

"Lights are ready!" the key grip announced. I turned around and rushed back to my place, losing a bootie in the process. I reached my position, grateful that no one noticed my absence. Five minutes later, we still hadn't shot anything.

"Where's the director?" someone important asked.

"In the can," the assistant director solemnly replied.

"Oohhh…" Mr. Important said, as if he were informed the director was meeting with the Pope at that instant.

A few moments later, the director returned and was told the lighting problem had been fixed.

"OK, everybody!" the director yelled at the extras. "Your motive is to get to the other side of the studio." He turned to the camera man. "I want a long, sweeping shot."

"How long?" the camera man asked.

"At least three minutes," the director replied.

"We don't have enough film. I'll have to change reels."

"Camera reload!" the director announced, and went to pour himself a coffee. *Now's my chance,* I thought, and tried to work with the wind as I swayed over to my assistant director. He was very busy chatting up the attractive make-up artist. I was leery of letting her look at me as we were strictly instructed not to wear any cosmetics and as usual, I tried to sneak a little mascara. A girl's gotta have something, doesn't she?

"Do I have time to run to my purse?" I imploringly asked.

"Are you wearing mascara?" the make-up girl asked in a whine.

"No," I lied.

"Then what's that all over your face?" she asked. So much for sneaking mascara to look a BIT attractive.

"We'll be ready in a sec," the A.D. informed me.

"Yeah, hurry up and wait," I said and stormed off. I could see they were not impressed with my attitude but I was starting to not give a royal damn one way or the other. I got back to my spot and decided to have a little cry. By the time the camera was ready to roll, my eyes had swollen shut from the massive bawl I'd granted myself.

After the director had satisfied himself with fourteen takes of his long, sweeping shot, he decided he wanted some close-ups. By this time I looked a mess. My hair was plastered to my head, my lips were chapped and my face looked like I had been holding my breath for 40 minutes. For the first-time ever in the acting world, an actor (namely me) tried their best NOT to get a close-up. I was very unprofessional. I sputtered curses at the film crew and felt very Garbo-ish, crying, "Leave me alone!" The camera, for one day in my life, loved me.

When the movie came out, there were six close-up shots of either me or the Elephant Man, but I don't recall him being on set that day. I even got billing in the film as 'The Ugly Girl'. Paul, for a while, had a lot of casting directors calling him and asking for "that ugly girl." But by the time I got the chance to see them, my face had long lost its swollen look, and no matter how hard I tried, I just couldn't seem to look as ugly anymore. The casting directors would tell me, "You're ugly, but not as ugly as we'd hoped." I turned out to be a flash in the pan. My mother managed to see that flick but she refused to believe that pitiful creature was me. "I never had a kid that homely," she declared. Mom never stuck around for the credits.

"Yeah, Paul, that was glory alright, but I'm serious this time. I'm sick of extra work. I know that's your bread and butter but I am going to refuse it from now on. I mean it."

Paul sat back in his groaning chair and gave me a long, shrewd look. He was an actor in his younger days and I could see he was emoting the 'deep thought' look. I sat under his scrutinizing stare until I thought I would yell "Cut!"

He finally spoke. "OK, Alice. Since you want to speak so

badly, I may have something for you. Five days' work, twenty bucks an hour, plenty of talking. You want it?"

"Yes, Paul!" What did he think I'd been complaining about?

"Alrighty then. You start tomorrow, 9 a.m., at The House of Bull."

* * *

I wanted to speak and I got my wish. I talked non-stop for five days in a role I never wish to repeat. I was a pork chop. It wasn't even an acting job, just some publicity gimmick. I stood in front of The House of Bull handing out flyers advertising the Special of the Day.

"Lamb chops today, folks! $11.95! Come on in to The House of Bull!" I repeated that line about 900 times today. Do you know the kind of looks you get when you're urging people to come into the restaurant at 9 a.m. in the morning? I'd press flyers into their hands and watch them walk away and throw the flyer to the ground. I really tried hard the first couple days but was hurt by some people's reactions to me. Finally I looked at it in perspective and realized I'd react in the same way if I was being accosted by an eight-foot-high pork chop.

The phone rang. "Alice, sweetheart!" said my agent, Paul. "What are you doing?"

"Nothing. Why?"

"I need you for a job tonight. Someone cancelled on me. Can you do it?" he urgently requested.

"Extra work?" I rather hopefully enquired.

"No, publicity work," he answered.

"Paul, I will not be a pork chop ever again. That was the most degrading job ever," I sternly told him.

"No, no...nothing like that. It's for the opening of a play down at The Royal Alex Theatre. *Three Men on a Horse*?"

I quickly considered it. Opening night meant there'd be all

sorts of influential showbiz types there. It might be worth my while. "I'll do it," I said.

I took extra care with my hair and make-up. Looking quite glamorous, I showed up at the theatre and asked for Mr. Empress, the publicity director. He didn't give me a second glance; just told me to get my ass into the costume. It almost sounded like he said, "Get into the ass costume," but I figured he was just speaking too quickly. I walked into the changing room and was greeted by the front end of a horse.

The horse spoke to me. "Finally! You're late, we have to be on the floor now. Get into the back end."

I couldn't believe it. I was a pork chop all week and to top it off, now I was a horse's ass. I may have been in the presence of Al Pacino that night, but I couldn't tell. All I could see were people's feet. I cheered myself up by telling myself that things couldn't get any worse; I was surely at rock bottom. Things had to get better.

And I did find 53 cents in change plus a silver charm that said 'Hollywood, Florida'. Close enough, I thought, and took it as a sign that every cloud has a silver lining.

* * *

Once again, I was sitting dejectedly in Paul's office. He'd called me earlier to tell me some money had come in. Not even the thought of a $200 check could raise my spirits, although Paul's 40-buck commission put him in a voluble mood.

"There's two big films starting on Monday, both using Toronto as New York," Paul enthused. "You know what that means? New York streets, which are always so busy, translates to...? C'mon, you know...Crowd scenes! Lots of extra work! If you really stay in the background, behind a newspaper, wearing sunglasses, out of camera range, then we'll probably be able to book you for a few days." Paul was already counting the dollar signs. I just sat there, glumly looking at him.

"What's the matter? You're not saying anything," Paul eventually noticed.

I acted startled, "Oh, yeah! I forgot! I know how to speak," I said sarcastically.

"So, whaddaya think? Wanna work next week?" Paul asked.

"Yes, Paul, I always want to work. But I don't want to stay OUT of camera range, I want to be right in front of the damn thing. I want to say something!" the broken record repeated. "What am I doing wrong?"

"Well, let's think about that," Paul suggested. "Who's your favorite actress? Who do you admire the most?"

I considered his question. "Hhmmm, Marilyn Monroe is one of my idols. So is Meryl Streep, Drew Barrymore, Susan Lucci, that girl who did three Humble Throat commercials... Pretty well anyone working steady is an idol of mine, Paul."

Paul leaned back in his overstuffed plush leather chair. Every time he shifted in that chair, his girth caused it to let forth a squeal. "Let's see...I could try sending you out on theatre auditions. They're usually at least six weeks work, often more. That's steady work."

"I'll do theatre!" Why didn't he suggest that two years ago, when I'd started in this godforsaken business?

"Doin' theatre is a great way to learn your craft. I'm not knocking it. But I have my reasons for not wanting you to do it. It don't pay. And if it don't pay you, then it sure don't pay me." For a while there, Paul was almost sounding human, but then he remembered his fondness for bucks.

"How little can they pay?" I asked. "Right now, I'm often working four hours a day for ten bucks an hour."

"And sometimes you hit the jackpot and get paid union rates. You've had a couple $300 days. Often in theatre, you'll earn in two weeks what you can make in one day on film." Paul definitely had a point there. I have a pet – a mongrel cat called

Lunchpail. During lean times, either Lunchpail and I share the same can of 'Miss Meow' or he eats what I eat – white rice and popcorn.

Then again, I could use the acting practice. Maybe if I was allowed to work steadily, I'd get to be a better actress and then I'd land that desired speaking role on film. "Paul, let me get just one play. Just for the experience. Then we'll concentrate on film." I came alive for the first time that day. Deep inside, I somehow knew this was a wise career move.

Paul's face looked as if he were chewing a sour antacid pill. Maybe he was. "Oh, alright," he agreed. "I'll see what I can do about lining up some theatre auditions. In the meanwhile, you'll do extra work."

Was he asking me or telling me?

* * *

It had been three weeks since the theatre discussion in Paul's office. During that time, Paul had me working eight days a week. I took that as a sign he was confident I'd land a theatre gig. Before I did though, Paul was going to make damn sure he'd work me for every cent he could get out of me.

I was a New York citizen almost the entire time. Trying to make Paul happy, I was always ducking the camera. Not that we got on camera very much. Most of the time, the 80 background performers set up camp in a vacant parking lot the film company so graciously allotted us. On my fourth day I got wise and brought a lawn chair to work with me.

Paul honored me one day with a visit on set. Of course he had a check for me and needed his $29.70 commission. I saw him approaching my camp, which consisted of my lawn chair, my *Complete Works of Shakespeare* (as I prepared for my theatre career), my Styrofoam coffee cup, and my 'acting bag', which mainly held food, as extras (contrary to popular belief) cannot live on donuts alone.

I didn't bother to get up; I was too bored. Paul was excited though. "I saw George Clooney!" he effused. I shrugged my shoulder in indifference.

"So? I see him every day," I yawned. "The thrill wears off after a while." In all honesty, the closest I'd come to him was 500 feet. The camera was usually on him and I was usually the farthest thing the camera could see, if it could see me at all.

"Alice, you're looking quite tanned," Paul commented on my blistered, thrice-sunburned face. "Must be all this sun you're getting."

Boy, Paul was a real Sherlock Holmes. The extras either sat in the parking lot most of the day or were at work on the street. Either way, we were always in 90-degree Fahrenheit weather. The only shade you got was when you used one of the two Johnny-on-the-Spot washrooms, which got quite rank around 11 a.m.

The heat was beginning to affect Paul. His face had rivers of sweat running down it. "Jeez, it's hot," he noted. "Alice, you want a break from this job? I got a call from a film looking for tanned beach bunnies. You interested?"

What I would have liked was a day off but I was enjoying my new wealth. Lunchpail got a flea collar and I splurged on a huge fern. Next I wanted to have new head-shot photos taken, as I was still using the one taken three years ago when I had braces.

Being a beach bunny might be fun. At least it'd be a change of scenery. "I'd love a break. Where is it?"

"Cherry Beach, tomorrow, 7 a.m. Bring your bikini."

I don't own a bikini. I showed up on the set of *Limbo Bimbo* at the appointed time and showed the costume man my attractive one-piece swimsuit. As I knew he would, and without saying a word, he dug into a rack of bathing suits and pulled out a high-tech modern bikini for me. I wished I'd brought my shaver with me. I wondered if the make-up lady would cover up the pimples on my ass.

This time, although I was still in the heat, I'd exchanged pavement for sand. We seemed to be shooting some kind of limbo contest. It was a sixties movie with a contemporary look. I noticed there weren't too many extras and thought, *Good, maybe I'll get lots of camera time.* And I certainly did, but the camera was pointed everywhere else but at my face. Over and over, I was a-limboing and the camera, whilst shooting me, seemed to be coming from weird angles. I had a queasy feeling they were getting some good T & A shots.

I limboed until the sun set. In my opinion, they shot it backwards. They should have begun shooting with us in the low limbo position, when our backs were still fresh and rested. By the end of the day, if we'd worked our way up to the high-broom position, we could almost walk under erect. (I'd become a limbo expert.) But I had to do it their way. So by the end of the shoot, I was squeezing myself under the broom which was held about two feet high. When I tried to straighten up and walk around, I measured four feet. I couldn't uncurl my back which had locked into a back-arch position. On the crowded subway going home that night, I had to lie across three other people's laps. The film company allowed me to keep the bathing suit though, which I'd probably wear once in the privacy of my apartment.

Paul, true to his word, did manage to turn up one theatre audition. It was for a children's play, the story of 'Little Red Riding Hood'. I really wanted this job and since I'd heard that theatre today is innovative, I decided I'd show them a Red Riding Hood no one could ever forget. I played Ms. Hood as a young heroine plagued by puberty...claustrophobic in the mysterious forest...yet strangely attracted to the big, bad wolf. I know I gave the original character a mild twist but I wanted them to see that I'd given the part a lot of thought. I didn't get called back.

It had been my last day on the Clooney film. I dragged my butt through the front door and started running a cold bath. I hadn't even gotten on set once. Instead, I learned how to play chess.

The phone beckoned. "Alice! Glad I caught you! Fun job tomorrow! You get to wear a Martian suit and you'll be working at a landfill north of the city." I think Paul purposely saves these jobs for me. I think he goes looking for them.

"Paul, I am too tired. Give me just one day off, please," I begged. "I've worked twenty-one days in a row. I need a break."

"I'll give you a minute to think about it," Paul said.

"No, Paul. Sorry."

"If you say so. Well, if you aren't going to work, then I have a theatre audition for you tomorrow."

* * *

I arrived 45 minutes early for my audition, absolutely determined to win the role. My intensity scared the other hopeful applicants away from me – they were seeing a hungry actor. The room held about a dozen fellow thespians who all seemed to know one another. One poor soul, dressed in a holly black turtleneck sweater and black patched jeans, was reciting his resume to another.

"I just finished *Save the Whales* and before that I toured for six months in *Just Say No*, which I had to start one day after my tour of *Charlie Brown* ended. That was just this year, too," he bragged. I figured he must have been so busy, he had no time to buy new clothes. "How 'bout you?" he asked the poncho-clad, bearded hippie sitting in front of his chair.

"I did a tour of *Jesus is Our Friend* about six months ago. We rolled the truck in a blizzard though and killed a couple actors, so the tour got cancelled. I've been on Welfare since," he agreeably replied.

The door opened and an anorexic, elderly man dragged himself in. In slow motion, he sat in the chair next to me. I could smell an odor wafting off him. Oh no, did he pee his pants? Was that old B.O. ? Nooo, it smelled like grease. Sneaking a look at him, I thought I detected a thin sheen of oil on his skin. He immediately fell asleep.

One of the girls, wearing an Indian wraparound cotton skirt, woke up the new arrival. "Danny! How's your *Winnie the Pooh* tour going?" she asked.

"We have a week left. I have to get another show right away. I owe the phone company 600 bucks." Danny looked worried. I sensed another hungry actor. Obsessed with keeping the odds in my favor, I decided this actor would have to drop out of the race.

"I hate to tell you this, but they're looking for actors under 30," I said with false sympathy.

Danny looked at me strangely. "I'm 22."

I was about to question the authenticity of his answer when I was distracted by a twosome that had just walked in. They filed past me. The woman in front was contorting her face – grimacing, bugging her eyes, widely opening her mouth. The man following her kept snapping his mouth open, saying one syllable, "Ma!"

Ohhh, sad, I thought. Some poor mother had to bring her mentally disabled child to her audition. They chose the last two vacant seats which were on the other side of me. The woman turned to face me and with every face and neck bone stretched taut, she perfectly enunciated, "Are – they – on – time?"

Her partner looked over at me and with quizzical eyes, he said, "May Me My Mo Moo."

I bluntly stared back at them and could feel laughter starting to boil. *Don't laugh, Alice, there's something wrong with these people. They've obviously come to the wrong address.* Yet I couldn't avert my face from hers. She waited for my answer with her nostrils flaring in opposite time to her stretching tongue. Fighting the urge to guffaw, I tore my gaze off her face only to have it land on the man's. Again, with a questioning look, he asked, "May Me My Mo Moo?"

That did it. I began to giggle and in the attempt to suppress it, it was coming out like nose expulsions of air. I looked around at the others in the room, hoping I wasn't the only crass one to be laughing at the retards. I caught the braggart's eye and he looked at me and said,"Bbbrrrr", his lips a blur. He looked away and said the same thing. I didn't find the room cold at all, but the boaster sounded like he was freezing to death.

Something hit my foot. I glanced down and saw the hippie stretched out on the floor between the seats. He seemed to be reaching for something with every ounce of strength in his soul, then suddenly he compressed himself into a tiny ball, a fetal innocent. Was he having some kind of flashback to that accident he was talking about? But then he did it again.

The blasts of air emitting from my nose slowed down. Maybe I wasn't in a roomful of mentally disturbed people. Maybe I was in a roomful of professional actors. Maybe they were the same thing. I wondered if I should be doing something equally stupid and decided to pretend my nasal clearing would be my warm-up exercise. I started snorting with a practiced conviction.

A woman walked out of a room and just before my nose started to bleed, she called out, "Alice Kumplunkem?" I stood up and gave one last nose blast to let the woman have a glimpse into how professional I was...and wished I hadn't. Suddenly I needed a Kleenex. Wiping my nose and chin with my blouse, I followed the lady into an empty room furnished only by a table and three chairs.

"Have a seat," the lady said. "I'm Eliza Spottle and this is my husband, Rauger. He's the director and I handle administration. Please," she kindly requested again, "have a seat."

Gee, what a nice person, I thought. I looked at her with an enchanted look on my face and then slowly swung my head to look at her husband in the same way. I was greeted by a steely-eyed look. Rauger was sitting hunched over in his chair, his fists placed directly in front of him on the table. As soon as he saw that he had my attention, he began barking questions at me.

"How's your back?"

Be on guard, Alice. You want this job, remember? Sell yourself.
"Just fine," I answered. Besides, I don't think he wanted to hear about that old slipped disc problem.

"Can you drive a truck?" he fired at me.

"Yes...sir," I replied. "Growing up in Oak Paw, Saskatchewan, you learn how to drive on a standard transmission pick-up truck. I was..."

"You like fries?" He interrupted my tidbit of the past.

"Pardon...sir?"

"Fries! French fries! You like them?" he yelled at me.

Loaded question, Alice. Maybe they only hired vegetarians, judging by the looks of the applicants for the position. Not that I'm crazy about fries, but....

"Yes, sir! I love fries, sir!" I felt like some sad sap of a buck private, cowering before the tyrannical drill sergeant.

"You better, 'cuz when you're pullin' into a truck stop at three in the morning, don't expect to find a fruit salad. There's two actors needed for this job and besides doing all the driving and finding your own places to stay, you'll also be expected to put up the set and pull it down when you're done. And those kids are monsters, do you understand me? They are the ENEMY."

I saluted. "Yes, sir!"

He nodded, pleased with my response. "Can you act?"

"Yes, sir!"

"Then get out on that floor and show me your stuff, soldier. Be smart about it!" he ordered me. I jumped up and marched into the center of the room.

With a visible effort, I tried to relax. I had decided to do a monologue from the play *A Streetcar Named Desire*. I know Blanch Dubois is 20 years older than me, but it's such a strong piece for an actor to do.

With a final reminding thought of how desperately I wanted

a real acting job, complete with lines, I decided to give my monologue every ounce of emotion the lines called for. I stretched my arms out yearningly in hope; I flung myself to the floor in despair; I beat my chest in anger. With a final flourish, I ended my piece, looked at the Spottle's and managed to squeeze a tear out of my sad, imploring eyes.

Fifteen long seconds later, I was still looking at them with the same hound-dog expression. I had finished my piece but I didn't know if I was to tell them or if they were supposed to applaud or if they realized when a piece had ended. Maybe they thought I was taking a dramatic pause and had more monologue to go? In a split second, my hangdog face changed into Miss Bubbly Actress. I sat there and smiled and tried to look like Alice Kumplunkem instead of Blanche.

The husband slowly turned to his wife. "She's very physical," Eliza commented.

That seemed to comfort Rauger somewhat. He picked up a script sitting in front of him. "See this script? You will read the part of 'Betsy Bunny'. I will be Farmer Dell opposite you. Ready?" he asked just as he handed me the script.

I wanted to ask for at least a minute to skim it over but didn't want to cause waves. "Uh...ready," I said.

"Page 12, top of the page. I'll start. 'There's that rabbit in my garden again!'" he commanded.

I saw my line. "'Oh, no! There's Farmer Dell. I'm not supposed to be eating his carrots!'" I quickly said.

"Come on, girl! Get into character!" Rauger shouted. "'I'll have to get my gun!'"

I looked at him in terror. Was I that bad? I searched Page 12 for my next line and in a squeaky bunny voice, I delivered it. "'Oh, no! He's gone to get his gun! I must hop away!'"

"Give it life, girl! The farmer's gonna blow you away!" Rauger directed me. I began running to the four corners of the room, running for my life. "You're a bunny, girl!" Rauger reminded me.

What a faux pas! Watch me lose the role because of my stupidity. Driven into a frenzy, in a last-ditch bid to claim the role, I began bounding around the room on all fours. I thought I may be resembling a jackrabbit more than a bunny, but I was possessed.

"'There you are, bunny! I've got you now!'" Rauger played his part perfectly.

The script called for me to halt and plead for my life. In my demented hopping, I'd twisted my ankle and was grateful to stop. In severe pain, I gasped out my line. "'Oh, no! Please, Farmer Dell, don't shoot me. Why can't we be friends?'"

I collapsed to the floor. What the hell, I thought, maybe it would look like the bunny gave up hope for life. *Please, Rauger, let's be friends! I'll work for nothing, I'll even give up the role, just don't make me leap for my life anymore.*

Eliza spoke up. "That'll be fine, Alice. Please, have a seat," she again kindly offered. I bravely concealed my limp as I gratefully walked to a chair. I felt whipped; my spirit broken.

"We'll let you in on a little secret," Eliza confided. "You're definitely right for the role of Betsy. Now, there's three weeks rehearsal and three months of touring. Unfortunately, we're unable to pay for rehearsal time." She said that last bit so regretfully that I took pity on her.

"Aaww...that's alright," I told her. There, there.

"We perform all over Ontario but there are some shows in Toronto. Usually there's about ten shows a week and you'd get fifty dollars a show, plus fifty dollars a day per diem when you're out of town. How does that sound to you?" Eliza pleasantly asked me.

What a feeling flowed through me. *Why, she's negotiating a contract with me! I'm being given the chance to call some financial shots.* "That sounds wonderful," I replied, smitten.

"Good," Eliza purred, happy we'd come to a mutual agreement. "We'll be making a final decision tomorrow and will let you know then. Thank you for coming. I'll walk you out."

Eliza walked me to the door. Even though I realized I didn't have the part yet, I felt contented. I wanted to nestle in her arms. "Thank you, Eliza," I breathlessly said as I floated out.

Eliza called out a name. "Barney Woodstock?"

The hippie rose from his yoga position. "Hi, Eliza," he greeted her with what looked like cupid arrows flying from his eyes. He walked forward but stopped in the doorway, his body rigid. "Rauger, sir!" Barney stood at attention a full ten seconds before goose-stepping into the room.

Ass kisser, I thought.

* * *

Three days after the audition and no call. Paul was threatening to get an unlisted number. "I'll call YOU if you get it. Besides, if we haven't heard by now, you probably didn't get it," Paul optimistically reassured me.

"But I did so well at the audition!" I wailed.

"Sit tight, be patient. There's five thousand other actors who'd like that job, too. In the meanwhile, do you want to do a modelling job?"

A modelling job! Those words were like magic to a girl who finally had to pay someone to take her on a date. My mother wouldn't even buy my school pictures until my final year, and that was because they came out blurry, making me appear slightly exotically attractive. Someone wanted to take pictures of me and would pay me? What a novel idea. I liked it.

Then I remembered Paul's penchant for off-color jobs. "Paul, this isn't for nudie magazines or anything, is it?" I asked leerily.

"Of course not. I got outta that business years ago. This is for some computer magazine. 20 bucks an hour. Want it?" Paul impatiently asked.

What harm could a computer magazine do? Attractive wages, too. "When and where?" I enquired.

"Tomorrow morning, 8 a.m. Professional Business Machines in Scarborough," Paul said. I hated Scarborough. It took three buses and two subways to get there.

"Thanks, Paul," I said. "Phone me if that theatre company calls."

"No kidding!" Paul hung up.

I got up at 5 a.m. the next morning and gave myself a couple hours to get ready. I decided to go with the 'secretary look' and wore the navy blue matching skirt and jacket that had seen about 45 'secretary extra' jobs. My hair was worn in a tight bun, showing that I meant business about my work, and my face, which I'd worked on the longest, sported the current 'no-make-up-look' fad. I chose sensible earrings, a sensible watch and sensible shoes.

I gave myself just enough time to reach my destination. The business office was located a 20-minute walk from the bus stop. I wished I'd worn lower heels. As I walked in at 8 a.m. on the dot, I hoped someone put the coffee on. I was already beginning to feel sleepy.

"Hi, I'm Alice Kumplunkem. I'm here to do a (relish, relish) modelling assignment," I preened before the receptionist.

"They're ready for you. Just down the hall. Last door on your left," the receptionist said, noticeably unimpressed.

I made my way down the hall to the last door and opened it. Facing me was a warehouse room filled to overflowing with computers, monitors, keyboards of every shape and size. A young man rushed forward. "Are you the model?"

"Yes," I replied. Couldn't he tell?

"Come on," the young man said, taking my arm. "Let's get going. This is Shawn, the photographer." I was introduced to a lanky fellow with six cameras around his neck.

"Hi, I'm Alice. Is my hair and make-up OK?" I professionally enquired.

Shawn gave me a quick once-over. "Your hair should be

more...I don't know...teased," he said. Of course! Secretaries don't wear buns anymore; that's a thing of the past! Nowadays, they're more modern; you could probably get away with a Mohawk.

"Shall I run and fix it?" I anxiously asked.

"Nah, that's just my personal taste," Shawn replied. "It's OK for the shoot. We're only going to see your hands."

"Enough chitchat," the young man said. "Let's get this shoot over with. Alice, sit in that chair, place your hands on the keyboard and Shawn will snap a few pics. Then wheel yourself over to the next keyboard and we'll do the same thing. Let's get to it."

I went to work. I sat in front of one computer, my fingers pretending to punch keys. I'd hear the camera click a half-dozen times then I'd move on to the next business machine. Same routine. By Computer #23, I started typing out, 'Profession Business Machines sucks the big one." I noticed I hadn't bothered to glamorize my nails. In a nervous state since auditioning for that theatre job, I had bitten all my nails down to the quick. As a matter of fact, a Band-Aid covered my baby finger where I had started chewing on the skin around the nail.

I had just rolled my chair over my foot en route to the next keyboard when the assistant called out, "No! That's it! No more photos! Your job's finished now." I glanced at my watch. Astonished, I noticed that not even two hours had gone by. The assistant also glanced at a stopwatch that hung around his neck. "An hour and fifty-five minutes. Aahh, let's make it two hours," he magnanimously said. "It was a good shoot. Thanks, guys."

I was dismissed. Two hours! All this time and energy for forty bucks, minus Paul's commission. Why did Paul give me these jobs? Had he no respect for me: My disillusionment with the modelling life began to build into a resentment of Paul. I couldn't wait to get home, get on the phone and rail at him.

After 90 minutes of mass transit, I trudged up the steps to my apartment. My phone was ringing! It could be the theatre company! *Please, please,* I prayed, *let me have the part.* I fumbled with the keys and finally managed to let myself in. I dove for the phone. "Hello?" I hopefully answered.

"Alice, Paul here."

The anger came rushing back. "Paul, you're rich! I made you eight bucks today. Why don't you tell me..."

Paul interrupted me. "Alice, you got that theatre job. The Bugs Bunny role."

I stared off, rhapsodic with emotion. "I'm Betsy Bunny?"

Paul continued, in a cold voice. "I was afraid something like this would happen. Remember, Alice, one play and then it's back to work."

* * *

Rehearsals for *Unity in the World* began in two days. In the interim I was filled to overflowing with peace and contentment. I had work! I allowed nothing to faze me. Not the fact that I wasn't going to be paid for the next three weeks work nor the fact that my mom didn't give a shit about my golden opportunity. I'd made enough cash from extra work lately to just squeak past the next few weeks and my mother is a scumbucket anyways.

I had placed a long-distance call to her in Oak Paw. "Hi, Mom, it's Alice."

"Is this collect?" she greeted me.

"No, I'm paying. I've been making some money," I reassured her.

"So, what do you want?" my mom asked. She has to warm up her maternal love. Takes her a while to get going.

"I just wanted to tell you I landed a big part. It's in a play and I have one of the main characters," I proudly boasted. I didn't bother mentioning that there were only two characters.

"Will I be able to rent it at the video store?" Mom asked.

"No, it's a play," I said. "Live theatre."

"You mean like that crap the kids put on every year at the school? Those talent-night things? They're boring." Mom couldn't contain her enthusiasm.

"Well, it's almost four months' work. I'm happy I got it," I petulantly said.

"You getting paid?" Mother asked suspiciously.

"A little bit," I replied.

"Well, if you need money...," my mother began.

Oh, here it comes! She does care somewhat for me. "Yes, Mother?" I tenderly asked.

"Don't forget, I have none. It's been nice talking to you, Alice," Mother continued, "but try not to call after 8 p.m. anymore. You know I'm watching TV then." She hung up on me.

I slowly put the receiver down. I considered calling her back and disowning her. Instead, I decided to practice my role for a while. I hopped around my living room until the neighbors complained.

* * *

Rehearsals fazed me. I showed up dressed in what I thought to be an appropriate theatre rehearsal costume. I wore black tights, a colorful billowing skirt, black turtleneck and my hair in a ponytail. Standing in the doorway of the community center building, I wondered where I would find the rehearsal space.

I noticed a sign posted on the wall. "Betsy and Farmer – Rehearsal in Basement – Locker Room Area," it read. How nice to be singled out! That sign could just as well have read "Rehearsals for Alice Kumplunkem, STAR of *Unity in the World*, will be held in our fully furnished Basement. No Autographs, Please."

With a spring in my step, I headed down the stairs leading to the basement. As I neared the bottom I smelled a faintly distinguishable odor. *Is that the smell of children making their own glue from flour and water? Noooo. Homemade silly putty? Nooo. Gee, that almost smells like...pot.*

I reached the bottom step and could distinctly smell ganga coming from under the steps. I wondered if I should just move on but then a righteous feeling overcame me. These kids shouldn't be doing that! And as a potential role model for the children, Betsy Bunny should try and set them on the road to becoming upstanding young citizens.

I looked under the steps and saw a single man crouched there. He was quickly sucking in last little gasps on his roach. I didn't expect to find a bum under the steps. I slowly backed away when the bearded face looked up at me.

"Oh, hi. Hey, I remember you," he said.

"No, I don't think so...," I told him. I wasn't in the mood to be picked up by some street nut.

He came out of his hiding place and straightened up. "Yeah," he assured me. "You were at the audition. You must be Betsy. I'm Farmer Dell."

"Oh," I said, a touch dismayed. "I'm Alice Kumplunkem."

He looked at me oddly for an instant then started giggling. He worked himself up into a good laugh for a couple minutes then slowly stopped. He must have laughed himself to tears because his eyes were gravely bloodshot. "I'm Barney Woodstock," he introduced himself. "We should get to rehearsal. Rauger is a fanatic about punctuality."

With that, he led the way down the hall. I wished I didn't have to walk in at the same time as Barney, as he reeked of marijuana. I was looking forward to seeing Eliza Spottle though. I had decided to cultivate her as my friend.

We came to a door marked 'Locker Room' and entered. I saw Rauger pacing the floor and a quick scan showed that Eliza wasn't there. Our esteemed director, Rauger, glanced up and saw his new recruits. Barney immediately stood at attention, compelling me to straighten my posture.

Rauger immediately started his diatribe. "We are about to

start three weeks of intensive training. You will be pushed to your highest physical limit. You will be allowed mere minutes each day to refuel yourselves. You will report on time every day and be expected to stay twelve hours. I want energy from you every minute of our working day. In three weeks I want a dynamite show and I will not settle for less. Do I make myself clear?"

"Yes, sir!" Barney snapped. I nodded my head but that wasn't enough for Rauger. I quickly voiced the same response as Barney.

"Good," Rauger said. "There's a big gymnasium on the other side of these doors. I want you to warm up. Twenty laps around the gym. Now!"

Every day was like the day before. Show up on time, stand at attention while you were orally abused, then do a minor version of a triathlon. After that, we rehearsed the play over and over. That was when Barney got to rest. He played the farmer rather sluggishly, which pleased our director. Rauger wanted CONTRAST; that was his favorite word. Since Betsy was always hopping and leaping about, she was the 'energy force'. Rauger said that if that was all the kids saw, just pure energy, it would incite them to violence. Thus, the farmer had to slow things down. Barney rarely moved from one position.

Somewhat astonishingly, a show began to form. Barney and I began looking at our scripts less and less. My lines were quite inane. Most of the time I was just saying, "Oh, no!" Before we knew it, Rauger announced that we'd be having a dress rehearsal. From a dusty trunk he pulled out our costumes. Barney's wasn't much different from his usual attire – he was given an old pair of coveralls.

"Kids will believe anything," Rauger said as he rummaged for my costume. "Put overalls on a guy and he's automatically a farmer. But Alice, the kids aren't stupid. They'll never buy you're a bunny unless you look like a bunny." He handed me the rabbit ensemble – a tight gray flannel body with a huge pompom sewn onto the butt. It was like one of those pajamas-with-feet.

Then Rauger pulled out a huge bunny head. I wasn't exactly pleased with the expression on the rabbit's face. I had been playing Betsy as a political activist for equality amongst all animals and this costume looked like I was a contestant in the 'Miss Buck-Toothed Bunny Pageant'. Taking the head from Rauger, I noticed it had a zipper running up the back of it. The front was made of a hard plastic but the back was a soft material. I tried it on.

"How does it look?" My words boomed back at me hollowly.

"You're going to have to speak loudly to be heard," the director informed me.

I tried projecting my voice. "How does it look?" I hollered.

Barney looked at me, cocked his head and said, "Huh?"

"How does it look?" I hollered at him again.

"You did a...?" Barney still didn't understand me.

"Look! Look! How does it look?" I persisted.

"Lude? You did a lude? Hey, Alice," Barney whispered, his eyes darting at our director. "It's no big deal to me but I wouldn't let Raug know."

"Alright, break's over. Let's try working with these costumes," Rauger dictated. I savored my steps as I walked to the stage area, as I knew I'd be hopping for the next four hours.

After a strenuous rehearsal session, I discovered the trick to my costume. The rabbit head completely muffled my words. Barney kept slowing up the show's pace to stare, cock his head and say, "Huh?" He should know my response lines already; I knew all of his. Finally, I tried shortening my sentences. Instead of saying, "Oh, goody, I see more carrots! How I love carrots!" I would instead say, "Mmm! Carrots! Mmm!" Barney seemed able to deal with that level of conversation and Rauger thought it added to my character. I felt Betsy had denigrated to the most insipid, brainless, vapid rabbit in the flock, but Rauger assured me it was perfect for children's theatre.

The three-week rehearsal period was drawing to a close. On our last afternoon, Rauger informed us we would be doing a preview show the following Monday morning. Following that, we would be going out on the road for three weeks. Eliza wafted in on that announcement.

"Eliza!" I cried out, as if I'd just discovered she was my real mother.

"Hello, Betsy. Hello, Farmer Dell," she greeted us, and twittered a bit. I guffawed loudly as if she'd made a big funny. In the sweetest voice she proceeded to tell us our upcoming agenda. "On Monday at ten, you'll go to the Riverdale Library and put on a preview show – sort of a final rehearsal with an audience. After the show, you'll pack up immediately and drive up to Mount Albert, which is about two hours from Toronto. Then you'll continue driving north for the next three weeks as we have shows booked for you. Good job, you two."

"This is the last time I'll have to set my eyes on you two," Rauger jumped in. "I've done my job. Now do yours. Don't disappoint me."

"I'll meet you here Monday morning," Eliza informed us. "You can load the props into the truck and then we'll proceed to the library. After the show, I'll give you your maps, your schedule and your per diem money." I quivered at the thought of my $50 a day. Already I was devising plans on how to bank most of it. "See you around eight Monday morning?" Eliza asked. I loved how she begged us to differ. Barney and I both nodded. "Fine, then. Have a lovely weekend. And," she added solemnly, "get plenty of rest."

* * *

Our preview show at the library went swell! I was terribly nervous. When I slipped my bunny head on, I could hear my breath coming in pants. Glancing through the curtains, I could see about fifty children and maybe twenty parents. At least it was a fairly small house.

We were greeted warmly by the library staff when we'd entered with Eliza. After the stage was set up, a librarian came over with juice and coffee. I was ever-so-grateful but Barney was annoying me with his rude behavior. He barely acknowledged the lady as he dug at something tangled in his matted beard. As soon as she left, Barney triumphantly pulled out what looked to be a dead beetle.

"Wow! Look what I found!" he excitedly crowed. "A bud!"

"Yuck, for gross," I grimaced. "Don't you shampoo your beard?" I hated bugs and was worried about hygiene in our tour truck.

"It's a bud, a marijuana bud," Barney explained.

Children were starting to walk into the theatre area. "Hide it!" I screeched. Barney was not contributing to my state of calmness.

Yet the show went so well, I would have gone out and did it again. The children laughed in all the right places and Barney and I didn't fluff too many lines. Afterwards many children, parents by their side, lined up to laud us.

"Tell Betsy Bunny how much you liked the show, Trevor," said Trevor's father. He gave the young son a tap on the shoulder.

"I liked the show," the young boy said.

Another parent and child stepped forward. "This is Betsy Bunny! You liked Betsy, didn't you, Katie?" the mother said.

Katie stuck out a big lip and shook her head negatively. Her mother gave her a mild shove.

"Katie....," she warned. Katie, looking frightened now, nodded her head up and down.

When the last child had left, I pulled off my mask and looked at Barney. Sweat was pouring off me and my hair was lank. I felt a camaraderie with my acting partner. "Well, chum, shall we pull down the set?"

"You go ahead," Barney told me. "I'm going to roll one."

Eliza greeted us in the main room of the library. "That was a terrific show," she commented.

"Great audience!" I exclaimed. "So well-behaved! I can't wait to do more shows in Toronto." I also wanted to get back to Toronto as soon as possible to make sure Lunchpail was still alive. I had to leave him in my agent's care on the condition that I allow Paul to book Lunchpail should any cat-acting jobs come along. I agreed, but if that cat started making more than me, I was getting out of the business.

Eliza gave us an envelope full of 50-dollar bills. "Here's your per diem money. Don't spend it all in one place," she said. I laughed, thinking she was such a wit. "Drive carefully. We don't want any more wrecked trucks." With that, she bid us a fond adieu.

We pulled into Mount Albert a couple hours later. It looked to be a town with a population of six. The only place of business was a shack with a weather-beaten sign claiming it was the Mount Albert Center.

"That's where we have to go," I said, looking at our schedule. "Doesn't look like much."

Barney and I entered what appeared to be a curling rink. The caretaker raced forward. "You the guys puttin' on a show for the kids?"

"Yes," I said with dignity. "We're the theatre company who will be performing a play for the children."

The caretaker led us into the curling area, a dingy two-lane sod-covered space. "Aren't you lucky we don't have the ice in?" the caretaker noted. "I guess youse guys will set up at one end and the kids at the other?"

"Sure," Barney agreed.

"I'm gonna git goin' then," the caretaker said, glancing at his pocket watch. "There's daytime bingo goin' on in Honeydew. That's where all the older folk are. I'll be back to lock up." With that, he made his exit.

Sitting behind our curtain, we could hear the kids coming in. I risked a peek. "There's a few kids but no parents or teachers," I observed.

Barney actually showed signs of being perturbed. "Oh, oh," he said. "Not a good sign."

Fragments of conversation drifted our way from the audience. "This is going to be a sissy play, I just know it," someone said.

"Let's skip it and play handball against the wall outside," the friend replied.

Someone else had a different suggestion. "I heard Billy wants to fight Johnny today. I bet they scrap here since there'll be no supervisors around to stop it. Everyone's in Honeydew for that Big Money Bingo."

The good feeling I was left with from our Toronto morning show was being acidly dissolved. "Ready to go on?" Barney asked. I had been studying the scene before me through a part in the curtains and now I clutched them for dear life.

"B...B...Barney, I don't see more than five kids under 12 out there. There's at least three couples making out. Oh, God...one kid just got sick..." I was rooted to the spot in petrification.

Barney meandered onto the stage without me. The kids quieted down as they looked at him. *They're KIDS, Alice, and they want to be entertained. Go out and make them happy!* I bounded onto the stage.

"You call that a rabbit?" one youngster called out. "That's a girl in a rabbit suit. You can see the tits!" The class clown was greeted by laughter.

The next 40 minutes were the toughest I've ever had to endure. I had to keep reminding myself to watch out for the wooden plank that served to separate the two curling rinks and our stage in the process. The court jester was 'on' that day; he didn't let a bon mot slide by. At one point, a Grade Two boy vomited across the front of our stage. He queasily looked up and said, "I've got the flu." Shortly after that, I started hearing a slurping noise. I couldn't place where the sound was coming from until I noticed most of the audience staring towards the bank of the rink. I strained my bunny neck and saw one couple going at in with a vengeance. The 14-year-old boy was implanting quite an impressive hickey on his date's neck. Every few seconds I'd look that way to check on the hickey's progression. After a couple minutes, a loud pop was heard. The entire audience turned to see the result – a dark purple outline of Africa. Mild applause was heard. Then the girl went to work on his neck.

At least there were four kindergarten kids paying us some attention. I played my heart out to them and wished the rink raconteur would stop corrupting them with his lewd remarks. Suddenly the back door burst open.

"Johnny and Billy are going at it outside!" some kid yelled. That cleared the place. Everyone got up and ran outside at full speed just as Betsy Bunny was telling the farmer about peace and unity. Barney and I were left alone in the room with a single kindergarten child.

She looked at us. With a tooth missing and her hair in pigtails, she said in a good Dirty Harry impression, "I'm still here. Finish the show."

Barney and I performed the last five minutes. When we ended, the Farmer and Betsy Bunny in a friendly hug, the punk simply got up and walked out. I think she knew it was over.

The kids trooped back in just as Barney and I were packing up the last of our set. Immediately they started complaining. "Hey! We didn't get to see how it ended! Finish the show! We'll tell!"

I was concerned for our safety but after a few seconds the kids got bored with us. "Bus is here!" someone yelled and before you could say, "Lickety split, you bad kids," they were on their way back to their kennels.

"Come on," I said to Barney, "let's get out of this town." We picked up a load to haul out to our truck.

"Oh, fuck!" Barney swore. "Those bastards!"

"What?" I asked. I had a load of boxes in front of my eyes. I put them down and followed Barney's gaze. "Oh, those bunch of Nazi brats!" I sputtered. The Mount Albert Mafia had deflated all four of our tires.

After a lengthy delay, Barney and I drove to the town where our next show would be performed – Squint, Ontario. I was looking forward to a nice bath and a good book. We hadn't been able to leave Mount Albert until early evening. "Squint should be the next town," I said, judging by my map of Ontario.

We pulled into a town illuminated by a couple streetlights. "There's no hotel here," I noticed uneasily.

"We'll have to drive to the next town," Barney said.

In the seventh town after Squint, we arrived in North Bay which offered four or five hotels in a strip. Barney stopped at the first one.

"Give me your 50 bucks," I suggested, tired and now just longing for the bath. "I'll get the accommodations."

Barney gave me his money. "Try and get a deal," he advised. I went into the hotel's office.

Five minutes later I was back at the truck. "Barney!" I wailed. "They want 100 bucks for one room!"

"That's the going rate," Barney said.

"Let's try the next hotel," I suggested.

The fifth hotel, along with the previous four, wanted $100 a room. "But that's twice my per diem money!" I complained to Barney.

"No, it isn't," Barney replied. "It's our combined per diem money for the day. You're not gonna get a room to yourself for 50 bucks unless we tour in Mexico. We have to share a room and we have to work a deal." Barney went in.

I sat in the truck, my prudish upbringing coming back to

haunt me. Share a room with a man? Almost a total stranger? What if he tries something? I prayed Barney would get a room with two beds.

Before long, Barney was back. "I got it for 90," he said, giving me my change. I had five dollars to spend the next day on food.

I wondered if I'd packed pajamas.

* * *

I entered my apartment by throwing myself onto the lime-green carpet. I gave it a resounding smack. "Home!" I went around kissing my appliances and furniture. I never thought I'd live to see the day I'd be happy to see my post-Goodwill decorated flat.

I opened the fridge to see what kind of healthy food I had inside. Nothing but a bag of potatoes with long tendrils sprouting from them. I slammed the door shut. No more potatoes! I'd had French fries for lunch and dinner every day for the last three weeks. I reminisced about the first leg of our tour.

"Barney," I'd say, scanning a menu. "Everything costs more than five dollars."

"How much are fries?" he'd ask. He was on the same diet as I.

"Three dollars."

"We'll have two waters and two orders of fries," Barney would usually end up telling the restaurant employee. If we had money left, we'd treat ourselves the next day to a fancy breakfast of toast and coffee.

And while nothing was quite as horrendous as our first road show, we still managed to run into difficulties. One night we drove until 2 a.m. looking for a place to stay. "Alice, I'm falling asleep," Barney said, at the end of his rope. "Either you drive again or we sleep in the truck."

I had been studying the road intensely. Northern Ontario roads are so desolate and lonely; nothing to keep you company but the moose crossing signs. "I'll drive," I said. I wasn't about to park the truck where a wild moose might attack me.

As soon as I'd taken the wheel, Barney fell asleep. Some co-pilot. I had a brainstorm. I'd drive to the school, park the truck in the parking lot, and we'd sleep there. I couldn't wait to get there; I kept seeing eyes darting at me from the side of the road. Finally, exhausted, I made out the schoolhouse in the dark. I drove into the lot, shut the truck off and immediately joined Barney in slumberland.

I awoke from a wild dream. I dreamt I was still seeing darting eyes but now they were the eyes of children. I kept shaking myself to wake up until I realized I was already awake. Dozens of children were staring through our windshield. I had parked under the basketball hoop on their playground. The teacher in charge of watching the playground strode over to have a word with us. Before she could reach us I considered gunning the truck out of there, but my getaway path was littered with children.

Barney woke up when the lady rapped her knuckles on my window. He looked at me reproachfully. I tried to laugh a little. "At least I saved us 90 bucks..." The Spottles received word of our unbecoming conduct.

And how about the day our schedule called for us to report to the Lady of Our Lord Church in Ste. Francis. Our truck, which had been running badly lately, chugged into town. Banners were hung everywhere, proclaiming this to be 'Revive Religion' Day. "Look, Barney!" I shrilled in delight. There was a poster advertising our play, *Unity in the World*.

As we tried to find a place to park in the crowded lot, we were hailed by the townsfolk. "Welcome to Ste. Francis! God be with you! Can't wait to see your enlightening show!"

Barney had a grave look of concern on his face.

"Barney, lighten up!" I urged. "This is great! May God be with you." I was loving thy fellow man.

"May the force be with you," Barney mumbled in return.

I was delighted to see a large crowd had gathered for our play. There must have been an adult for every child. After the donation plate had been passed around (of which we wouldn't see any), Barney and I went on.

After just a few lines, I noticed a change in the climate. The audience had quieted right down and were staring at us in disbelief. Barney was sweating and I started hearing snippets of outraged conversation. "...a bunny? ... He's got a gun! ...Our children shouldn't be seeing this..."

One man stood up. "I thought we were going to see *Unity in the World*?"

I broke character long enough to say, "This is it."

"Your title is misleading!" he shouted. For effect, he pointed the long arm of righteousness at us. "You have MISLED us! You are doing the work of the DEVIL!"

I begged to differ but was struck by a ripe tomato. Barney took a good shot to the knee by a cauliflower. A veritable julienne salad began pelting us.

"Run!" Barney shouted, already on his way. I completely broke character as I ran on two legs to the truck. Barney jumped in the driver's seat and turned on the ignition.

Nothing. "Come on, you piece of junk! Start!" Barney screamed.

"Please, God, let us get out of here. Please, God, let the truck start," I prayed. Just before I was about to promise God I'd get out of the acting business forever, the truck started. I'm still holding a grudge against Him for not allowing me to make that promise.

The angry crowd surged toward us. The man who had started it was at the forefront. "Devil's henchmen!" he shouted, waving a rosary above his head like a lasso. Barney raced the truck out of the lot as more vegetables were hurled at us.

"Barney!" I remembered. "Our set!"

"Our life comes first," Barney said. "We'll worry about the set later."

We hid in the hills all day. As evening drew near we could hear gospel singing. Barney and I decided to slink back into town. It appeared everyone was at the revivalist meeting so we went back to the church and tore down our spotted, rotting set.

Yeah, I definitely had enough of Northern Ontario for a while. I was anxious for the polite audiences of Toronto, where I would thankfully be working for the next week.

* * *

Toronto greeted us with open arms. Thank goodness, because then I could see the stilettos, daggers and brass knuckles tucked into their clothing. I saw Grade Three children more mature than I.

Barney met me at the inner-city school. I was waiting for him in the girls' locker room off the gym, already dressed for work. Barney strode in, looking dangerous. He was wearing a tight black leather jacket and pointy cowboy boots. His muscle shirt had a logo reading 'Fuck the System'.

"What's with the boots, Barney?" I asked.

As if to prove his point, Barney killed a cockroach in the corner of the locker room. "Protection," he muttered. I didn't know he hated bugs too.

Barney pulled his overalls out of the trunk. He simply put them on over his ensemble. "Barney, you're gonna die of heatstroke," I warned him. I was only too aware of the sweat I worked up every show.

"Don't leave anything they can steal," Barney advised. "I'm gonna hang out in the schoolyard after we set up...see if I can score anything. You gonna guard the set?"

I walked into the staff room to get Barney and I a coffee before we set up. I saw a couple pots percolating on the counter. One pot was marked 'Special Coffee'. My taste buds jumped – that was probably some fancy Irish cream or amaretto-flavored blend of coffee. After my first cup I knew it was heavily rum-flavored. That coffee was spiked.

Barney re-appeared five minutes before the show was to begin. The cavernous gymnasium was still empty. Barney sat motionless, his eyes on the clock. Feeling as if I were in a *Twilight Zone* version of *High Noon*, I tried to calm my partner down. "Relax, Barn. We're in Toronto again. Civilization." The clock struck 10 a.m. "Where is everybody?" I wondered.

The many doors leading into the gym were thrown open. Hundreds of children rushed the stage. I leapt for cover behind one of the trunks backstage. Barney joined me.

We could hear mass pandemonium. No one seemed to be coming backstage to murder us though. I looked over at Barney who was a quivering, spineless mess. "Barney!" I yelled over the din. "Don't they have any teachers out there?"

No sooner had I said that when a haggard woman ran backstage. Barney and I both cowered. "They're ready for you!" she panted. With fear pounding in our hearts, Barney and I slowly made our way around the curtain.

Our stage was littered with spitballs. It seemed to be the current Grade Four fad. Teachers were wrestling with randy students; one was dragged out in a headlock. The cacophony never let up. At one point Barney was distracted by a seven-year-old trying to pass him something. "Farmer Dell," I squeaked in my Betsy voice, trying to grab his attention. He was in a whispered conversation with the minor. "Farmer Dell!" I shouted, slipping into my aggravated Alice voice. I saw him reaching for his wallet. "Barney, for fuck's sake!" I yelled, which finally caused him to look at me. He obviously couldn't remember his next line. After some thought, he jumped in with a line five pages further in the story. I went with it, knowing no one was folioing the play anyways.

As soon as the show finished, about one hundred kids crowded onto the stage area. Everyone was picking up props and looking backstage. It was like being surrounded by sheep. Barney, brandishing his pitchfork prop, hollered at them. "Everyone get outta here! Don't make me use this on you!" He jabbed the air menacingly. The kids looked at him mildly, some sliding their hands toward their back pockets. Barney advanced on them and they slowly walked off the stage, some pushing props to the floor to let us know where we stood with them.

In combat shock, Barney and I struck the set and went to load our truck. I suddenly felt a pang of longing for the silly shenanigans of the Mount Albert tykes. These Toronto hooligans didn't bother disfiguring our truck; they merely stole it.

After arresting two Grade Eight boys for joyriding, the cops returned our truck to us. Throughout the week we came to realize those kids took it easy on us that first show. Besides having to deal with prison-bound children, Barney and I had to battle Toronto rush-hour traffic twice a day.

"Ah, your face, my ass!" Barney yelled at a driver who was trying to squeeze into our lane.

"Barney, watch your mouth," I told him.

"Ah, your face, my breath," he replied. The week's events were having its effects on my partner and me.

"Speaking of your breath, it DOES stink," I retorted.

"You ever have to smell your bunny suit?" Barney asked. "I hate having to hug you at the end. Let's just go for a handshake from now on. Shit, we're in the city now, Alice. Can't you find a Laundromat?"

That did it. We didn't speak for two days unless we had to when we were performing. I was afraid Barney would actually load his gun. I DID wash my suit now and then; it's just that I worked hard at being a bunny and was drenched from perspiration after every performance.

I was packing for the next three weeks. This time we were touring Southern Ontario. My phone rang and I hoped it was my agent, Paul, changing his mind about caring for my cat. Seems

Lunchpail and Paul's leather couch had a roustabout and Lunchpail came out the victor. I answered the phone.

"Alice! Guess who?"

"Velda!" It was my best friend. "You're back! How was the Bahamas?"

"Beautiful! You should see my tan! What are you doing tomorrow?" she asked. "Why don't you drop by?"

"I can't," I said, then smugly added, "I'm working. Touring with a children's show."

"Oh, well. I'm in town for three weeks. Then I'm off to Alberta to shoot a western." She giggled. "I can't even ride a horse!"

Boy, that galled me. I can ride a horse well enough to enter the Kentucky Derby but Velda gets by on her good looks. "Velda, I hate to be asking as soon as you return but could you look after Lunchpail for me? I'll be back on the 20th," I said.

"Welllll...I guess so. I leave on the 21st so it should be no problem. We'll catch up the night you get back," Velda said.

I sure had missed Velda. Even though she got all the breaks, she would still be there for me to cry on her shoulder when my career was going nowhere. Velda couldn't care less about being an actress; she didn't go looking for work, the jobs usually came to her. She would be content to go on with her former job as an Avon cosmetics representative. Sometimes, after one of my complaining jags, she wouldn't even bother to tell me she'd been chosen Miss Ontario or had just gotten a recurring character role on the only American production being shot in town. I couldn't wait to talk to her when I got back from down South.

Although the children in Southern Ontario seemed better behaved, the parents seemed over-productive. The gymnasiums were filled to capacity with their issue. Eliza had forewarned us that these schools also requested a question and answer period at the end of our shows. My poor bunny voice was shot from continuously trying to squeak loud enough for the back row to hear. Barney took control of these sessions.

Q. "Why didn't Farmer Dell just shoot the rabbit?"
A. "I really can't answer that."
Q. "Are you and Betsy married?"
A. "Are you serious?"
Q. "How old are you?"
A. "I'm 25 and Alice is 28."
Q. "Wow, you guys look way older."

Near the end of that tour, I was changing my costume for the ride to the next town, Windsor, a regular metropolis. I went to unzip my bunny head when the zipper caught in my hair. "Yow!" I screeched in pain. "My hair is caught in the zipper!" I wailed to Barney.

"Yeah, I know it's my turn to drive," Barney replied.

"No, you goof! My hair is caught in the zipper," I repeated.

"Alice, take the goddam head off. I can't make out what you're saying," Barney wisely told me. In a remarkable display of charades, I managed to inform my partner that I was unable to take the rabbit head off. "Hang on, I'll go get some scissors," Barney said.

"No!!" I yelled, Betsy shaking her head wildly back and forth. I was given a bad haircut a couple years ago as an extra on a shoot where I wasn't even used. It had taken me this long to grow my hair out.

"What, then?" Barney impatiently asked. He wasn't able to take the goddam mask off either and grew bored with me. He wasn't the one suffering the dilemma obviously. It was decided that I'd just wear my head on the drive to Windsor; maybe I could somehow loosen the zipper en route.

Barney checked us into the Sleep-E-Z (Sleep-E-Zed to us Canucks) Motel and I snuck into my room, still wearing my head. After we'd watched our three hours of sitcoms on TV, I finally gave up. By now a huge chunk of my hair was caught. I sign-languaged to Barney that I wanted him to find me some scissors.

He left but was back in moments. "They don't trust me to return them. You have to go to the office," Barney said, resettling onto his bed to watch *The Big Bang Theory* for the second time that day.

I headed off towards the motel office but was dismayed to see a sign posted on the locked door.

'I'm at restaurant across street. Boris.' it read.

I walked to the side of the road and tentatively looked both ways. The highway was busy with transport trucks and it didn't look like I'd get a chance to cross. I could see truckers giving me second glances, wondering if they really saw a rabbit that big. Finally I scampered through a break in the traffic and went into the restaurant.

I opened the door and 30 burly truck drivers stopped eating to look at me. "Boris?" I squeaked, then remembered that bunny head or not, I was really Alice Kumplunkem. "Boris!" I yelled.

The waitress came over. "The bars are in town, dear," she informed me, thinking I'd already had one too many.

"Bo-Ris," I slowly enunciated. A man at a table looked at his friends and then slowly stood up.

"I'm Boris," he suspiciously said.

"Scissors! Sci-Ssors!" I was speaking as if I were still on stage.

"I'm sorry," the waitress said as she tried to steer me out. "We're not a licensed establishment."

I resorted to my sign language. I frantically made cutting motions. "Oh, you're the girl who wanted scissors!" Boris eventually said. "Fran, you must have scissors here," he said to the waitress.

"Shore do," she drawled. We were in Southern Ontario after all. "Come with me, hon." She led me to the cash register area. "Sorry, but Ah'm gonna have to cut a huge chunk of your pretty hair off."

I nodded my head, the mask beginning to weigh heavily on my neck. With one snip, I saw six inches of my glossy mouse-colored hair fall to the ground. I immediately felt for the zipper. It wasn't attached to my hair anymore and I went to zip the head off.

The zipper went about an inch of the way up and stopped again. I yanked but I could tell it wasn't stuck on my hair. I gestured to Fran to see what the matter was. "Hon, your zipper is just plain broken now. You'll never get that mouse head off," Fran told me.

"I'm not a mouse, I'm a rabbit!" I angrily informed her.

"Two burgers and a shake, you said?" Fran asked, taking her order pad out of her apron.

I ran out of the restaurant and back to the highway. A truck blared his horn to prevent me from becoming roadkill. I walked back into the room.

Barney barely glanced up from *Seinfeld*. "Didja get the mask off?" he enquired.

"DOES IT LOOK LIKE IT?" I yelled and started bawling. I stopped when I realized I couldn't get a Kleenex under the mask to blow my nose. "Barney, the zipper is broken now. Can you try and fix it?"

I sat on his bed and pointed at the zipper. Barney looked at the problem and said, "Alice, the zipper is broken now. I'll try and fix it."

Barney finally kicked me off his bed a couple hours later. "I just can't unzip it. I'm tired. I'm going to sleep."

"What should I do?" I wailed, wanting to cry again. I was also hungry and wanted to eat.

"I can't understand you. You know that. So don't talk to me no more." Barney crawled under his sheets. "Good night, Betsy."

The only thing left for me to do was try to Sleep-E-Z. Lying on my back, snuffling a bit and feeling sorry for myself, I finally managed to drop off into a fitful sleep. I awoke a dozen times, waking Barney up with my muffled groans.

"I had a bad dream! I was in this elevator that kept going

down but it wouldn't let me off," I gasped, trying to catch my breath. Barney just looked at me and went back to sleep.

A while later, I woke up screaming from another dream. Barney jumped out of his bed at the sound of my cries. "I was on this beach and kids were covering me with sand. They wouldn't stop! They were burying me alive!" I reviewed my dream.

"Go to sleep, Alice," Barney grumpily said as he crawled back into his bed.

My sleep was invaded by another nightmare. I knocked the bedside lamp to the floor in my struggle to wake up. Barney was again lovingly by my side. "Barney, this time I dreamt..." I began, but was stopped by Barney's hands on my throat.

"Alice, if you wake me up one more time, I swear I'm gonna pop you one," he threatened. He glared at me evilly and then went back to his bed. I stayed up the rest of the night trying to interpret my dreams.

In the morning Barney ran across to the restaurant and returned with two coffees. I took one, lifted it to my lips and realized I couldn't drink it. Barney, seeing my predicament, said, "That's right. You can't drink anything with that mask on, can you? You can't eat anything either." Why was he telling me what I already knew? I huffed in disgust and could distinctly detect morning breath.

"Hey, I've got an idea. Hold still and I'll give you a good shot to the face. It'll be hard enough to knock that damn thing off," Barney said as he drew his fist back to put his idea into action.

I went into a tirade. "Are you nuts? This head won't come off unless we cut it off, you idiot. I don't need any of your simpleton ideas. 'Knock it off,' he says. I'd like to knock you off! I'll just wear it 'til after the show then I don't care what the Spottle's say, I'm cutting this mask off." By this point I was getting slightly nauseated by the noxious gas in my mask.

Barney waited a second then said, "Come again?"

Did you know, ladies, that if you don't bother with your face or hair whatsoever, you can get out of the house in under four minutes?

I didn't think I'd have the energy to finish our morning show. I was faint with hunger and holding my phony carrot was only rubbing salt into the wound. Parched; food and fresh air were the only thoughts in my mind.

As soon as Barney answered the last question ("Did you shoot Betsy Bunny in the leg? She wasn't even jumping near the end of the show.") I rushed into the staff room.

The teachers were enjoying a post-show coffee. "Can someone please help me cut this mask off?" I said upon entering. They all just looked at me, a couple cupping their ears. I had forgotten to use my Betsy Bunny lingo and newly acquired sign-language skills. I eventually got them to understand my need. One generous lady got up.

"Let me help," she offered. "There's scissors in here somewhere." I stood watching the teachers eat tarts the home-ec students had prepared. My stomach let out a huge growl. The teachers heard and they all turned to glance at my butt.

"That was my stomach," I corrected them.

"You're excused," an elderly teacher granted me absolution.

"Found them!" the lady said, brandishing scissors. "Turn around and I'll cut the mask off." I did as she suggested. It didn't take long; in seconds I was freed! The stale air of the staff room, smelling of coffee and mold, hit me like an ocean breeze.

I turned around to face my savior. "Thank you!" I gushed.

She got a look on her face as if I'd given her a left hook, then staggered to her chair. A couple of teachers covered their faces, one man covered his mouth with a napkin and two more ran out of the room.

I met Barney on my way out of the staff room. He gaped at me and kept walking. "Barney?" I said, hurt by his reaction.

"I don't know you, man," Barney whispered, putting distance between us. I had a sneaky suspicion my breath might be a bit bad, perhaps rancid, so I walked into the little girl's room.

I looked into the mirror and gagged. My face looked like one of those bloated corpses you see washing up on shore. *I don't know you either,* I thought, taking Barney's side. I went to the use the toilet but forgot I was in an elementary school where they build the loos a foot lower for the young 'uns, and almost broke my tailbone.

For the last three shows of that tour, I had to wear a huge rubber band around my head to keep the bunny mask on. It gave Betsy a pinched look but I wasn't worrying about the zipper anymore. After the show the kids were awfully impressed with my cool Toronto-style punk haircut. It was now being worn long on both sides with a six-inch shorter swatch up the middle.

Trudging up the stairs to my apartment, I heard a loud mewling. Lunchpail? I got to the top and saw my cat tied to the doorknob of my flat. His water bowl and food dish were also out there but were licked dry.

"Lunchpail? What are you doing out here?" I asked, going to pet him. He shot his paw at my hand, leaving a long scratch. He was definitely mad about something. I saw a note taped to my door.

"Dear Alice," the note read. "I got called to Alberta early! Had to leave on the 17th! I called your agent to see if he could take care of cat but he said you called him and would be back on the 18th instead. I just missed you!! So Lunchpail only stayed out for one night. You should leave me a key!!! See you in a month or so. Luv ya! Velda."

I wondered what Lunchpail would say when I told him I had no cat food in the apartment. He should have told Velda to lay newspaper on the floor if his litter box wasn't available. And Paul, that liar! I never called him! Oh, well...at least I was home again. Only one tour left and then my freedom.

* * *

Barney was waiting for me to leave my apartment. I was in a quandary as to what to do with my cat. "Barney," I pleaded, "let me take him with us. He's a good cat."

"No way, Alice," Barney bluntly put it. Paul had also refused to take care of him, saying he was going to Miami for the next three weeks. I knew I could find him at home every single day if I called but I didn't push it. None of my other so-called friends wanted the responsibility either.

I wasn't worried about my fern, which had been flourishing. I had rigged up a kind of irrigation system and it seemed to be working. I looked at Lunchpail and a last-ditch plan formed itself.

"Alright, Pail, follow me," I said as I led him from room to room. First I went into the kitchen. "I'll fill all these bowls with food," I said as I dished cat food into every bowl and dish I owned. Then I went into the bathroom and turned on the tub's faucet a bit, just so a slow stream of water flowed out. "And here is where you'll drink your water," I informed my cat. "I'll be back soon. Just 21 days. Be good and...live."

Barney and I left long before sunrise for the most western point of Ontario. This time we were doing shows in towns we'd been unable to cover previously in the tour. There were libraries, recreation centers and schools spread out over the entire province. Our gas allowance had been quadrupled.

One night we had been driving for six hours and I decided to catch a few winks. We were on our way from Niagara Falls, where it was usually quite balmy, to Sudbury where it still snowed in May. I was well into reel two of a dream when I became aware I was coughing.

My conscious mind flitted a thought into my subconscious scenario. *Must be all those cigarettes,* I mused. Barney and I were both staunch non-smokers before we began the tour. Now we were working up to a pack a day each. Smoking looked so cool on the school kids. Besides, we needed something to relieve the boredom, even if it was remembering to take a puff before the cigarette burned to the end. I still hadn't quite gotten the hang of smoking; for one thing I couldn't put them out properly. Either they were still smoking after I butted them out or I'd burn my index finger in a concentrated effort to extinguish it.

What a nightmare I was suddenly having! My throat was starting to catch fire and my body was rocking from side to side. I struggled to awaken, only to find real life even more of a nightmare.

As soon as my eyes opened, they began tearing from the smoke in the truck. Flames were licking up from the seat. "Barney!! Fire!!" I screamed. The truck veered to the right and I ended up sliding onto the hotspot. "Stop, Barney!" I yelled.

Barney paid me no heed. His head was slumped onto his chest, one hand on the wheel, the other holding a cigarette that was burning a huge hole in the truck's upholstery.

I was confused. Should I grab the wheel or should I stamp out the fire? In complete hysterics, I started shrieking, "Barney! Barney! Barney! Barney!"

He awoke and immediately pretended that he hadn't fallen asleep. He brought his cigarette to his lips to take a drag. Meanwhile, the truck began fishtailing. I braced myself, praying the seatbelt would stop me from flying through the windshield when we hit one of the rock cuts by the side of the road. Barney noticed the smoke and more than likely felt some heat by his butt. "WHAT THE HELL ARE YOU DOING, BITCH?" he freaked out at me.

Now that burned. As soon as I knew whether I'd live through this, I planned on giving Barney a couple days of silent treatment. Barney finally slammed on the brakes, sending the truck into a spin. We came to a halt mere inches from the mini-mountains on the side of the road, our truck pointed back in the direction of Niagara Falls.

I counted my blessings for a moment then yelled at Barney.

"You fell asleep at the wheel, you DOPE!" I opened the door to air out the truck.

Barney started stamping out the seat fire with his Birkenstock's. "Maybe if you'd drive a bit more, I wouldn't get so tired, you COW."

I returned with an armful of snow and threw it on the seat. "You started the fire, ASSHOLE!" I shouted. "This is all your fault!"

"You're a whiny old NAG," Barney said.

"You're a burnt-out HIPPIE," I countered.

"You can be a real CUNT," he replied.

"You're a fucking FAGGOT!" I answered.

That was just the appetizers leading to the worst fight Barney and I had yet on tour. I felt sure we would come to fisticuffs and I wanted him. Eventually the yelling was starting to affect our already overworked damaged voices. Suddenly I did something I didn't want to do – I began to cry.

Barney obviously thought I'd pulled a dirty move. "Aahhh...come on. Let's get to Sudbury already. You drive," he muttered as he got back into the truck. I got into the new bucket seat, lit a cigarette and took off.

Our last show was to be held in Northern Ontario in a desolate area known as the Pocolocum Indian Reservation. I don't want to appear prejudiced but I was nervous about this show. "Why do you think this is the last show to be scheduled?" I asked Barney. We were again on civil terms although Barney still hadn't consented to take the blame for the charred hole in the middle of the truck seat. "For some reason, I fear for my scalp."

"What are you worried about?" Barney asked.

I took a little nip out of the whiskey bottle I had bought that morning. I'd hidden it all day in the hole in the seat of the truck, but now Barney saw it out in the open. "They're full-blooded Indians," I replied.

"Well, then, I wouldn't bring any liquor into town," Barney prejudicedly warned. "Come on, Alice! One show left! You don't need that stuff," he said fatherly, as he rolled a joint while steering with his knees.

The reservation itself didn't help my anxiety. It was almost entirely made up of trailer homes. Packs of dogs roamed the streets and everyone stopped what they were doing to stare at us as we drove by. "Barn, let's skip this show," I said. "I have a bad feeling."

"Don't be such a bigot, Alice," Barney said. "Unity in the World, remember?"

We were greeted like royalty when we arrived at the dilapidated school. I was wary though, and never had my back to anyone. I think my eyes started squinting. Through the curtain backstage, I watched the children enter in an orderly manner. They all sat quietly, hands in their laps, no one uttering a sound. "Watch it, Barn," I cautioned. "Looks like an ambush."

Showtime! I bounded on, wondering if some youngster brought his bow and arrow. Look, Ma! Rabbit stew! I waited for the pierce but instead heard laughter wafting from the audience.

More than anywhere else we'd toured, these kids really appreciated the show. I thought the hug between Betsy and Farmer Dell at the end, considering this was our last show, had extra poignancy. As soon as the children started clapping, Barney shoved me away from him. "Thank God I don't have to smell that stinky suit anymore," he touchingly said.

After the kids had finished helping us load our truck and we'd signed autographs like we were big rock stars, Barney and I drove off. We were Toronto-bound! If we sped a little, we figured we'd make it in under eight hours.

The cop clocked me at 130 km/h in a 90 km/h zone. I jumped out of the truck before the officer reached me as I didn't want him smelling the seven joints Barney had smoked so far. "Do you know how fast you were going?" the cop asked.

"About a hundred k's?" I hopefully replied. He snorted and handed me a ticket for my entire week's pay.

By the time we arrived in Toronto, it was late and my good feeling had waned quite a bit. Barney and I had one last fight for old time's sake when he refused to stop for a piss break because we were only two hours out of Toronto. To prove I was right, I had an accident.

Reaching my apartment late that night, I trudged up the stairs and put my key in the lock. The door grudgingly opened, seeming to drag on something. I looked and saw a greenish dry puddle. Peering around the room, I saw puddles everywhere.

"Lunchpail?" I called out as I went into the kitchen. Every bowl had been licked clean. I stepped into a wet mess and noticed green leaves sticking to my foot. "Yuk! What the...?!" I said as I went into the living room.

Lunchpail was in the process of ralphing up a new puddle, green leaves spewing out of his mouth. I went to grab him but thought, *What's one more puddle? And what's that green stuff? Did his food go bad?*

Lunchpail finished vomiting and then walked towards my fern. "Lunchpail!" I hollered as he started chewing at the few remaining leaves. The fern was demolished. I was now irrigating a stalk.

After cleaning up about eighty piles of cat puke, I surmised (judging by the freshness of the piles) that Lunchpail had been hungry for about a week. Some piles were hard and crusty while some were still warm and moist.

I wondered if I should let myself have an all-out depression. The tour had been murder on my system; my nails wouldn't grow, I hadn't gotten my period in three months, my voice was just a rasp and I had the worse case of acne this side of a pizza. Now Lunchpail looked like he needed his stomach pumped.

Then I remembered my pact with Paul. One play and that's it! Giving Lunchpail some frozen hamburger to eat, I thought happily of the offer the Spottle's had made me.

"If you want to do the next tour," Eliza sweetly said, "we'd love to have you back."

I didn't exactly say yes or no. I said, "I think I'll throw myself in front of the subway before that would happen."

I left it up to them to decipher what I meant.

CHAPTER TWO

"You have a crowd scene tomorrow in Scarborough, on Tuesday you'll be a housewife in a supermarket, and on Wednesday, a high-school student," Paul dictated my agenda for the week.

"More extra work, huh?" I said with distaste.

"You said you'd go back to film after that tour," Paul reminded me.

"Yeah, yeah, I know. But, Paul," I hesitantly went on, "I want to change a few things." I had been thinking of the play I'd just finished. All weekend, I relived my lines. 'Oh, no! Farmer! Run!' My mouth started watering at the thought of spoken lines again. I broached my thoughts carefully to Paul. "I think, Paul, that you...WE have to work harder at promoting me. I've been doing extra work for close to three years now. It's time I had a shot at a line in some bigger things, like the American shows shooting here."

Paul interrupted. "Alice, you're not in the union. They can't hire you."

"Well, how do I get in the union?" I asked.

"You have to do six union jobs," Paul replied.

I huffed. "Catch-22, isn't it?"

"You have to start on smaller films, namely non-union and low-budget," Paul stated. "Sometimes they pay even less than extra work."

"That's alright!" I excitedly said. Now Paul huffed. I pressed on. "At least that'd be lines! I could put it on my resume. You know I can't put background work on resumes. Can't you try and find me a job like that? One with lines?" I was pushing Paul.

"Hhmmm...I may know of one, come to think of it. Look, I'll make a few calls. Meanwhile, you'll do more extra work?"

"Just a few more," I said before Paul could hang up on me. "I really want to move up in this business."

I called Paul on my second day of extra work. I wanted to cancel Wednesday's job. I'd already had enough of background work and didn't particularly feel like seeing the inside of a school again. "Hi, Paul, it's Alice."

"Aren't you at work," he anxiously asked.

"Of course I'm at work," I bitchily replied. "Can't you hear my brats?" The assistant director took one look at me and assigned me three small children, all under five, as my own kids. I guess I still hadn't quite recovered from the tour. Two of the children were constantly wailing for their real moms and the other kept wanting to play hide n' seek. He'd already been hiding for an hour and I was enjoying his absence.

"Look, Paul, I'm cancelling tomorrow, OK?" I informed him. "I just can't get my appetite back for extra work."

"If you cancel tomorrow, then I'll cancel Thursday," Paul childishly replied.

"What's Thursday?" I asked.

"Only an ACTING JOB," Paul said. "No audition necessary. Mind you, it's only one line but there's your start."

My heart fluttered; I thought I might faint. *An acting job! Oh, Lord be praised!* "Oh, thank you, Paul!" I effused. "What's the film? Where do I get a script?"

"The film...uh...*Bed of Blood*," Paul said. "Horror flick, I guess. I'm supposed to just give you your line. You don't need the script."

"Give it to me," I said.

"Huh? How did you know?" Paul asked, astounded.

"Know what? Give it to me," I repeated.

"Yeah," Paul said.

"'Yeah'? That's my line?" I was confused.

"Yeah," Paul agreed. "What a good guess. Call me tomorrow...from your extra shoot...and I'll have more details."

I walked back euphorically, almost stopping to say hi to Cameron Diaz. After all, weren't we now in the same league?

Instead, I went back to the holding pen to gloat to my fellow extras.

* * *

"Yeah? Yeah?" I snarled to myself in the mirror. I'd been rehearsing my line – my word – incessantly since I was aware of my new part. Sometimes I'd innocently whisper, "Yeah?" sometimes I'd just agree, "Yeah." I wish I knew what the scene was about.

I showed up at the studio at the appointed hour of 7 a.m. I was ushered into a hair and make-up room where I noticed a few ladies in various stages of undress. Pretty casual, I thought. I decided to keep my smock tightly drawn.

"Who're you?" one of the girls haughtily demanded. She was already made up and could afford to put on airs.

"Alice Kumplunken," I timidly replied.

"No, who are you in the movie?" Miss Nose in the Air wanted to know. Obviously she was the lead actor and I was some lowly bit player who didn't know much more than the film's title.

The make-up lady saved the day for me. "She's the masochist," she said, bored, having seen it all. The other girls giggled. All except for a girl sitting in the corner of a couch, weeping. She wore fishnet stockings and little else.

"At least she doesn't have nudity," Fishnet whimpered.

"Don't you?" a buxom brunette asked me.

"NO!" I snapped back, insulted.

The assistant director came into the room. "OK, everyone! On set!" he yelled. The girls got up and filed past him, no one bothering to go to wardrobe for their costume. The A.D. didn't make any bones about his ogling.

"I've still got to do her face and hair," the make-up lady said, pointing to me.

"There's still time for her," the A.D. said, checking his call sheet.

"What about my wardrobe?" I enquired.

"What've you got on under your smock?" he asked.

"N...nothing!" I replied, affronted.

"So what are you supposed to wear?" he asked.

"Something!"

"Well, go to wardrobe when you're done here. He'll find you something," the A.D. finally answered a question.

The make-up lady was rather harsh with my make-up. Black lips, heavy black eyeliner and teased hair. I wanted to ask her about this masochist remark but she was engaged in heavy conversation with her assistant.

"Jerome is sleeping with Janis, that's what I heard."

"He is, but she's sneaking around with Mark."

"Not Mark! He's gay! I thought he was with the props guy."

"The props guy is married! Didn't you know? His wife is our star."

I declined her kind offer of piercing my tongue. "Well, then, I guess you're done," she said, walking out with her mate.

Someone pointed out where wardrobe was located. I walked in and saw a man sewing sequin onto a bra. "Hi," I said, trying to appear warm and friendly regardless of how my face looked. "I'm here for my wardrobe?"

He looked up. "Who're you in the script?"

I looked ashamed. "I don't know."

He didn't appear to care. "What's your name?" he asked.

"Alice Kumplunkem," I replied.

He checked his call sheet. "Oh, the masochist! I'm just finishing your bra." He held it up. The sequins on the black bra turned out to be spikes.

"Is that it?" I asked, aghast.

"Naaah...we have the whole number for you," he said. He proceeded to put the bra on me plus a rubber skirt, thigh-high leather boots and to top it off, a dog collar. I was embarrassed when I saw myself in a full-length mirror.

I heh-hehed a little then said, "Would it be possible to look at a script?"

The A.D. ran into the room. "You're needed on set now!"

I followed him, feeling more foolish with each step. All the crew stopped to stare at me. "Whooo! Whip me, mama! Bite me! Spank me!" I zapped a disintegrating look at the creep who said that.

He turned out to be the director. "OK, Alice, see that bed? I want you to sit right in the corner, tight to the wall. Pedro here, he's the killer. He's going to come in with a bat. You see him, say your line and that's the scene. Short and sweet. Got it?" the director rat-a-tatted at me.

Sounded simple enough. A killer was coming after me; I should be scared. I wondered how my line fit in.

"Action!" was called. Pedro approached me, slapping his bat menacingly against his palms. I looked up at him fearfully and, wondering what he wanted, said, "Yes?"

The script girl cut the scene short. "Wrong line!" she shouted. She was right! I was supposed to say, 'Yeah'!

Before I was fired, I blurted out an apology. "I'm sorry, I'll get it right next time."

"Alright, take two," the director said. "Action!"

The killer came at me again. I gave it all I had; I cowered, covered my face with a pillow and, one eye peeking out, asked, "Yeah?"

"Give it to me!" the script girl yelled. "That's your line!"

"Cut!" the director yelled. "Alice, your line is 'Give it to me.' You like pain. You want it. I want you to slide up the wall real sexy and beg for it. Got it? Action!"

My mind was swirling. Pedro came at me again, I slid without realizing I was doing it and said, "Give it to me," in a flat voice.

"Cut! Print! Thanks, Alice, you're wrapped. Moving on to the lesbians in the shower scene!" The director dismissed me.

I walked away, wondering if we'd done the scene yet and should I perhaps mention I no longer wanted the part? Everything happened so quick. Oh well, it was done and over with and like the lady said, at least I didn't have to do nudity.

I left the studio and caught a bus home. It was 9 a.m. and everybody was going to work. I felt so dirty among them.

* * *

It was the Christmas break for the film business. That meant we were in mid-November and should get back to work around mid-February. Even if I wanted to do extra work, there was none to be had. I had to budget my money carefully. I was still left with a bad taste in my mouth about my one speaking part to date, although I couldn't quite figure out why. Maybe my acting ability had rusted. I decided to take a few classes. Paul said the trick was to take a class being taught by a casting director; that way they got a chance to see your work. Only one was being taught by a casting director – Bluto Parker. I signed up. The other classes I planned on attending were Relaxing in Front of the Camera and How to Breathe During an Audition.

* * *

Did I ever mention that I had a boyfriend? His name's Joe. Not much to look at but he sure gets work. I was looking forward to his arrival from Africa, where he'd landed a five-week shoot that turned into five months. I was going to spend Christmas with him, doing what we usually do. Make big plans to go out and then end up staying home, ordering pizza and a movie. It was a comfortable relationship.

I got an email from Joe. My man wouldn't be home for Christmas. He got another film that started immediately so he was just going to skip from Africa to Italy. Seemed the 'movie girlfriend' from the African film landed a role in an Italian film, but insisted that Joe be her co-star. The producers met her demand. It was hard to believe that just a year before, Joe wrote, produced, directed and starred in a one-man show that just took off. I begged him to write a role in it for me but he didn't. Who knows what might have happened then? Maybe I'd be in France. Maybe the show would have bombed. I wished Joe all the best but I was jealous. My self-esteem was low.

Since I wasn't going to get any lovin' from my beau this Christmas, I decided to find it elsewhere. I booked a plane flight home to Oak Paw. "Mom! I'm coming home this Christmas!" I said when I called her.

"Where you gonna sleep?" my mother replied.

"Uh...in my old room, I thought,"

"Well, I've turned that into the junk room," Mother complained.

"Gee, don't we have a couch at least?" She drove me crazy sometimes. I was starting to wish I'd made this call before booking my flight.

"Oh, I guess so," Mom gave in. "Sometimes I like to fall asleep there too, you know."

"For cris' sake, Mom!" I yelled. "I'll sleep on the floor then! Maybe I just won't come!"

"Listen, Alice," my mother warned me, "I won't put up with that behavior when you get here. You may as well just stay there if you're going to act this way."

"I'm sorry," I backed down. "Look, I'll see you on the 22nd. Don't worry," as if she would, "I'll make my own way to Oak Paw from the Saskatoon airport. See you then." I hung up quickly, just before the pent-up roar escaped my lips. I love my mother (I think... Aren't we supposed to?) but sometimes I daydream of gleeful matricide.

Instead, after I'd calmed down, I went out Christmas shopping. I entered a joke shop and bought my mother some lovely gifts. Cigarettes that blow up in your face, candies with a pepper center and perfume that was really spray-on itching powder.

Money well-spent.

* * *

I was living a *Family Guy* episode. No, I wasn't dreaming again. I was home for Christmas. I was experiencing a horrid tradition called Christmas dinner.

Mother had the usual assorted relatives over for her annual display of culinary skills. The turkey was dry as dust, we had four different jellied salads to choose from (my favorite being the lime Jell-O with mini marshmallows), her famous root vegetable salad, with candied fruit thrown in, mashed potatoes mixed with an entire container of margarine, and canned everything else, including the ham.

This year there were sixteen people crammed into our tiny house, including my sister Louise and her five brats. Each were a year apart and if one wasn't fighting with the other, the other was fighting with the youngest. The last-born was five and I've yet to see him not crying. Louise stopped raising her children after the fourth was born. Every now and then though, the maternal urge would hit her and she'd remember she was a mother. I'd be talking to her and Megan would be yelling at Simon and Louise's hand would just shoot out and smack Megan. She wouldn't miss a word of the conversation. Other than those few times though, her kids ran wild. The oldest was ten and was smoking at the kitchen table.

Speaking of the kitchen table, that is where the Grand Inquisition began. The family was curious about my showbiz career. When I had decided to move to Toronto and become an actress, my mother tried to discourage me. When that failed, she had every relative I owned try to dissuade me.

"Alice, it's alright to dream, but you're goin' too far!" from Aunt Stella. "What's wrong with your nice job at the factory?"

"Alice, I might do ya, but you're no Megan Fox, ya know," from Cousin Jerry.

But I went ahead with my dream anyways and now they all wanted a progress report. The questions were relentless. I kept trying to change the subject but I couldn't shake them. "Yeah, I do work pretty steady," I said, then looked at my brother-in-law. "So, Frank, how's the scrap heap business?"

"Fine, do you ever get to work with any big stars?" he replied.

I decided to make a big deal out of some of my better extra jobs, making it sound like I was one of the major characters. "Oh, yeah, about a month ago I had dinner with Tom Hanks." Really, I was on a lunchbreak on a film he was starring in. Maybe we were eating at the same time, but he was being catered to in his deluxe Winnebago and I was eating my box lunch in a stairwell of the warehouse we were shooting in. "I also worked with George Clooney. One of the greats."

"I think Charlie Sheen is one of the greats!" Louise gushed.

My great-aunt Ginny sat next to me. Every year she was seated next to me. She was about 98 years old and I could see right through her skin. She weighed about as much as Mom's turkey and ate like a horse, most of it ending up on me somehow. I always had to fix her a plate because it was too heavy for her to carry to the table. "Do they manage to make you look any better?" she asked.

"Sometimes I'm quite beautiful. When you get to set..." (and I knew they had no idea what common film words like 'set', 'Winnie', and 'crew' meant, but I wanted to assert some power), "...when you get to set, they have people there to do your hair, your make-up, everything. All you have to do is brush your teeth."

Aunt Ginny was all agog. But then she had spasms of delight when power windows were invented. "Do you ever get to work anywhere unusual?" she asked.

"There's lots of location work," I said, again not bothering to mention that these included morgues, back alleys and gravel pits. "I even have to go out of the city on some jobs."

"Do they pick you up for work too?" Aunt Ginny asked, all aquiver.

"Uh...sometimes we're brought to the shoot in a Winnebago," I replied, neglecting to add that I usually had to travel an hour and a half by public transit to get to the pick-up point. And when I did board the bus, I had to find a place to sit among the other 30 extras.

"And do you get your own dressing room?" Ginny dominated the queries.

I hesitated to answer but seeing as how she just couldn't butter her bun until she heard my comment, I kept talking. "Sometimes. And then sometimes you have to share a room." Yeah, with 100 other extras. Aunt Ginny just oohed and dug into her meal before it got cold.

Aunt Gladys' husband had been giving me funny looks all day and it was starting to make me uncomfortable. This was Aunt Gladys' third husband and I have to admit, I didn't much care for him, or her second, while I'm at it. After divorcing dear Uncle Sid, her taste got decidedly worse. Her latest, Vito Pennelli, had an undefinable presence. He was too smooth, too slick, a bit too greasy, oozy and languid. I guess it was definable. Aunt Gladys said he was a private investor but I harbored suspicions he was a gangster.

Mom, bless her heart, ordered me to go downstairs and bring up some more wine. I was glad to escape Twenty Questions Times Five and eagerly pushed my chair away from the table.

"I'll help you," Uncle Vito offered.

"It's OK, I can manage," I said.

"Please, allow me," he said, pushing his chair away from the table. He had been seated across me and it felt like a showdown.

"No, really, it's OK," I insisted.

"Oh, Alice! Stop being such a big star and show your Uncle Vito our basement," my mother butted in.

"But, Mom, it's only four cement walls and a dirt floor. Nothing fancy!"

"Aaaaliccce.....," Mother said warningly. I could tell my defense was arousing the relatives' curiosity so I dropped the subject.

We descended the stairs into the damp basement. The hair on my neck was standing up; I was tense. I was getting the creeps from my new Uncle Vito. I saw the wine in the old crate where Mom has always hidden her booze. "Our wine cellar, ha ha," I said as I grabbed two bottles. Uncle Vito's hands reached out and I automatically passed them to him.

Instead of taking the bottles, Vito wrapped his sweaty palms around my hands. "Uh...ha, ha," I laughed, even more fakishly than the first time.

He only persisted in holding my hands and giving me what he thought was a romantic look. I read lecherous. I couldn't pull my hands away without dropping the wine. Mom splurged and spent almost $8 a bottle.

"Does our movie star want to give her new uncle Vito a kiss?" Vito asked, giving me an olive oil-eyed look.

"Why don't we wait until we get under the mistletoe upstairs?" I joked. "Besides, I hardly know you."

"Oh, I'm sure you're quite accustomed to kissing strange men...and not only on the lips," he replied, pulling me closer.

His last comment didn't sound very innocent. As a matter of fact, it had a rather perverse connotation. As he was drawing me closer, I pulled the wine bottles up so that they were pressed top to bottom against our chests.

"We should get the wine upstairs," I spoke rapidly. "Everyone is so thirsty. Oh! Look at this! Mom bought AUNT GLADYS' favorite wine!" Hint, hint.

"Don't play the prude with me," Vito growled, dropping my hands and becoming quite intense. "I saw *Whispering Limbs*."

"Whi...what? I didn't do anything with that name."

"Sure you did. You were wearing an S&M outfit. I saw it at a stag. You were good," Vito critiqued. He had something there...but I still denied it.

"I think you're mistaking me for some..."

"Loved the bra with the spikes. The dog collar," Vito recalled.

He had me. I DID do a movie like that. But that was only five weeks ago! Could it have come out that fast? I thought it was called *Blood Bed* or something. I hung my head in shame. "Yeah. I did it."

"Why don't we go upstairs and talk to the relatives about that movie? Or any other ones I haven't seen, Miss PORNO star," Vito suggested.

"No! And I only did that one! I swear!"

"Tell that to your priest," Vito said. "So you don't want me to tell them?"

"No! Of course not!" I vehemently answered.

"Then I won't. But it's gonna cost you."

"Cost me? Oh, fuck, I'll give you a kiss already," I sputtered.

"No. Better. I want 200 dollars a month, every month, until...well, say until you want your dear family to know about them films."

I was shocked. This was blackmail! I was a victim of a crime! "Come on! You're joking!" I laughed at Vito. He only gave a slight negative shake of his head. I tried to bargain him down.

"Make it 50 bucks! Alright...100!"

"200 payable to me every month. They'll be wanting this wine," Vito said as he took the bottles out of my hands. I was fuming with anger but damn, I was going to have to pay. How'd I land in a mess like this? I only wanted to better myself in the movie business, not end up dealing with the mob.

I followed Vito up the stairs, killing the desire to push him back down. More relatives were entering the house. "Alice!" my aunt Fiona greeted me. "How's showbiz?"

"If I have to answer one more question about showbiz," I yelled, "I swear I'll puke!"

I ruined Christmas.

* * *

My best friend Velda and I were splitting a slice of pecan pie at some ritzy dessert place. Velda was graciously allowing me to be seen with her. Her star was rapidly rising and I harbored suspicions that I would soon be left by the wayside. I took a bite of sweet, gooey pie while Velda pressed a few crumbs onto her fork. I saw her arm shoot out.

"Bluto!" she trilled. She slipped her fork into her mouth and let it slide slowly, rather disgustingly, out. On her, it looked sexy. I turned to see who caught her eye and saw Bluto Parker approach us. Bluto Parker, the big casting director! I took his class! I tried to chew my mouthful of pie a bit faster.

"Velda, darling, how are you?" Bluto asked.

"Fabulous," Velda replied. We were really being Hollywood North today. "This is my friend, Alice Kumplunkem."

I stuck my hand out and tried to say hello but my jaws were wired shut by the pecan filling. I desperately tried to get my mouth opened.

Bluto touched my fingertips. "Nice to meet you," he said.

What did he mean, 'meet me'? I took his frigging acting class. Didn't he remember me? It was only a couple weeks ago. He'd really taken an interest in me; he was always making me re-do scenes. I thought he believed I had potential since he suggested I take more acting classes.

"Bluto, honey, I don't want to keep you, but do you have any word on *Stewardesses of the Americas*?" Velda batted her lashes which prodded Bluto to answer.

"Well, I can't say anything for certain...yet...but I can tell you one thing. It's looking quite promising."

"Oooohhh!" Velda gasped, in l950s delight.

"I have to run. Shane Scott, the director of *For Once and For All* and *Sometimes I Cry* is joining me for croissants. Ciao!" Bluto flitted off just as my teeth, with a cavity-causing pop, sprang apart.

"Bluto!" I shouted. Too late. He was already seating himself at a plate-sized table. I looked at Velda with anguish but she was busy looking at herself in her compact mirror.

She glanced at me. "Fix your face, Alice. A big director might notice us."

"Do you think he can wait the six weeks for the bandages to come off?" I sarcastically replied. "What's this Stewardesses thing you two were talking about?"

Velda signaled for another cup of coffee. It was one of those places where you went to see and be seen, but you made sure you got your money's worth out of a $6.50 cup of coffee. No charge for refills. "It's a TV series about this bunch of girls who live together and they also happen to work as stewardesses for the same airline. I had a callback a couple days ago."

"Think there'd be anything in it for me?" I asked hopefully.

"Are you kidding!? Tons of female roles! They're looking at every girl in the city. I'm surprised you didn't get an audition."

I wasn't all that surprised, but I was mad. Mad at Paul and mad at Bluto and mad at Velda. And since Velda was treating, I ordered a slice of $l4 cheesecake.

* * *

I was in Paul's office, so hyper I couldn't stop pacing. "Paul, Velda told me every actress in town is trying out for this show! Why didn't you get me an audition?"

"I tried, Alice, but Bluto refused to see you," Paul replied.

"Why?" I wailed. "I took his class. He knows my work. I bet he doesn't like me."

"He loooves you!" Paul tried to console me.

"Enough of that bullshit!" I screamed. "Everyone LOOVVVES me, that's what you always say! Tell me the truth for once."

"OK," Paul calmly said. "He hates you."

I gaped. "Really?" Paul solemnly nodded. Boy, I wanted the truth, but did he have to be so blunt? Yeah, the truth hurts. Matter of fact, I was momentarily devastated. Silent tears started streaming down my face. "Should I quit the business?"

"It's up to you," Paul answered. Strange opening for a pep talk, I thought.

"What I want to do is cry. I think I'm going to," I warned. I could feel huge sobs starting to wrack my body.

Paul grabbed the phone. "No, please, no, Alice. Let's not have any of that. It's too theatrical. Look, Bluto doesn't know it yet, but he owes me one. Let me make a call."

I held off on the waterworks. Truth is, I was quite proud of my agent. He was about to swing some kind of deal on my behalf. "Bluto!" Paul yelled into the phone. "I got a meeting with the entertainment reporter of the Daily Moon, that gossip writer, Sophie Tellus. I just wanted to get one fact straight...that was Shane Scott the director I saw you with at BumBoys, wasn't it?... Whaddaya mean, don't tell Sophie? ... I'll say you were probably researching for locations... You still don't want me to say anything? Gee, that was the only tidbit I had for the ol' gal. Maybe we can come to an arrangement? I won't say anything to Sophie and you see one of my talent for 'Stewardessess'... No, you missed one, Alice Kumplunkem...come on, she can't be that bad...OK, that sounds fair enough. We got a deal." Paul hung up.

"Did I get an audition?" I faintly asked.

"Well, sort of. It's actually a pre-audition."

"What the hell is a pre-audition?"

"Something Bluto does once in a while," Paul informed me.

"He'll have you come in and read a few scenes, just for his benefit. Then he'll judge whether you're actually good enough to be shown to a director."

"I don't know if I like the sounds of that," I replied. "Nobody I know has ever had to pre-audition. It's like auditioning for an audition."

"Best I could do," Paul said. "There's a couple scenes for you to pick up at Bluto's office. Outer office, I'm to tell you. Your time is 9 a.m. tomorrow."

At least I had a fighting chance. Before I left, I asked, "Paul, what were YOU doing at BumBoys?"

"One of my guys is a dancer there," he nonchalantly answered. "I caught his show."

Geez, Paul never saw me as Betsy Bunny and I was in Toronto for three weeks with the show. At least then he would have seen me at work and could have seen for himself I CAN ACT. Now I had to prove it to Bluto Parker.

* * *

I was still on the stoop outside Parker's Casting at 9:30 a.m. No Bluto and no co-actor. I couldn't bear to run my lines even one more time. The two scenes I was given to enact were pretty heavy. One was a love scene and the other was an impassioned argument. I had been studying them for hours. I finally called it quits at 3 a.m. but set the alarm for 5 a.m. to further prepare myself.

An overweight man ambled up the walk. Since it wasn't the anorexic Bluto, I assumed it was my co-star. Wanting to start off on a jovial note, I called out to him with his character name. "Hello, Nico!"

He gave me a snooty look. "I'm Tad, Bluto's assistant." His holier-than-thou attitude was a requisite if you wanted to work for Bluto Parker.

He didn't say anything else; just slipped a key into the door's lock and entered the office. I slipped in behind him before he could shut me out. "I'm Alice Kumplunkem," I announced myself.

There was still no response from him. His type of people really got my goat. Well, at least he didn't react badly to my name as some are wont to do. Around two in the morning, I got to thinking about the possibility that my name was hampering my career. It's Alice KumPLUNKem. I toyed around with the idea of changing my name to Jasmine Rothchild or Katania Cheyenne but decided against it. I had this belief that I should make it in this biz with my own name, contrary to my mother's wishes. But for the next few weeks, I was going to try saying Alice KUMplunkem.

Deciding that Tad was of no help, I sat in one of the pink Louis IV-style settees. After a few minutes, Tad must have realized I wasn't going to leave so he sighed and asked, "Can I help you?"

I sighed back and said, "I don't know. I have a 9 a.m. appointment to read for Bluto."

At that moment Bluto breezed in. He stopped dead when he saw me and pouted. "Oh, yes," he seemed to recall. "Well, let's get it over with. Come into my office."

I still hadn't seen any fellow actor and with some trepidation, I surmised that Tad would be my boyfriend in the scene. Tad spoke up. "Shall I hold your calls, Bluto?"

"Oh, heavens, of course not," Bluto retorted as he swept into the office. I followed, trying to quell the butterflies in my stomach. As if that wasn't enough, my knees were so weak they threatened to give way. Bluto sat himself behind his desk and picked up some papers. "Shall we begin with the love scene?" he asked.

I was busy digging in my bag for my photo and resume. I glanced up and asked, "Don't we have to wait for the other actor?"

"Alice, please, I'm a very busy man," Bluto said with a contracted-sphincter look. "I'll be reading the scene opposite you."

I got rattled. I was to read a LOVE scene with Bluto Parker who I knew in reality HATED me?

Boyoboy, Alice, this will take real acting. I took a deep breath, walked to the center of the room, turned my back and did a few actory things. Rolled my shoulders a couple times, put my fingers to my temples. I stood still for a brief moment before turning around to begin the scene.

"'Nico! You came back to me!'" I gushed, throwing myself against the desk. The script had called for Nico and I to embrace but Bluto's desk was an impediment.

Bluto leaned back in his chair and crossed his legs. "'How could I stay away from you? You mean everything to me,'" my Nico said in a severely monotonous voice.

Pick up the pace, buddy! The next line was a dandy and I put most of the acting into my eyes. I knelt before his desk. "'Oh, my darling, I'll love you 'til the day I die,'" I emoted, my ears tearing up. *Good stuff, Alice,* I mentally congratulated myself.

"'Oh, my precious, will you be my wife?'" the robot asked. Before I could give my predesigned line, Bluto's phone rang. He put more emotion into his "Hello" than into Nico's lovely-written lines. "Yeah, she's still available," he said. My heart jumped. Me? "You want Velda Springfield for six episodes. I'll get back to you after I speak to her agent." He hung up and looked down at me. "You may continue."

Lucky Velda! My knees were getting sore from where I had been kneeling for some time. I continued the scene. "Velda's my best friend, you know…'oh, Nico!'" I cried as I stiffly jumped up. "'You don't know how long I've waited for those words! Yes, oh, yes! When?'" Since it was impossible to follow the script directions requiring us to twirl around in each other's arms, I just did my own little tailspin.

"'As soon as possible, my little dove.' Shall we move on to the next scene?" Bluto/Nico replied. I could tell Bluto had ended the scene because his last line had some emphasis to it. If this guy had been an actor, he would have been doing lousier than I. No wonder he taught acting. How does that saying go? Those who can't, teach?

Oh, don't get catty, Alice. But who cares? This guy ain't even trying. He's not giving me any kind of break. I took the bull by the horns. "Bluto, I feel I must tell you..." I said quite straightforwardly, "I know how you feel about me."

"Alice, I told you, I'm very busy. I don't wish to discuss personal matters."

"My agent said you hated me and hated my acting," I said. It hurt just repeating it.

"Do you have a problem with that?" Bluto asked.

"Well...yeah!" I sputtered. "For one thing, I think it's getting in the way of this scene."

"Alice," Bluto said condescendingly, "if you are ANY kind of an ACTOR, you must learn to deal with these matters. Now, do you want to continue or call it a day?"

Alright. I'd show him what kind of actor I was. He wanted to do the argument scene, I'd give him an argument. "'Nico, I found out you've been cheating on me with Lisa!'" I yelled.

Bluto got up, walked to his window and drew the blind. "Don't rain....," he muttered. Then he glanced at his script. "'Honey, I wanted to tell you...'"

The script read that he take me in his arms and I shake him off. His arms weren't anywhere near me so I stormed up to him and gave his arm a jerk. "'You've been lying to me for weeks!'" I now gave his body a rough shake to put more effect into my delivery.

Bluto gave me an alarmed look then stammered out his line. "'Listen, you mean more to me than Lisa. It's just that....'"

"'Just nothing!'" I screamed, giving his wastebasket one hell of a kick. "'I can't listen to any more of your lies!'" I sprayed spittle into his face.

"I think this reading...," Bluto began. I don't know if that was his next line or not; I was cooking and there was no stopping me. I blazed on with my final speech.

"'I want you out NOW! I never want to see your face again, you FAGGOT!'" I bellowed as I slapped him in the face. *Oooopps...*

Did I really slap him? And hey, did I hear myself call him 'faggot'? Please tell me I said 'two-timer' as the script dictated. I stood stock-still, puffing a little.

Bluto stared at me. Through gritted teeth, he said, "That...will...be...all, Alice. Good...bye." His face was also beet red except for a white palm-print.

I fawned my way out of his office. "Thank you, Bluto...Mr. Parker. What a good actor you are! Hope I see you soon...."

* * *

Velda was over, in a state of euphoria. She'd gotten the wonderful news that she was cast in the stupid stewardess show. She brought over donuts and a couple frozen cheesecakes. "Come on, Alice!" she enthused. "Let's celebrate!" *Right, Velda. You'll eat the holes in the donuts and make one forkful of cheesecake last an hour and I'll devour the rest.* "Let's go and rent some videos and just laze around all day," she suggested. "I'm not going to get to see much of you for the next couple months."

"Sure, let's go," I replied with a lack of excitement. I just didn't have a good feeling from that audi...excuse me, pre-auditon. The phone rang.

"Alice, it's Paul," my agent said. "Bluto just called me."

My heart jumped. Maybe I had a part! Wait, I didn't read for the director. Maybe I had an audition! "And...?" I said with bated breath."

"And it looks like he wants to press charges."

"Wh...what? I don't get it," I stammered.

"What you may get is one to five in the pen. He said you got pretty rough with him."

"Paul! I was acting!" Wasn't I? I was delivering the script lines though I may have embellished a bit with the physical part. It felt so right though.

"Well, Alice, I'm going to see him later today. I'll try and calm him down. In the meantime, obviously you won't be getting any audition. I must say, I'm quite disappointed. I thought you were more professional than that." Paul hung up on me.

I turned to Velda. "Well, let's go already!" I said. "I probably won't be seeing much of you for the next couple YEARS. I'm going to JAIL!"

Good ol' Velda put aside her elation as she consoled me. How could I let Velda's good fortunes come in the way of our friendship? "Listen, Alice," Velda said as she rubbed my back, "if it'll make you feel better, I'll see if I can get you on the show as an extra."

* * *

Velda and I ended up at the video store after all. She confessed that she wanted to research her role and was busy hunting for the old *Airport* movies. I was wandering aimlessly. I couldn't even find a flick that I was an extra in. Sometimes it's fun trying to find yourself in a crowd scene. In the last video I'd rented, I spotted a close-up of my armpit. I found myself in the adult section and scurried through, not wanting to be seen there.

A title caught my eye. *Whispering Limbs.* My God! Wasn't that the film I was being blackmailed for?! How dare some inept goof of an employee put it on the shelf?! I furtively glanced around and saw no one in sight. Grabbing the video, I snuck it under my snug sweater then went off in search of Velda.

I spotted her considering the *Airplane* comedy. "Come on, Vel, let's get outta here," I said out of the corner of my mouth.

"Alice, what's that square thing under your sweater?" Velda immediately asked. Damn, I was caught. At least it was by Velda and not a store dick.

I pulled the video case out. Time to fess up. "Velda, I did this trashy movie, a skin flick. I found it in the porno section just now."

"Alice, this store doesn't have a porno section. So if it's on the shelf, it can't be that bad," Velda noted. "Why did you have it hidden?"

"Uh...I was, like...trying to steal it."

"Oh, Alice," Velda laughed. "All you would have stolen is an empty video case. They keep all the cassettes behind the counter. Come on, let's rent it."

I ate one of the cheesecakes and three donuts before my scene came up in *Whispering Limbs*. So far the film had been pretty schlocky but it wasn't nearly as bad as I'd been led to believe. Suddenly, there I was in that ridiculous costume. I cringed and glanced over at Velda. She was still watching rather uninterestedly. "Velda," I whispered, "there I am..."

Velda looked harder at the screen. "That's you? I never would've guessed." We watched my scene, which lasted all of 30 seconds. As soon as it was over, I switched the tape off. Velda immediately gave me her verdict. "It was kind of a sick film, definitely not a role I'd take, but I wouldn't get too concerned over it."

"Would you pay 200 a month to hush it up?" I asked.

"I don't know what you're talking about but hey...you had a line. You should get a copy of that scene to show to people," Velda suggested.

I wasn't that proud of my scene. I looked like a prime slut. But what I was going to do was put a stop to those payments I was making to Uncle Vito. Or else put the money to good use by contacting a rival gang member of his. Surely one of them would take my money to beat the shit out of Vito.

* * *

I did it! I finally got a lead role! Grant you, it wasn't a Spielberg spectacular but it could have been the beginning of things to come. It was the lead role in a non-union video. That resulted in the fact that I wasn't going to be paid, and I'd have to work a twenty-hour day, and the whole crew would consist of four second-year film students and a rich guy would be the producer, director and star. I could accept those conditions because it was EXPOSURE. And never mind that, I could honestly say in future conversations, "Have you heard of *The Beast Experiment*? No? Oh, cuz I had the lead in that." Real nonchalant, just a mention-it-in-passing conversation piece.

I'd be playing the wife of the caveman, obviously making me a cavewoman. It was amazing how I got the job. Paul saw an ad in 'Savage Lovers' magazine, of all places, and sent them my photo and resume.

The day I went in for my audition, I was asked to put my dance leotard on. Yikes! I wasn't prepared to dance! I was wearing the wrong clothes for anything remotely connected to dancing. I had one of Velda's skirts on which fit me like a girdle and this cute leather top that showed my chest off to great advantage, meaning it flattened them out a bit. Still, they insisted they must see me in that damn leotard. "We just happen to have an extra one if you've forgotten yours. Why don't you try it on?" they casually suggested.

What luck! And to think I was going to blow the audition due to plain stupidity. An actor should be prepared, quoth Stanislavsky...or someone in his field.

They handed me the leotard...or should I say the hankie and

two Band-Aids? I queasily looked up at them and saw a challenge.

"Thank you," I said professionally as I pinched the clothing from Mr. Virgo's outstretched hand. "I'll be back in five minutes."

In the bathroom of the house, I surveyed the situation. My eyes tried not to look at the pile of hair in the tub and the two cockroaches chitchatting on the bar of soap. Five minutes to get into their idea of wardrobe. I had a moment of panic when I realized it was completely impossible to wear a brassiere. There went one life-support system. But I didn't have time to panic; I'd have to squish and poke myself into the top. Unless I could wear the top as a bottom and the bottom as a top... Nah, wouldn't work. The bottom fit, sort of, and I could get away with the fact that I'd been meaning to shave for a couple months if I stood ten feet away. If they noticed, I'd say I was getting into character for the cavewoman.

The top was a different matter. Now, I'm a 38DD and the bra they handed me had a tag on it. Just to torment myself, I wasted five seconds to look at the tag. I didn't allow for reaction time though. *Aagghh! 32B!* The bright side was that I made use of the tag to cover myself an extra centimeter. Knowing there was absolutely nothing I could do about the situation, I crammed myself into the bra, made sure the most obvious parts of my breasts weren't showing and went out.

I had lost my composure. I dragged my feet on the way in, head hung low. I dropped into a chair and let them have their fill looking at me. I couldn't speak; I couldn't even put on the usual bubbly, sparkling routine an actor does to impress potential employers. "See me! I'm full of energy! I never bitch! I never sleep! I never eat! I don't even go to the washroom! I'm the perfect guy to have on your film!" No, I didn't even bother to suck in my gut.

Mr. Virgo finally broke the silence. "You fill the suit. You're hired."

***

I'm so glad to be home! Today was the worst day I have ever spent in this degrading, cheap, no-money useless business. Bring entertainment to millions of DVD owners? Phoeey! Read a book.

I reported to the pick-up point at 5 a.m. Public transit was not running this early so I spent Lunchpail's cat food money for a whole month to reach God's Country by cab. I'd be back to eating popcorn and rice again for a while and Lunchpail could enjoy the same people-food. I didn't see him doing anything to earn his room and board so he could suffer right along with me.

Our meagre crew soon assembled. Besides the film students and the producer/star/director, there were three other cavemen and an older lady who was to play my cavemother. We spent the next 45 minutes all crowded into the back of a Rent-a-Wreck van, looking for a convenience store that was open so the boss could buy cigarettes. We also picked up some six-hour-old coffee and then drove to our location. Their plan was that we were going to take advantage of the first light and they meant the very first ray.

The van was parked and the crew immediately dispersed, leaving some bewildered caveactors sitting in the vehicle. I logically figured we should be going into hair and make-up and since I was the star, I wanted them to get started on me as soon as possible. I stepped out of the van into pitch-blackness. The only light I could see was coming from the producer/director/star's bald pate. I approached him and asked about make-up. Hero, which is what I shall call him as that was his character in the script, gave me his first direction. "Go talk to Sergio."

I found Sergio on the third try. It's difficult with such a small crew. Besides hair and make-up, Sergio was also in charge of the props, the food, and was the driver of the van.

"We want a real natural look in this film since you're caveguys and no one wore make-up in them days," Sergio said.

"Well, did you bring anything?" I politely enquired. "Or shall we do it ourselves?"

He pulled out a kit and opened it. Amongst the bones, clubs, a couple bags of day-old donuts and a case of the most generic brand of soda pop to be bought in a dollar store, he found a can of hairspray and a container of baby powder. "Wait," he said as he scrounged some more. He finally found a comb among the sandwiches. "There you go. Put the powder on your face so you don't sweat."

I thanked him kindly and left without the goods. I figured it was every man for himself today and I'd make sure I looked my best. It was still pretty dark out, and quite chilly to boot. I tried to make out what kind of location we were at but there still wasn't enough light. All I could make out was the parking lot we were in. As I approached the van, the entire crew left on some fact-finding mission.

I sat on an apple crate in the van and pulled out my compact. The truck was only equipped with two front seats. Jug, one of the caveguy actors, was in the driver's seat. The other seat was occupied by the elderly lady. Only polite, I guess, lucky wench. "Jug, could you turn on the interior lights, please?" I asked.

Jug seemed like a nice kid. Real young and eager to please. I counted on him being my friend for today. He searched high and low for the switch. "Sorry, I can't find it," he said. "What'd you lose?"

"Nothing. I'd like to put on my make-up. I think we have to do it ourselves."

Jug looked terrified at my remark. I suspected he was on his first acting job. "Maybe I can sit up front and look for the switch?" I suggested.

We exchanged seats and after a few seconds, I found the switch. The only thing illuminated was the ashtray. I attempted some make-up and then decided it was going to have to be the natural look after all. Everyone was sleeping except for Jug and I and after five minutes of eerie silence, I decided to whilst the time away in conversation with him. We turned to each other and at the same time, we both spoke.

"Have you read the script yet?"

We laughed and felt like old friends already. In no time we were gossiping about the shoot. I was right; novice actor. Turned out he was an attendant at a carwash and was vacuuming out a pick-up truck once when he stumbled upon the same magazine my agent had found. He felt like fate was speaking out to him, telling him it was time to change his life around and reach for one of his dreams. Ever since he'd sat engrossed by Zak Efron in *High School Musical*, Jug wanted to be in pictures. And just the fact that he'd opened up such a filthy magazine (my stomach ulcer twitched at his description) was proof enough that he was getting a message from someone up above. He was pleased as punch to have gotten the very first job he tried out for. Personally, I don't think I would have cast him. He was very personable but his look didn't match the one I had in mind for a caveman. For one thing, those thick glasses he wore and his red-haired brushcut reminded me more of a character from *Revenge of the Nerds*.

Shortly after, Sergio came running to the van. "Everyone! Get into costume! We shoot in fifteen minutes!"

Sure enough, the sun was rising. I could see we were parked by a lake. The sunrise wasn't very glorious as it was obscured by the black, threatening clouds. The lake was in constant turmoil, huge waves crashing onto the shore. Ocean spray filled the air.

The only sight in sight were huge bluffs rising hundreds of feet into the air. They were majestic until the very top, where they were eroding and falling back to the earth beneath them. I looked for any other type of attraction and saw nothing but the sand and stone bluffs. I guessed, since we were dressed like cavepeople, and the bluffs could look like 10,000,000 B.C., that we were shooting here today. I wished I'd read a script.

"Hey, Serge!" I yelled out the window, since I saw him retreating back to the set. "Where do we change?"

"In the van!" he yelled.

I'm an actor, I figured. I'm supposed to be immodest about such things as nudity and ugly panties and menstruation. Just as I was rolling the window back up, I thought it funny that the ocean spray reached all the way to the parking lot. And was it ever cold! I looked at Sergio's back and saw him stick his hands into his pockets all the way up to his elbows, and hunch his head almost completely into his jacket. I figured out the clouds weren't threatening anymore; they'd gone ahead and done their dirty deed.

After making everyone cross their hearts and hope to die that they wouldn't peek, I stooped my way into the back of the van. The cavemother came with me. She was a petite old thing, maybe 4'11" and with grey hair. She was fortunate enough to be able to stand erect in the van. "I guess we girls have to stick together," she said sweetly. I wondered what the hell she could have been doing with a 'Savage Lovers' magazine.

We searched for our costumes. Eva finally found hers in a green garbage bag amid other garbage bags. Fur-covered item after fur-covered item was pulled out. "My goodness," Eva whined. "It'll take me longer than 15 minutes to get dressed."

I found my wardrobe in a baggie under Eva's purse. It was sealed with florescent tape so I assumed they especially wanted to make sure I'd find mine. I dressed in a matter of seconds and waited until Granny was finished. She was beginning to look like a human buffalo. She was ensconced in fur apparel from the hood completely covering her head to the mucklucks they provided for her feet.

Taking a break from all the velcro-ing she was doing, she glanced up at me. "My gosh, dearie, shouldn't you be getting dressed? Don't worry about me," she kindly suggested.

How I hated to tell her I was already dressed. I didn't want this saintly lady to think badly of me, and I couldn't very well say,

"This is all I'm wearing as I'm the sex object in this flick," could I? So I told a fib. "Oh, I guess I'm still half asleep. Yes, I should finish dressing."

She resumed hers and I wondered what else I could wear, if only to gain a few minutes more grace with her. I spotted the seat-cover on the driver's seat. It was a ragged, oil-stained, blue fake-fur cover. While Granny's back was turned, I whispered to Jug, "Jug, get up, you're sitting on my costume!"

He rose and I pulled the cover off the seat. I had a moment's sanity when I realized I was sure to be caught; what animal could I have killed to wear its blue fur? But then I figured there were already a few discernible peculiarities happening, so there was a chance I'd get away with it.

Granny turned to look as I was trying to find a way to drape the cover around my body in a becoming manner. I ended up stepping into the elastic fasteners at each end and wore it like a potato-sack stole.

Granny tsk-tsked. "You'll freeze your fanny, dearie." I could only shrug helplessly as the whole lot of us exchanged seats. The ladies sat up front while the cavemen grunted into their wardrobe. It turned out that there was a garbage bag awaiting each of them, filled with fur apparel. If you ever saw the film, you probably thought you were seeing a water buffalo, three grizzly bears, and a quivering, defenseless shaved gazelle.

Sergio came running back into the van. We were already behind schedule as we were given 20 minutes instead of 15 to dress. He didn't bother to shout at us through the window this time; he just opened the van door on the run and leapt into the driver's seat next to me, causing me to knock into Granny, causing her to miss a purl in her knitting. Sergio sat there for about 30 seconds, his face and hands pushed right up into the heaters on the dash. He gave us a sidelong glance. "Get onto set and put that seat-cover back where you found it."

We were indeed a motley crew as we filed from the van.

Sergio was cracking open a bottle of Scotch but hey...it was 7:30 a.m. already. Since we had no idea where we were to go amid the sand piles, we just followed the sound of voices. I disobeyed Sergio and kept the seat-cover on. For some reason, we'd be walking towards the voices when suddenly it seemed like the voices would be coming from behind us instead. Eventually we realized that the sand cliffs were distorting the sounds and we'd managed to get lost.

We were undecided as to what to do. One of the cavemen, Skum (his character name), thought we should spark up a joint and let them find us by the smell. I guess he thought it a fine idea as he went immediately into action with Plan A.

Jug took Skum's suggestion seriously but offered an alternative plan. He thought we should collect firewood and build a fire; maybe someone would spot the smoke or we could even send smoke signals. Seeing as how I seemed to be the only one approaching the frostbite stage, I suggested we all combine our voices and hope they would locate us.

"Help! We're lost! Help!" the five of us started screaming. After a couple minutes, I made another suggestion. "Everyone! Try to project your voices!"

Skum scoffed. "Yeah, right, Miss Joker. How can we project if there's no camera?"

Amateurs, I thought. Rank amateurs. I never knew exactly what that term meant but in Skum's case, rank certainly seemed to fit.

Sergio suddenly came running over a sandpile. "What's goin' on? Get on set!" He took off and we all went running after him en herd to make sure we kept him in sight.

The rest of the day simply went from bad to worse. None of us got to look at a script. I think I figured out the plotline though. It went something like this: All the cavemen are vying for my attention but my mother wants me to become a cavenun. Hero appears, I fall for him, so does my mother, and she eventually allows him to drag me off by the hair into the sunset. You may find it to be a rather violent film as Hero does away with my other caveadmirers one by one by bludgeoning them all with Styrofoam rocks.

I froze my butt off all day and every one of the film crew offered to wrap his arms around me to keep me warm. I thought I'd give Jug the honors. He was the only one who didn't throw a lewd remark in with the offer, so I knew Jug was either shy or gay (or just a nice guy?) and I'd settle for him. I told him how real his acting was. He was the first to die and he actually looked in severe pain when he was bludgeoned.

"I wasn't acting," Jug denied. "That Hero guy hit me so hard, his fist went through the Styrofoam. I took a good punch to the nose." Every actor after that had the same look as Jug. I guess our Hero was a method actor.

The rain eventually tapered off to a mist and it warmed up to five degrees above zero. The frozen sandpiles thawed out a bit and we ended up slip-sliding in mud for most of the day. I secretly appreciated the mud. Once it dried on you, it made for some sort of protection against the cold.

We were slightly behind schedule when we completed our last shot – the Hero dragging me off into the revised moonset to make me his wife. It was once again -12 below and the ground was frozen. Hero played method actor with me too. I was yanked by my hair over the mud and rocks and got scraped from top to bottom. Embarrassingly, my bikini top became snagged on a root and the clasp that held it together was torn away. At that point though, I was covered with so much mud that nobody noticed.

We packed up all our stuff. I was tired of looking at these people. My body ached and I just wanted to go home. We had all been promised a ride right to our front doors and Mr. Virgo, aka Hero, approached me.

"Alice, fine work today. Especially that last scene," he smiled. "I'll give you a lift home."

I was happy to ride in a Toyota Corolla instead of the van, with everyone cold and muddy and smelly. We left immediately. I tried not to fall asleep as soon as the car warmed up.

"So," Mr. Virgo opened the conversation, "have you ever considered doing nude photography?"

"No."

"You SHOULD consider it. You have just the body for one of our magazines."

"Which one?"

"There's many! 'Breasts', 'Huge Breasts', 'Big Breasts', 'Boobs', 'Huge Boobs', 'Big...'"

"I get the point," I interrupted. "But I don't think I'm interested."

During the hour-long drive to my place, Mr. Virgo didn't let up. "We could start easy. Simple camera, simple lighting. I have a digital camera at home and all you would need is an ordinary light, like a lamp you would find in a bedroom."

I humored him a bit. "And who'd be the photographer? Sergio?"

"Oh, no," he seriously replied. "I'm also a photographer."

I bet, I thought. I wasn't too impressed with his directing or acting. But when we got to my place, I gave it the ol' college try at being a professional actress. "Well, thank you very much, Mr. Virgo, for giving me this wonderful acting role."

"No problem," he replied. "Shall we say next Saturday, 11 p.m.?"

I wearily shook my head no and went inside to kick my cat.

CHAPTER THREE

Paul was perturbed. He didn't like the idea of my taking work for no pay. "Are you SURE you didn't get ANY money for that video?"

"Paul, all I can give you is 20 per cent of my cold," I nasally shot back. I was in a vile mood. I woke up in one, stayed in one all day and decided to pay Paul a visit in one. It helped what I was determined to tell him. If he couldn't get me one decent speaking part, I was going to get out. Not only out of his agency but out of the business.

Paul took a long look at me. I seethed back at him. "Alice, don't tell me you've come here to give me one of your speeches," he whined.

"What if?" I snarled. "I'll make it short and sweet. If I don't get a good, PG-rated line soon, I'm quitting. Thank you for your time." I got up to leave. Had to blow my nose anyways.

"Alice, Alice," Paul said consolingly. "Look, I've been thinking. Maybe you do have some talent. I'm going to make a long-distance call on your behalf." He nodded his head, already acknowledging the heartfelt thanks he thought I should give him.

"To who?" I sneered.

"I have a contact in New York. I think it's time to ask him for a favor."

Yeah, right, Paul. New York. He should have said, "I might be able to land you a local CBC one-liner" and I would have bought it. But even I couldn't buy Alice Kumplunkem in New York. Yeah, I'd be hot competition for those Actor's Studio graduates.

Still, I needled Paul. "And when will I know?"

"Give me a week. Until then, can I book you for extra work?"

Gee, did he actually end that sentence with a question mark? And a week wasn't all that long. "I suppose," I reluctantly agreed, a mucous bubble expanding at the end of my sentence. My vile mood returned, as I remembered why I'd gotten a cold in the first place. "But one week ONLY, and that's FINAL."

* * *

I gave Paul three weeks. The biz was pretty slow and I'd only gotten two extra jobs. There is absolutely nothing to say about them; they were so mundane. Get on set, wait four hours, do a five-minute bit where you just cross the room, have lunch, go back to set, wait four more hours, do another five-minute bit where you do another cross, then wrap for the day. Both jobs were for $12 an hour, opposed to the union extras who raked in $33 an hour plus overtime plus meal penalties plus whatever else that union entitled them to. Bigshot extras. God, I wanted to be like them. On the positive side though, I became a pretty good euchre player.

After nursing my cold for a few days, I decided to check out the employment possibilities in the 'real' world. (The question most asked of an actor by their family: "When are you going to get a real job?") Well, hot damn if I wasn't qualified to be much more than a welfare recipient. I couldn't deliver pizza as I didn't have a car. I couldn't be a courier because I didn't have a bike, computers were beyond my understanding and phone sex was out of the question.

I got hired at a supermarket. Stock person. I spent all day ripping crates open and putting huge cans of juice on the shelves. I thought I finished quite quickly until I was reminded that I had to have all labels facing forward. Back down they came, where they stayed, littering the aisle. I quit. They didn't even pay me.

I was sitting at home with the newspaper's classifieds in front of me. That section was the only portion of the paper I used. I was circling things everywhere – cheaper places for me and Lunchpail to live, jobs to check out, seeing who wanted to buy what furniture I had left. I was poor now. Lunchpail had been ignoring me for days. I had jestingly said to him, "Sheesh, Pail, the cheapest place for you to live right now might be the Humane Society." He took it to heart.

The phone rang. For some reason, I sensed it was Paul and I steeled myself, knowing I had to be strong.

"Alice, sweetheart! Fun job! Only 20 extras required and you get your own Winnebago."

"Each?"

"Of course not. But there's only 20 extras. Get there early and you'll get a chair."

He almost hooked me. A winny compared to a roomful of stacking chairs...I had to sell my CDs to make this month's rent...two weeks to go on the pawn ticket to get my bedroom suite out of hock...Mom wants me to pay for that appendix operation I had when I was six...

NO!!!

"Sorry, Paul. No more. If you can't come up with a decent audition for a speaking part, then please don't bother to call me anymore." I hung up on him. I couldn't believe I stood strong! I felt elated.

A week later I felt deflated. Every carton of milk I bought expired the day it was supposed to, the couch I'd been sleeping on sprung a spring at both ends and the worst, the very worst, was that I got a 'Dear Alice' letter from Joe the schmo.

Dear Alice, it basically said, *I will be coming back to Toronto very soon but please don't call me. I'm returning with Beulah who is now my fiancée. Good luck in your career. Joe.* He didn't even bother writing 'Love Joe', if only for old time's sake. I can't say the news surprised me because I had been feeling niggling doubts for some time, but it did irk me something fierce. I'd been moping around the apartment ever since, feeling very sorry for myself and eating nothing but junk food.

With an energy one only sees in emancipated people, I

answered my ringing phone.

"Alice! It's Paul the Persistent! New York came through. Next Monday, 3 p.m. New soap called *Monday to Sunday*." He went on with the details. It was to be a *Big Chill* meets *Modern Family* kind of show and my look fit one of the characters they hadn't been able to cast yet.

I slowly felt hope seep back into my life. I even felt chivalrous enough to ask Paul if he needed me for any extra work in the meanwhile.

"Sorry, hon. Got nothing to offer you right now."

I wished I hadn't asked.

* * *

I spent that phone call until Monday afternoon dieting. I took the Greyhound Bus into New York and didn't talk to a single stranger or pimp all the way. I kept my return ticket (hoping I wouldn't need it) and my meagre spending money close to my breast. I arrived with two hours to spare before my audition and with a bad case of nerves, decided to while the time away at a restaurant in the vicinity. I gorged on fried chicken with an extra helping of fries and gravy. It didn't seem to help my frayed nerves but it sure gave me a good case of gas.

At a quarter to three, I stood before the imposing structure that was Largemar Productions. With a deep breath and a final fart, I walked through the portals. You would have thought I was entering the White House, for Pete's sake. A uniformed doorman opened the door for me then immediately directed me to a reception desk. A veritable Loni Anderson receptionist enquired as to my business with Largemar.

"I'm here to audition for your soap opera," I answered smugly.

"Which one?" Loni glitteringly asked. "We do five."

"Uh...*Monday to Sunday*."

"Our new one! Sure to be a smash hit! Watch for it!" Loni trilled by rote.

"Well, I hope to be in it," I quipped.

"The auditions are on the fortieth floor. The receptionist there will direct you to the proper area."

"Thank you," I said. I stood a moment longer, hoping she'd tell me to break my leg or something. Not a word. Ah, she was probably up for the same role. I headed for the express elevator.

I got off rather green in the gills. It took precisely three seconds to get to the fortieth floor and my stomach contents threatened to exit the elevator before I did. As soon as I had my gagging under control, I spoke to the new receptionist. "Hi, I'm here (burp) to audition for *Monday to* (belch) *Sunday.*"

This gal was Ice Queen 2009. "Down the hall to the end. The casting director will check you in." She immediately went back to some typing. Sheesh, this one probably had a callback for my role already.

Down the hall, to the end, to a door with a sign proclaiming that I was in the audition area, please enter. I paused a moment to have a private pep talk. *OK Alice, this is it. Act like you've never acted before. Smile a lot. Sparkle your eyes. Relax, Alice, relax. Settle down, gut, settle down. OK, let's go in. Alright, three more breaths. Now, LET'S GO GET 'EM!*

I opened the door and was confronted by a sorry sight. Twenty overweight, out-of-fashion, dumpy European women faced me. I felt like I was in the House of Mirrors. A bizarre feeling washed over me; I felt like bursting into tears.

A luscious blonde entered through another door, followed by my twin. All eyes in the room drank in the blonde, including mine. Perfect figure, perfect hair, perfect teeth. An unusual insight hit me... Why, she was probably just like me once, but then some sugar daddy spent millions on liposuction, rhinoplasty, dental care, breast reduction, waxing, hair, etc. on her. But then I realized it to only be a fantasy when a more truthful insight hit me. If she originally looked like me, how would she have really found a sugar daddy?

"Beverly Bohunk?" Miss Perfect asked. Beverly hesitantly stood up. You would have thought she was going to the electric chair. "You'll be going in next. Just hold on a moment."

She approached me. "Hi! What's your name?" she asked.

Oh, great. The name game again. *Hey, Alice, cut it out! You're letting this scene get to you. You're better than them! Stand out! Besides, your name isn't going to sound any worse than Beverly Bohunk's and nobody snickered then.* "Alice Kumplunkem!" I proudly stated.

Miss Perfect checked her list and marked me off. "We're running a bit behind schedule," she said. "There's a scene on the table for you to study. Alright, Beverly, come on in." She spun off before I could speak. I'm glad, because I had the urge to endear myself to her by telling her she had the looks to be an actress. I'm sure every second Bohunk in the room probably said it and I didn't want to be part of that crowd. And please, I'm sure I had to be the best-looking Polack of the bunch.

I had my lines down pat when my turn came along at 4:45. I had the questionable pleasure of watching a constant procession of slovenly-looking sad sacks come and go. Miss Perfect, still shining bright, announced that I could go in. I followed her and saw five people sitting behind a table laden with food. How nice! They were trying to put us actors at ease. Miss Perfect announced me and I walked forward. And kept walking forward until I was right in front of the table. Mmmm...strawberries, pate, chocolates, all sorts of goodies. I reached for a custard tart.

"Those are for US," a huge-bellied man said. *Aux fuck! Faux pas!* I quickly back-pedaled back to Miss Perfect who gave me a frown, causing a single furrow to interrupt her flawless features.

"That man is Abe Goldstein," Miss Perfect said, "the owner of Largemar. In order after him are Troy LeRue and Abby Flute, the executive producers of the show. Sam Wymer is the producer and

Fred Guyler is the director. I'm the casting director. We'll be deciding if you're suitable for the role."

"Oh you're so pretty you should be an actress," I quickly squeezed in.

"I'll be reading opposite you. Did you bring your photo and resume?" she asked.

OH, OH. "Uh...didn't my agent send you one?" I beseechingly asked.

The casting director acted as if she'd heard this excuse once too often. She heaved a huge sigh, as did two others around the table. "I imagine there's one around," she muttered. "You should always bring a photo and resume to all auditions."

"Yes, I'll remember that," I vowed to her. "I could phone my agent and have him get one to you immediately."

"Well, let's just see how the audition goes," Miss Perfect said. "Anytime you're ready."

Ohhh, I so wanted to please them and already I'd committed two no-no's. I opened my mouth to speak and couldn't, for the life of me, remember my first line. I looked like I was in pain as I desperately searched my mind for that elusive line.

"Where's your script?" Miss Perfect asked a touch clippingly.

"I left it in the waiting room," I confessed. Thing is, I deliberately left it there. I wanted to impress them by walking in scriptless, to show them how quick a study I was.

Abe Goldstein groaned aloud. "I'll run and get it!" I quickly offered.

The director picked up some papers and without a word, handed them over to me. I grabbed them, ran back beside the casting director and played my heart out to Abe Goldstein. I'd deliver a line to Miss Perfect then jerk my head to catch Abe's response. He was just sneaking sidelong glances at everyone, which only served to make me more manic.

Halfway through the scene, I noticed an unintroduced man. He was manning a video camera, capturing my performance.

Now I was shaken. Had I known I'd be on camera, I'd have...what? Tried to act better? In the scene we were enacting, I was talking to my evil sister about our mother's will. I'm playing this newly discovered daughter and I'm begging for some piece of this will.

Now, after having discovered this camera, I'd deliver some heartrending line and end it with an oozing Marilyn Monroe smile. I couldn't help it; my inner soul knew I should act in anguish but my face was beyond my control. It was trying to...ugh...make love to the camera.

Finally, after an eternity, we ended the scene. I slipped in one more quick Marilyn smile replete with pose before the cameraman clicked off his recorder. There was a dead silence. "Shall I do it again?" I asked.

"Oh, no, no," all five at the table concurred.

Miss Perfect gave them a cool, appraising glance, lasting all of a second. "Thank you, Alice," she said.

She was edging me towards the exit. "Shall I send you my photo and res—" No time to finish the sentence.

"No, no, that won't be necessary," Miss Perfect interjected. She was definitely ushering me out. She didn't even bother to escort me into the waiting area. The door was firmly shut behind me as soon as I'd cleared it.

But maybe...dare I dream? Was she to be in on a discussion about me? My availability? How quickly they could get me? I stood still for a moment, hoping to catch a tidbit.

"Where's SHE from?"

"Toronto, Canada."

"You know, they wonder why all the American stars are taking over their shows, and why we hire about one Canadian a decade. My God! If that girl is any indication of the talent from Canada..."

I fled.

My mind was doing nothing but zoning and I felt like I was on the verge of spontaneous combustion. I wanted to do it in private though. I staggered down the hall to a door called Marilyn. (Agh! Bamboo shoots under the nails!) There was an identical door next to it which read Clark. I assumed this was Largemar's cute way of saying Men's and Ladies' washrooms.

As I pushed my way through Marilyn, I had a moment of clarity. I stopped dead with the thought which was almost teletyping itself into my brain. You...have...just...made... a...laughing...stock...of...your...self...in...front...of...the...biggest... employers...in...the...business...I...repeat...

I calmly stepped through the door. When I was on the other side, I accelerated its slow-closing swing by throwing my body against it. "WHY MEEEE??? Oh my God, it was all recorded on videotape! For years to come, people are going to watch that audition and get the belly laugh of their life!" I tried wisecracking to keep from crying. "Whoopee! I'll beat out Joan Rivers for comedy video of the year!"

I banged on a washroom door. "Face it! You can't act! Stick to the background where you belong!"

I pounded my fist on the hand dryer. "First you're doing films with a six-dollar budget, then you somehow manage to do a porno film and now you think you're so big-league, it's time for the soaps! Fat chance, fatso!"

I dried my hands. "Velda can't decide if she wants her fur coat in black or white. My boyfriend, oh sorry – make that EX-boyfriend, can't wait to drop me for some witch doctor's kid and I'm the court jester for Largemar Productions. My mother doesn't believe I'm really her kid, my agent obviously looks on me in an unkind light, and yet I think I'm so special, I'm going to blow Marilyn Monroe outta the water!"

The dryer stopped. I also stopped my tirade. I looked into the mirror and felt like throttling the throat of that loser reflected. The criminal urge was so strong that I actually reached out to my image. Catching myself, I slapped the mirror a few times. I finally broke into tears and slid down between the matching pink sinks. I rested my cheek on the pipes, which I barely noticed were not given the same painstakingly pink paint job as above.

I wailed for a while. Every now and then I'd throw in another spoken reason for me to wallow in self-pity. Suddenly I stopped. My eyes focused on a pair of legs directly across from me. Realizing someone had just overheard my monologue on my crisis of a life, I figured it was likely a lady fearful of this madwoman.

"It's alright," I said in a wooden voice. "It's safe to come out." I was afraid to stand up, knowing the violent state I was actually in. And since this lady now knew my intimate secrets, I didn't exactly want to face her. I just remained sprawled under the sinks.

A disgustingly trim woman dressed in ultra-gaudy Rodeo Drive clothes walked out of the stall. Her hair color was so beautiful, you knew it had to be fake. As she stood above me, I was pleased to see that she had a hair protruding from a mole placed oh-so-becomingly by her mouth.

"I wasn't afraid," she spoke with a fancy Vassar College accent. "You've certainly had to struggle through life."

Yeah, so what, lady? Have you ever had to struggle? Would you struggle if I tried to pull that greasy hair out of your mole? I felt wicked. I felt like doing it; I knew it would grow back twice as long. Instead, I just sniffed a big one.

"My name is Karen D'Amato," she introduced herself. "I'm a producer over at Sebrings."

Spare me, I thought. Just go down the hall to the Largemar audition room, watch my tape and then spare yourself. She continued, "And you are...?"

I felt compelled to answer. "Alice...snuffle...Kumplunkem."

"I'll be in touch," she said, looked in the mirror, patted her already sleek hair, and exited.

Be in touch? What for? I had enough of New York. I caught the bus back to Toronto, my tail between my legs.

* * *

I was back in my beloved, coldhearted Toronto. I was living in squalor and depression and wanted to be left alone, thank you. As a matter of fact, I was debating whether I should seek asylum in Iran or Siberia, or just an asylum. I felt like an infectious, pus-filled sore. Obviously I wasn't wanted in my home country or the land of opportunity. No one wanted me. Not even Lunchpail.

I was gone from Toronto less than 30 hours and in that time, not wanting to be outdone by New York, my Toronto life fell apart. I entered my apartment and the first thing to greet me was a note from my landlady. How I hate when they enter your apartment without prior permission. The note said she wanted to see me as soon as possible.

I went down to her spacious suite and presented myself. She asked me to come in and I immediately saw my dear cat Lunchpail curled up in front of the fireplace, a bowl of cream within reach. "Lunchpail!?" I cried out. He glanced at me and snobbily turned his head away again.

"He's not called Lunchpail anymore," Mrs. Beautt informed me. "What a ridiculous name for a cat. He is now known as Winthrop the Third."

"Sez who?" I asked. What in the hell was she pulling? "I don't get it," I said, meaning every word.

"I went up to your apartment to enquire about this month's rent, and the large amount owing on LAST month's, and I heard this awful meowing," Mrs. Beautt exaggerated. "I felt it within reason to use my passkey and I found this poor cat STARVING." She glared at me with venom.

"Oh, I DOUBT it. I was only gone a DAY," I retorted. Mind you, I didn't have much cat food to begin with when I left.

"And the SMELL in your apartment! We do have health laws

to obey," my landlady continued. Well, she did have a point there. It was pretty acidic. I'd been making a bag of kitty litter last a helluva long time, changing his box only when I absolutely had to. Such as when he began shitting in my sugar bowl.

I didn't know what to say. I could fight for custody. Hell, he was MY cat – I could just take him back! I looked at Lunchpail who stood up and stretched. *Fuck, Pail, are you grinning?* I could see he'd been given a bath and sported a gay red flea collar. He ambled over towards some space-age tent which I realized was a fancy litter box. Yeah, he was a happy cat here. What alternative life could I offer him? Deserter.

"Fine, Mrs. Beautt," I said. "You can have him. Just take care of him." I turned to leave.

"Alice, the rent. I want it ALL in one week or you'll be evicted. I'm giving you verbal notice and," she rummaged in a pile of letters, "written notice." I was handed said notice. I sputtered a bit, then grabbed it and turned on my heel. I didn't feel like being nice to her and why the hell should I?

The next dilemma was that my phone was cut off. OK, OK, I didn't pay that bill either. And if I didn't pay the heating bill, that would be the next to go in a couple days. I used a couple precious quarters to phone my agent.

"Paul, it's Alice. Look, I bombed big in New York. Just don't ask," I pleaded.

"I don't have to," Paul quietly responded. "I've heard from them already."

"Well, I won't ask for any more speaking parts, I promise. Paul, I need an extra job real bad. I'll even take the $10-an-hour ones. Do you have anything?"

"Alice, it's dead right now. There's nothing to offer you. Call me in a week." He hung up.

So I spent the week holed up in my flat. I didn't wash my hair and it hung lankly around my shoulders. I decided to spend my last few cents just on chocolate and potato chips. My face had broken out like mad but did I care? Well, I cared enough to have a good zit-picking session.

I had just finished squeezing every last blackhead I could find. My face was red and blotchy. I sat and waited for the inevitable. Mrs. Beautt was expected any moment, probably accompanied by eviction enforcers.

Sure enough, there was the knock. I took my time getting to the door. I opened it with a resigned look on my face. Resigned to the fact that as of tomorrow, I'd be living on the street, all my belongings in a borrowed shopping cart. *Please be kind and spare some change when you pass by.*

Standing there was the lady from the Largemar ladies' room.

"Hello, Alice," she said. "If you remember, I'm Karen D'Amato. I'm a producer for *Tomorrow Will Come*, the soap opera." *Great. Now I'm being turned down for roles I haven't even tried out for yet. Word does get around fast in that town.* She continued, "I was in the washroom at Largemar when you did your Scarlett O'Hara number."

Oh, I see. She doesn't want me to stay away from her auditions, she only wants me to pay a couple grand for the destruction I caused in her precious powder room. "Yeah, look," I said, "I know I caused a few bucks worth of damage. Uh...I'm a bit strapped for cash at the moment. Maybe we can work something out, like maybe I can work for you for no money...till it's paid off, ya know?" I didn't put much excitement into my offer. I figured, if you want to throw me in jail, go right ahead. It was a place to live.

"Well," she said, looking awfully unangry, "you're right on one point. I DO want you to work for me, but it won't be for nothing! Based on what I heard from you in the ladies' room, I'd like to hire you as the executive consultant to the writers on my show. I do hope you're available?"

Available?! My next gig was to be at Sing Sing but hey, I think I can get out of it. On the inside I was already planning the celebration party but on the outside, I was acting real cool. You know how they do it in the movies – making it seem like I would maybe consider the proposition but maybe I was quite satisfied with Paul's People. I lowered a shoulder, curled my lips, scratched my neck (Lunchpail's fleas had found a new home) and casually asked, "What's the pay like?"

"There'd be an increase every three months, but I was thinking of a starting weekly salary of $3000, if that's agree..."

"Fine!" I interrupted. "We have a deal! When can I start?" I was shaking her hand furiously with both of mine.

"Anytime. Book a flight with American Airlines, charged to Sebrings, of course, and let me know when you're in town. We'll arrange for your work permit and...," she continued, pulling an envelope out of her pocket, "here is a retainer check for $3000. Welcome aboard."

With that, she left. I stood there, reveling in my newfound success. I had a job! Suddenly my iron shoulderpads turned into regular lightweight (wash by hand) foam. I was so grateful to Ms. D'Amato! Why, even her mole hair had looked a rather pleasing shade of Raven Black #32.

Something nagged at my mind. I pushed it into the corner. *I love thy neighbor! (except for that bitch Beautt) All is right with the world!* That same nagging thought returned. I put it in a half-nelson. I was on top...it was on top...I was...it was... Aagh! I was pinned.

The thought made itself known loud and clear. I had to leave Paul's People. It was going to be a tricky situation; since I hadn't gotten the acting job, Paul didn't get any commission. In the meanwhile, I was going on to a much better show-business job. He couldn't touch me. I owed him something, but it wasn't money. He wasn't going to like the fact that I was now a step up on him in the biz. He'd dumped on me so often; now he was to be the dumpee. I could do it though, because I was going to New York City to be an executive consultant, whatever the hell that was.

Eat my dust, Paul.

* * *

New York, New York. What a contradiction.

This is what my days consisted of: I'd leave my ritzy sky-high apartment, dressed in the finest clothes my salary could buy, which means that I was finally buying clothes first-hand. I'd jump into a cab summoned by my solicitous doorman. I'd be let off at Sebrings Productions, my palatial place of employment, where I'd be heartily greeted by Chester, keeper of the gate for Sebrings. I'd walk past my receptionist, Lilli, who'd breathily gush a wonderful, super, meaningful good morning to me. I'd put my belongings in my swank private office then head to the huge meeting room marked 'Writers – Alice Kumplunken, Executive Consultant'. I'd stop to marvel once more at my name in lights then, hoping that today might be different from the others, I'd open the door, stride in and take my place at the head of the table. That is where the glamour ended and the grind began.

"Were you raped? Or at least something close to that?"

"What indecent things have you done in your career climb?"

"How many men have left you?"

"What makes you such a loser?"

And on and on and on. Every day, nine to twelve and then two to six, I'd sit there having to honestly answer the most demeaning questions thrown at me. It hurt. The grosser, disgusting, saddening and sickening items I shared seemed to please them the most. Just before my breaking point, the writing staff would gleefully scrabble to their notepads and shout out ideas.

The two head writers, Mary and Bill, were going at it head to head. "Let's have Gino and Dina get robbed as soon as Gino presents Dina with the engagement ring," Bill shouted at Mary.

"Oh, Gino!" Mary enacted. "Save me!"

"No!" Bill yelled. "Let's have Gino put the ring in her champagne glass and Dina accidentally swallows it!"

"Oh, Gino!" Mary began choking. "Save me!"

There definitely was a high energy in the room. I was left, forgotten about, alone to recall the buried, ugly lowlights of my life that I'd been forced to reminisce about. It was all too obvious why I'd been selected for this position. It was because I had LIVED. I had suffered grief and agony and humiliation. These people merely had spouses and children and a mortgage. They were BORING. I was ALIVE. God, I wanted to be like them.

Suddenly, I could tell a scene had been written. They'd gather in their seats, stare at me like I was a bug under a microscope, and then one would usually start.

"Are your parents alive?" Bill asked. He was so tense, you would have thought he was back in Vietnam.

I hesitated a bit with my answer. At first I was tempted to say my mother was dead and my father was alive. Nothing against Ma, but...uh...well...well, she might watch the show and see herself in it. Lordy, she may cut me out of her will, which will solely consist of money that I gave her. As soon as she found out what my salary was, she made me feel so guilty that I promised to send her home $500 a week. All that notwithstanding, I liked my father's memory.

"My mother's alive, my father's dead," I answered. *Oh, did I notice a twitch of interest?*

"How'd he die?" Mary asked sans compassion. "How old were you?"

"Let's see," I tried to remember that painful era. "I guess I was eight years old. Dad...oh, my silly Dad... He was always trying to help people. Anyways...uh...one day this neighbor of ours was plowing his field. His cattle got loose and Dad saw them. He went to tell the farmer and of course the guy was mad. So I guess Dad, figuring he had to help, offered to plow while the guy went to get his cows. 'Cuz see, Dad was scared of cows. He'd never have made a farmer. Dad drove the local school bus. I remember him driving it.

"Anyways, the farmer says thanks and Dad gets up on the tractor. Now, he could drive a bus but he'd never been on a tractor. Somehow he managed to jam it into high gear, the tractor took off with a jump...Dad...fell off...he fell to the ground...I wanted to help him..." It was hard to continue. The memory came rushing back.

"How could you help him? Were you there?" Mary asked. Everyone poised on the edges of their chairs, awaiting my answer. I could only nod.

"Did you see him DIE?" they asked en masse.

"I was going to tell him Mom said not to go doin' anybody no favors. I was just passing the farmer and told him his cows were loose and he said I know and then we heard the tractor roar. We both looked and it was like I saw it in slow motion. Dad fell backwards and at first he just hit the ground and was a bit stunned, I guess. He was about to get up and I swear I could see that sheepish grin coming over his face. But...for some reason...the tractor did a circle and ran him down. Then it did it again. At first the farmer and I...we were just paralyzed...but then we ran to try and help Dad. Except that fucking tractor was keeping us away. It was like a fucking dog protecting his bone. Dad...finally...didn't need our help anymore. He was plowed six feet under."

BOOM! My writers went into action. It was good timing because I couldn't continue. I sat in my chair bawling while the writers began their usual routine.

"Let's have Peter Clifton die," Bill suggested. "His fan mail's been way down."

"No, we don't have the OK from the producers yet," Mary replied. "Besides, Peter doesn't have any children."

"Wait!" Bill said. "I'm on to a good thing. Let's have Peter discover he has a little girl, and he's on his way to meet her, and he gets in a tractor crash...no, it's not coming..." Bill banged his skull.

"Yes! Yes! But he'll get in a plane crash, and the daughter can see it on the news...," Mary continued Bill's train of thought.

"No! The plane will crash into the lake where she just happens to be swimming, and they won't be able to find Peter's body..."

"And maybe he's alive and maybe he isn't!" Mary gleefully finished the scene. There'd be a mad flurry of keystroking. Mary finally glanced at her watch. "It's almost lunch. This afternoon, we have to figure out the cliffhanger scene for Friday. I think Beluga should attempt suicide."

Everyone nodded their agreement. Beluga was the character who had the most of my miseries assigned to her. At first, I thought there'd be only one character based on me but I was told it was too unbelievable that so much hardship could befall one person. My unfortunate life was to be spread out over a few characters but poor Beluga took the brunt of it. And get this – they wanted to come up with a name similar to mine, so what sounds like Alice Kumplunkem? Beluga Gotyerdinski? They seemed to think.

I gave one of my very rare executive commands. "OK. Lunch."

"See ya later," Bill said to me... "Think about suicide."

This type of thing happened every day. They'd file out for lunch and I'd be left trying to sweep up my dignity. I could have quit, couldn't I? They weren't holding a gun to my head. No, they were holding a paycheck.

I'd pull out my low-cal yogurt, an apple and an ounce of cheese and eat in a pensive silence. Then, feeling quite down in the dumps and oh-so-sorry for myself, I'd leave the building and walk two streets over where there was a junk-food heaven haven. One day I'd have 31 flavors, the next day I'd have a whopper of a sandwich, the next day a bucket. I was drowning my sorrows in root beers and frosty shakes.

Then I'd head back to the office, undo the top button of my skirt, and talk to my writers cum psychiatrists. Once 6 p.m. rolled around, what I privately called 'your hour's up' time, I was a broken women. All the writers would jovially leave, still talking about ideas for the show. No one ever said good-bye to me; I was treated like the mats under their rolling office chairs. And every evening, moments after they'd leave, I'd get a burst of ferocious pride.

"Alright, Al," I'd say aloud, "you're not that bad off. You're rich. You're in New York. You could have lots of friends."

I'd gather my things, leave my hell on earth, and that's when, every night, a whole different lifestyle would begin.

* * *

Depending on how lonely I was, I'd either head for Piles o' Pies, Little Shop of Donuts or Mascots. Piles o' Pies sold a lot of pies, piles of them as a matter of fact. Quite delicious too. At first that was the main attraction for me, but I was aware of this black girl who was the cashier. She always seemed to be studying me.

At first Raunda didn't want to have anything to do with me. I couldn't get her to say more than three words back to me. I persisted in hanging out at the cafe though, buying a slice of pie and a coffee for anyone who'd care to sit and talk to me. Finally, one night, after a man had negotiated with me for two slices of Boston Cream and an herbal tea, Raunda actually spoke to me as she handed me my change.

"You must have lots of money to buy so many pies," she said.

"I do," I replied. "I could buy piles of them if I wanted."

"Meet me after work," Raunda decreed. "I get off at nine."

It turned out that Raunda would be my friend. She intuitively seemed to know my situation. She said she was Rastafarian but I could find no such country in the atlas at work. I suspected she was African but she probably clued into the fiasco with my ex,

Joe the Jerk, and didn't want to hurt my feelings.

The deal, Raunda announced, was that I could hang out with her, but see, she liked to smoke a lot of pot, but it was expensive and she wasn't making that much coin at the pie stand, so if I'd buy it, she'd smoke it in my presence.

Eventually we became good enough buddies that I'd get to smoke some too. As a matter of fact, we'd smoke non-stop from the moment we entered her flat. Speaking of her flat, it was nothing compared to my fully furnished suite. Raunda's consisted of two rooms with a communal bathroom down the hall. At first I was terrified of the place, not to speak of the area she lived in. Raunda used six keys to let herself in and as soon as we'd entered, I heard what sounded like a murder in progress.

"Call the cops, Raunda!" I whispered, ready to pelt out of the place at any second. Raunda didn't seem fazed though.

"Let's go in my room," Raunda suggested. We were standing in a kitchen that was smaller than my bathtub, where a month's worth of dishes were collecting mold. Two doorways faced us. One was a red door, firmly closed, and the other merely had a beaded curtain. Raunda parted the beads. "Come on," she said.

"Raunda!" I stage-whispered. The room had gotten strangely silent. "I don't hear anything now. Something happened!"

"Yeah, the guy came," Raunda replied mysteriously.

I suffered a momentary heart attack when the red door suddenly opened. A black girl, who I assumed was Raunda's room-mate, walked out. She was followed by a well-dressed white guy. "Hi," I introduced myself. "I'm Alice, Raunda's friend."

The white guy just rudely pushed past me and left the apartment. Then the room-mate did something that turned my stomach. She opened an overflowing garbage can and calmly dropped in a used condom. She looked at me, catching my disgusted face. I looked into her eyes and what with their bloodshot appearance, along with her orange lipstick and unkempt hair, I thought she was the most evil-looking person I'd ever seen. "Safe sex, huh?" I feebly joked.

"I pay most of the rent here and I don't want you hanging out in the kitchen," she declared.

I really feared for my life. "May I go into Raunda's room, please? Ma'am?"

Raunda's voice rang out. "You comin' or not, Alice? Hi, Sugar."

"See you in a bit, Raunda. I'll be home early. It's pretty fuckin' slow out there tonight," Sugar (give me a break!) replied and left.

Raunda came out to lock the six locks. "Was that her boyfriend?" I politely asked.

"Don't be so naive. You really are from Toronto, aren't you?"

So, as I soon discovered, Sugar was a real, live prostitute. At first I have to admit that I was quite affronted. I didn't realize I was so pure. As an extra, I've played a hooker more times than anything else, but now I realized how off the mark I was. Nowadays, you can ask me the going rate for anything – round the world, BJ, anything – and I could give you a pretty good price. Hey! Not that I was into it! You just couldn't help overhearing when Sugar would bring in one of her dates. First it was the haggling over the price, then it was the oohs and aahhhss and then it was the squeak of the garbage can opening. They never spent much time in the red-doored room.

I felt fairly safe in Raunda's room. I don't think it was originally meant to be a room. I think it was supposed to be just a storage space. All that fit in there was a mattress on the floor with a TV at the foot of it and her clothes piled at the other end. No windows or other such luxuries. Not even a lightbulb. We got some light from the kitchen and she used a lot of candles.

Raunda and I would turn on the TV set as soon as we got there, light up the scented candles and ignite a few sticks of incense. Raunda would roll a joint the size of a $10 stogie. Then she'd roll one for herself. Now, I'm not old-fashioned; I've been around, I've smoked joints before. But these were usually pencil-thin and smoked amongst five other people, and I would get a nice, silly buzz. NOW, Raunda and I would smoke our spliffs and as soon as we were done, my eyes bleeding, my balance gone, unable to breathe properly from my scorched throat, as soon as we were done, Raunda would roll another couple. We'd smoke them too.

I'd talk quite a bit throughout the evening. Raunda apparently didn't have any stories of her own so she never interrupted. Midway through the 1 a.m. late-night movie, I'd usually pass out from one too many brain cells dying too fast. Raunda would never wake me up in the morning. I'd get up late and have no time to make it to my apartment before work. I'd enter the workplace wearing the same clothes I'd worn the day before, which delighted my writers no end.

After a night at Raunda's, I'd spend the next day with a smoke hangover, coughing a huge hack that had people across the street looking at me. It sounded like I'd contracted a good case of tuberculosis. All day long I'd drink sodas or juice or milk shakes, anything to soothe my throat. That evening, I'd head for Little Shop of Donuts.

* * *

One night, on my way home after work, I walked past a donut shop and thought I'd have a coffee and a bag of day-olds. I suffered a pang of guilt when I thought about eating a whole bag of donuts but justified it by thinking I was saving money by buying day-old. Then I remembered that I was rich; I could eat chocolate éclairs if I wanted. Coffee and donuts were sort of my sign though; it reminded me of what I really stood for – Extra Work. It seemed life was somehow better back then. At least I was suffering humiliating experiences for the first time, not the second time for millions of TV viewers to see.

As usual, I sat at a table seating for four. I set out napkins and donuts for four people then expectantly sat down for my pre-dinner appetizer. I was only half-listening to a couple guys sitting on stools at the counter.

"So he's sellin' newspapers on the corner every day for twenty years, never says boo to anyone, and at night, get this, he's the Shoe Kisser the cops have been lookin' for the last two years."

"Ya don't mean that weirdo on 5th and Exeter?"

"That's the guy! I heard he's made out with sixty or more pairs of shoes on broads," said the older man of the two. The crack of his ass was showing about a yard over his belt.

"They should shoot those fuckin' perverts. Or let me at him," said a mild-looking skinny guy. Judging by his macho line, he was probably Clark Kent. He glanced over at the waitress to see if she'd caught his threat.

My ears had perked up during their conversation. Every morning, I'd buy my newspaper from the very same man they were discussing. He'd never raise his head; just keep his eyes pointed downward. I thought he was shy and probably needed a friend as badly as I did. I'd often toyed with the idea of inviting him up for a home-cooked TV dinner one night. Matter of fact, I had next Tuesday at eight in mind.

I decided to speak up. "Did you guys know him too? Want a donut?"

In time I came to know Andre and Petie quite well. Andre was the dominant force in that relationship, although I couldn't quite figure out why. To hear him talk, he was making it with every third woman in New York, and that was because the other two-thirds were gay. That's what he claimed. His beer gut was of award-winning proportions and none of his jeans fit. Even if he was standing up, you could still insert a quarter into his back end. His hairstyle was stuck in the '50s. Andre was slicking on Brylcreem as often as he lit up a cigarette.

Petie was his best buddy – a tall, anorexic, acne-plagued

dude. I don't think I've used the word 'dude' more than a couple times in my life, but that word jumps into my head when I think of Petie. He was quite nice, almost vulnerable in a way. He hated his Afro hairstyle so much, was almost ashamed of it, so he always hid it by wearing filthy white caps with stupid slogans. You could see he revered Andre. His favorite cap said 'Kiss me! I'm with him!' and he truly believed the cap would work in Andre's presence. Petie often complained along with Andre about how hateful shaving was. I think it was rather a religious experience with Petie though, as it took him three weeks just to grow some peach fuzz. One day I thought I'd make him feel special by calling him Peter, but I was told it was a sissy name.

Besides Petie and Andre, our foursome consisted of Muriel, the counter-girl at Little Shop of Donuts. She was sort of seeing Andre whenever he wasn't busy with any other available woman, but I could tell Petie had a huge crush on her. Muriel was what you could call a 'hard' woman. She wore make-up and nail polish and nice clothes, but on Muriel it was all blue eyeshadow and chipped brown polish and size 7 clothes on a size 14 body. She wore lipliner but someone forgot to tell her she was supposed to fill it in with lipstick. The moment we were introduced, she took me under her wing. She wasn't in the same league as Velda but she did serve a useful purpose.

I'd usually see them twice a week, and sometimes for lunch too. I'd become a caffeine addict. We never made any plans to meet. Usually I'd get the urge to go there and when I arrived, Andre and Petie were usually there already. Muriel had no choice; she worked there. I offered to pick up the tab once in an earlier meet and since that day, I never had to offer again. They just let me pick it up every time. Mind you, they didn't abuse my pocketbook, but then how many donuts can you eat? And the coffee was free after the first cup. I didn't mind spending money on them; I was happy now to have three more friends. And where a night with Raunda would cost me $120, the guys usually ran me about 10 bucks.

Life at the donut shop was pretty laid back. No one ever did much more than read the daily newspapers then talk about what they'd just read. After a while, Andre and Petie'd go off in a corner to discuss "next day's business". That's when Muriel and I would girl talk. "What kind of business are they in?" I'd asked Muriel.

"Your guess is as good as mine," she replied. "Hey, like the new watch Petie gave me? It says Gucci but it really ain't. It's a genuine fake." Muriel displayed a watch encrusted in diamonds. If Muriel was wearing it, it had to be a fake. But sheeesh, Petie kept giving Muriel such nice gifts. One day it was a blouse, the next day a hind rump of beef.

I was starting to develop a little crush on Petie. I don't know why; maybe I felt sorry for him. He so adored Muriel, but Muriel and Andre were making it, and sooner or later, it was going to get to Petie. I offered myself as a substitute for his affections. "Petie, why don't you and I just kind of...go out sort of...alone one of these nights?"

Muriel and Andre had gotten up to go to the washroom together. I saw the yearning look in Petie's eyes and knew the time was right to strike. Petie stammered, "You and me? Go out? Alone?"

He put it quite succinctly. "Yes," I said, warming up to the idea, "we could go to a nice restaurant or..."

"I can't go out with you!" Petie yelled for all in the shop to hear. "You're one of them dykes!"

"Petie, shush! I'm not gay!"

"Yes, you are," Petie insisted.

"I am not!" I denied.

"You are," Petie emphatically informed me. "Andre said so."

"Oh, if Andre says so, then it must be true," I replied sarcastically.

"Yes!" Petie agreed. "Andre said he hasn't gone to bed with

you yet and you made no moves on him, so you must be gay."

I haven't gone to bed with him YET? Was I destined to? Oh, that thought was scarier than going to work every day. Even with the three-inch heels on the cowboy boots he wore, pants always tucked in, I was still taller. I'd TURN gay just to avoid copulation with Andre.

"Petie, forget I asked," I said. "For the record though, I'm not gay. I just thought that since Andre's with Muriel..."

"I KNOW that!" Petie shot in, putting on a brave front.

"Well, I just thought we could do something together," I petulantly finished.

"We are. We're drinkin' coffee," Petie said as if I was missing a card in my deck. At that moment Muriel walked out of the bathroom, squealing as she dodged Andre's butt-pinching fingers. Petie's attention was diverted.

Yeah. That was all we ever did. Drink coffee. I took a good look at Petie and wondered why I wanted to go out with him. He had three huge zits running down the front of his nose, his teeth looked a bit furry and there were bits of donut in his hair. I glanced into my coffee cup. Just a sip left. Then I knew for a fact that I would get up, walk to the counter and have Muriel pour me another one. Then I'd drink that cup. These guys were boring. That's why I asked Petie out; because I was bored.

I stood up. "I think I'll go home."

"So soon?" Muriel asked.

"I wanted to ask you if Sebrings needed some spare DVD players," Andre said.

"Stick around, I'll treat ya to a jam-filled," Petie offered.

Why, they cared! I sat back down, a goofy grin spreading across my face. I was gonna come back here more often.

* * *

One night at the donut shop, Andre was bitching about how

thirsty he was for a beer. He had a small fit when Muriel poured him another cup of coffee. "Enough already! If I wanted another cup, I'd ask for one. I want a beer." I could tell he hurt Muriel's feelings, so she was moody after that. "Petie, give me a cigarette," Andre ordered. He was always bumming smokes off Petie.

"Sorry, Andre, I'm all out," Petie had to admit. He was broke too.

"Come on, Muriel, lend me 20 bucks out of the till," Andre said.

"I can't do that. I'll lose my job," Muriel snapped.

"Come on, I'll pay you back tomorrow. What's 20 bucks?" Andre kept trying to coax her but Muriel refused.

After a while, no one felt much like talking. The few hundred dollars I had in my wallet started feeling like a few million. I thought I'd lose my newfound buddies if I didn't offer to share it with them in some small way. "Andre, if you want, I could give you some money for a beer."

"Great! Come on, Petie. Let's get outta here," Andre was quick to reply.

I upped the offer. "Look, if you take me with you, I'll treat."

"That's awfully nice of you, Alice, but I don't know if you want to go where we'll be going," Andre said. "Why don't you just stay and keep Muriel company."

"Because it's boring here!" I retorted, then gave Muriel an apologetic look.

"Honey, I know it's boring. But I don't think you want to be goin' with the boys. Stay here and I'll treat you to anything you want," Muriel kindly offered.

Anything I wanted? At Little Shop of Donuts, that meant I might have my fifth donut of the night or my twelfth coffee. And what did she want me hanging around for? Was she scared I'd try and pick Andre up? Hardly. I was starting to think I had my crush on Petie again. That's what I really wanted...a little lovin'.

Sure I had a few friends now, but I was still sleeping alone. Not that that was a new experience. Suffice to say womanly urges were starting to overcome me. I was dying for a little kiss even.

"OK then. Forget I made any offers," I said, standing up. "See you guys around."

Andre couldn't let this financial gain slip through his fingers. "Alright, you can come with us. But I'm tellin' ya, I'm real thirsty. See ya, Muriel. We're goin' across the street."

"Sure," Muriel quietly said. "See you."

Andre stopped to look at her for a moment. I think he felt guilty about leaving her behind. "Maybe I'll see you later," he said. "You still on the rag?"

I was embarrassed for Muriel but she only nodded. "Well, I'll see you tomorrow then." With that, Andre ushered us out.

I was excited. Right on! A night on the town! I looked across the street to see what bar we were going to. There were only two; a gay bar called The Backdoor and another bar called Mascots that advertised 'Racy Girls! Continuous Action!' The latter is where Andre led us. He stopped us at the entrance and puffed himself up. I could tell he imagined himself a big man. "OK, guys, no drooling, got that?" We both nodded, although I have no idea why I did. "Alice, I don't want you cramping my style. Let me have some money right now."

"Sure," I complied. "How much?"

Andre looked at Petie and did some figuring. "Let's see...six beers each, a few table dances...tips...got a couple hundred on you?"

I handed it over and we entered. It was pitch black in there and I stood still for a few minutes, letting my eyes adjust to the light. When they did, I could see men looking at me. I glanced at Petie, who was enthralled by the stage show. Andre was already settling himself down at a table and I ran to join him.

I wasn't the only girl in the place. There were about twenty others, most of them naked. So I was in a strip joint. I tried to make the best of it. A song came over the speakers and I said, "Oh, I just love this song!"

"If you wanna dance," Andre noted, "there's only one place to do it."

Just then a stunning girl walked by. She had on a G-string and a bra with her boobs poking out through the middle. She was lugging some kind of stool on her shoulder. Andre went into spasms.

"Petie! Didja see her? What a slut! I'd like to stick her up with my piece," Andre said. For some reason, both my dates had become quite crude ever since we'd entered the bar. "Shall we have her do a little dance in our pants?"

"I've got such a boner just looking at her," Petie declared.

"Petie!" I exclaimed. He was rapidly losing favor in my eyes. But he ignored me. The same girl walked by again and Andre grabbed her by the panties, sticking a bill into the elastic.

She merely stopped, made sure it was real money, then put her stool down in front of our table. She stepped on top of it and began her dance. I tried to push my chair back but I was crowded in by other men taking advantage of our purchase. The dancer was positioned right in front of my face, gyrating to the music. I don't want to be rude, and she was very pretty, but she had the worst vaginal odor. I simply couldn't help but notice; I swear I was no more than three inches away. And what was that? A crab? I leaned my head way back and the space was filled by Andre's head, making sure he got his money's worth of visual excitement. And damn if he wasn't drooling.

The song ended and our girl got off her pedestal. She hooked up her G-string, picked up her stool and was gone without a word. Andre looked at both of us excitedly. "Didja like that, Petie? How 'bout you, Alice?"

"Andre," Petie confided in a whisper. "I came."

That did it. I no longer wanted Petie. "I'm going to play some pinball games," I said. As I stood up, a dead ringer for Al Pacino as he looked in *Scarface* passed by. We had a deep look into each other's eyes and I'm sure something passed between us. With him, I think the look was "What the hell is a nice girl like you doing here?" I think my look said, "I'm so lonely. Won't you fuck me?" I scurried off to the pinball games but not before I heard Andre bellow, "Silvio! I haven't seen you in years! Where the hell you bin?"

My luck was terrible at the pinball machine. My highest score was 3000 and I needed 1,000,000 to win a free game. It was cheaper than a table dance though, and then I gave my head a shake when that thought entered my mind. Why was I still so hung up on money? I kept forgetting how rich I was now. Old habits are hard to break, I guess.

Andre came up to me and watched me play a game. I was deep in concentration. I could tell he wanted something but he took his time asking. Finally he casually said, "I think Silvio likes you."

My heart skipped a beat; the ball went through the chute. "What gives you that idea?" I asked, hoping it was Silvio who gave him that idea. I shot another ball into the playing area.

"He likes big tits," Andre replied. I risked a quick glance at him, but his look told me he was still buttering me up.

I went back to my game; this round was going better than my last few games. Barely listening to Andre, I asked, "How do you know him?"

"I used to see him around a lot," Andre replied. "You know, on the street. I haven't seen him for a while though. He was doing time in a pen in Utah."

Andre said that last line as if he'd just told me Silvio spent the last few years selling shoes in Idaho. "What!?" I screeched. The ball slipped through the chute again and my game was over. I gave the machine a slap.

Andre rushed to reassure me. "Oh, it was nothing. Just a little indecent exposure charge."

"That's not nothing," I replied. "That's pretty sick."

"Not when you know the story, Alice," Andre patiently said. "See, he just came from work – he's the deejay here – and when you see so much nudity around, it can affect you. So one day he left and...uh...I guess the atmosphere from the strip club was still in him and...well...his peter was hanging out of his pants and he didn't see anything wrong with it. But I guess some frigid bitch did and she called the cops. It was really a bum rap, and he had to go to jail for two years 'cuz of her."

Did I buy that story? I looked at Andre with an exaggerated questioning look on my face. "He wants to meet you," Andre said. OK, I bought it.

"Really?" I asked. "Now?"

"Yeah," Andre said.

"Alright, I guess so." I was suddenly shy.

"'cept, Alice, Petie and I need to ask you a favor."

"What?"

"Do you have much money left on you?"

"A bit," I hesitantly replied.

"Do you have another 200?" Andre hopefully asked. "Petie and I...well...we made a couple dates with some strippers. We need more money though."

I handed over two c-notes, pretending that I was paying for the introduction service. I knew I wouldn't get paid back. "Where you taking them?" I asked.

"Oh, just to the dressing room. This should buy us at least 15 minutes. We'll meet you back at the table. Silvio's there now." With that, Andre took off for his rendezvous.

I slowly walked back to the table. What was I going to say to Silvio? I practiced smooth lines. "So how was Utah?" No, stay away from jail talk. "How'd you get that ear-to-mouth scar?" No, he might be sensitive about that. "Been working here long?" No, because then he might want to talk about my job. I decided to just wing it.

"Hi," I said, sliding into my seat.

Silvio was watching one of the dancers. He barely glanced at me. "Hi."

That was the extent of our conversation. I was starting to feel like I had been had. Minutes later, my friends (ha!) returned. Andre was in a jubilant mood; Petie looked like he had been crying.

"So, how're you two lover-birds makin' out?" Andre asked cutely. I gave him an evil look. We weren't making out.

"Fine," Silvio replied, the liar!

"Well, I'm fuckin' tired, or...," he leered at Petie, "...tired of fuckin'!" They both had a good laugh over that. "We're gonna go. Comin', Alice?"

No, I was going to sit in a strip joint by myself. Of course I was coming. I looked at Silvio and threw off a "See ya."

"How 'bout tomorrow night? Meet me here at midnight," Silvio replied.

I was thrown back into my Nervous Nellie state. Midnight was pretty late. And this guy was an ex-con. And I'd have to walk into the strip joint by myself. And I...

And I was horny. "See you tomorrow," I agreed. I didn't even mind when Andre said he needed money for cab fare.

* * *

Silvio became my steady boyfriend. He made it very clear that I wasn't his steady girlfriend though. Really, I barely liked the guy but he was nice enough to let me take him to dinners and movies so I kept him.

We both knew the real reason I wanted him in the first place. Sadly, that became the worst part of our relationship. Our first date, when I met him at the strip joint, was so bizarre. I mainly hung out with him and when he got a break from deejaying, he said to me, "Wanna go fuck in the office?"

I was a little insulted, but I didn't want to lose him so soon, so I made a suggestion. "Why don't we go back to my place?"

"Because I only get 15 minutes for a break," Silvio replied.

I didn't want him thinking I was a prude but I just wasn't that free n' easy. Nevertheless, I allowed him to lead me to the office. I had just taken my top off, still trying to think of a way to get out of the situation, when the club's manager walked in.

"For fuck sake, Silvio! I'm not running a motel here! If I catch you boffing any more girls in here, you're fired!" The manager was livid.

I wanted to save Silvio's job. "We didn't boff, sir," I said.

"Just get the hell out of here!" the manager ordered. "I got work to do."

I hustled out, still buttoning my blouse. I bumped into a stripper who grabbed me by the shoulders. They're all pretty tough chicks and I cowered. "Oh, good!" the stripper smiled. "You did him already!" Just then Silvio edged his way past us and the lady relaxed her hold on me. Her smile disappeared and with a muttered expletive, she walked into the office.

So Silvio ended up coming to my apartment that night. I was ready for him, ravenous even. I was a wild woman. Three hours later, he still couldn't get an erection. I tried not to let it bother me; he probably had some deep, hidden reason.

"Patty, you just don't seem to excite me," Silvio said.

"Sorry, RICHARD," I pouted.

"Oh, didn't I call you Patty? Sorry," Silvio apologized.

"Yeah, you DID call me Patty! My name's ALICE," I replied. I wanted to add, "And who is this Patty anyways?" but I didn't think we'd progressed far enough into our relationship.

"Right. Alice. You told me that, didn't you? Well, I'm gonna split," Silvio said, getting dressed.

"Oh! Spend the night! We don't have to do anything," I begged, as if we hadn't been trying. I became a sniveling fishwife. I just wanted to lie beside a man. True, I had to wake up in two hours for work, and I didn't trust him enough to let him keep sleeping in my apartment, but I didn't want our date to end just yet.

"No, I'm gonna go," Silvio decided.

"Will I see you again?" I asked, right out of a movie.

"I don't know. I wanna get laid, you know," I was informed.

"So do I!" I hastened to say, letting him know I was putty in his hands.

"Well then, we'll have to work at this problem we have."

"I'll work! Anything you say!" Putty. Silly, silly putty.

So sex with Silvio became a constant experiment. Sometimes I got lucky and was awarded coital bliss. That is, if I could reach it in the 30 seconds it took Silvio. The best method, we'd discovered, was when I played 'Pedestrian'. I'd pretend to walk past this strange man in a raincoat, and he'd flash me, and I'd shriek. It worried me that he had once been arrested for this type of behavior but at least we were keeping it off the streets. My sexy lingerie had no effect on him, nor did my striptease. Once I let him take Polaroids of me and he still couldn't get it up, so we didn't try that again. Mainly because he wouldn't give me the photos back. Now, all this isn't my idea of good sex; hell, I love the missionary position. It was just the price I had to pay in the hope of sex period.

* * *

Yup, New York is a big city, even to a with-it Toronto girl like me. All the scary stories you hear? Well, they're all true.

I hadn't seen Raunda in a couple days so I moseyed on over after work one day. Lo and behold, there was a strange girl working the till.

I approached her. "'Scuse me, where's Raunda?"

"Off sick with a throat infection," I was told.

I hung out and ate a slice of pie, wondering if this girl felt like being my friend. She was more interested in her *Us* Magazine.

Feeling restless, I decided to wander over to the donut shop. Lo and behold, Petie and Andre weren't there. I sat at the counter and ordered the usual. I always started off with a blueberry-filled donut. "So where're the boys?" I asked Muriel.

Muriel was a bitch. "Oh, they got some fancy deal cooking with some low-life." I didn't think anyone could get any lower than Andre. "Andre says he has girls all over town, but who does he come to for money all the time? Me!" I sort of wanted to say that wasn't true; I'd loaned Andre about three grand so far. Muriel was probably glad I was there. She had an ear to grind to the ground. "I know they're up to no good. They'll end up shot or in jail. I should just drop that man for good." I thought so too, but I know that's not what Muriel wanted to hear. She wanted me to say how wonderful Andre actually was and how lucky she was to have him, but I didn't want to go to hell with such lies.

Instead, I decided to leave. I could go home but I had nothing to do there. I'd seen Silvio the night before and nothing was consummated, so I decided to ask him if I could hang out with him. Making sure no one saw me, I ducked into Mascots. Even at 7 p.m., the place was filled. I looked into the deejay booth but there was some strange man with a straw up his nose in there. That wasn't unusual. Silvio didn't work every day but he usually hung around the place on his time off. I approached one of the strippers. "Excuse me, Miss Nude Scranton? Have you seen Silvio around?"

"Silvio?" she mused. "The guy with the scar?" I nodded. "No, he hasn't been in today." Someone beckoned her over with a $10 bill and after informing me she hated Neil Sedaka music, she went over.

Well, so much for Silvio. I didn't know where he lived. I didn't even have his phone number. Come to think of it, I didn't even know his last name. I guess I had to go home after all.

Or did I? It was still so early still. Maybe it was time to make another friend. I liked the thought. I started walking around the streets of New York, trying to decide who to bestow my appreciation on. A kid whizzed past me on a skateboard, catching my elbow. I saw a group of them in a parking lot and walked over.

No one had hair. There were enough safety pins in their clothes to diaper all the babies in New York. Intuition told me they were skinheads. I eavesdropped on a couple kids and the conversation was all about glue and if they should pierce a second hole in their tongue. I was wondering if I was too old for the skinhead scene when an androgynous type approached me. "Whaddaya think you're looking at, lady?" Yeah, too old. I continued my walk.

I found myself in Times Square, as good a place to meet people as anywhere else. Sure enough, there was someone I sort of knew, the alternate deejay at Mascot's. Still feeling a pang for poon tang, I walked up to him. He was into a heavy conversation with a guy that looked like he was a bodyguard for a living.

"Hi! I hate to interrupt, but I sort of know you..." I began.

"From where?" the deejay was quick to ask.

"Mascots?" I replied. "I'm Silvio's...one of Silvio's girlfriends. You haven't seen him, have you?"

The deejay and the bodyguard exchanged a look. The deejay became very nice to me. "Well, it just so happens I'll be seeing him in a bit. If you can do me a favor, I'll make sure he gets a message."

A favor? "What kind of favor?"

"I've gotta deliver this briefcase to a friend, but I've got no time," the deejay said. "If you'll drop the case off and meet me back here in an hour, I'll be able to tell you where to find Silvio."

Sounded like a good deal. Besides, I had nothing else to do. "Sure," I agreed.

"You're a nice lady," the deejay said. "I'll have to tell Silvio that. OK, just deliver this to Bruno at 4344 Sixth. Got that?"

"Bruno. 4344 Sixth," I repeated, taking the briefcase. "See you in an hour."

"I'm counting on you now," the deejay said. Aaaww, he was kind of cute when he said that. I gave him a flirtatious wave good-bye and headed off to Bruno's.

Sixth Avenue wasn't too far away. En route, I passed one of those restaurants that has loud music and a dance floor. I guess if you wanted to pass the time between courses, you could always take a whirl on the dance floor. I slowed as I passed the window. The place was filled with pretty people all my age. Everyone was having a good time.

I was drawn in. Just a quick coffee, I thought. I needed a dose of handsome men to look at. I wished they'd look at me. I sat at a seating for two and placed my order. I let my shoulders move to the music; a slight indication that I was in the mood to dance should anyone be interested.

Curiosity overcame me. I kept looking at the briefcase and wondering what it held. Oh, for Pete's sake, it was just a briefcase. Bruno probably forgot his work at the office. Bruno was most likely the manager of the strip joint. I wondered what they paid those strippers? I know they made a killing off table dancing alone. Hhmmm, would the briefcase contents tell?

I put the case on the table in front of me and snapped it open. There was today's newspaper. Well, something to read while I drank my coffee. I pulled it out and underneath the newspapers were all these bags.

Bags of white powder. I stared at them, my mind trying to register something. Numbly, my brain ticked away, then like a bolt...COCAINE!

"Here's your coffee," my waitress said.

I slammed the case shut. I was scared to touch it, lest it spill open. The case took up the entire table top. "Your coffee, ma'am?" I was reminded.

"Yes, uhhh...." Why was I panting? "Just set it on top." The waitress shrugged her shoulders and placed the cup and saucer on top of the briefcase. "Will there be anything else?" she further asked.

I had to think. And I always thought better on a full stomach. "Uh...just bring me the pasta special." I don't even like pasta that much, which just goes to show you I wasn't thinking clearly.

My coffee remained untouched. My mind was repetitively racing...*I'm carrying cocaine...I've got cocaine on me...someone gave me cocaine to deliver...this is cocaine under my cup...*

Besides that, my personal seating area looked a mess. The newspaper had fallen apart around my feet when it dropped from my fingers. I would have put it back into the case but I was too petrified to open it. I ate my pasta off the briefcase too.

My hour went by and I still hadn't moved. I couldn't sit there forever, I thought, but I could sit for another hour and decided what to do. The waitress took away my dishes and a busboy came over to wipe the top of my briefcase. I wondered if he was a narc. I had to get out of that restaurant! I furtively glanced around; no one was looking. Quickly I snapped the case shut, threw money down for my meal and was gone in under 15 seconds. I was become paranoid, and I don't even use cocaine.

What to do? What to do? I walked the streets for a while, clutching the case as if I were carrying the Lindberg baby. No one paid me any heed though, and I finally figured out that as I was still in my fancy work duds, a briefcase didn't look too out of the ordinary. I relaxed my hold and my facial muscles. Still, I couldn't help thinking...*I've got cocaine on me...I'm carrying cocaine...*

I eventually ended up in Central Park. I meandered in a daze for a while until I spotted a park bench. Sitting down, I told myself, 'THINK!" What I was carrying was contraband, therefore a crime, and therefore, being a fairly good citizen, I should report it to the authorities.

A man sat next to me. He was about 45, carrying his own briefcase. He looked at me then quietly said, "You lookin'? Want weed? Hash?"

I stood up, quite affronted, and walked away.

At the park entrance I saw a police officer and ran over to him. Relief was in sight.

He looked at me when I reached him and simply said, "What?" He didn't look to be having a good day.

I opened my mouth and then snapped it shut. What was I going to say? "Hello, sir. I'm carrying a briefcase full of cocaine. Would you care to take it off my hands?" I'm sure those handcuffs would be snapped on sooner than you could say Ma Parker.

So I opened my mouth again and dumbly asked, "Is this Central Park?"

"Yeah," the man in blue replied.

"Thank you," I said and walked away from the park. It was all I could do not to run like mad.

Raunda! Maybe she'd want it! She liked her drugs. It was quite dark out already but I headed to her home-turf, deep in the heart of Harlem. I hated that area; I was such a stand-out. I wished I were a hooker. I wished I were a junkie. Just being black would have been an advantage.

The more I thought about it, the more I knew Raunda would like the 'present' I brought her. I rushed up the three flights of piss-stained stairs to Raunda's flat and started banging on her door. A little peephole slid open. Raunda's voice came to me. "Alice? What are you doing here?"

Just let me in already!! "I brought you a present. I heard you were sick."

The door locks sounded and Raunda opened the door. "I got a real bad throat infection. I can hardly swallow. What'd you bring me?"

"Drugs!" I triumphantly said, muscling my way into the flat.

Her eyes lit up. "Really? Real drugs like smoke, or drugstore drugs?"

"Cocaine," I said, thrusting the case at her.

"Cocaine? Why'd you bring me coke? I don't touch that shit. Why didn't you bring me some smoke?" Raunda whined. So much for gratitude. "Well, maybe I can trade it with Sugar for some weed." I handed her the case. "Why are you giving me your briefcase?"

"That's the coke."

"What?!" Raunda exclaimed. She flipped the latches and just stared at the mounds of coke. "Alice, I know you're rich, but you're not a millionaire. Where'd you get this?"

I was going to lie but the truth tumbled out. Raunda was really pissed off. "So you figured you'd dump the stuff on me? Well, I don't want it. Give it to someone else, but not me. I want it out of my place NOW. God, you're so hick, Alice. Don't you think you might be in some trouble by now?"

Oh, wow. I didn't even think about that. Raunda shut the case and opened the door. "Sorry, Alice, but until you fix this situation, you'd better not come around here. We've already had three murders in the building this year." The door's locks couldn't lock fast enough behind me.

I headed back to Times Square. I hoped the deejay would be waiting for me although I was over three hours late for our appointment. I waited in the shadows of the sex-shop where I'd earlier seen him. Some guy passed me, gave me a long look, then raced to a pay phone. Call it paranoia, call it intuition, but I left in a hurry.

I walked over to Mascots. Please, deejay, be there and take this stuff off my hands. I walked into the deejay booth and there was my Silvio.

"Silvio! I need your help," I said, starting to cry a little.

"Alice! Fuck, you're in such shit right now. What'd you do with the COKE, MAN?" Not even a hello kiss.

"It's right here," I meekly said, holding the briefcase out to him. He withdrew as if I'd handed him a live grenade.

"Get it OUT of here!" Silvio shrilled. "If you get busted with that, the club will close down, I'll lose my job...I'm not even supposed to be working tonight, but Vince is out looking for you. Bruno's looking for you. Fuck, half the scum in New York is looking for you."

"What should I do with it?" I whimpered. I was so tired of this dilemma.

"You dumb cunt!" Silvio yelled, and I could tell it wasn't the dirty talk he used in my bed. "What were you supposed to do with it in the FIRST place?"

"Give it to Bruno," I correctly answered.

"So DO it. I don't even want to see you until this blows over. Fuck, you're so stupid! You're dead meat, Alice." He shook his head. "You KNOW, you told Vince you were my girlfriend. So if you don't deliver, they're going to ask me where you live. I'll have to tell them."

Why did I have a sneaking suspicion he'd already told them? I left for Sixth Avenue.

4344 Sixth Avenue was an import business. Made sense, I thought. I was six hours late in delivering. Of course there was a sign reading 'Closed'; it was the middle of the night. Still, I could see a few burly types standing around inside. I timidly knocked on the door.

An ex-boxer opened the door. "I'm looking for Bruno," I said and was promptly yanked in. That sort of told me I was in deep trouble. I had to come up with a good story if I didn't want to end up swimming with the fishes. "Take it easy!" I yelled. "I just came from the hospital!"

A wizened old man croaked from the corner. "I'm Bruno. Where's the case?"

"Right here," I said. "Don't you want to know what happened to me?"

"Check if it's all there, Fingers," Bruno commanded.

"See, I was on my way over here, but this car ran a red..."

"Looks OK, Boss," Fingers said. *No, I snorted a kilo on the way over.* Of course it was all there.

"I'm OK now, but they thought I'd fractured...."

"You don't know how lucky you are to be alive," Bruno said.

"I know! I was pretty shaken up at...."

"Hatchet, call off the dogs," the don said. "Look, lady, you don't know me and you don't know where to find me. Got that?" Bruno was being silly, I thought. He was Bruno at 4344 Sixth Ave.

His tone of voice told me that I'd better play along though. "Sure, Bruno."

He gave me a long look then said, "She can live." Nah, he must have said "she can leave". I walked to the door and no one tried to stop me. I opened it as my back tensed for a hail of bullets. None came. I walked out, went around the corner and pissed my pants.

Something told me I shouldn't go home for a couple days. Happy to be alive, I checked into the fanciest Holiday Time Hotel I could find. After bolting my door and putting a chair under the doorknob, I crawled into bed and reviewed the night's events.

How did it all start anyways? Because Ms. Alice wasn't happy with the friends she had, she had to go looking for more. *See what trouble you caused yourself?* Maybe I didn't have the most desirable friends in the world, but they were my friends nonetheless. So Raunda was a pot-fiend who took advantage of my wealth; so my donut-shop cronies were a bit boring; so Silvio made me lick his toes after he'd worn the same socks for a week. They accepted me as I was and I appreciated that.

If only I'd known them longer, I could have told them that.

CHAPTER FOUR

Beluga Gotyerdinski committed suicide. No, not the character. She was too big an audience draw. The actress playing her, Valerie Krymkyw, went out in grand dramatic style.

Valerie Krymkyw was no dummy. She may have had that appearance but she knew her worth. She got paid the big bucks and received star treatment. She had it all, except for looks. So this morning her limo driver goes to pick her up and she's not her customary 15 minutes late. He gave her a few more minutes then had the doorman let him into her apartment.

It wasn't a pretty sight. Valerie was in a silk peignoir, face painted, hair to die for. Blood ran down her arms in already coagulated rivers. There was a rose by her face and she was holding a scroll tied with pink ribbon. At the foot of the bed was a mound of paper which turned out to be the day's shooting script on *Tomorrow Will Come*. She'd been dead for hours from severe razor nick.

The limo driver knew a good thing when he saw it. Before calling the studio, he called the press. Someone from the press suggested he call the cops. By the limo driver's misplaced priorities, the paparazzi had a great stroke of luck. They found Valerie Krymkyw's suicide letter.

Dear Shelby, the letter began. Shelby was her personal secretary who worked out of her apartment. Shelby said he tried to phone in sick that day but she'd apparently already left (in a big way) so he simply left a message at the studio.

Darling, the letter continued, *you know me – I'm the most together person you could ever hope to find, definitely not the type to commit suicide. However, I've been letting Beluga get to me. That poor thing! I'm well aware that it's only make-believe,"* Sez who, I wondered? Excuse me, please, continue reading her death throes letter, *but some nights I come home so depressed. One week I had two abortions! Oh, I mean to say, Beluga did. Tomorrow's script calls for her fiancé to leave her for another man! When will this poor character's suffering stop? She just lost another fiancé two months ago! People see me on the street and commiserate with me. I just can't go through with tomorrow's show. Please, the writers MUST kill off Beluga. No woman should have a life like that.* Well, I had to agree with her there. OK, OK, we're coming to the final stretch anyways. *I had to do this, Shelby. It's Beluga's only salvation. Please make sure you call the press but don't talk to the Post. They said I was terrible in* Sunset Sinner, *the last movie I appeared in and I'll never forgive them for that. And try to get me on the cover of People. You've been a dear, Shelby, and my will shall reflect that. Say good-bye to Beluga! Farewell, all! Love, Valerie Krym*—bloodstain. I imagine she'd signed her full name but her blood blotted it out. I don't know – it was one of the photos displayed in the newspapers.

An executive meeting was immediately called and unfortunately Valerie wouldn't be getting her last wish. By a vote of nine to one (mine being the dissenting vote), it was decided to keep the Beluga character in the show. Auditions were being held the same day as the funeral.

We didn't get much work done that day, which was a pleasing side-effect of the suicide. All sorts of press kept interrupting us. Their questions were probing but they were kinder on me than my writers were. I thought I handled the interviews quite well. I put lots of emphasis on the fact that I was the executive consultant to the writers and only met Valerie once (and that was only in an elevator) and my last name was spelled with a 'K'. It was all quite exciting, although I really did feel bad that Valerie had to go to such extremes to prove a point. Why didn't she just set up a meeting to talk to us?

The next morning, I picked up a newspaper from my usual stand and handed the change to the vendor. He slapped the coins from my hand, spit, and said, "I don't want your stinkin' money." That's as nice as New Yorkers get, I guess.

I walked into Sebrings Productions and instead of the usual hearty greetings, I was met with averted faces and suddenly busy people. I saw newspapers everywhere. I surmised that Valerie's death was still big news. On the elevator ride up, I opened my paper to see what else they had to say about ol' Valerie and the first headline I read was 'Head Writer to Blame for Star's Suicide'. Oh, no! But which head writer? Bill or Mary? I scanned the story some more and to my horror, saw that I'd been demoted.

I was now called the 'Head Writer'. Based on information received, the reporters discovered that a lot of the storyline, Beluga's in particular, was based on my life. The story basically said that if I hadn't been such a fifth-rate person, Valerie Krymkyw might still be alive today.

The elevator door opened onto a beehive. Everyone was running around with a newspaper and I swear I heard my name mentioned more than twice. My private secretary let out a huge gasp and pointed straight at me. All eyes turned and everyone froze.

"Good morning," I said.

Everyone scampered away. I entered my secretary's office just as she slid behind her desk.

"Good morning, Alice!" she said, as if she hadn't already seen me yet.

"Good morning, Lilli. Have you read the paper today?"

"No, why?" she out and out lied.

"Never mind," I said and started to walk out.

"Do you have something for me to do today?" Lilli asked.

Did I ever have something for her to do? She had a tough job being my personal secretary. File nails at 11 a.m., talk to boyfriend at noon, lunch with the girls for a couple hours, open my mail for a minute, and get off early for one appointment or another. How many facial peelings can one woman have?

"Of course not," I said. Then a disturbing idea hit me. "Wait, you can do something for me. Buy me every daily newspaper in this city."

I walked into the writers' conference room. My writers were already shouting ideas back and forth. Hhmmm...they were usually still drinking coffee at this time. Scenes were just flying. All of next week's shows had been written when someone finally acknowledge me at lunchtime.

"Oh, Alice, it's lunchtime," Mary reported.

"So it is," I replied, giving them all a very suspicious look. Everyone cleared the room. Damn it! I didn't say they could break for lunch! It was one of the few reasons I stayed with the job. Something was definitely up. And where the hell were my newspapers?

I stormed into the main reception room and damn if the entire floor hadn't gone for lunch. I saw a stack of newspapers on my desk.

Good Lord in Heaven, grant me a lawyer. The first headline I read was 'Charges Pending in Star's Death'. I scanned the story and my jaw dropped. If I was reading between the lines correctly, my fellow writers dumped the death on me. I was to be the scapegoat.

The next headline was ludicrous. 'Head Writer Jealous of Star; Gets Her Revenge'. That story claimed Valerie refused my romantic advances, so I got even by writing especially heart-breaking scenes for her.

An unusual sound caught my attention. What was it? I walked back into the reception room where the reception was better. Why, it sounded like a chant. I scurried over to the huge picture windows and glanced down.

Four thousand housewives, many pushing baby-laden strollers, were gathered below. I couldn't make out the placards they were carrying, but had this funny feeling they didn't say 'Ban Abortion'. In my 13th floor suite (cleverly designed as the 14th floor), I couldn't quite make out what they were saying.

But why were they trying to bust into Sebrings Productions? The cops were fighting them off quite brutally. Chester the doorman was also in the thick of it. What WERE they saying? "Kum-kumkum kid kim-ku" was all I could make out.

I walked back into my seldom-used office and noticed my window was designed so that you could slide it open. Well, the mysterious chant would soon be revealed. I slid the window open and was bombarded by "KUMPLUNKEM KILLED KRYMKYW!" Over and over.

"I did not!" I yelled out the window, but no one seemed to hear me. I tried using the executive treatment on them and ordered, "Go on! Go home!" Zip response. They were too intent on running my name through the mud.

The rest of my lunch was spent watching the crowd gathering below. I had planned on going out for some chicken nuggets but this looked like a lynch mob. So I sat in my safe, well-protected office watching the group who wanted to come in and tear me limb from limb. Surreal feeling.

Oh gee, lunch must be over! There was Mary and Bill fighting their way into work. *Go ahead, Bill, tell them YOU'RE really the head writer! Come on, Mary, tell them YOU'RE the one who made Beluga get herpes when all Alice Kumplunkem ever said she caught was impetigo.* But nooo, with Chester acting as halfback, they were magically transported into the building.

The afternoon became even more surrealistic. One second no one was on my floor, the next second it was pandemonium every time I looked. Once again, my help wasn't needed. I sat back and took a well-deserved break from psychoanalysis. We all pretended to ignore the chant from outside. If they didn't stop soon, I was going to jump out my office window and squash one of the suckers.

Miraculously, the gathering below dispersed at a quarter to four. Oh, of course, it was almost time for *Tomorrow Will Come*. Well, ha ha on them, I was going to get some revenge. Today's episode was taped days ago and the same ol' Valerie Krymkyw will still be playing Beluga. No surprises. Although Beluga does discover she's adopted in this episode. And see what I mean? I was NEVER adopted. Only once did my mother farm me out to a foster home, and that was only for a few months after Daddy died.

Lilli walked into the conference room. Wasn't she usually gone by this time? "Alice, there's some people here to see you," she told me. She wasn't very efficient. *What kind of people, Lilli? They wouldn't happen to be axe murderers now, would they?* "They're in the lobby," she stated.

"Show them to my office, Lilli," I said.

"Oh, there's way too many for your office," Lilli informed me and walked out.

I walked into our lobby and thankfully, just as I entered the room, I saw a camera. Immediately I threw my hands in front of my face – an animal instinct. FLASH! POP! FLASH! You would have thought I was someone important. I turned around and hightailed it to my office.

And sonofagun if they didn't give chase! There were a trillion questions being shouted at me. I made it to my office and locked the door behind me. Just hours earlier, my office had been such a safe retreat. *Come on, people! You're not going to break down my door now, are you?*

I ran to my intercom and paged Lilli. "Whaaat?" Lilli bitched. "I'm busy!"

Lilli! I'm your boss, for cryin' out loud! Jeezus, she was gonna get herself fired yet. "Lilli, this is ridiculous!" I said. "Look, tell them I'll answer a few questions but I'm not going to face them. They can phone me, alright?"

"This is the Herald," a voice came over the intercom. "Is it true that you led a life the exact same as Beluga?"

"No, I should hope not. Beluga had a much worse life."

"Entertainment Extra here," my intercom interview

continued. "What do you think of the accusations being thrown at you?"

"They're all lies! I didn't even know Valerie Krymkyw!"

"International Inquirer. Is it true you and Valerie were secretly lovers?"

"NO!"

The questions went on for close to two hours. My skin was crawling; judging from the reporters' questions, I think I was in trouble. Sheesh, I never thought a simple suicide could reach such proportions. I took one last question.

"Have you been charged with anything yet?"

"Why should I be? For FUCK SAKE, Valerie committed suicide! I didn't know her. I had nothing to do with it. Now leave me alone! I'm not answering any more questions. Lilli, send them away. Good-bye!" I wished I could slam down a phone but instead I clicked off the intercom with what force I could muster.

A few still persisted, but not for long. "Miss Kumplunkem, are you an illegal alien?" Now, what kind of trashy newspaper would be asking me that? Next thing you know, I'll be from Mars. I didn't answer and eventually my intercom was silent. I tested it. "Lilli? Are they gone?" No answer, so I assumed Lilli had left too, probably giving an insider's scoop along the way.

It was almost 6 p.m. so I walked to the writer's room to dismiss them. My goodness, the executive producer was standing in the doorway. I heard Bill's voice. "We've been ignoring her all day. She hasn't given us any ideas."

"Excuse me," I said as I slipped past the big boss. I gave the writers another one of my suspicious looks. Why weren't they letting me in on the big joke?

"Alice," the boss said, "I've got some bad news."

"Am I fired?"

"No, no. WE know how valuable you are to *Tomorrow Will Come*, but THEY don't. You see, we are under tremendous pressure at the moment. So, until things settle down, Sebrings thinks it would be a good idea if you were to take a leave of absence. A paid one, of course." Of course. Otherwise, some rival soap opera might bid for my services. It is a cutthroat business. "We'll be letting you know when your services will be required again."

I gathered a few belongings and left the building. Chester showed me a nifty back way out. I needed a friend right now. My life was collapsing around me. I didn't care who was available. I'd find Raundra and drown my sorrows in cannabis; I'd go for beers with Andre; hell, I'd even let Silvio have his flagellation fantasy.

Piles o' Pies was closest. Raunda was just getting off work. She took one look at me and understood. "Come on," she said. "It'll cost more but it's the best stuff you can smoke." She made a quick buy and headed off in the direction of her place.

"Raunda, please don't take this personal," I said, "but I don't want to go into Harlem tonight. This hasn't been my day and I just KNOW I'd be asking for more trouble if we go there."

"Where, then?" Raunda was always impatient to get high.

"Let's go to my place," I suggested. I know it wasn't Raunda's favorite hangout; the security cameras bothered her. But since we were just around the corner, Raunda agreed.

We were just about to smoke our second joint when my apartment buzzer sounded. I went over to the intercom and said hello.

"Alice Kumplunkem?"

"Yes," I said, belatedly wishing I'd stop doing that.

"Police. May we come up and ask you a few questions?"

What could I say to that? No, I'm busy smoking pot? You say, "Yes, of course you may come up." Then I ran into my living room. "Raunda! It's the cops!" She was as terrified as I. She grabbed the bag of pot and bolted out of the place. I ran into the hall with her and almost entered the stairwell when I wondered why we were running. I called after Raunda but to no avail.

I walked back into the apartment and the first thing to hit me was the aroma. I may as well have had a neon sign proclaiming 'Pot Was Smoked Here!' Flying to the windows, I flung them open. I bolted to the bathroom and grabbed my can of air freshener. It was still full because when you live alone, who do you freshen the air for? I sprayed that can until I heard a knock at the door. I doused perfume on myself and went to let in New York's finest.

As soon as I saw them, I thought to myself, *I am very, very high*. I could almost feel blood dripping out of my eyes. "Come in," I said and led them into my living room. The air was still misty from the spray and it stung the eyes.

One of the cops spoke. "Thanks for seeing us. We're just conducting a routine investigation."

"Into what?" I asked, then stopped talking. My eyes had spotted a white, rolled-up paper that had fallen onto the floor by the coffee table. That wasn't...that was. It was the joint Raunda and I had been about to light. I ripped my eyes away from it and focused on what the cop was saying.

"We're looking into the death of Valerie Krymkyw," he said.

"Yes, I can understand that," I enunciated, wondering what I was talking about. Could I just walk over and pick it up nonchalantly? Should I ask them if they dropped it, 'cuz it sure wasn't there before?

The officer continued. "We have to ask you a few questions to determine if you tried to murder her."

MURDER HER? Suddenly that lil ol' joint seemed so inconsequential. I tried to deal with the officers coherently but I was so stoned, I may have confessed to it. *Please believe me, Mr. Policeman, I am so very innocent.* I guess they thought so too, because they left without me.

As soon as that door shut behind them, I dove to the floor, picked up the joint and lit it. The phone rang. Now what? I answered and it was my dear mother.

"Alice," she immediately went into a nag, "they had your

name on Entertainment Tonight. What's going on? Now you're murdering people for a living?" I tried to deny it but she wouldn't give me the chance to break in. "They didn't get a good shot of you though; you covered your face. But, Alice, if you're gonna be on TV, don't wear yellow! That's never been your color. And obviously you've gained at least 20 pounds since you moved to New York. And for chrissake, do something with your hair! It..."

I hung up on her.

If I was going to be charged for murder, why couldn't it have been...?

The phone rang again but it went unanswered. I wasn't going to talk to anyone else. Now I had a new 'worst day of my life'. I picked up my purse and headed back to my favorite Holiday Time Hotel.

I was going to hole up for a while.

* * *

I took what spare cash I had on me, which amounted to a little over 1400 dollars. When I checked into the Holiday Time, I was decked out in sunglasses, hat, scarf, and collar pulled up. Then I tried something illegal, but I heard it's done all the time.

"Fill out the registration card," the reception clerk said.

Under name: Trish Halapeno. Something pretty. Something exotic. Something so far removed from my real nationality.

Under address: Winnipeg, Manitoba. As I was checking into a hotel, I could realistically be travelling. And if I had to speak, my prairie accent would be believable.

I put primo bullshit in every space requiring information about me. The clerk picked up the card when I'd finished and gave it a long look. My breath caught; my criminal career wasn't off to a good start.

"How many days will you be staying here?" he asked.

"At least two...maybe more," I replied.

"And how will you be paying?" he enquired.

"Cash."

The transaction went smoothly after that. I was given my room key for a suite on the top floor. And there I stayed.

I didn't want to see anyone, including hotel staff. Every time I ordered from the various delivery services offered in New York, I paid cash and dressed up in my Mata Hari disguise. A 'Do Not Disturb' sign hung on my doorknob 24/7. My room was littered in Pegli's Pizza cartons, Wong's Ribs and Super Sub wrappers. I watched a lot of TV.

I had been given quite a scare. Why was everyone after me? After two days, I dressed up and went downstairs. The reception clerk (Oh, no! A different guy!) was busy with a customer. I picked up a newspaper from a table and buried my face in it. 'Kumplunkem Hiding From Press', with a sub-heading, 'What IS She Trying to Hide?' I was the subject of an editorial in the New York Times. Now that was big-time. Whoop-tee-doo.

I decided to check if I was in any other papers. Through rose-colored glasses I read in the Post that 'charges against Alice Kumplunkem have been dropped, although the overweight, prematurely greying Kumplunkem continues to elude the media.' Well, I was glad to hear about the charges, but what did the media want to talk to me about? I wanted to be left alone! *Oh, and by the way, I am NOT going gray.* The newspaper used a photo of me that had been snapped the afternoon all the press converged on me. On that morning, I had tried to spruce up my thick, unruly hair. I decided to wear a light blue ribbon in it. In the photo, you can't see my face but my hair takes up a good third of the picture. The ribbon wasn't very apparent, although it DID look like I had two long streaks of silver. And OK, I looked fat. But doesn't the camera add ten pounds?

In another newspaper, I saw a letter to the editor concerning me. I read it and wished it had given an address under Mrs.

Edith Racine's name. I wanted to pay her a visit and give her a good punch in the nose. One of her lines: 'There was no need for Beluga to suffer as much as she did, and I truly believe Alice Kumplunkem, the head writer, put Valerie Krymkyw under a terrible strain.' She whined for two whole columns.

The reception clerk let out a fake cough. I guess I had been loitering for a while. I walked up to him. Considering I was still hot news, I decided to stay for another three days. I told the clerk my intentions.

"And you are...?" he asked.

Good question. Who WAS I again? "Uuhhh...Room 1209," I brilliantly said. The clerk pulled out my card.

"Trish Halapeno?" he reminded me.

"That's it," I said.

Cash again. That's OK. I still had plenty. I went back to my *Saw 4* movie. You call that a horror flick? I was living a horror flick.

Three days later, feeling bloated and pimply, I simply donned a scarf and went back down to the lobby. I figured my hair was the biggest giveaway. Before talking to the reception clerk, I walked over to the newspapers. Good, good...nothing in the Times. Nothing in the Herald. Oh, shit, the Post had a picture of me! My 8 x 10 glossy audition photo. Paul probably sent it as revenge. Looking at it, I really didn't think I resembled that photo. I paid big bucks for a make-up artist the day of the photo shoot and she almost made me look pretty. My lips were so obviously liplined and filled with a crimson color. Every last blemish had artfully been made invisible, and my nose had been so heavily shadowed as to make it almost look normal-sized. My hair wasn't so attractive though. I'd gotten one of those beauty-school students to cut it for $8, and I don't think she passed the course. She'd cut my locks off to my chinline, giving me 1 foot by 1 foot hair. It looked like I was wearing a brown helmet.

Still, that story was on Page 47. I was becoming old news, but I was still news. I paid for two more days.

I went back up to my stagnant room. My body craved sunshine and food with vitamins in it. I crawled back onto my mussed bed and by rote, picked up the remote. Flip. Flip. Nothing on TV. Man, holing up was so boring. I decided to watch the news for a change.

The news! Why hadn't I thought of that before? I could have been keeping a better update on my situation if I'd watched the news. But, judging by the few shows I watched that day, I was too late. No one discussed me.

Judgment day came. I was broke. Should I venture out to a bank machine? Should I try and stay another day? Or should I go home? I decided to let the newspapers tell me. The TV news said, "Go on home, Alice, it's safe." Yup, the newspapers told me the same thing. With a big smile, ripping off my headscarf, I skipped up to my room.

I tore the yellowing 'Do Not Disturb' sign off my doorknob and the maids were there in an instant. Letting them get a good look at my face, I said, "I'm checking out. You can clean it in half an hour."

They looked at my room in disgust. One turned to the other and said, "I'll clean this room if you do the eighth floor."

The other considered a moment then said, "Sounds fair."

I packed in a jiffy since I didn't bring much. I couldn't wait to get into clean underwear. I walked up to the clerk and told him I wanted to check out.

"Your room number?" he asked.

"1209."

He pulled my file up on the computer. "You owe $21.50 in phone charges," he told me.

Ooops. I was lucky if I had 10 bucks for cab fare. Oh, but I had my credit cards! They came by the truckload when I got my new job. I knew I'd only get in trouble with so many, so I threw most of them out and kept only a couple. Since this wasn't Bloomingdale's, I gave him my Gold Card. There was no limit to the amount I could charge to that card.

He took the plastic and went to run it through the machine. Something caught his attention. Giving me a good glare, he opened a drawer, pulled out a pair of scissors and cut my Gold Card in half. Shit! He knows who I am!

"I didn't kill her!" was all I could think of to say.

He gave me a funny look. "You're registered as Trish Halapeno but the card you gave me had a different name. Either it's stolen or there's something fishy going on. Holiday Time Hotel doesn't need business from con artists like you. If you don't leave, I'm calling the police." He was wielding those scissors quite threateningly so I left without explanation.

Good-bye, my private Sing Sing! Even though I only had enough money to get halfway home, and the sunlight hurt my eyes, I wasn't recognized by anyone. I was a nobody again and for once, it was a pleasant feeling.

* * *

The first thing I did was replenish my wallet. I was in the mood for some ACTION. I put on a sweater that had a neckline down to my clavicle bone, allowing some cleavage to show. I put on my jeans with the zippers on the ankles, unzipped so my ankles could breathe. I put lots of make-up on my zits and went to see my pals.

The first stop was Piles O' Pies. The cafe was empty. Raunda was engrossed in a novel. I stepped up to the counter and said, "Give me a pile of pie, please." Oh, I felt witty tonight!

"Alice!" Raunda cooed in her low voice. "I was almost starting to worry about you." She was being funny too! My friend Raunda. "What are you up to tonight?" she asked.

"I'm not sure. I might see Silvio." I was dressed to please him anyways. "Depends." Cool dude talk.

"Check back with me," Raunda suggested. "So, where ya

bin?"

"Didn't you hear? About the Krymkyw lady dying and me being charged..."

"I read the papers," Raunda said. "But that was all last week. We've had a plane crash, an earthquake, and an assassination attempt since you last made front page."

"Well, I couldn't take the press, man." I used that word, 'man', a lot around Raunda. "They were like vultures!"

"So...what? You went into hiding?" Raunda asked.

"At the Holiday Time Hotel. Don't stay there. Shitty place." I thought I'd start a little crusade against Holiday Time. "By the way, I'm on a health kick now. Give me a slice of pie with fruit in it."

"We have a great apple strudel," Raunda suggested.

"OK. That and a blueberry pie."

I ate my dessert and talked to Raunda. Conversation was smooth and easy between us. I truly felt I had one excellent comrade. I left her my usual tip – $10 – and said, "Catch you later."

I was going to slip into Mascots but saw the gang at Little Shop of Donuts. I checked to make sure my burgundy lipstick was in place and crossed the street.

"Hiya, guys!" I greeted them as I opened the door. Muriel was behind the counter. Andre and Petie were at their conference table. There was a stranger sitting with them and all three heads were bent low in conversation.

"Alice!" Muriel whispered. She jerked at me to sit down.

"Whaaa..?" I said but Muriel gestured to shut up.

She poured me a quick coffee, keeping an eagle eye on the boys. She was tensed up because she spilled some liquid when she set the cup down.

"They're up to no good," Muriel said through clenched lips. "See that guy?"

I dropped a napkin and took another look, although I'd seen

him when I came in. "Yeah?" I replied.

"He's the biggest crook on the street," Muriel said. Ooohh, drama in the donut shop!

"What's Andre and Petie doing with him?" I asked.

"I haven't been able to find out yet, but I'm telling' ya, it ain't legal," Muriel said. "Andre's been acting real hyper these days. It must be big."

The stranger got up. I couldn't help but stare as he walked out. Andre and Petie grabbed their cups and brought them to the counter. Muriel was about to refill them but Andre covered the top of his cup. "No more," he said. "We got a meeting."

"You just HAD a meeting," Muriel said.

"And so maybe I got another," Andre shot back. "C'mon, Petie, let's get outta here."

"Hi, guys," I said.

"Andre, what were you talking about to that guy?" Muriel just had to know.

"Can't a guy talk?" Andre retorted. He wasn't being very nice to his gal Muriel tonight. "Don't start with the questions, Muriel."

"Hi, Petie," I said.

"You better not be runnin' no deals outta my shop!" Muriel yelled.

"Shut up!" Andre yelled back. "And it ain't your shop! It belongs to that drunk Ramon."

"Are you coming by later?" Muriel asked.

"I don't know! I got things on my mind!" Andre snarled. "Petie, let's go!" Petie had been gawking at the little scrap between the lovers. I had a feeling he wanted to fight for Muriel's honor.

"OK," Petie said. "See you, Muriel. Oh, hi, Alice." Andre was already out the door so Petie ran to catch up.

Muriel launched into another commentary – her observations on Andre. I snuck a look at my coffee cup and saw it was barely touched. Aaww, I'd have to finish it and listen to Muriel. I liked the lady, except when she had problems. "It used to be just watches and sports jackets, but then it got to TVs and computers. Now what? I bet it's a bank job. It has the smell of a bank job. My last husband went to jail for bank robbing. I thought Andre was classier than that..." On and on. I finished my coffee and waited for an opportunity to jump in.

Finally a customer walked in. Muriel stopped talking when she had to figure out his change. "I've gotta go, Muriel," I said. "I'll probably see you later." Although I doubted it.

"Alice, was that you in the paper last week?" Muriel asked out of the blue.

"Yeah."

"Andre was looking for you," Muriel recalled. "He thought you were going to jail and he wanted to borrow some money before you went away."

"How considerate," I sarcastically responded.

"He's been like that all week," Muriel began. "One day..."

"I gotta go, Muriel," I repeated. I hated to interrupt but I could see she wasn't interested in my crime saga. "See ya soon."

Mascots looked the same as it always did. Half-filled with men, a stripper going through her routine, a few working table dancers. No matter what time of day or night, the scene never changed. I could see why Silvio got bored with his job.

I walked up the steps and opened the door to the deejay booth. Silvio was standing there, watching the stripper, halfheartedly masturbating. At first he was startled to see me but then a sly grin spread over his face.

"Alice! I haven't seen you in a few days," he said.

"A whole week, actually," I said. He looked kind of good standing there, his pecker hard in his hand. "So what are you doing after work?" I asked suggestively.

He got the hint. "Wanna get fucked?"

"Yes, please, if it's possible," I said. When I laid in my Holiday

Time Hotel bed every night, I fantasized that Silvio got it up every time we had sex.

"I got this idea. It's already turning me on."

"What?" I nervously asked.

"Wait 'til the dancer finishes. Meanwhile, get undressed."

"Here?" I giggled nervously. Silvio nodded. *OK, now we're into sex in weird places.* A new kick for me. The weirdest spot for me so far had been the couch. I guessed I could try this.

The dancer finished her number and Silvio fiddled with the electronic system. He winked at me and said, "House music." With a flick of a switch, music with a rhythmic beat blared out. Funk or whatever you call it. "Watch what I do," Silvio advised me. He turned a microphone on and just said, "Yeah, baby. Oh, baby." It sounded pretty good with the music. "Try it," he said to me.

I walked up to the mike and said, "Yeah, baby, oh, baby." Neat! I was a singer! I turned to smile at Silvio when I felt him slide his member into me. I gave a little amplified gasp.

"Yeah, that's right," Silvio whispered in my ear. "I'm gonna give it to you good and I wanna hear you sing it over the mike."

I had never felt Silvio so big and it hurt standing up. I hadn't exactly been ready for him either. "Yow! Ouch! Agh!" went out over the music. I heard it loud and clear, so shut up.

"Come on, come on," Silvio urged me on.

I felt he wanted me to perform so I emitted a few "Oh, yes!" and "Feels so good!". With perfect timing, the song ended just as Silvio came with a bloodcurdling whoop. In a second, he was out of me and changing the tune. I scrambled to get dressed.

"So what are you doing tonight, Silvio?" I asked. I still wanted to spend a little quality time with him.

"See that blonde?" Silvio grinned, pointing. "The one table dancing in the corner?"

"Yeah," I said.

"She's hot, huh? I watched her while we were fucking. I got a date with her tonight."

"Lucky you," I said, perhaps a touch hurt.

"Alice, you better get out of here. The boss doesn't like it if you spend too much time in here."

"I'm going. Well, have fun tonight, Silvio. I hope you can get it up!" I said maliciously, before storming off. I was getting pretty tired of Silvio being my boyfriend. He was lacking in the social graces.

Raunda won the draw. She'd be the one to enjoy my friendship. In anticipation of the evening, I bought a milkshake on the way over to Piles o' Pies. Oh well, I hadn't killed any brain cells in a while. This day had already been exciting enough for me and I was ready to just kick back with Raunda and get stupid.

* * *

My euphoric feeling returned when I saw Raunda. She was just getting off work. For once I beat her to the punch. "Feel like gettin' high?"

Raunda looked dumbfounded, as if I'd read her mind. Then she laughed. "Whaddaya think?"

"Where do we have to go?" I asked. Raunda had about nine places where we could look. I never met her contacts; usually I waited on a bench or in a coffee shop.

"St. Ignatius Hotel," Raunda thought would be the ideal place. Although I'd never witnessed it, I knew the deal here. Raunda knew a dealer who lived in a room on the main floor. Raunda would give the secret knock, the window'd slide open, Raunda would give them my money, and she'd get the equivalent in weed. It was usually a quick transaction so I sat on a nearby bus-stop bench.

Two buses had already passed and no sign of Raunda. She wouldn't have taken off with my money, would she? Nah, she was my friend. Even though it was only 7 p.m., it was dark out already. A scary thought wormed into my mind...maybe something happened to Raunda! In a dark alley, alone, carrying over a hundred bucks... *Go save her, Alice!* Or at least go find out what's keeping her.

I snuck a peek into the alley. Yup, pretty dark. I could dimly make out a figure. Raunda? I edged in a bit and still couldn't make out who it was. Inch by inch I stealthily went ahead. Finally I knew it was a black person and my confidence increased. I walked forward just as I saw something handed through the window to the person standing there. Oh, yes, it was Raunda.

"Hi," I calmly said. The window slammed shut and Raunda jumped a foot high.

"Alice!" Raunda gasped. "Don't ever do that!"

"You were taking so long, I got worried," I said.

"Shit. I didn't even see you come up!" Raunda was still on the first topic.

"Yeah, it's pretty dark in here," I had to admit. "What took you so long?"

"He just got a delivery and he had to cut it up," Raunda replied. "I didn't think it'd take that long. Let's get on the street."

"So did you get it?" I asked.

"Yeah, here it is," Raunda said, flashing the bag of pot at me. We started to walk forward and almost bumped into the two men in dark blue walking toward us.

One officer quickly turned his flashlight on us. The other drew his gun. Both Raunda's and my arms involuntarily went up. Raunda's hat still gripped the bot of pot. The flashlight shot its beam upwards and Raunda dropped it.

"The black girl has the pot!" one officer confirmed.

"Right!" the other said. "Now don't you girls move a muscle. We seen with our eyes that there's a drug deal going on here. We have every right to search you." He put his gun back into its holster. "Keep 'em covered, Rob."

The policeman, who was about 50 years old and looked like a

secret drinker, approached Raunda. She never carried a purse. He gave her a frisk and didn't find anything. "Well, I know you were the one with the pot, so that's a possession charge right there," the cop said. "Where's your ID?"

"I don't carry any," Raunda said, then outright lied, "I'm Grace Jackson, 3435 Finchley Avenue."

"We'll see," the cop said. "I think we'll be hauling you down to the station." Then he turned to look at me.

"Alice Kumplunkem," I immediately said. I could have said Trish Halapeno but I was carrying ID to prove otherwise.

I started to dig in my purse to prove my identity when the cop yelled, "Keep your hands in sight!" The other cop drew his gun. Both my hands flew upwards and my purse spilled open onto the pavement. The cop ran to pick it up and search it. Satisfied I wasn't carrying a weapon, he gave me a quick ticklish frisk. Then he picked my wallet up off the ground.

"Alice Kumplunkem," he read. Then he noticed that my billfold was overflowing with dollars. "Whoa, whoa, what's this?" He made a quick count. "Over five hundred dollars here, Rob. I think we found ourselves a drug pusher here."

"ME?!?" I shot back incredulously. I noticed a window curtain part imperceptibly and an indistinct face peek out. I wanted to say, "I think that's the pusher there!" and point at the window. Was it a bad idea? Was he a good friend of Raunda's? Would I be considered a snitch? "I'm not a drug dealer," I said. "I'm an executive consultant."

"To the drug kingpin?" the other cop asked. What a dummy. No wonder all he was good for was holding a flashlight on us.

"I think you'll both be coming with us," the first cop decided. He slapped a pair of handcuffs on me. I felt piles of pie coming up.

"This isn't necessary," I pleaded.

"Rob, cuff the black girl," the cop said, as if there were hundreds of white girls standing around. Bigot.

Officer Rob looked pretty eager to please. He cuffed Raunda then asked, "What about the marijuana, Charlie?"

What a dope. I could have told him the exact thing Officer Charlie told him. "We'll be taking it in for evidence."

We took the scenic route to Precinct #45. We cruised past Sebrings. "I work there," I said, wondering if I still did. Past my elegant apartment we drove. "I live there," I proudly stated. Nothing helped. We were hauled into the police station like common criminals.

The officers led us into a barren room. "You'll wait in here until a matron can search you," Officer Charlie stated.

Raunda looked strange; defiant, majestic, African. She looked almost beautiful there. I guess the cops thought so too. Officer Charlie slid a look at Officer Rob. "I hope our search was thorough enough, Robbo."

Officer Rob caught his drift. "I hope they're not concealing weapons."

"Right. Maybe we'd better give them another quick search," Charlie concluded.

They both went for Raunda. What pigs! You could obviously tell they were feeling her up. Oh, God, and I was next.

They did a pretty thorough search on Raunda, I figured, and had yet to start on me. Hell, they already found the drugs on Raunda.

"You still have to search me," I reminded them.

"Alice!" Raunda shouted. "You're not hiding anything! They found what they were after already."

"I know, but..." But what? Was I envious that I wasn't being manhandled? *Come on, guys! You should be searching me! Besides, I'm white like you!* (The bigot in me coming out?)

"Ow! Fuck right off!" Raunda yelled at Officer Charlie, slapping his hand away. *Careful, Raunda! Assaulting a police officer isn't going to help our case.*

"OK, they're clean," Officer Charlie said. "Let's let the matrons at them."

The matrons were very efficient and gave me a thorough strip search. What the hell am I gonna hide in my rear, for chrissake, and would I be smoking it after I took it out? I have never felt such embarrassment in my life. I couldn't even look at Raunda after they left the room.

Our arresting officers returned. "Come on," Charlie said. "Fingerprint and photo time."

"Oh, shit," Raunda muttered to me. "I'm cooked."

We were led into another room and processed. This was a different photo shoot than I'd ever experienced. You had one chance to take a good picture. After inking our fingers and smudging them over some paper, we were then taken to a cell.

"You'll be staying here until we run your names through the system," Officer Charlie said. "Gotta check if there's any outstanding warrants on you."

I'd had enough. "Listen! I'm Alice Kumplunkem! I had lots of money on me because I'm rich! Maybe you heard of me..." I shut my mouth. I was going to say I'd made all the newspapers last week but I didn't want to remind them I was temporarily up for murder.

"Back in a flash," Officer Charlie said.

They left and Raunda crawled onto the bottom bunk. I began pacing. "What are we going to do, Raunda? They're checking up on us!"

"What've you got to fear?" Raunda asked quietly.

"Uh...nothing, I guess. Neither do you, right?" I asked.

"Shhhh, the walls have ears," Raunda said. "Let's just hope for a computer foul-up." She turned her back and faced the wall. I don't think she wanted to sleep; just to be left alone to think. The party was over.

Around 1 a.m., a guard checked up on us. "Excuse me," I said from my top bunk, "I think someone forgot about us. We were supposed to have our names run through a computer?"

"Computer's down," the guard said. "You'll probably be here for the night."

For the night? I had envisioned sleeping in my own bed. And wasn't I allowed a phone call? But then, who would I call? I punched my unpillowcased pillow, pulled the dingy gray cotton blanket around me, and settled in for the night.

A loud rude noise awakened us at eight o'clock the next morning. "Kumplunkem!" a different officer shouted. "You're free to go."

"Great! Finally," I said as I jumped off the top bunk. The ankle zipper on my jeans caught in the blanket and tripped me up. I fell on Raunda. "Come on, Raunda...uh....Grace? Yeah, Grace. Let's go."

"Oh, no," the policeman said. "Raunda Hutch, alias Grace Jackson, stays."

"Why?" I demanded to know.

"Well, it seems your friend was ordered to leave the country the LAST time she was busted for possession. Didn't make the boat, didja, Grace?" the cop called over to her. "This time we make sure our illegal immigrant makes it home. We're going to put her on a plane and wave bye-bye."

I had a feeling the cop was being condescending to me. I walked over to Raunda and sat beside her on the bunk. "What if I take the possession charge?" I whispered. "Will that help?"

"You kidding? You'll be deported back to Canada!" Raunda said. "Besides, they nailed me. They got that old warrant on me. I was supposed to go back last year."

"So that's it?" I asked. "I"m never going to see you again?" *Say it ain't so, Joe.*

"Guess not. It's been nice knowin' you, Alice." She stuck her hand out.

Nice knowing me? It was such a pleasure having you for a friend, Raunda! I love you! I need you! Don't leave me!

I took her hand and shook it, then impulsively threw my arms around her. I wanted to have a good soul-sister cry with her.

"Let's go. No lesbo action here." The cop banged the bars.

The last image I have of my friend Raunda is of her sitting on the bunk, having a cell door slammed between us. I was in shock. My best bud was being deported to Rastafaria.

* * *

I spent all day moping. I couldn't believe it. I'd lost my best chum. I wished there was some way I could help her out but I was at a loss. How could such an anticipated relaxing evening turn into such a nightmare? The fact that I'd spent a night in jail had yet to register; I was in a spin over losing the best girlfriend I'd had since Velda.

Around nine in the evening, I pulled myself away from the fridge and gave myself a good talking-to. "OK. It HAPPENED. Shit HAPPENS. But it's OVER. Maybe you DID lose your best friend, but you still have FOUR more. Treat them well and you won't lose these." I didn't think Silvio or my donut-shop pal were illegal immigrants. "Come on, Alice, let's get our act together and see what's going on at Little Shop."

I bundled up since it was chilly and took a walk down the block. I could see into the donut shop's window from across the street. Shit, Muriel was there but not the boys. Should I go back home? *No, Alice,* I again reminded myself. *Muriel is your FRIEND, although you like her better with Andre and Petie around. Let's go see her and hope she's in a better mood tonight.*

As soon as I opened the door, I knew something was up with Muriel. She was busy filling up the sugar containers. I could see the napkin holders stuffed already and every table gleaming. Muriel was a good waitress but she didn't keep a tidy shop. She usually liked to lean back against the hot chocolate maker, an unlit long Virginia Menthol Slim 100 behind her ear, eating spoon-sized donuts. She would trace her lips with the color of the day, backcomb her hair in the reflection from the coffee machine, and shoot the shit. Yes, this was a new, improved Muriel.

She ran behind the counter to serve me. "Alice!" she cried. "You have to stay here with me! I don't care what you're doing tonight. You have to stay!"

Wow, she really needed me. I decided to be a true blue friend and do what I could for her. "I'm not doing anything else tonight," I told her.

"Coffee?" she asked, already pouring it.

"Sure."

It was set down in a flash and this time she spilled more than a drop. I could have fit another cup of coffee into my mug.

"Yow!" I exclaimed as some coffee sloshed onto my pants.

"Sorry," Muriel automatically said, already wiping the counter with a rag. Her eyes were looking out the window. Then she grabbed the pot and started pouring more coffee into my mug. I watched the coffee overflow and glanced up at Muriel. Again her eyes were checking the windows.

"That's enough, Muriel," I said. I had enough coffee in my saucer to fill an extra cup. A couple homeless people got up to leave and Muriel ran over to clear their table. She checked the street from the window view.

Hhmm. Something was definitely up. I think that's why the place was so clean; lots of window areas to tidy. I decided to ask a few questions. "Can I have a banana-cream donut, Muriel?"

"Sorry," she said again. Keep this up, Muriel, and you might not get a tip. "Here you go," she said, whipping the donut at me.

"You're pretty jumpy tonight," I observed.

She was scraping her brown nail polish off. "Can you tell?" she asked. I nodded. "I wish I had a Valium. Do you know where to get one?"

I reared back. Oh, no! No more drug business for me. I was off drugs for life. "No," I replied. "I don't even know what a Valium looks like."

Muriel craned her neck towards the window again. "Where are they?"

I knew she meant Andre and Petie. "Yeah," I agreed, "where are they tonight?"

"That's what I'd like to know!" Muriel almost shouted. "Jeez, Alice, if Andre isn't back here by 10, I am in BIG TROUBLE."

"He still has almost an hour," I informed her.

"He was SUPPOSED to be here now," she said. "Oh God! I can't believe I'm so stupid!"

What? To be going out with Andre? Neither can I. But Muriel looked ready to bawl. "What's up?" I asked.

"Alice, you know how Andre is always bugging me to give him money from the till, and how I never do?"

I nodded. It was true; Andre did always pester Muriel but she wasn't dumb – she wasn't going to give away the owner's earnings.

"Well, I gave him money tonight," Muriel confessed. "Every cent in the till."

"Muriel!" I gasped. "Why would you do that?"

"He wouldn't let up!" Muriel declared. "After this one time, he said he'd never have to ask again. He'd be rich by tonight. But would he tell me what's going on? No! All I know is he needed $300 for some guy's SERVICES."

Ready to help out, I reached for my wallet. According to Officer Charlie's calculations, I had $500 on me. Shit! Where was my purse? I checked the floor by my stool. It wasn't there. I mentally retraced my steps and realized I'd not come directly here from there. When I left the house in such a determined frame of mind, I neglected to bring my purse. My ID, bank card, lipstick and house keys were sitting on my kitchen table. I didn't even have $2.50 for my coffee and donut.

"Damn!" I said. "I left my purse at home!"

"That's the least of our worries," Muriel said. NEVER did she

EVER want to hear of my woes. "If Ramon gets back before Andre, I'm dead. Ramon's not gonna find any money in the till and what am I gonna say?"

"Maybe you can say you were robbed?" I suggested.

"Oh, God! I don't want any cops called! I hate cops!" Muriel fretfully said. Boy, was she ever working in the wrong place. "I never told you I did time once, did I?" Muriel threw out. "Well, I did. I'm on probation right now."

Gawd! A female ex-con! "What'd you go to jail for?" I asked.

"Because of my ex, the bank robber. He hid the money at our place and after he got caught, I hid the money somewhere else. I figured I was entitled to it. Hell, he earned it! Anyways, he blabbed to someone that I still had it and the next thing you know, the cops find it and I'm arrested." Muriel took another look out the window. "Oh, Andre, hurry!"

"Is Petie in on this?" I asked.

"Of course!" Muriel replied. "What's Laurel without Hardy?"

Suddenly we heard an alarm. Both of us froze and looked at one another. One of the regulars got up and took a look outside. Muriel began trembling.

"It's the pawn shop," the regular reported.

Muriel relaxed a bit. "The pawn shop? Who'd want to break into that?"

I shrugged. "Whoever wants stereos and jewelry and..."

I stopped speaking. Muriel gave me a queasy look. "Andre wouldn't..."

Andre would. Our attention was drawn to the window where some outdoor action was taking place. It only took two seconds for Andre and Petie to pass our vision but I can still see it in slow-motion in my mind. The boys were being taken away in custody. One cop had Petie in the lead, and Petie was yelling and being a macho bad guy and he even managed to glance into the donut shop window once. Andre was being led along, dejected, caught by the long arm of the law. He also looked into the window, and

I could see direct eye contact was made with Muriel. He seemed to be giving her a longing glance.

Muriel almost collapsed. "Andre!"

We both went running to the door but the only thing we could see was a good-bye moon from Andre as he bent down to get into the squad car. Muriel kissed $300 good-bye.

Ramon, the owner of Little Shop of Donuts, came staggering out of Mascots to see what was going on. A small crowd had gathered to watch Andre and Petie's finest moment. Muriel saw him and shrieked, "Oh, Mother of Christ, it's Ramon!" She clutched at me. "Alice! What should I do?"

"I don't know!" I shrieked back. All I knew was that I didn't want to be a part of this scenario anymore. Things were starting to get a little hot.

"I know, I'll get outta town," Muriel decided. "Watch for Ramon. I'm getting my bag." Muriel ran off behind the counter.

A customer was waiting. "How much for a cruller, ma'am?"

"Three hundred bucks," Muriel said, stopping briefly to serve him should he buy it. He laughed, thinking she was joking, so she grabbed her purse and coat and asked, "Coast clear? I'm gonna make a dash for it."

"Muriel, I don't want to be an accomplice to anything," I said, wimping out of this crime.

"IS RAMON COMING?" Muriel urgently demanded.

I took a peek and Ramon was about two feet away from the entrance. "YES!" I yelled back at Muriel. She ran behind the counter, thinking she'd use the back door to make her escape.

"Muriel!" Ramon's voice stopped her. "Was that your boyfriend being put into the back of a police car?"

"I didn't see anything," Muriel lied.

"What are you doing with your coat on?" Ramon noticed. "Where you goin'?"

"Nowhere," came Muriel's lame response.

"How was business tonight?" Ramon asked.

"Slow." Muriel continued her fibbing. The place was half-packed but maybe Muriel saw it as half-empty. Ramon walked over to the cash register. I was standing by the door and thought this would be a good time to leave. Muriel's panicked look rooted me to the spot though.

The cash register drawer slid open and Ramon just stared. Finally he looked up at Muriel and said, "Twelve dollars?"

"It was slow," Muriel repeated.

"I take in at least 400 on a slow night, Muriel. Where's the money?" Ramon looked mean and was starting to get angry. "Empty your purse," he commanded. Muriel just stood there, wringing the strap. Ramon grabbed it and searched it. "WHERE'S the MONEY, Muriel?"

"I had to lend it to someone. I'll pay you back, I swear," Muriel started to beg. "It was only $300. Hold my salary. I'll work extra shifts. I promise you'll get your money back."

"This is something you and your boyfriend cooked up, isn't it? How long you two been ripping me off?" Muriel tried to make a run for it but Ramon caught hold of her arm. "Bitch! You're staying right here until the cops come!" He roughly pinned her against the coffee machine and pulled out his cellphone.

"Don't call the cops!" Muriel started to cry. "I'll do anything, Ramon!" I still couldn't move from my spot, mortified by the drama unfolding.

"Police?" Ramon asked into his phone. "Yeah, I caught a thief in my donut shop...I think this has something to do with those two guys the cops caught on 16th a few minutes ago...Little Shop of Donuts...16th and Main...Oh, yeah, I got her, she's not going anywhere...Couple minutes? I'll have some donuts for them."

Either I left now or I helped bust Muriel out. The last thing I wanted to see were more cops. Why was there so much crime happening around me? What kind of friends was I picking? I knew Muriel would go back into the slammer for this. Oh, Muriel...all for love, wasn't it? Poor girl. She was crying for real now, mascara running down her face. Ramon was yelling at her, demanding to know what had taken place.

I decided to slip out. I couldn't even say good-bye as I didn't want Ramon thinking I was in cahoots with her. Now that I think of it, I didn't get to say good-bye to Andre or Petie either. I guess they were also heading for some jail time. I didn't get the chance to ever kiss Petie or party with Muriel somewhere away from the donut shop or collect the couple grand Andre owed me. I never got around to telling Raunda how dear she was to me. One second I had friends and the next instant, they were gone.

The cop car came squealing around the corner and I exited. I put a look on my face like I was a bimbo, not a criminal. Am I a criminal? The cops barely glanced at me. I decided to go to a liquor store before going home.

I had a big lump in my throat and wanted to wash it down with whiskey.

* * *

The bottle became my best friend. Just that one bottle, mind you. I stayed home for a couple days and got blotto four times. I did the usual bad drunk routine; cried a lot, moaned about my life. I killed the bottle one morning then passed out for a couple hours. I woke up with a wicked hangover.

I think it was a migraine actually. I could hardly breathe, it hurt so bad. I desperately searched the medicine cabinet for the 1000-tablet bottle of Tylenol Extra-Strength I'd purchased. It hurt my brain just remembering I'd brought the bottle to work, where I usually got my first headache by lunchtime.

I parted my heavily drawn curtains and looked outside. Although it was very overcast, what light there was made me wince. New York was soaked in rain. The traffic noises were usually muted in my skyrise apartment but today the sound came through as if amplified. I didn't feel like going out for aspirin.

I writhed on the floor for an hour and then gave up. I needed painkillers! In agony, I donned outdoor apparel. Keeping my severe headache in mind, I wore my Holiday Time Hotel get-up, although for a different reason this time. The huge sunglasses were to block out any light and the scarf bound about my head was to muffle noises. I took my umbrella and dragged myself out of the apartment.

I knew there was a pharmacy down the block and around the corner. I was just passing the high-rise car-park on the corner when I almost collided with two disgusted women.

"That was just sick!" one lady said.

"The perverts in this city!" the other exclaimed. "Makes you want to move to Minnesota."

"He WAVED it at us!" the first one cried.

"Then he made it swing in a circle!" the other remembered.

"I am so sickened," the first lady said. "I wish my husband had been with us. He would have killed him."

They went out of earshot. Thank goodness; they'd been pretty shrill although it was an interesting conversation.

I rounded the corner, the drugstore sign in sight. God, I hate neon. Today anyways. "Psssst, lady! Hey, lady," a whispered voice came at me. I wondered where the voice was coming from and glanced around. "Lady, right here," the voice said.

I looked up and saw a man on the second level of the car-park. He had on a raincoat but it was wide open. The guy had his penis in his hand and sure enough, he was performing tricks with it. "Like it?" he asked.

"You're sick!" I said, repulsed. His voice sounded familiar though. I took a better look and saw a long scar running along his half-hidden face.

"SILVIO?" I asked aloud. He stopped twirling his member and let it hang limply in his fingers. Come to think of it, I recognized that too. "That IS you, Silvio!"

"Do I know you?" he asked.

"It's me," I said. "Alice."

"Shit, I didn't even recognize you."

"Silvio, what are you doing?"

"Just killing some time before work," he said.

"You're flashing people! That's so sick. And hey, you already did time for that!" I couldn't believe how dumb my boyfriend was. "Don't you realize the trouble you could get in?"

"Don't YOU realize I NEED to do this!" he pouted. "It relieves me of my sexual frustration."

He looked at me defiantly. I wondered if I still wanted him for a boyfriend. Right now my mind was just filled with complete loathing for him. I shook my head and repeated, "It's sick."

Any thoughts I'd had concerning my relationship with Silvio were registered redundant. Out of nowhere, he was nabbed by one of them sneaky cops.

The two women were right behind the officer. "You didn't think we'd report you, did you?" one woman triumphantly crowed. "People like you belong in jail. You're SICK!"

The votes were in. Silvio was definitely sick. He put up a slight struggle and it was rather pitiful seeing his nudity flashing around, but he was no match for the burly cop.

Silvio was read his rights. Then the cop looked at me. "You can stay and give a statement," he said, "but you don't have to. We have two good witnesses right here."

"I'll pass," I said and simply walked away. What WAS it with me and cops? I was some kind of jinx. All my friends saw me and then went straight to jail. Do not pass go. Go to Alice Kumplunkem Place and then go directly to jail. Well, the jinx would be off. I had no more friends left.

And to top it all off, I got my job back.

CHAPTER FIVE

The ringing of the phone woke me up. I still had a headache, hours later. I took my 32nd Tylenol aspirin. *Go away, phone!* Since the caller insisted on trying me every ninety seconds, I finally answered. "Hello," I said groggily.

"Is this Alice Kumplunkem?" I was asked.

What the heck. "Yes, it is," I replied.

"Hold on one moment for Mr. Rigby," she said, and put me on hold. I started sweating; I wanted to hang up. Mr. Rigby was the big boss at Sebrings. He was probably going to fire me. Or worse yet, give me my job back.

"Alice!" Mr. Rigby jovially said. "Comin' in today?"

"Uhh...can I? Am I allowed?" I asked, quite seriously.

Mr. Rigby took it the wrong way. "Alice, Alice, you KNOW we had to do that. We had to protect the image of the show." What image, I wondered? Every character was a slut and all were on third marriages. "But now things have quieted down and the writers are desperate for new ideas." I bet they were. They needed their daily dose of Alice Atrocities.

"Well, I guess I could come in today," I said. "Umm...so everything will be the same?" I'd grown accustomed to my executive consultant title.

Again Mr. Rigby took it wrong. "Alright, alright, we owe you. How does an extra 1000 a week sound?"

Well, how did he think it sounded? What a bonus out of the blue! For the first time in ages, my voice got some life back into it. "That sounds fine, Mr. Rigby. Thank you!"

"Right. Gotta run! See you at work," Rigby clicked off.

I rushed to get ready and took a few more Tylenols before I left. Why did I have to have a headache when I was almost in a good mood? This was the second day I had the same hangover. Remind me never to buy bourbon again.

Chester the doorman grandly swept open the doors to Sebrings Productions. Absolutely everyone said hello to me. I began to get a cozy feeling. They missed me! My secretary, Lilli, actually stood up when I entered the reception area. "Good morning, Lilli," I said, erasing any grudges I may have been holding against her.

"Good morning! Welcome back!" Lilli beamed. "Your mail is on your desk..."

"I got mail?" I asked.

"I sorted through all of it. There was a lot of hate mail from that silly thing that happened, so I threw it out. Other than that, you got a letter," Lilli said. "I didn't know if you wanted to see any of the press clippings from last week, but if you do, I sent a whole batch down to Publicity."

"Maybe later," I said, like when I'm old and grey.

"And you have a meeting at 11 a.m..."

"I have a meeting?" I asked even more incredulously.

"With Farnia Forya," Lilli informed me. "She's the new Beluga."

"Well, alright," I said. "I'll see you later."

"Alice, can I leave at three?" Lilli asked, true to form. "I have an appointment with my pedicurist."

"I suppose," I said. I was still in a fairly good mood and wanted to add, "Just don't make it a habit," but my jokes always fell on deaf ears.

I walked into my office to hang my coat and saw a bouquet of roses on my desk. I rushed for the card. "From the Gang at Sebrings". How sweet! I'd never received flowers before and didn't really know what to do with them. There seemed to be lots of water in the vase so I guessed you were supposed to smell them. I sniffed for a minute then realized they were also pretty to look at. I would keep them in my office until they crumbled from old age, I swore.

Then I spotted the letter. It was from Largemar Productions. I slit it open and saw it was from Troy LeRue, an executive producer from *Monday to Sunday*. I was afraid to read it, wondering if this wasn't some blackmail attempt from my horrid audition with them. I still felt like I had a felonious aura around me – I was destined to lead a life of crime from now on.

I scanned the letter and all sorts of figures jumped out at me. 6 months, $6000 a week, 5% royalties, so on and so forth. With interest, I sat down to scan this fascinating missive. And holy cow if my self-esteem didn't shoot up by 1000 degrees.

Largemar Productions were greatly interested in my consulting services. They were prepared to make me an offer and it was much better than Sebrings. Could it be possible I might get even richer? They were anxious to have my reply by December 15, so that I may start January 5. I guess they were going to give the current executive consultant the boot. Well! I had over a month to decide. With a satisfied grin, I tucked the letter into my purse.

"Hi, everyone," I said as I walked into the writers' room. Everyone was present and accounted for.

"Alice! Welcome back!" Mary said and gaw-lee! She presented me with more roses! "These are from all the writers, just to let you know how much we missed you."

"Thank you!" I said.

Bill wheeled in a cake, decorated in the likeness of the old Beluga character. Rather macabre, but I liked the words written in icing – 'Welcome back, Alice! We need you!'

"Aww, thanks, everyone. This is wonderful," I gushed. I felt a tear slip down my face.

"I'm making coffee," one of the underlings said. "Would you like one, Alice?"

"I would, thank you, Frank," I almost whimpered.

Mary cut the cake and we had a short party. I told them I was given a raise and Bill slapped me on the back. "They should give you one!" he agreed. "You're worth every penny they're paying you."

We had all finished a second cup of coffee and I could sense they were waiting for something. Perhaps I was expected to give an executive direction. "Well," I tried, "shall we get to work?"

Every one of them whooped and ran to their chairs. Once seated, all cast an intense eye upon me. Bill solemnly spoke. "Alright, Alice, we have to concentrate on the Beluga Gotyerdinski character. How can we fit the new girl in believably?"

"That's what I wanted to talk about – the new Beluga," I said. "Why don't we lighten up on her a bit?"

"No, I say we don't," Bill said.

"Leave her the way she was," another writer said.

"If anything, there should be even more drama in her life," Mary thought.

So much for my suggestion. Bill came up to me and scrutinized my face. "I know!" he shouted. "Beluga gets major plastic surgery. Tell us, Alice, why you never got that nose of yours fixed?"

I hated my nose. It had a huge, ball-shaped bump in the middle of it. "I was going to have it fixed once," I said, "'cept I could never come up with the funds. I had even booked the hospital time and the doctor. I was very serious about having it done but my old acting agent changed my mind. I was famous for a while as 'The Ugliest Girl Alive' and Paul thought the nose helped."

"Did you feel embarrassed by your nose?" Mary asked.

"I guess," I said. "I remember when I was younger and would go into dressing rooms in the department stores. Sometimes I'd find one that had those angled mirrors, and I'd catch a reflection of my profile. I'd run out of those rooms in tears. Same as when I'd get my hair cut and they'd show me the side view. There was that big nose again. For ages when I was going out with Joe, I'd try to never let him see me in profile. I'd be facing him even when we went to the movies." My nose was starting to feel larger by the second. It felt like it was covering my entire face.

After the nose story was over, they wanted to know why I never got my chin done. It receded a bit; I only had an inch between my jawline and bottom lip. Next they asked why I didn't get my teeth straightened. I had a bit of an overbite... OK, OK, I have buck teeth. I was glad to move away from Oak Paw and my 'Beaver' nickname. Anger coursed through me as I told them my mother was too cheap to pay for braces, especially when the dentist told her I needed them for six years. When I moved to Toronto, I found a dentist who could get me cheap braces. I don't know if they were second-hand or what, but after two years of wearing them, I got another dentist to pry them out of my aching mouth.

Then Mary said, "Alice, haven't you heard of liposuction?"

"What's wrong with my lips?" I demanded to know. As far as I was concerned, they were purely ordinary. My best feature.

"It's a method of sucking fat off your thighs and your behind..."

"I wasn't always fat!" I said. "I DON'T need liposuction. I just need to go on a diet!"

My buzzer rang. Lilli informed me I had a visitor. It was time for my meeting and I was glad to leave this discussion. "If you'll excuse me," I said icily, "I have a meeting."

"No problem," Bill replied. "I think we have enough to write a scene."

"So we're going to have Beluga go through major reconstructive surgery?" Mary asked.

"Yeah," Bill said. "Picture this...Beluga is in a car, racing to meet her doctor..."

"She's discovered she's pregnant again and wants to keep the baby this time!" Mary jumped in.

"Except she crashes and she has to have her whole body rebuilt..." Bill continued.

"But she loses the baby!" Mary concluded.

I shook my head and slipped out. My headache was back.

* * *

A woman who fairly resembled Miss Guatemela walked into my office. She caught me in the act of swallowing a couple Tylenols. "Hi, Ms. Kumplunkem, I'm Farnia Forya," she said, extending her hand.

I shook it and said, "I'm Alice Kumplunkem." She kept standing and I didn't know what else to say to her. "Have a seat," I thought to say.

She sat down and we looked at each other. She wore a bright grin so I donned the same thing. No one was speaking. I had no idea why I had to meet with her. To make small talk, I said, "So you're the new Beluga?"

"Yes," Farnia said, "and I'm so happy I got the part! I wanted to meet with you so I could tell you something." Aha, so she arranged this get-together. I tensed, knowing she may threaten to beat me up if the new Beluga wasn't made more likeable. "I'd like to say that you have nothing to worry about with me. I'll do anything you write and I won't cause any problems at all. So I don't care what you make happen to Beluga, I'll play it with a smile on my face." That'd be terrible acting, I thought. What if Beluga broke her legs?

But then I figured she was probably getting paid some pretty big bucks to make her come into my office and encourage me to belittle Beluga. Write anything, just don't kill her off, huh, Farnia? I felt a sinking in my stomach. "Uh, Farnia, who else have you been meeting with?" I asked.

"Oh, everyone!" she trilled. "I even met with the OWNER of Sebrings! Mr. Rigby!"

"How nice but did you meet with my writing staff by any chance?"

"Yes, yesterday," she beamed. "I basically told them the same thing I'm telling you now." She cocked her head and smiled, thinking she was such a good girl.

"Wonderful," I said, not meaning it. "Well, is there anything else?"

"Just that I'd like to thank you for letting me take up some of your valuable time," Farnia said, still smiling. "Thank you for seeing me." She skipped out.

I had no time to ask her to stay. When she mentioned my valuable time, all I could think of was the time being spent with my writers. I hated that room. I hated being with those people. I spent up to half an hour just going for a piss when I was at work. Although I thought Miss Forya was an ass-kisser, I'd much rather have her sucking up to me than what I had to go through with my writing staff. Those guys were bloodsuckers!

I couldn't recall if I took a Tylenol or not so just to be on the safe side, I took two more. I glanced at my watch. Good, 45 minutes to lunch. I dragged myself back into the writing room.

"Alice!" Bill pounced immediately. "There's just so much work to do on this Beluga character! We have an idea for a scene we have to finish by lunch."

"I just met Farnia..." I began.

"Yes, wonderful actress," Bill said. "Now, we want you to think hard..."

"I noticed....," I began again.

"Have you ever been goosed?" Bill asked.

I thought...*GOOSED?* I had wanted to ask them how they were going to match the two Beluga's skin tones. Farnia Forya's was definitely olive-tinted whereas Valerie Krymkyw's was rather ivory-colored. But what the hell was Bill talking about?

"High-school kids did it a lot," Mary stroked my memory. "You know...poke each other in the rear with brooms, et cetera."

"Yeah, I KNOW what goosing is, and NO, I have never been goosed," I retorted. Sometimes I really hated their questions.

The writers were silent a moment then Bill shouted. "A tightie! Have you ever gotten a tightie?"

"A tightie is...," Mary began.

"I know what a tightie is!" I yelled. "And no...." I stopped. A memory surfaced. An ugly Grade-Six memory. I was going to keep silent but then remembered that's what I was being paid for – to divulge these agonies. "Well, come to think of it, I was given a bad tightie once," I said.

"Were you cut?" Bill asked.

"Cut?? No! Just extremely embarrassed," I replied.

"That's OK. That's good. Go on," Bill encouraged me.

"It goes back to when I was 10 years old. That's when I got my first period." One of the writers looked confused, so I elaborated. "My menstrual cycle began. And Mom wasn't too pleased about it. She didn't like the extra expense. So she showed me her napkin pads and told me to wear them and they were awful. So big! I would get chafed wearing them. Anyways, I was in Grade Six and tighties were the big gag then. This kid in my class – Lyle – snuck up behind me when I was at my locker. He gave my panties a good yank. That's another thing about my mother! She always bought me old-lady panties up to my belly button. All the girls in school got to wear mini-panties; I saw in the shower room. Anyways, MY panties were always sticking out over my pants, and Lyle took advantage of it. But this day I had my period and was wearing one of Mom's big Kotex pads. When Lyle grabbed my panties, he also grabbed the end of the pad and pulled it halfway out." I winced, still remembering my shock. "He looked at it and called me gross and then went around telling everyone in school that I wore a diaper." I stopped talking, recalling the jeers and taunts I'd put up with until Grade Eight.

The writers were silent for a moment. "Let's give Beluga toxic shock syndrome!" Mary suggested.

"We'll use that she got goosed but in the wrong place..." Bill started.

"And she was wearing a tampon and it lodged in her for 15 years!" Mary continued the storyline.

Yeah, I was back at work alright. I leaned forward and smelled the roses.

* * *

My life became meaningless. I turned into a couch potato and ate mounds of carcinogenic food and gained 10 more pounds. I was pretty depressed. And to top it off, I still couldn't get rid of THAT FUCKING HEADACHE. I was popping Extra-Strength Tylenols every half-hour. Sometimes it would subside to a dull roar but at times, like when work let out, it was a fire-breathing monster in my skull.

One day at work I asked my writers to let me off early because of my skull-splitter. They looked a touch worried. "Alice, Beluga has to find a way to get out of that cave," Bill reminded me.

"Is it that bad?" Mary asked.

"It's the worst it's been in three weeks," I groaned.

"You've had a headache that long?" Mary asked. I could only nod. "You should go see a doctor," Mary suggested.

"Hoooo no!" I replied. "I know what your doctors charge for their services." By 'your' I meant 'American', and they knew it.

"But you're covered," Mary said. "That's one of the benefits of this job."

I didn't know that. "Great," I said. "I'll make an appointment somewhere."

"Oh, Lilli can do that," Mary said.

"She can?" I didn't know that either.

"Sure," Mary replied. "Sebrings uses a whole slew of doctors. Why don't you have Lilli make an appointment for tomorrow on your lunch break?"

"I guess so," I said.

"That's settled then," Bill said. "Alice, talk to us about problem BO."

Sure enough, Lilli booked an appointment for me to see Dr. Hilaire. I guess they thought I was someone important because I only had to wait 20 minutes to see him. I talked to Dr. Hilaire and told him I had this major ongoing headache. He asked me a few questions and then started filling out a prescription form.

"I'm giving you a prescription for Tylenol 2s," Dr. Hilaire said. "They have codeine in them and are much, much stronger than over-the-counter Tylenols. Take one whenever you feel a headache coming on." He handed me the form.

"They never COME ON," I said. "They CAME and haven't LEFT. Shouldn't I be given a brain scan or something?"

"I don't think that's necessary," the good doctor said. "You are under considerable stress, very lonely, overweight and suffer from low self-esteem." He may as well have added I was no catch. "It's not a wonder you have these headaches."

"Head ache," I corrected him. I stood up. "Thank you."

I left a little miffed at this so-called doctor. I didn't care for his diagnosis and decided to seek a second opinion. I headed for the nearest pharmacy to get those Tylenol 2s. I may not have agreed with the doctor's view of me, but I was desperate for any type of cure.

Lilli made me a second appointment and I went the following day. Sure enough, Doctor Hilaire did give me the wrong prescription. Dr. Fong prescribed Tylenol 3s.

"Dr. Fong," I said, "I don't think Tylenols are going to help..."

"Ohhh, yes!" Dr. Fong interrupted. "Tyrenol 3s very strong."

"But I took a Tylenol 2 this morning...."

"Tyrenol 3 much stronger!" Dr. Fong cheered for his drug of choice.

"Okayyyy...I'll try them. Jeez, am I not covered for brain scans or what?" I started to walk out in a bit of a huff again.

"Wait, I give you another prescription!" Dr. Fong called me

back. What?! Did he change his diagnosis just like that? He started scribbling then handed me a second prescription form.

"What's this?" I asked.

"Diet pills."

* * *

My life became even more meaningless. I spent my time away from work in a spacey void. During work, if I felt the slightest twinge of a headache, I'd pop a Tylenol 2. A 3 made me too incoherent. But as soon as quitting time rolled around, I'd go for a Tylenol 3. Matter of fact, I didn't even know if I had a headache anymore. But I did know that if I didn't have one, an afternoon with my writers would surely bring one on. They were being simply ruthless since I returned from my exile.

The only way I knew that this spacey void had any energy was from this buzz I always seemed to have. My skin was creepy-crawly and I wanted to DO SOMETHING, but didn't know what. Usually what I DID was sit in front of my TV, pine for a friend, and not eat. Those diet pills were Diet Pill 3s, I do believe.

One night I was sitting at home feeling sorry for myself. For something to do, I took a speedball – my own version. A diet pill and a Tylenol 3. Actually I took two Tylenols to one diet pill. Lately the Tylenols didn't seem to be having the same effect. I was feeling extra itchy. I knew I should just stop taking Tylenols to see if I still had a headache, but I grew to like the sheltered feeling I got from them. And I wasn't about to give up those diet pills. I'd lost ten pounds in two weeks, although I suspected they were responsible for giving me this racing feeling.

I was mulling over the fact that I was rich and not spending any money. I was banking piles of cash, as I'm sure my mother was too. I had no friends to spend it on and I didn't want any. Friends! Pshaw! More trouble than they were worth. God! It felt like my bones wanted to jump right out of my skin! I decided to unglue myself from the couch and go for a walk.

The first thing to pop into my mind was Pile o' Pies. My stomach lurched a negative; pies or donuts for that matter didn't appeal to me. I decided to go buy myself an outfit to fit my new svelte 183-pound figure.

Piles o' Pies was on the way to Bloomingdales. Wasn't it? I walked past the building again and looked in the window of the cafe. I saw a bunch of safes – some were so big, you probably would hide masterpiece paintings in them. I glanced up at the sign and it said 'Safes to Go'. I may have felt a pang of nostalgia had I seen the quaint cloth-covered tables with fake antique chairs, but they were gone. All I felt was a strange mind quirk, as if it were all a dream.

Little Shop of Donuts was still there. I went out of my way just to make sure. I thought I'd sit and have a coffee and check out the waitress who was replacing Muriel. I saw a couple old cronies who I knew always hung out there. We'd never spoken and I wasn't about to start. I sat at the counter.

"Whaddaya want?" the waitress asked me. She was barely an adult, maybe 19. Her Farrah Fawcett hair almost obliterated the perfect features on her blemish-free face. Her polyester uniform showed the clearly defined curves of her athletic figure. Innocence shone from her. She had no business working in this coffee shop.

"A coffee," I said.

She placed it in front of me, with none of the style Muriel displayed. "Buck sixty," my waitress said. I paid her and she went to stand at the other end of the counter.

I tried to drink my coffee but I felt like everyone was staring at me. "That girl is ALONE," I imagined one said. "She USED to talk when she came in here," I bet one regular said to the other. I couldn't take it; I imagined the new waitress to be watching me and I didn't want her to catch me looking back. I stared into my cup and felt my nerves tingle.

My body, of its own volition, decided it was time to get out of that place. I didn't have a nostalgic feeling at all; I don't think I even liked the place anymore.

I was glad to get away from their prying eyes and out in the open. I noticed Mascots across the street. *Go three for three, Alice?* Nahhhh, I never liked that place to begin with.

I decided to continue with my original mission – to spend some money. I hitched up my pants and went off to Bloomingdales to buy a belt.

* * *

"How old were you when you got your first kiss?"

"Did you ever have any uncles or brothers who molested you?"

"Excuse me a moment," I said, "I have to think about these questions." I got up to go to the washroom, where I hid my bottle of Tylenols. I popped a few more 2s and looked thirstily forward to quitting time when I could start in on the 3s. My mind was constantly numb these days; in a vacuum. I don't think my writers knew what was going on though, as the diet pills gave my body a lot of action. I continually found myself drumming my fingers or swinging a leg back and forth. 10 more pounds fell off me.

I knew I was hooked on those drugs. I'm not dumb. Yes, they definitely were a crutch. But what did I see written on a washroom wall? "If drugs are a crutch, then life's a broken leg." But really, my normal life did resemble a broken leg and what with these miracle drugs I was taking, I'd lost 20 pounds already and was able to deal with my writers. Life was still pretty shitty but it just didn't seem to hurt as much anymore.

I still had a couple days to make up mind on the Largemar offer. If I wasn't so brain-dead, I knew the extra money and benefits appealed to me. Another part of me said that it would just be more of the same routine. Question and Wound Period. Anyhow, I was too lethargic to make a decision.

It was another hour until lunch. My stomach craved a burger and fries but the diet pills in my system shot my brain a signal that said, "No! The stomach is not hungry!" Besides, I'd already forced a bran muffin down my throat that morning. I didn't care for the diet pills but I wasn't going off them. Sure, they made me irritable, short-tempered, nasty and constipated, but I definitely noticed cheekbones coming out on my pudgy face.

I went into my office to grab a stick of gum. Chewing gum was another action-filled trick I used to fool my writers. Besides, a stick of gum quelled my hunger. The first thing I noticed was that my beloved roses were gone.

I didn't bother using the intercom; I rushed into the reception area and screamed at my secretary, "Lilli! What happened to my roses?"

"Alice, they were brown and crispy already!" she said. "I told the cleaning guy he could take them away."

Fuck you, Lilli, who gives the orders around here? I loved those roses! They were the only things that gave me a sense of peace.

I stalked to my writers' room, letting Lilli know I wasn't pleased. Fine. I had my roses in the writers' room and I used those a lot more than the ones in my office.

They were gone. I yelled at the room in general. "Where are my roses??"

"They were crumbling all over the table," Bill said. "I told Zeke he could get rid of them. Now, about those uncles...?"

If looks could kill, they'd have made me one happy mass murderess.

* * *

The phone woke me up at 8 a.m. I used to get up earlier on workdays but lately I didn't bother much with my appearance before I left the apartment. My mother was calling. It was two hours earlier in Oak Paw; what was she doing up this early? Then I remembered that she always got up early to get my sister Louise's kids to school. Louise needed her beauty sleep, Ma explained.

"Alice, are you coming home for Christmas?" my mother immediately asked.

Oohh, how sweet of her to wonder! Mother-daughter feelings swept over me and I wanted to tell her of the fright I'd had. The night before, I think I had a little overdose. I recall taking three Tylonel 3s and then I remember nothing else. I don't know what happened; if I slept or sat there with my eyes open. All I know is I looked at my watch and four hours had passed me by.

"Yes, I'll be there on the 24th," I said. I was staying until the 26th. That was long enough to spend in Oak Paw with my mother. "Mom, I have to tell you..."

"Good," Mother said. "I want a special Christmas present from you." *Yes, I guess I should get started with my Christmas shopping.* St. Nick's was only eleven days away. I thought my mother would like a nice track suit. "Carol Sigurdson got one for Christmas and she saw it already and showed it to me and I want you to buy me one now, only a little nicer."

"Buy you what?" I asked.

"I want a fur coat. A mink would be just right."

Wow, I thought I'd be splurging if I bought her a new TV set. "Those cost about 10 grand, Mom," I said. I don't think she realized they were that much.

"I know," Mom said. "But you're making a lot of money. Your sister doesn't make that much and she's buying me a coffee maker." *Yeah, but Mom, she's always over at your house drinking your coffee.*

"I'll look into it, Mom," I said.

"Alice, I WANT a fur coat!" she whined. "You have a very good job..."

"It's not a good job!" I yelled. "It's a shitty job. I hate it!"

"I'll see you Christmas Eve, Alice," Mom said. "I hope to see you carrying a nice, big, furry present for me. Good-bye, dear," she said, a final suck-up effect because she's never called me that before, and hung up.

I went straight for my pills. Fuck the bran muffin.

* * *

"We just got word from Mr. Rigby," Bill said as I grouchily entered the writers' room. I'd just finished screaming at Lilli. She made me stand in front of her desk until she'd finished the phone conversation with her boyfriend. After she hung up, I yelled at her that if someone didn't show a little more respect, then someone would be losing their job. I don't think she knew who I meant. Why couldn't I just fire her? After roughing her up a bit first, of course.

"What'd Rigby want?" I asked. Usually I deferred to him by calling him Mr. Rigby, out of respect, but today I just wasn't feeling very respectful to anybody.

"The new Beluga is not working out," Bill said. "The ratings have gone down and they figure it's because of her. They're recasting today and we have to come up with some scenes that'll grab the viewers."

"Fine," I said.

"Alright then. I think the new Beluga should be fatter," Bill said.

"Oh, definitely," Mary agreed. "Alice, I know you're on diet pills. What finally told you that you were too fat?"

"Whaddaya say to Beluga having no fashion sense whatsoever?" Bill suggested.

"Perfect!" Mary agreed. "Alice, where do you shop?"

Frank, the underlingest of them all and usually just a coffee-getter, even had an idea. "Alice, you haven't talked about your friends at all these days. Why are they avoiding you?"

"Shall we give Beluga a boyfriend?" another minor writer wondered.

"Let's make her a lesbian," Bill thought.

"No, let's keep it closer to Alice's life," Mary decreed. "Let's give Beluga that guy Alice goes out with!"

"Oh, that greaser punk...the stripper," Bill recalled.

I had been watching this conversation like a ping pong game. I was simply agog. How could they sit there and discuss me as if I were vermin? I finally shouted at them, "He wasn't a stripper! Besides, I dropped him! Got that? I did the dropping. And the reason I have no friends is because they all went to jail; I didn't chase them away. Furthermore, you ungracious slobs, I buy my clothes at Bloomingdales and pay top dollar, so I do have some fashion sense!" I looked down at what I was wearing – an orange blouse with a big coffee stain, old shapeless white pants, and my winter galoshes. "And I'm really sick to death of hearing how fat I am! I've lost 20 pounds already."

"You're still on the heavy side," Mary had to point out.

"Listen, you guys, I'm tired of sitting here and letting you walk all over me," I warned them.

"You HAVE to," Bill said. "That's why they pay you so much; it's your job."

"There's a LIMIT, for chrissake!" I yelled. "If things don't improve around here concerning me, a few people are going to lose their jobs. OK? Do I make myself clear?" There. I laid my threat on the table.

"You can't fire us, Alice," Bill smugly said. "You don't have the authority. Only Rigby can fire us. Now shut up and let's get to work."

Shut up? SHUT UP? How dare he!? And now I found out I couldn't fire anyone, not even Lilli? I was apoplectic.

"I have a great idea for the new Beluga's initial appearance!" Mary said. "Listen...she enters a beauty contest of all things... and comes in last place!"

"We'll show her in the swimsuit competition!" Bill said.

"And of course the question period, so she can come up with the usual dumb answer," Mary continued.

I had it. I had enough. I erupted.

"That does it!! Fuck off, you guys! I can't stand this bogus work anymore. You're nothing but glossed-over gossip rag reporters!" I felt something for the first time in days; a rush of adrenaline. It seemed a trifle much though. I was in advanced hyperactive mode.

The writers stopped to look at me, then Bill encouraged me. "Come on, Alice, get it off your chest." They all sat down expectantly, notepads at the ready.

"There's nothing left to get off my chest!" I said. "I've sold you every memory I own!"

"We want to know what you're feeling right now," Mary said, casting Bill a hopeful look.

"You want to know what I'm feeling? I feel like I hate every one of you and I hate Sebrings and Rigby and Beluga!"

"Yes! Beluga can have those feelings!" Bill said to Mary. "What brought all this on, Alice?"

"You guys did! I can't stand working here anymore; it's the worst job I've ever had and I won't take it anymore. I'm getting out of here," I said, making a decision.

"Beluga can become a hermit," Mary suggested. "What else, Alice? Do you feel like killing yourself?" What it felt like was that I was having a nervous breakdown and damn if they weren't galvanizing me. Damn if it wasn't a long time in coming.

I ran into my office and opened my desk drawer. My contract with Sebrings was right on top. I grabbed it and ran back into the writers' room. "See this?" I said. "It's my contract for this godawful job. Look!" I proceeded to tear it into tiny bits. "I'm quitting. I don't care what happens. Sue me, but you fuckheads won't have Alice Kumplunkem to push around anymore." I scooped up the tiny bits of paper and threw it into their stunned faces.

"Alice, this could have serious repercussions," Bill warned.

"I DON'T CARE! I QUIT! YOU HEAR ME? I QUIT I QUIT I QUIT!!!" I turned around and walked back to my office. I was still fuming as I grabbed my coat. Lilli paged me on the intercom.

"Alice, Largemar Productions on Line 3," Lilli said.

I grabbed up the phone. "What?"

"Troy LeRue here," a man identified himself. "It's December 15, and we were wondering if you'd given any thought to our offer. How's it going at Sebrings?"

"Ohhh, just fine," I said sarcastically. "Matter of fact, I just quit. And I'm sooo happy!"

"Oh, we are too! Can we hope that you'll be coming to Largemar?" Mr. LeRue asked.

 Oh, sure. Out of the frying pan and into the fire. Was he serious? "No, I will not work for Largemar either," I said. "I'm getting right out of show business because IT SUCKS. So to hell with you guys too!"

"We can increase our offer," Mr. LeRue said.

"Go ahead. Offer me a million bucks a week. I wouldn't do this job again for ANYTHING, so leave me the fuck alone!" I hung up on Largemar.

Storming out of my office, I noticed Lilli painting her nails in full view. How professional. I wanted to slap her as a grand exit gesture but feeling mean and out of control, I simply said, "Lilli, you're fired."

"Whaaa....?" she asked, looking extremely worried. Good! I WAS capable of firing her. I didn't know if it'd have any effect as I no longer worked for Sebrings, but it was worth saying it just to see her fret.

I went home to nurse my breakdown.

* * *

And it was a good thing I was home. I wasn't being myself at all. A cab driver picked me up outside of Sebrings and told me his sister worked there. That launched me into a diatribe against Sebrings and then against show business then against taxi companies and then against families. My doorman wished me a Merry Christmas and I snarled that it wasn't Christmas yet and who needed Christmas anyways? I took the elevator up and pressed every floor button before it went back down. I got into my suite and started pacing.

"You're outta there, Alice. Told 'em to go to hell in a big way, didn't ya? The bastards, you don't need them." It was all a pep talk but I wasn't feeling any better. I still felt like I was coming apart and I was still angry and I didn't want to feel this way.

I called my mother. "Yah-lo!" she answered.

"Mom, it's me, Alice," I said, starting to sob. "I quit my job, Mom. I just had to; it was so awful..."

"You QUIT your job?" my mother shrieked. "Oh for God's sake, Alice, what are we supposed to do for money now?"

"I don't care about stupid money!" I cried. "I'm rich!"

"It costs a lot to live in that fancy city," Mom reminded me. "Just make sure you buy me that coat before you spend it all."

"Mom, I'm scared! I don't feel right! I feel funny...like I want to really hurt somebody! A fur coat is the last thing on my mind!"

"Well, it's the only thing on my mind, Alice," Mother said. "Don't you dare come home if you don't have a fur coat for me."

"Alright then!" I screamed. "I just won't come home then!"

"Fine, then you can ship it to me," my mother said. "And Alice, another thing concerns me. How are you going to send me my money if you don't have a job?"

"Your money? It's my money! You didn't deserve one cent! Use THAT money to buy a fucking fur coat already. And thank you very much, Mother DEAR, for helping me with my problems. I knew I could count on you. Have a merry Christmas." I slammed the phone down so hard the receiver cracked. I prayed her eardrum did too.

I liked the look of that broken phone. I picked up a rack of dried dishes and slammed them down too. Then I grabbed scissors and cut up my clothes. Aaahh, I'd found something destructive to do with my time.

An hour later, the apartment was trashed. I was ready to start on the neighbor's but tried to get a grip on myself. It wasn't easy. I was definitely having a nervous breakdown but was sane enough to realize it.

I found the 'P' section in the yellow pages I'd ripped apart. I found an address and packed a small overnight case. My two big bottles of Tylenols and jug of diet pills took up most of the space. I fought an urge to set fire to the apartment and went downstairs to hail a cab.

I was checking myself into a psychiatric institution.

* * *

Bound in a straitjacket, I was hauled into a tiny cell by two young guards. No, that is not what happens once you present yourself at a psychiatric hospital. And it wouldn't have happened to me except they tried to take my overnight bag away.

It started off well enough. The cab drove me to Lyman's Institute for the Criminally Insane. I chose that particular place because I figured I was fully capable of committing a crime at the moment. Besides, wasn't I already some kind of criminal? The cabby didn't say a word to me after I'd given him the address and I sat in the back seat, trembling. *Get me there...hurry... you'll be OK in a while, Alice...*

The nurse at the front desk admitted me very properly. "Your name?"

"Alice Kumplunkem and I think I'm having a nervous breakdown," I panted.

"Fine. Haven't you simply considered a hospital for this, or some other psychiatric institution?" Nurse Lavally asked.

"No, this one suits me," I replied. "Believe me. Ma'am, uh...I'd like to stop feeling this way."

"Alright. We have extra beds. How will you be paying for this?" she asked.

"Uh...I'm covered by Sebrings Productions for medical expenses," I said. Surely I had some benefits coming to me; I'd only used up two doctor appointments.

"Next of kin?" the nurse asked.

I started sobbing and could barely gasp out, "Sorry...I can't stop crying..."

"Nothing unusual," Lavally reassured me. "Next of kin?"

"No, none," I said. None worth mentioning anyways.

"Just sign your name here, here and here," Nurse Lavally said, turning some papers around to face me. "The last place you sign says that you have voluntarily committed yourself."

I gripped the pen in both hands. Sheesh, I tore a phone book in half in my rage; how did she expect me to delicately handle a pen? I scratched out an A.K. "Can I see a doctor now?" I anxiously asked.

"In a moment. I'll just take that bag from you..."

"WHAT?" I said, clutching my case to me.

"We have to search your bag for drugs or weapons..."

"No one's taking this bag from me!" I declared. I noticed the nurse furtively press a button under the countertop. "I SAW THAT!" I yelled.

"Miss Kumplunkem, it is a rule here that we search the bags. Your bag will be returned to you. Now we don't want any trouble here, do we?" Nurse Lavally questioned.

"I'm not causing trouble! You are! I don't have anything in this bag! Just a nightgown and my pills. They're PRESCRIPTION. I MUST take them!" I could have gone on but the two young guards came running up to me.

"Everything OK, Nurse Lavally?" one asked.

"Could you please give me this lady's bag, Ted?" Lavally asked.

"Maybe I'll just check out," I said.

"You just checked IN," the nurse told me. "Now the doctor will have to check you OUT. Her bag, boys."

"YOU ARE NOT TAKNG MY BAG!" I shrieked. I tried to make a break for it but I was nabbed. I clawed, scratched, kicked, gouged, punched, slapped, bit and swore at the guards in an attempt to keep my bag. All to no avail. One finally broke the straps and handed the best part of my bag to Nurse Lavally. She in turn handed him a straitjacket which I tried to fight off, but I was just too tired from the first struggle.

It's hard to have a nervous breakdown in a straitjacket. You're bound up, so all the energy rushes to your brain. Nurse Lavally walked into the cell I'd been placed in. I was yelling so hard, I was red in the face. "Get me a doctor before I blow up for real! I'm sick! I need help!"

"You don't have to tell me that," the nurse said. "The doctor is busy right now. I'm going to give you a heavy sedative and when you wake up, you will have your damn bag back. Your straitjacket will have been removed and your clothes will have been searched, as well as your bag. There is absolutely nothing in this room with which to harm yourself. And until you fall asleep, these guards will be keeping an eye on you." That said and done, she forced a big tablet down my throat.

She left and I ranted at the guards for a while. They ignored me and discussed the local hockey team's results. Before long, it became a real effort to call them bastards, and when I did say it, that one word took five seconds to leave my mouth. I stopped my harassment and just sailed on the wings of a drug to precious, peaceful sleep.

*　*　*

I woke up hungry. The straitjacket had been removed, true to the promise made me. So had the wallet I carried in my pocket. By habit, I began craving a few Tylenols. After all, I was awake. Usually my three-course breakfast consisted of three Tylenol 2s, a bran muffin to provide fiber to produce a couple poop pellets, then a couple diet pills. That was usually enough to hold me until lunch.

Suddenly my pangs became acute. My pills were completely out of reach! How was I going to get one? I started panicking. What if I couldn't get one?! What then? Maybe...yeah! I'd go see the nurse and pull another freakout. That would be good for a sedative at least.

I tried the door, only to find I was locked in. I yanked on it and then started banging on the door, yelling through the opening. "Hey! Nurse! Guard! Someone! Hey! Hey!"

"Hey hey for the Monkees!" another voice chimed in.

I ignored it. "Helloooo?" I called out.

"Hello, I love you, won't you tell me your name?" the voice sang.

"Shuddup!" I yelled at whoever the jerk was.

"Shuddup yourself!" she yelled back. "We're trying to sleep!"

A guard came up. "Oh, it's you. Finally woke up, huh?" It was one of the guards from the night before.

"You're still working? What time is it?" I asked.

"Midnight. You checked in last night. Been asleep over 24 hours."

"No wonder I'm so hungry," I marveled.

"I'll be right back with your supper. Then the doctor wants to see you," the guard said before walking off.

A supper! The thought of food appealed to me more than a Tylenol. Then I stopped short. Why, I didn't have a headache! None whatsoever. I was totally clear-headed. If I could fight the withdrawal symptoms, then I'd be free of Tylenols! However, I still wanted to lose 30 more pounds.

The guard returned and spoke through the opening of the door. "Move away now. Move back." I meekly stood in the far corner and awaited my room-service meal. "Doctor will be up in ten minutes," the guard informed me.

He didn't leave the room so I stayed in the corner. "Go ahead," he said. "Eat. I have to watch you in case you try something."

I moved towards the food. "Every time I eat?" I asked.

"Until you're moved into the next ward. Then you'll eat your meals in the cafeteria, although there are guards there too. After meals, you get searched for hidden utensils." My guard appeared to like his job. "We only have three of these mattress rooms. They're used for active criminally insane or for people like you."

"Like me?" I asked as I began to eat my supper. One boiled potato, no butter, carrots (and too many at that), a boiled piece of chicken and some Jell-O. I licked my plate clean.

"People who give us a rough time when they come in," the guard replied. "We don't know what peak of insanity they've reached and so that we don't get sued, we take the precaution of putting them in here."

"Do you always work nights?" I asked.

"Always," he said. "4 p.m. to 4 a.m. We move from ward to ward though. Same shift, different pile." He laughed and I laughed along with him, although I didn't get the joke. I was just so happy to feel sane again.

"What's your name?" I asked.

"Pegli," he replied. "Well, I'll take your tray now." He opened the door just as the doctor appeared. I was dismayed to see Pegli leaving.

"Any trouble?" the doctor asked.

"None, but you can never tell with these people," Pegli said and left.

The doctor entered my padded cell. "Hello, I'm Dr. Stavefield," he said. He looked at a chart he was carrying. "Goodness, it says you voluntarily committed yourself. Why?"

"I had a nervous breakdown," I explained. "I truly believed I was dangerous."

"Well, we need more citizens like you," Dr. Stavefield commended me. "Why don't you come with me and we'll give you an examination. Guard!" he shouted down the hall.

"Oh, that's alright," I reassured him. "I don't feel dangerous anymore."

He was still being nice. "Just a precaution, you understand, until I can assess your mental status."

"Of course," I said. The guard appeared – Pegli again – and I was led out of my cell. This was the first time I really focused on the place I was now residing. It actually did resemble a hospital. I was in a room at the very end of the corridor. Every room had a window that you could look through. Not very private, I thought. We passed the nurse's desk and I saw Nurse Lavally counting out pills. My glands salivated.

I wanted to see what kind of loony went behind these doors. I angled my steps closer toward one of the rooms then stopped. "Aren't these the new kind of fluorescent lights?" I asked and pointed up.

Pegli and Dr. Stavefield stopped briefly and looked up. I spun my head to look into a window. All I saw was a fat man picking his nose. If that was a sign of insanity, then a third of the car drivers in New York were lunatics.

"I couldn't say," Dr. Stavefield said. "Come on, let's go."

We went up a flight of stairs and then began going up to the third floor. "What's on the second floor?" I asked.

"That's the men's ward," Pegli said, proud of his institution. "If you check out with the doctor, you get the fourth floor."

"What about the first floor?" I enquired, not that I was overly fond of my cell.

"That's the mattress rooms and cells for the people who still need to be constantly monitored," Pegli said. "The fourth floor is open; it's got about forty beds and only one guard."

"We'll give you a little tour," Dr. Stavefield said. "I'll show you the third floor; that's the kitchen, eating area and recreation area. Of course we can't show you the second floor as women aren't allowed to mingle with the men."

"Of course," I said again. Pegli opened the third-floor door for the doctor and I. It was eerie seeing the place at night. Deathly silent and still. I began to feel nervous about Pegli and the doctor; after all, they were complete strangers.

"I've seen enough," I said.

We went up one more floor. "This is the women's ward," Pegli said. There was a small staff lounge, a nurse's area and a huge open space filled with cots. I saw one woman dart from another's bed as we entered.

"Where's the guard?" Dr. Stavefield wondered.

"Probably on his break," Pegli thought. Everyone was in bed and under the covers. It was still fairly early – just past midnight – but it was clearly past lights-out time.

I noticed a women's washroom. "Excuse me...?" I said. I really had to take a piss.

"Oh, no," Dr. Stavefied held me back. "Save it for the urine sample, please."

I thought I could hold on that long. We went up one more flight of stairs. "Top floor," the doctor said. "The best for last! This is where I spend most of my time, in the laboratory. We have the finest equipment in New York City." Dr. Stavefield was vainglorious about this floor. He introduced me to superior blood pressure machines and the latest in electrograms.

Finally, "And here's my examination room."

"Great why don't we get started?" I asked, my legs crossed. My bladder was ready to burst. "Where's the container for the urine sample?"

After washing his hands (subtle torture), Dr. Stavefield took one out of a cupboard and passed it to me. I grabbed it and started off towards the washroom. "Wait, Alice," the doctor halted me. "Take this robe and change into it." I ran back and snatched it from him.

As soon as I saw the toilet, I involuntarily started pissing myself. I threw the robe on the floor, undid my pants, squatted over the seat and began filling the container. In no time, my hand got hot. *Oh shit! I'm overflowing the thing!* I yanked my hand out from under myself and spilled some pee on my robe. Piss on it. I was glad to empty my bladder. I capped the full-to-the-brim urine jar and changed into my robe.

The doctor ran me through a battery of tests then sat me down and had a talk with me. I told him a few of the circumstances that led me to Lyman's Institute for the Criminally Insane. The doctor examined a couple x-rays then studied me for a moment.

"Alice, since you checked yourself in, you can also check yourself out. I've given my examination and legally, you'd be allowed on the streets of New York," the doctor said. "However, I'd like you to consider staying. I've found heavy traces of Tylenols and diet pills in your system and I'd say you were an addict..."

"I need them!" I said.

"You don't NEED them, Alice," the doctor sternly said.

"OK, I don't need the Tylenols. I'm off them anyways. But let me stick to the diet pills!" I begged. "I need to lose 30 more pounds!"

"You don't need pills to lose weight. There are more sensible diets," Stavefield said. Yeah, like carrots for breakfast, lettuce for lunch and celery for supper. "I'd like to treat you for your pill dependency, put you on a proper nutritional diet, monitor your nervous breakdown..."

"Oh, am I still having one?" I asked.

"It could flare up again. And I'd like to see if we can't make this ulcer disappear," the doctor concluded.

"I'VE got an ULCER?" I asked disbelievingly.

"You're surprised?" the doctor questioned. "After what I've just been told?"

I guess I wasn't. "How do I know when I'm better?" I asked.

"We'll let you know," Stavefield said. "Now, I'm going to assign you to the fourth floor. A word of advice though – the ladies you'll be bunking with all have a criminal history. It would be wise not to form any close friendships. Keep your eyes open, stay alert, and you should be alright."

"Thanks, doctor," I said. *Thanks for putting me at ease.*

"Pegli, set her up on the fourth floor," Dr. Stavefield called out to my guard. "Have a good night's sleep, Alice."

* * *

I couldn't sleep. It wasn't because I'd just woken up two hours earlier from a 24-hour nap; I was nervous one of my fellow sleepers was hiding a machete under her mattress. I did have the option of checking myself out of the joint but I was even more scared of the City of New York. I started shaking again just at the thought.

Morning finally rolled around. Before anyone woke up, I used the washroom and freshened up. There were no guards around; probably on the change of shift.

I was just finishing taking a tinkle when I heard someone come into the stall next to me. "That you, Gravedigger?" a voice asked. Ice started running through my veins. What kind of human – a woman at that – would have a name like that? I pulled up my pants and ran out without washing my hands.

Everyone eventually woke up. I stayed in bed, not bothering to mingle. I was sneaking peeks at them but was terrified they'd catch me staring. So far I could see I was living with a motley crew. I've never seen so many scars on so few people, and all of them seemed to sport multiple tattoos.

A few of us stayed in bed. The girl in the bed next to me

started crying. Bawling. Wailing. The guard walked up to the bed. "Dottie!" she threatened. "I'll send you down to the mattress room..."

Dottie held it down to a slight whimper until the guard walked out of the room. She started up again until a fellow patient walked up to her. "SHADDAP!" she yelled. Dottie stopped. She was only moaning when the same inmate returned and gave her a chop to the head. I didn't say a word about this brutality; I was just going to mind my own beeswax.

A loud bell went off. Everyone lined up. I was the only one left lying in bed. The guard walked up to me. She was at least 300 pounds in weight and all her buttons were bulging. Her breasts were flattened into a square box from her tight, Extra-Large uniform top. She looked like she was a boxer before becoming a security guard. Her only redeeming feature was a head of tightly permed black coils. "WHO are YOU?" she asked me. "The Queen of Sheba? You goin' to lie in bed all day?"

"I'm new here," I whispered.

"So? You eat like everyone else, dontcha? Get in line!" she yelled, prodding me then walking away. Waddling away. A large layer of blubber spilled out above and below her clearly defined bra-line. I didn't think I was going to like her.

I got into the line-up and stood about four feet from the girl closest to me. She looked like a walking case of leprosy. Her neck, arms and ankles were oozing with pus-filled scabs. We were marched into the dining room.

Two ladies in grease-splattered aprons served us. Their every movement was automatic; I could see there was no asking for extra bacon. I was given a severely undercooked fried egg, two pieces of burnt-to-a-crisp bacon and a slice of unbuttered bread. White. I wondered if this diet was to be any more sensible than my usual fare. A cup of watered-down coffee came with the meal.

Since I was last in line, everyone had seated themselves before me. I took my tray and gave a quick circumspect look around the room. There was one empty table in the dead-center. Keeping my head down, I walked over to it. I had just sat down when I saw the security guard walking over to me. Now what had I done? Then I saw she was also carrying a breakfast tray. She took a seat at the opposite end of the table. I looked at her tray with envy. Three platefuls? And how'd she get her bread toasted?

Everyone finished eating in a matter of minutes. Still, we had to sit there for a full hour. I wished I had a book to read. I think we stayed that long so that our chunky guard could finish her meal. She got up one time and I thought, *Good, back to our room.* Instead, she came back with another trayful.

Finally, she burped out loud and looked at a pocket watch attached to her utility belt. Leaning her head back, with a projection worthy of a theatre gig, she hollered, "LINE UP!"

I stood up quickly to let her know I wasn't royalty, but managed to stall getting into the line-up. Once again I was last in line, behind the third-world refugee. She was scratching a scab off her throat.

We bypassed our living quarters. We were simply led into the hall and into an open room. There were a few couches, a television set, games on shelves. Everyone stood in a line facing a door though. I peeked out from my position and saw the guard open the door and look up. "Well, it's only drizzling. You're goin' out today." We all filed out the door and down a rickety set of iron steps to a big yard. There was a wall dividing the property in half. I could make out men shouting on the other side.

The guard followed me down the steps. I got to the bottom and heard her grunt. I turned around and saw she'd managed to squeeze herself into a sitting position on the stairwell. "GO PLAY!" she commanded. I wandered off to an unoccupied corner of the dividing wall.

I was standing there when out of nowhere I heard a male voice. "That you, Gravedigger?" Somehow it was coming from the wall. A folded piece of paper waved at me and I saw there was a chink in the wall. Two tough-looking babes started walking towards me so I decided to pay a visit to the empty space under the stairwell.

I surveyed the scene. There were a few loners like myself, a few exercisers, a few huddlers. Suddenly there was a loud booming and I glanced above. The security guard was walking back upstairs and I thought she was going to fall through. Obviously she didn't know I was under the stairwell as she let a fart rip.

As soon as the door slammed behind her, there was a mass exodus to the far corner of the yard – my initial hanging-out area. I felt a rise of excitement in the air. I almost had the urge to walk over and see what the hullabaloo was about. Before I took my first step, I heard the door above me open and I froze. Obviously the guard would notice the crowd in the corner.

But, where there was none a second ago, now a fight was in progress between the two girls I'd seen walk over to me earlier. The other dozen girls had formed a circle and were egging them on.

CRASH! CRASH! This time I did run out from under the stairwell as the guard came lumbering down. The fight had broken up by the time she got there, and nobody was saying anything. I turned around to go back under the steps but two gals had taken my place and were grabbing a quick smooch.

I walked around, my eyes pointed at the ground. I saw the Scab Girl sprawled on the ground, her back against the wall. No one seemed to be bothering her so I struck the same pose a few feet away. I was getting sleepy now and was glad when our Sarah Bernhardt-contender hollered, "LINE UP!"

Back into the cafeteria we went. I was amazed at how hungry I'd gotten doing nothing. The same cooks now doled out a spoonful of...chili? Stew? Chunky Soup? It rather looked like pig slop. For fruit, we had a choice – bruised apple or black banana.

I passed.

I was headed back to the empty table when that fat guard just bristled past me. I guess she wanted to sit there too. I didn't want to make it look like I was joining her so I simply sat in the empty chair I had been pushed into. The table was filled with inmates but I ignored them all. I was really quite enthralled with my meal. In one bite, I had a big chunk of pork fat. In the next was a piece of pasta. The next had a bone.

I watched the guard slurp the rest of her soup. She had the bowl brought up to her lips. As soon as her lunch was over, her head went back and I knew what was coming. Before she could utter her directive, I stood up and headed for the door. I was going to try being first in line this time.

Thankfully, we were led back into our cot-filled room. I headed directly for my bed. Although I was yawning over and over, I still didn't go to sleep. I trusted these girls less when they were awake, never mind asleep. I still didn't speak to anyone. Call me a snob but I was following doctor's orders. The girl next to me – Dottie – started her sobbing again and was repeatedly told to shut up. At least she was keeping me awake.

A nurse walked into the room and the guard yelled her favorite order. Most of the institution's patrons lined up but I noticed a few remained where they were. I decided I would too. The guard rushed up to me so I scrambled out of bed. I was almost in line when she reached out and shoved me the last couple feet. "I don't know who you are but..." She didn't continue her threat. But what? If I don't behave, I'll go to the mattress room? Big deal. I rather liked it there, what I recall of it. This guard was really starting to get on my nerves.

We were moving ahead extremely slowly. When I got closer, I saw we were in a line-up for pills from the nurse. Well, why didn't they tell me that in the first place? Why did I get that funny feeling whenever I saw pills? Weak brain circuit, I guess. The nurse would check the patient's name, pop open a corresponding case and hand the woman some pills and a glass of water. After downing the pills, you next had to walk over to the guard, who would search your mouth. Well, if they were going to give me pills, I guess I'd have to take them.

I reached the nurse. "Your name?" she asked.

"Alice Kumplunkem," I said. *Hurry up, dearie.*

She ran her finger down a list of names on the board she carried. "Oh, here you are! Yes, Dr. Stavefield recommends absolutely no medication. You needn't get in line next time."

I shot the guard a dirty look. She made me get in line, yet her face showed no remorse, the shit locker.

"I'll be seeing you tomorrow, Gilda," the nurse said to the guard. "You get off soon, don't you?"

"Two more hours," Gilda the guard replied. "My kids are taking me out for supper tonight," she bragged. I hoped they'd take her to a Chinese restaurant so she'd get hungry an hour later.

The guard shift change came and we got a very disinterested guard. I was so sleepy and bored. These girls, with the exception of the sap in the bed next to me, all seemed as sane as I. Playing cards, reading, sleeping, all quite non-violent. To stay awake, I tried to figure out who Gravedigger was.

The guard, Stanley, called supper. This was our third meal of the day, and already it was becoming routine. I got in line, eighth from the last, and marched to the cafeteria. We were given a vinegary coleslaw, a piece of meat loaf and a spoonful of Brussels sprouts. Dessert was the leftover fruit from lunch. I was ravenous again and this time I took an apple. I ate between the bruises.

Supper came to a close and I was wondering what was next in store. Our room again? It was too dark to go 'play' outside. I figured it would be TV time. Sure enough, our conga line ended up in the recreation room.

The couches were filled quickly so a few girls went into a

cupboard and pulled out some folding chairs. I followed suit. When in Rome... A general circle was formed and everyone sat down for God knows what. I was seated mere inches from the tough-looking girl I'd seen up close in the yard. She wasn't ugly or anything; she just looked like she'd be able to handle herself in a back alley alone at dark. She looked like a two-bit hooker. Her hair was quite nice though. Somehow she managed to have it looking quite vampy although I'd seen no curling irons or hairspray anywhere in the institution.

Dr. Stavefield entered the room. "Hello, everyone," he greeted us. "How are you all?" There were a few mumbled responses. My "Fine" came out loud and clear. "Yes, has everyone met Alice?" the doctor asked. *Yeah, right, doc, I'm going to go around handing out my business card, after what you told me.* No, I hadn't met ANYONE. Again, a few mumbled replies. "Well," the doctor continued, "who feels like talking tonight? Anyone got anything to get off their chests?" No one spoke. "Alice?" *No!*

I didn't want to speak! I shook my head. "Gravedigger?" the doctor asked.

All heads swiveled towards me. Was I Gravedigger after all? Why?? Then I saw their eyes were focused on the gal next to me, the tough one. "I got nothing to say," she said.

"Why don't you start off our session until everyone feels comfortable enough to talk?" the doctor suggested.

"Why can't Alice start?" Gravedigger asked. I cringed; I wanted no friction between her and I.

"Because this is Alice's first night with our group. She has a right to be shy. I'm sure you remember your first visit with us," the doctor had her recall.

"I remember what I DID to have to come here," Gravedigger chose to remember. "That fucking bitch..."

"Are you sure you want to talk about this?" the doctor asked.

"Hey! You asked me to talk and this is what I now feel like talking about!" Gravedigger retorted. "I don't know why I have to spend more than three years in this place!"

"Gravedigger, you were on parole from prison for your first slice and dice job," the doctor calmly said. "You committed another violent crime while on parole so it became quite obvious you were a sick person. Now, you've made a lot of headway while you've been here and your case will be studied in the new year. If all goes well, you'll be released. Who'd like to speak next?"

A girl timidly put up her hand. "I know Pussie is spreading germs," she said, looking over at the Scab Girl, who I guess was called Pussie. Not like the cat but like the stuff that oozes out of sores.

"Now, Katrina, you know your tendency to over-exaggerate everything," Dr. Stavefield said. I don't know about that one, Doc. I tended to agree with Katrina.

"Where can I get some drugs....?" Pussie wanted to know.

"Pus...uh, Florence, you are getting drugs – a low form of methadone," Stavefield said. What? Why her and not me? "There is no possible way for you to stick a needle into yourself. Not only are the needles under lock and key, but the scar tissue over your veins is too thick for them."

"I KNOOOWW she's spreading germs!" Katrina whined.

"Katrina," the doctor sternly said. "There ARE germs everywhere, but they aren't going to kill you. Are you going to kill Pussie like you killed your baby?"

"There's germs in bath water!" Katrina declared.

"That didn't mean you had to pour three gallons of bleach into the water," the doctor grimly said. "Didn't you know those fumes would asphyxiate her?" I don't think Katrina was the doc's favorite. I was going to stay clear of Katrina though, or else take at least three showers a day for her benefit. I found out later that was where the germophobic spent most of her time.

"You shouldn't kill people by asphyxiation," one girl stated. "You should throw a hair dryer into the bath, like I did. Twice.

Then they jump!"

"No way!" another angrily yelled. "Not like that! Just shoot them! Plain and simple! Watch 'em die, them cocksuckers! MOTHERFUCKERS! I'll kill ya all! FUCKING FREAKS! I'll shoot ya in the fucking face, you..."

"Linda!" Dr. Stavefield shouted. "Enough!" Linda shut up but still glowered.

"I wanna get fucked," a voice said from the couch.

"Rebecca, you're close to getting out of here," the doctor said. "Let's not have any talk like that from you."

"I WANNA GET FUCKED!" Rebecca repeated. Well, so what, Rebecca? So did I but I wasn't making a big production out of it.

"Shut up, Rebecca," Gravedigger warned. I wondered why.

"You must fight your nymphomania," the doctor urged. "If you continue to prostitute yourself and then hold your tricks as sexual hostages, you will only end up back here."

Rebecca pouted and massaged herself. We all pretended to ignore her but it was making me sick.

"Well, this was a good session," the doctor said. "Enjoy your free time and I'll see you tomorrow." The doctor up and left.

Our guard turned on the TV and pulled a chair up to the set. I decided to watch some tube myself and was never so aware of all the sex and violence on TV these days. It perturbed me that most of the inmates seemed to also be watching. I couldn't stay awake any longer and was starting to nod off when the guard stood up and turned off the set.

"Ten o'clock. Let's go," he said in a monotone.

"I didn't get my methadone yet!" Pussie whined.

"You did too. At 3 p.m.," our guard, Stanley, said. "You're not conning me."

"I'll do ya," Pussie offered.

"That's why she's here," Gravedigger said to Rebecca. "She'll do anything for a fix."

"I'll do ya for nothing!" Rebecca jumped in.

"No, thanks," Stanley declined. "Come on, up to your room."

We headed back for our dorm. Although I was deathly afraid of my fellow lunatics, I was also bone-tired. I left myself to their mercy.

* * *

And woke up alive. To pandemonium. Gravedigger was beating up on the crybaby in the bed next to me. "Shut up already! I can't take this crying every day!" Smack to the eye. "If you don't shut your trap, I'll take a pair of scissors to ya!" Pow to the mouth. I don't know if it was the threat or the last punch that helped, but Crybaby hid under her blankets and didn't utter another sound.

"Gravedigger!" Katrina called out. "Guard's coming!" Gravedigger and Katrina ran off towards the washroom.

My nerves were shot first thing in the morning. I was too nervous to get out of bed and go for a leak. And again, I was just starving! My desire for pills was subsiding as my craving for a substantial meal grew. I heard a whimper and glanced over at the next bed.

Dottie was starting up again, even after the pummeling she took from Gravedigger. *Are you nuts, girl?* Fortunately for Dottie, Gravedigger was in the john so the guard (Gilda again) merely gave our sissy a shake.

She was silent a moment and I saw Gravedigger emerge from the washroom, yawn and crawl back into bed. Dottie started her whimpering again. It was starting to get louder and I saw Gravedigger sit up.

"What the hell's the matter?" I whispered, wanting her to shut her trap before I started thrashing her. She stopped crying and poked her head out from under the blankets.

"Who said that?" she asked, looking around.

"Me," I replied. "Why are you crying all the time? Christ."

"You don't really want to know," Dottie said, lip snarling.

Well, as a matter of fact, I was curious as to what possessed her to spend her every waking moment crying.

"Sure," I said all friendly-like, "tell me."

Her lip unfolded and her bloodshot eyes brightened a bit. "Really?" she said, unbelievingly. I nodded. "Let's sit together at breakfast and I'll tell you, OK?" I nodded again. Gee, a breakfast date.

In the line-up, Dottie stood right behind me. She was going to make sure I sat with her. Ever since I'd said I would listen to her story, she hadn't uttered a peep; just stared at me with puppy-dog eyes. I grabbed my breakfast tray and didn't look as my egg was slid onto a plate. I KNOW there was blood in the yolk; isn't that dangerous? Besides the egg, we had porridge and a slice of bread. I spotted a table near the back wall that was still empty and I walked over, Dottie trailing an inch from my tailbone.

She started speaking as soon as we sat down. "Here," she said, "you can have my egg. I don't want it." If it was possible, her egg looked worse than mine. I didn't want it either but I suspected she was making a gesture of friendship.

"Thanks," I said.

"I just want you to know that I appreciate the fact you want to hear my story," Dottie said. "You're the first one! Everyone thinks that because I cry all the time, that I'm crazy. But I'm not crazy."

"Neither am I," I said. "So what makes you cry so much?"

"No one's had the life I've had," Dottie said. Right away, I thought, *Oh yeah?* "The reason I'm in this place, in a criminal institution, is because I set fire to a house that my lover was in. He was going to leave me because I wouldn't leave my husband. My husband was a black witch though, and if I left him, he would cast a spell on me and eat our children. So I told him about the fire and he was proud of me and then he brought me to a witches' meeting and I told them, but there was an informant in the group. He went to the police but I escaped before they came into my house. I was in the back yard and found my can of gasoline and I lit my house on fire. I wanted them to find a body and think I was dead, but instead they found out it was my husband's body. So they found me living in a room on Skid Row and arrested me. I admitted that I committed a couple murders lately but I was upset that my life had so fallen to pieces, and I couldn't stop crying. They figured I belonged in a mental institution! If only I could have talked to someone like you, then I would have gone to a nice normal prison. This place is terrible! There are real lunatics here!"

"Yeah, a couple, I guess," I said. I was talking to one.

"Shit," Dottie said, glancing around. "Aretha...over there? She thinks she's the Virgin Mary and went around to over a hundred churches busting up statues of the Virgin because they didn't look like her. Toni? She's here 'cuz she was castrating bums while they slept...Sky because she wants to be a terrorist for any country...Why are you here anyways?"

I knew it was coming. I was in an institution filled with murderers and I was there because of a nervous breakdown. I pretended to still be chewing a mouthful of porridge while I decided what to tell her. If I told the truth, I might be considered a wimp and word would go around and then I'd end up as the new punching bag. Finally, after a swallow of coffee, I came up with an idea. I'd tell her the truth, but would slightly embellish it.

"Murder, drug dealing, armed robbery," I listed. "The cops were hounding me all the time and I finally had a nervous breakdown." I put it as flippantly as possible but Dottie wasn't overly impressed.

"Oh, you're probably just borderline crazy," she said.

"I don't think I'm crazy at all," I replied.

"Neither am I," Dottie said.

"Are you going to be doing any more crying?" I asked.

"Oh, no! I feel SO much better! And now that I don't feel like crying, the doctor will see I'm better and send me to a prison instead," Dottie said, actually quite happy now.

And so she should have been, with the hope of real prison in her future. When I got better, I'd get sent back to my life in NYC.

* * *

I tried to keep to myself again that day but Dottie would sit on my bed and have a chat every now and then. Other inmates were giving us weird looks. If it was possible, I was feeling even more nervous. Was Dottie a snitch and now I was in cahoots with her? Is that what they thought? But if I ignored Dottie, I just knew she'd find a way to torch my bed. I was in a no-win situation.

It was nearing the end of my second day at the institution. We'd eaten our supper, the blandest meal I'd ever eaten. Plain rice and a piece on unseasoned baked fish. Vanilla pudding for dessert. That made six white courses I'd eaten today. Lunch was the highlight of my day. At least the boiled cabbage had a hint of green to it.

Once again, it was session time with the doctor. I was seated between Dottie and Pussie. As we waited for the doctor, I felt Pussie brush her chair against mine. She got real close to me so I inched a bit nearer to Dottie. I glanced at Pussie, hoping she wouldn't notice and get insulted and kill me. I almost lost my pudding. There was a huge mound of pus settling on her collarbone. It dripped in a slow-travelling river from a picked-off scab near her chin.

I got up and took a tissue out of a box. Wadding it up, I drifted back to my seat and passed it over to Pussie. She came to life; she opened it up quickly and searched for its contents. Finding it empty, she looked at me quizzically.

"It's a Kleenex," I said. "You're...dripping from your chin." Pussie simply dropped the tissue on the floor.

Doctor Stavefield entered the room. "Hello, ladies," he greeted us. "Let's get right to it; I have a Christmas party to go to tonight, so I won't be able to spend much time with you. Who'd like to start?"

Gravedigger spoke up. "I don't know what Alice did but somehow, she managed to shut Dottie up. I'm speaking for most of us, and we'd like to thank Alice. I think Dottie is what was keeping half of us crazy and we finally had a pleasurable day here today."

"Well, that's a remarkable thing for you to say, Gravedigger," the doctor said. "It shows a valid human emotion and that's commendable. Matter of fact, I'm going to make a notation of that." He scribbled something down. "Do you have something to say, Alice?"

"You're welcome," I said. I was actually blushing, I was so grateful. Grateful that I was on Gravedigger's good side.

"Fine, but would you like to comment on anything?" Stavefield persisted.

Oh shit. My turn to speak. I didn't want these girls to think I was a softie so I decided to go for broke. Murder seemed to be the going thing and I went with it. "Uh...I really don't like that guard, Gilda. She bothers me." I said that last bit real spooky-like. "The last time someone bothered me so much, I made them commit suicide. The cops found out thooouughhh. They charged me with murrrderrr." For some reason, I was relaying this in a singsong manner. Maybe it was adding a crazy-like emphasis. "Then they got me for drug deeaalinggg..."

"You deal drugs!" Pussie exclaimed. "I need just a bit. Do you have some?"

Before the doctor could speak, I put on a tough act. "Nah, they nailed me when I got to this place. Took 500 pills off me." It was the truth.

The doctor was looking at me oddly. "Got a problem?" I asked belligerently. I didn't want to hurt the doctor – I rather liked him. But I could sense a growing appreciation of me in the room, and I played it to the hilt.

"No, no problem," the doctor murmured and made some notes on me. Uh oh. I hadn't been quite expecting that, but I'd made my play and the ball was in his court now. "Anyone else?" the doctor asked.

Pussie spoke up, but she spoke directly to me. "I'm here because of a drug problem. I don't know when to stop and have had over sixty overdoses. You know what got me in here? I broke into a pharmacy and I found so many good drugs and so many clean needles! I kept shooting up until I passed out. The pharmacist and two cops woke me up the next morning. That, and my bazillion prior convictions, got me in here."

"That's the most you've said since you did get here," Stavefield observed. "That's progress! I'm glad to hear you've decided your drug problem is real. Yes, I'll note that too." He scribbled some more and then stood up. "Excellent session, ladies. I'll see you tomorrow." He left.

I played shuffleboard with Gravedigger. She kept up a conversation and I sensed she was feeling me out. I kept lying like a rug.

* * *

Gravedigger woke me up with a light slap to the leg. I gasped and cowered, expecting my beating. Instead she good-naturedly said, "Get up, sleepyhead! It's almost time for breakfast!" I got out of bed and finally used the washroom in the morning; I felt courageous enough.

Pussie followed me in. "So, Alice," she whispered, "are you carrying?"

"Carrying?" I said aloud. "Carrying...what?"

"Anything," she replied.

I looked down and saw my toothbrush and paste in my hand. "Just this," I showed her.

"Shit. Do you have any connections in this place?" Pussie asked. It seemed she was coding her questions because I just wasn't getting her drift.

"I guess I know a few people," I replied. "If that's what you mean..."

"We have to work out a plan," Pussie said conspiringly.

"Sure," I lied. I figured she was just being a loony. She turned to exit and I dropped a broad hint. "Pussie, there's lots of toilet paper in the stall." Didn't she realize she was actually leaving a trail of pus?

She nodded, her eyes wide. "Yeahhh, that's where we'll hide whatever we get. Smart. Got it." She obviously didn't get it because she still walked out.

Breakfast was rather fun. I sat at a table with Dottie, Gravedigger and Rebecca. Everyone exchanged stories. I was actually sitting with people who had as many humiliations and degradations as I had. They were almost like kin. I humored them by telling them of different methods I'd use to kill Gilda.

I don't know why ol' Pegli had different piles because Gilda seemed to be permanently assigned to working the day shift in the women's ward. For some odd reason, she seemed to have it in for me. *I'm sorry, Gilda darling, but this is my first time in a mental institution, never mind a criminal one at that. Bear with me, s'il vous plait.*

I found myself asking Gravedigger what she was doing during 'yard time'. We were in the line-up, waiting for our turn to be searched for weapons, whether they be fork, knife or spoon.

"Rebecca and I got a meeting," she said.

That dumbfounded me. "You can have MEETINGS here?"

"We got a plan," Gravedigger said. "Maybe I'll tell you about it tonight." I nodded, although I wasn't sure I wanted to get involved in any plan. I didn't think I wanted to KNOW anything about the plan.

I walked around the yard and worked off my raison omelet. Pussie walked a bit with me but tired out after ten minutes. She sank to her spot on the wall and I meandered over to the stairwell. I was freezing and wanted to go inside. Granted, yard time had been reduced to an hour, but it was December in New York City! I stood quietly behind the large bulk of Gilda, squeezed into the staircase. She made a fine windblock.

I was only there a few minutes when a couple girls walked in front of me. They stopped and looked at me, only they didn't seem to be overly friendly. I recognized them as a couple of smoochers I'd been seeing; grabbing a kiss or a quick feel whenever they could. *So...I take it you want the stairwell?* Well, I wasn't into giving any of these girls at the institution a hard time, so I hunched all of my back muscles and wandered off into the cold.

"Hey! You! Come here!" Gilda commanded me.

I walked over. "What?" I said, not making a pretense of the fact I didn't much care for her.

She stuck her hand out. "Help me up," she said. Ohhh boy, I did not want to help her. I figured she was just too heavy to lift herself out so I walked closer and offered her my hand. I left it limp as she grabbed it and hoped no one was looking.

"Pull me!" she shrieked in a fierce whisper. "Pull me out!"

"Are you STUCK?" I stupidly asked. I found that to be hysterically funny and started laughing. It was the first belly laugh I'd had in three years. Gilda was fuming.

"If you don't get me out, I'll make sure you go to the mattress room," Gilda warned.

Big deal, I thought. Still, her attitude sobered me up enough to reply, "Oh? And maybe I'll just call all the girls over and we can all have a big laugh at you. Try and be nice once in a while. Maybe you'll get your way more often with us."

Gilda tried to soften up. "Alright, please help me out," she said quite artificially.

Nah, she bugged me now. "Look, it's fucking freezing out," I said. It's funny how quick you pick up prison jargon. "I'll pull you out if you call us in right after. Otherwise...I'll tell everyone."

"Fine," Gilda agreed. "Now get me out...please." She may have gotten the better end of the deal or else I may have just been weak from hunger. Lifting 300 pounds is harder than it used to be. Finally she came out with a rip. We looked at each other quizzically and I noticed a huge tear in her blouse. I don't think she saw it for the layers of fat. "Excuse yourself," she ordered.

Of course, no 'thank you' emitted from her lips. Instead, a second later, I got the full force of her "Line up!" I was first in line and followed her up the stairs. Through the rip in her shirt, I could see she was a 54DD. Her bra looked more like a harness.

Pussie sat with me at lunch and regaled me with this lovely dream she'd had – she'd died and was a ghost and nobody could see her when she broke into their homes and consumed their drugs. I suggested she mention the dream to the doctor at session time; maybe he could analyze it. "Not necessary," Pussie said. "I've analyzed it myself. Sign from God, showing me there is a heaven."

The turnip mash at lunch really filled me up so I thought I'd lie down for a nap. I was almost into dreamtime when I caught part of a whispered conversation. "You goin' on the list?" one girl asked.

"Oh yeah, count me in!" another girl excitedly replied.

"Good, that leaves three more names left to fill," the first girl said. I drifted off to sleep.

And was awakened by Gilda screaming, "Line up!" beside my bed. She turned to glower at me and I wondered what happened to our brief peace. I groggily got into line and heard one girl ask another, "Didja get on the list?"

The other girl had a spasm. "YES!" she whispered, clutching her body with both arms. I wondered what this list was about and if I was on it. Gravedigger got into the line behind me and started up a quiet conversation on the way to the mess hall.

"You're alright, Alice," she said. "I heard what you did to Gilda this morning in the yard."

I supposed she was referring to my helping Gilda out of a tight spot. You could say I was being a Good Samaritan, I guess.

"I was just there at the right time," I calmly conceded.

"Yeah, and you let her have it, didn't ya?" Gravedigger said. "Told her off good and proper. If I wasn't trying to get out of here, I'd have told her where to go months ago."

"How'd you hear about it?" I asked her.

"Rona and Daphne," she said. I looked confused. "You know, the two dykes. They were there. They heard everything."

"Who'd they tell?" I asked.

"Everybody," Gravedigger replied. "Which makes you a big gun around here." Yeah, and it also made a big reason for Gilda to pick on me some more. By now, she'd have heard a few details and she was gonna think I broke my end of the deal. "Listen, ol' Alice, ol' palomino," Gravedigger continued. "Remember this plan I told you I had? Sit with me after the doctor's visit and I'll fill you in, alright?"

"Sure," I said to Gravedigger, new palomino, buddyomine, friendomine!

I could tell people were making gestures of friendship during supper because I got more gifts of refried beans than I could possibly eat. I wasn't even going to eat my own.

In our recreation area, a spot was made vacant for me on the couch. I didn't mind the folding chairs but I knew the couch was considered a 'choice' seat. The doctor rushed in and informed us he had to finish some Christmas shopping. It wasn't a very good session, or a very long one. Katrina started crying because she found a black hair on her soap and she has blonde hair; thus someone is trying to poison her through her soap. I could tell the doctor didn't want to waste time on her; he told her to join the real world and then said if anyone didn't have any real problems to bring up, he'd see us tomorrow.

He left and I looked over at Gravedigger. She made a motion with her hand that told me to wait.

"Who wants a good game of shuffleboard?" Rebecca asked aloud.

I could see Pegli, who was finally our guard again, get excited. None of the girls responded so he piped up. "Come on, Rebecca, I'll take you on."

"Sure," Rebecca said then lewdly asked. "What are we playing for?"

Pegli laughed. "If you think you can beat me, I'll leave it up to you." Rebecca rushed to the table.

Gravedigger steered me to the opposite corner and took out a pack of playing cards. "Now that Rebecca's got his attention," Gravedigger said, "I can tell you about this plan. You wanna get fucked? By a man?"

I was startled but didn't allow it to show. "Of course," I said. I didn't want to appear any different from the other girls and I sure as hell didn't want them thinking I was a lesbian. Besides, after all is said and done, I did want to get fucked by a man. I always did.

"Good, 'cuz there's still room on the list," Gravedigger said. "See, a lot of us have been in here for years, and we haven't been with a man. That's the worst privilege being denied to us, and Rebecca and I came up with this plan. On Christmas Eve, ten lucky girls are gonna get laid."

"How?" I asked. "By who?"

"By ten lucky guys in the men's ward," Gravedigger replied.

"Do you know them?" I asked.

"No, but that doesn't matter. All that matters is what they have between their legs. I've been talking to this guy on the other side of the wall – his name's Rivo. We've been working this plan up for over a month now. Today he gave me a list of the men who are interested in fucking us and tomorrow, I give him our list."

"But how are we going to meet them?" I continued my line of questioning.

"That part's in the finalizing stages. On Christmas Eve, this place is really under-staffed. Whoever's working all get together at midnight for a little party. Now, Rebecca's being given pills to control her nymphomania; they're supposed to calm her right down. But she's been stashing them...."

"How?" I asked incredulously. "Gilda searches everyone's mouths..."

"What she doesn't know is that Rebecca is missing a tooth in the back of her mouth. She's been putting the pill there and it looks just like a tooth," Gravedigger proudly related. It was a unique device. "By Christmas Eve, we'll have almost 20 pills saved up...enough to knock out the guard assigned to patrol the WHOLE building."

"Sounds like a pretty good plan to me," I said. What did I expect? I was dealing with criminals.

Gravedigger secretly pulled a sheet of paper out of her pants. She snuck a look towards the shuffleboard table. I could see Pegli working up a sweat. Either he wasn't as good as he thought or Rebecca was trying really hard. Gravedigger shook her head. "I can't wait until she gets back on those pills. She's been getting hornier by the minute, and I'm worried she'll blow the plan. Anyways, wanna get on the list?"

I took a second before answering. It was a good plan, but I really didn't think it would work. So what harm would it do if I agreed to it? It was just foolish psycho talk anyways. "Yeah, well, I'm interested," I hedged.

"Who do you want?" Gravedigger asked. "John or Shackles?"

"Uh...just like that?" I asked. "I don't even know if they're...my type, ya know?"

"Type doesn't matter," Gravedigger said. "Remember, it's gonna be fast work. No time to get acquainted. We get in there, find our man, fuck him and scram. So who do you want?"

I chose the more exotic name. "Shackles," I said.

I went on the list.

***

It was December 23, the day before Plan Fuck went into action. I still didn't think the idea would actually succeed – I didn't think we'd even attempt it – but I was having a good time planning it. The key instigators – Gravedigger and Rebecca – seemed to think I was enough of a master criminal to help in its drafting stages.

Gilda walked into the room. "KUMPLUNKEM!" she hollered. She took a perverse pleasure in my name, although no one else called me that. My new nickname was 'Palomine'. Gravedigger had taken to calling me that and it had caught on. I really liked it.

"What?" I hollered back. I never acted very nice towards her and why should I? She was a total bitch to me.

"Get your ass over here, you cow!" she yelled, as if she should talk. "You're wanted in Stavefield's office – NOW!"

I looked over at Dottie's bed. "What for?" I asked her. Dottie shrugged. "Is this usual?" I whispered. She shook her head negatively.

I got off my bed to see what the doctor wanted me for. Gravedigger passed my cot. "Don't say anything about the plan," she muttered through clenched teeth. Just what I needed to hear. Now I knew what the doctor wanted to see me about. My knees went weak.

"Took your sweet time getting here, dincha?" Gilda greeted me. She was really in a grouchy mood today. Where was her Christmas spirit?

Walking to Stavefield's office felt like walking to the electric chair. I wondered how much they knew, and how much I could get away with. I came up with a good defense; we were PLANNING a crime to stay in criminal shape. We weren't actually going to COMMIT it. I would say to him, "How could I help it? I checked into an institute for the criminally insane. You're bound to be surrounded by criminals."

Gilda knocked on the doctor's door and I heard him say, "Come in." Gilda motioned me in and the doctor said, "Alice, I believe you know this man."

I turned and saw a man standing in the corner. For a moment I stared blankly at him. Then, with a flash, I recognized him. "Mr. Rigby!" I exclaimed. And "Oh shit!" Shit because they tracked me down. They wanted me back on that show. He was probably going to offer me double my old salary. That whole scene, which had almost been excised from my memory, flooded back. I began shaking.

Dr. Stavefield spoke. "Alice, on this form, it says you voluntarily committed yourself and that Sebrings Productions would pay for your stay." I nodded. Yes, that was correct.

"Why would Sebrings pay for it?" Rigby asked.

"Because I'm covered for medical expenses," I replied.

"But you quit," Rigby reminded me. "You tore up your contract in front of witnesses. Since YOU broke the contract, we were legally not bound to you anymore."

"Huh?" I said. I never did know anything about contracts; I usually just signed them. Tearing one up was just a dramatic defiant gesture.

"Any benefits you might have received from us ended one second after you tore up the contract," Rigby said evenly.

"Look, in all the time I worked for you, I had two measly doctor appointments," I said. "Surely you can pick up the tab for this...."

"Do you know how much this place costs!?" Rigby yelled. "We got a bill yesterday from Lyman's for...," and here he took it from his pocket, "6700 dollars for one week's stay!" I gasped, never realizing it could be so expensive. I figured, if I lived and ate like this in the real world, it would cost a tenth that amount.

Rigby tossed the bill on the doctor's desk and walked up to me. "You know, we really wanted you back on *Tomorrow Will Come*. We thought maybe you did need a rest. But then we find out you're in THIS place and demanding that we pay for it?! Well, Sebrings will not pay." He turned on his heel and walked out.

I reeled towards the doctor. "Oh, come on, doctor!" I said. "You can't tell me that all the inmates are paying $6700 a week to stay here!"

"No, they aren't personally paying that," Stavefield said. I could see he wasn't very pleased with me. "They have been committed by the courts and the government is paying for their stay. You're the only one here voluntarily; therefore, you are liable for the costs. Now, I'd like to know, how do you plan on paying for this?"

"I got the money!" I shouted. "I'm rich!" The doctor only smirked at that; I may as well have said I was Napolean. "I am! You can check my wallet, which you guys still have. I have bank machine slips in there. Check them, I have lots of money."

The doctor considered a moment. "If this is true, we will be contacting your bank. In the meantime, I suppose you'll want to check yourself out..."

"What?" I shrieked. "Wait, I don't know about that...." I pondered for a brief moment. Did I want to leave so soon? I was growing to like the joint. So the girls had a few idiosyncrasies. And besides, I didn't what to spend Christmas alone. "Look, I feel real strange after seeing that guy Rigby. Brings back baaad memories." I started acting a little bit loony to help my cause. "I'm not ready to leave. Check with the bank. I've got enough to stay for a few more weeks still."

"I'll check with the bank," Stavefield agreed, "but if you're lying, you'll be out of here by supper. Gilda! Bring her back to the ward."

I was glad that ordeal was over. I was anxious to get back to my pals, who were all in high spirits these days. I entered the ward and walked over to Gravedigger. "We're in the clear," I said.

"What was that all about?" she asked.

"Ah, they just pinned another crime on me," I said, very blasé. "Listen, I figured out a way to make the guard take the pills tomorrow night..."

* * *

December 24th. Hours before the plan went into effect. I was in the washroom, suffering from a nervous stomach. It was starting to feel like we might actually do it. I think everyone was afraid to be the first to call it quits. If no one spoke up in the next hour...

OH, NO! I wasn't going to be the one to tell nine horny girls that the plan was off. Hell, Rebecca was joking that she was going to try and do all 10 guys in 15 minutes. Dottie managed to get the final position on the list and she kept me awake half the night whispering about 'John'. "I wonder if he'll be tall and blond," Dottie mused. "I like them that way. I hope he's muscular and tanned. And blue eyes! I hope he has blue eyes!" In 15 minutes, Dottie, all you should hope for is that he has a hard-on. Gravedigger already considered herself and Rivo a hot item, although they had yet to see one another. No, I think these girls had been serious all along and now they had themselves a dynamite plan.

I finally came out of the stall for air. Pussie walked into the washroom. "Hi, Florence," I said. I no longer called her Pussie. She'd taken to hanging around with me and whenever I was in her presence, she'd make sure to blot herself. That was a real effort and I rewarded her by calling her by her given (as opposed to rightful) name. Florence stood in the doorway of the stall, grabbed a wad of tissue and started dabbing her inner arms. She didn't say a word, which was very normal with her. Around me though, she tended to open up. "Something wrong, Florence?"

She gave me an insolent glance. Finally, "I waited all week, 'Palomine'," she stated, saying my nickname sarcastically. "You never told me about the plan."

"Plan?" I asked. "What plan?" Of course I knew what plan – there was only THE plan – but I was under orders from Gravedigger not to talk to anyone but the 10 chosen.

"The Fuck Plan. For tonight. At midnight," Florence replied. Yup, she definitely knew about the plan, alright. No use denying it.

"How did YOU find out about it?" I asked.

"I heard Gravedigger and Rebecca talking about it," Florence said, upset. "They always talk around me like I'm stoned and can't hear. I may be brain-dead but I'm sure not stoned anymore."

"Look, no one on the list was supposed to talk about it," I said. "I would have told you but I couldn't. I'm sorry. Anyways, I didn't think you'd be interested in screwing anybody."

"I'm not," Florence said. "I'm dead there too. But I would have liked to help out. I'm real good at midnight crimes." She looked at me imploringly and for the first time, I really saw how young and scrawny she was. She just wanted to come along for the ride.

I nodded. "OK. For starters, I think we need a look-out," I said. I had brought up the look-out issue with the Chosen 10, but no one wanted to cut their screwing time short to take a minute-long shift.

Florence brightened. "That'd be great!" she said. "Thanks!"

"Another thing," I said. "We have 15 sedatives saved up to knock out whoever's on guard tonight. I'm worried about that. You're a professional...tell me, is that much going to kill him?"

Florence thought a moment then said, "No, it won't kill him, just knock him out for the night. But you should only give him 14."

I looked at her. "And give you the other one?" I asked. She simply nodded. "Just one?" I asked again.

"I'm a drug addict and I know I'm on my way to a full

recovery," Florence said solemnly. "But...it's Christmas."

She had a point. OK, so I'm no Nancy Reagan. But it WAS Christmas. If I was gonna get a dick, she could get a pill.

* * *

Gilda was working a double shift! A straight 24 hours. I guess when you're understaffed, you choose the toughest guard to mind the fort. I had a feeling Gilda's appointment added an extra measure of success to our plan.

Lights out came at 10:30 sharp. Pussie started her own guard duty and stood by the door. I placed a plate of date squares by the only light in the room – on a table by an occupied bed near the exit door. Five of us had saved our dessert from supper. We had been hoping for something more appealing, but it was either that or the chicken nuggets. Which showed that tonight's meal was a touch better than usual, but chocolate cake was not an option.

Time was running out. It was close to 11:30 and still no Gilda. Knowing our gluttonous guard, we'd placed sedatives in all five of the squares. Pussie had assured us that if she even ate two squares, she'd be out for a few hours. Gravedigger kept making periodic checks to see if Pussie was doing her job right.

Getting antsy, 'Digger was already coming up with Plan B. "Ok," she decided, "if Gilda doesn't show, we're going for it anyways. Fuck the consequences." I thought that was a pretty weak Plan B and wished we'd been smart enough to think of one earlier.

"Here she comes!" Pussie stage-whispered. We all dashed to our cots and pretended that we'd been asleep for an hour already. I affected a slight snore. Gilda entered the room. Through slitted eyelids, I watched her walk straight past the date squares. Shit! She wandered amongst the beds, counting bodies. All were accounted for and she turned to walk out. *Come on, Gilda, goodies! Twelve o'clock high.*

Yes! She paused when she saw the dessert. She turned her

head to look at us and I'm sure everyone in the room slammed their eyelids shut at the same time. She then turned back to the plate. *Come onnn, Gilda, they're not for Santa.* Her hand reached out and she picked one up. In one push, she crammed the whole square into her mouth. I guess they were up to her standards because she went for a second and then a third. I don't know what happened to the other two squares because she picked up the plate and walked out.

We waited five minutes and then Pussie stealthily slipped from her bed. She checked the exit and even wandered out a bit. On her return, she said, "Gilda's nowhere in sight."

"She ate three squares for sure," I said. "How long before she's knocked out, Florence?"

"It should be hitting her by now," Pussie said. "She's probably at the party, drinking her first glass of wine. She'll feel tired and think it's the wine hitting her."

"We give her 10 more minutes and then we move," Gravedigger said, taking charge. "Get ready, girls, we're about to meet our men."

By 'get ready', I thought she meant psyche up for our crime, but she started teasing her hair. Rebecca undid the buttons on her pajama top and then knotted the shirt under her breasts. I took out my toothpaste but knew that if I went into the washroom to brush my teeth, I'd end up spending 10 minutes on the potty instead. I just put some on my finger and brushed it over my teeth.

"Do the beds now," Gravedigger commanded. That was part of the plan; we mussed and shaped the beds to make it appear we were still asleep in them. I made mine a pleasing 115-pound figure. "OK," Gravedigger announced, "let's do it!"

I had a panic-stricken feeling. I wanted to drop out. Let Rebecca have my man. They could manage a ménage a trios. Somehow though, I found myself walking out the door. One of the Chosen 10.

The 10 of us walked in a very close-knit formation. Pussie scouted ahead; she'd reach turns in the hallway and peek out, then gesture for us to follow. We reached the stairwell. Pussie entered and silently ran down a flight. She ran back up. "Clear!" she said. I'd never seen her so energized.

We went down the stairs to the third floor and stopped. We were one floor away from the men's ward. Pussie scouted and again it was safe to descend. Pussie and Gravedigger went through the door together, the rest of us following in a huddle.

Gravedigger looked around, worry on her face. "We don't know the layout of this ward!" she frantically whispered.

Pussie had an idea. "Let's just assume it's the same floor plan as our ward," she said. "We'll pretend we're walking to our dorm."

It was a magnificent suggestion. It allowed you to forget visual sights and just concentrate on your sense of direction. It was a quiet but nerve-wracking trip. We reached a door where our dorm entrance would have been, if we were two floors up.

"This should be it," Gravedigger said. "I'm goin' in first. Wait here. Florence, you take the rear and stand watch, OK?"

"Right," Florence said, walking to the back. I wanted to move away from Rebecca; she'd started moaning already and I'm sure she was rubbing against me.

"Now, last-minute reminder," Gravedigger said. "If Gilda shows, Pussie runs in and tells us and we dive under the beds. Got it?" We nodded. She opened the door and walked in.

A minute later she rushed out, a grin on her face. "Come on in," she said. We entered and saw a group of ten men standing there. Quite a ragged bunch, and the only one I really found attractive was the guy with the wooden leg. I could see shaving wasn't a big deal around here. Not even combing your hair.

Rebecca pushed past me. "Who's Jonesy? Come on, come on! We only got 15 minutes!" A guy walked forward, grinning lecherously at her enthusiasm.

A different guy spoke up. "Who's Dottie?" he asked.

"Right here," she said. "Let's go to your place." They walked off arm in arm. He wasn't exactly the man of her dreams, but he was tanned. He was black.

Rivo and Gravedigger were standing next to one another, watching the proceedings. He had his hand in her pants already. The pairings were getting together rather quickly. Finally there were two eligible men left standing there. One was the wooden-legged man and I prayed he was mine, because the other guy didn't look like he'd finished evolving yet.

The guy with the leg of lumber spoke up, rather shyly. "Who's Alice?"

Oh, joy of joys! "Me!" I exclaimed. I walked up to him and smiled.

"I'm way over in the corner," he said. "Let's go. Oh, I'm Shackles, by the way."

"Odd name," I remarked. We headed over to his bed. I tried to ignore the seven copulating couples we passed en route. This was a rather public way to have sex but what did I expect? The romantic mattress suite?

"Yeah," Shackles said. "I used to try escaping every day. Finally they put wrist and leg shackles on me. One leg shackle was always too tight and I got gangrene in my ankle. The doctors got to it too late and I lost my leg."

I almost bumped into Rebecca. "You fuck him yet?" she asked.

"No," I said, rather embarrassed.

"Hurry then," she said before running off. Where was she going? Where was her man?

"Here's my cot," Shackles said and laid down. I sat on the edge. "Nervous?" he asked.

"Uh...yeah, a bit," I replied.

Shackles tenderly undid my pajama top buttons. "I'll be gentle," he assured me. He had my clothes off in no time. What a perfect lover he was! Kissed me all over, whispered my name lovingly, slipped an impressive erection into me and came in due time, which was after me. I only got one sliver. I knew there was only a minute or two remaining in our fifteen minutes. I nestled in Shackle's arms.

And was suddenly ripped from them. Rebecca stood there panting and rather messy. "Move over, Alice!" she gasped. "This is the last one. I'm gonna do it!" Shackles laughed as the blanket was torn away from his privates. "Oh, shit, you're soft!" Rebecca noticed. "Didn't you know I'd be by?"

She went to work on Shackles. You could tell she was a pro. Shackles was enough of a gentleman to glance up at me and whisper, "Thanks, Alice."

"You're welcome," I tenderly whispered back. "Merry Christmas."

Gravedigger came running up with Dottie. "Time's up!" she said. I gestured towards Rebecca. "I only gave her one minute with my guy," Gravedigger said. "She hit all ten after all! Let's go, Rebecca! We gotta get a move on!"

"Come on, you motherfucker!" Rebecca shouted. She was bouncing away on top of Shackles. The other seven girls, some with their dates still, wandered up. It was a regular sideshow. A tension built up among the crowd. We were a minute late in departure.

Pussie came running in. "Why aren't we moving?" she asked and then saw why. "Rebecca! We have to go!"

"I'm trying..." she said in a frenzy. "This guy's holding back!"

I looked at Shackles and saw a grin on his face. Yes, I think he was holding back. "Shackles," I said, "don't make us get into trouble."

He opened his eyes and saw who was speaking. He winked and then said, "Aaahhh!" Rebecca jumped off immediately.

"Let's move!" she said.

"Where's your pants?" Dottie asked her.

"By the exit door where I left 'em," Rebecca said. We made our way there, Rebecca bare-assed for all the ward to see. There were whispered hoots and hollers.

We got back to our ward in no time. We barely cared if we did see anyone as all of us felt pretty damn good. There were jokes and good-natured poking among the Chosen 10. Many had managed to do it twice. I admitted that mine was the best lover I'd ever had. We stayed up late in our ward, talking about the Great Fuck well into the wee morning hours.

Everyone stayed up but Pussie. She did a splendid job and was rewarded with one sedative from Gravedigger. She slept with a smile on her face and no doubt dreamt of sugar-plum pushers. Around 4 a.m., I found myself drifting off into a peaceful sleep. I felt sublime. I got to pull the wool over Gilda's eyes. I finally got to commit an actual crime. I found some real special friends.

And I got fucked for Christmas.

* * *

It was the day after New Year's. An even better Christmas present had arrived – my period. I don't think we included birth control methods in our plan. Rebecca was showing signs of worry already; she was like clockwork, she claimed. Every 26 days, 11 a.m. on the button. Well, she was a day and a half late. She took 10 chances in quick succession...what were her odds?

I was suffering either from post-Christmas depression or PMS. I craved chocolate and looked at my baggy clothes. I'd lost 18 pounds since I'd entered the institution. I was always hungry and felt awful. Dr. Stavefield was conducting his session with the ladies and picked up on my disinterest. "What's bothering you tonight, Alice?" he asked.

"Oh, nothing. I'm just hungry. I wish I could get pants that fit and I wish I could cut my bangs and I wish we could have butter on our bread." I indicated that I'd said my piece, now leave me alone.

"I could cut your hair," Gravedigger offered. "I used to be a professional hair stylist."

"I just need my bangs cut," I said. "If they gave me some scissors, I could do it myself."

The mention of scissors caused Dr. Stavefield to sit up and take notice. "But I could give you such a flattering hairstyle," Gravedigger persisted, then looked at the doctor. "You can stay and supervise, Doctor, and I'll prove to you that I'm alright now. How's about givin' me a chance?"

Dr. Stavefield consulted his clipboard. "You're due for re-evaluation pretty soon. Yes, this would be an excellent opportunity to see if you can trust yourself with scissors." He called to Pegli. "Pegli, find me some scissors!"

Gravedigger set up a chair for me and wrapped a tablecloth around my neck. She began playing with my hair and making comments. "Naturally curly, rather dry, much too long, round face..."

"I guess you could take an inch off the bottom," I said. Pegli returned with the scissors.

"Oh, no! I'm cutting half of your hair off; it's way too long for your features," Gravedigger informed me. Pegli quickly handed her the scissors and back-pedaled. "See, Doctor, my first cut will be right here...around her neck..."

I saw the doctor tense for action. "Now take it easy, Digger," he cautioned. I was ready to bolt from my chair when I heard a loud snip. I looked down and saw an eight-inch chunk of hair.

"Gravedigger!" I shouted. "I said only an inch! I look terrible with short hair!"

"See, Doctor," Gravedigger said, "she's giving me a hard time, just like those other ladies did. Now watch what I do." I started to crane my neck to see what she was up to when I heard another snip. More of my hair fell away.

I slumped against the back of my chair. "Well!" I sniped.

"Now that you've STARTED, I guess you may as well FINISH it." I wasn't leaving her a tip.

Gravedigger cut and snipped away. The doctor stood up. "Gravedigger, I'm going to leave the room for a few minutes," he said. "This is the real test. Now, of course Pegli will remain in here, but I'm placing my trust and confidence in you."

To do what, I thought? *Give me a stylish cut?* I felt beads of sweat run down my neck as I saw the doctor walk out. "What kind of test is this anyways?" I asked my hairdresser.

"I knew it as soon as you said you wanted your hair cut," Gravedigger began. "That's what I used to do for a living until I freaked out on a couple ladies. The first time, this teenybopper wanted this frumpy look and I gave her a proper cut, and she whined so much that I just jabbed her in the neck with my scissors. Guess I severed an artery, but she lived." Gravedigger paused a moment to study my hair. "The second time I was a little more brutal. This old bag wanted to look like Ivana Trump and nothing I did pleased her. I gave her Ivana's hairstyle but I couldn't do a thing about her face. She said she didn't look like Ivana and wouldn't pay me. She got the scissor treatment a little worse. She barely survived."

"Gravedigger..." I hesitantly began.

"Yeah, Palomine?"

Ohhh, I just had to trust her! "Am I looking any better?" I enquired.

"Oh, much!" she said. I could see a few nods from the girls.

The doctor entered the room just as Gravedigger was finishing up. "Now isn't that an improvement!" he exclaimed.

"Look in the mirror," Gravedigger suggested, quite proud of her work.

My head felt 20 pounds lighter. I approached the mirror and was amazed at the person reflected. Why, I could almost be called becoming!

"Thanks so much, Gravedigger!" I enthused, looking at my

hair from all angles. I no longer had bangs and was astounded at the lovely forehead I possessed. All my hair was pushed up and away from my face; sort of a windswept look. It gave me a devil-may-care, saucy appearance. I no longer looked like a human version of Bigfoot.

My joy knew no bounds...well, almost none. The final bound-breaker came when I heard the doctor say, "Pegli, you can take the scissors away from Gravedigger now."

* * *

Life at the ranch was peaceful, serene and routine. I was in heaven. My skin was clear, I'd almost reached my ideal weight, I was no longer addicted to diet pills or Tylenols, and I felt confident about myself around my friends. I was currently in the process of comforting Rebecca, telling her that lots of girls skip a period. But by Rebecca's calculations, she was a month pregnant.

The doctor came into the room with Stanley. "Alice, I'd like to speak to you for a moment privately. Stanley, you can stay in here." He walked into the outer hall and I shot a puzzled glance at the rest of the girls.

"What'd you do?" Rebecca asked.

I shrugged my shoulders and followed the doctor. I couldn't figure out why he would want to talk to me alone...unless it had to do with money. "What is it, Doctor?" I enquired.

He put it bluntly. "You have to check out of here tomorrow."

"WHAAAT?" I shrilled. "I'm not ready!!"

"Oh, Alice!" the doctor retorted. "You're no crazier than I am! This place has just been a rest haven for you."

"So? You haven't said anything until now," I replied. "You've been getting paid directly from my bank. Why can't we keep it that way?"

"Yes, we've been into your bank account, but unfortunately so have a number of other people," Stavefield said. "You seem to have forgotten a few outstanding debts, such as your swank apartment, your insurance policy and a handful of other places. As of this morning's bank statement, you are pretty close to being dead-broke."

I staggered against the wall. "Impossible! I'm rich!"

"No, I'm afraid you're not," the doctor sternly informed me. "I'm sorry, you'll have to leave by noon tomorrow."

I was devastated. "Let me tell the girls," I said. He nodded and entered the room to begin that night's session. I followed, pain showing all over my face. The girls were all staring at me during the doctor's visit; I couldn't speak. It was all I could do not to break down and weep.

Gravedigger didn't waste a second after the doctor left. She took me aside and whispered, "What's going on?"

"They're releasing me," I said and started whimpering.

"OH, LUCKY YOU!" she shouted, clapping me on the back. "When?"

"T...tomorrow," I replied. Why was she so happy? I was leaving my Utopia!

Word went around quickly. Everyone was so pleased for me except me. Gravedigger wrote down my address on the outside as she expected to be following me out next. Florence was teary already. "I can't tell you how much you've helped me," she said, hugging me. I bawled along with her.

After lights out, I laid in bed thinking. *They can't make me leave! I'll prove that I'm crazy!* I started devising a plan to stay. I thought long into the night and finally came up with a fairly foolproof plan.

It may also be foolhardy, but I was going to stay in that institution if it killed me.

* * *

The next day, hours before my pending departure, I went along with the girls in farewell talk. At breakfast, knowing I wouldn't be there for any more meals, I received almost everyone's slice of bread – a whole loaf's worth. I ate as much as possible but lately I think my stomach had shrunk to the size of a walnut. My mind was intent on my plan.

After yard time would normally come lunch, but I was due to be sent out into the real world before that. I wasn't sure who would be my victim but I was determined to attack and physically wound somebody before noon. Gilda was my first choice but I figured she'd pulverize me to a pulp, so I cast my hopes on the nurse. Sure, I'd be restrained and have to do time in the mattress room, but before long I'd be reunited with my pals. I hadn't even gone yet and I was missing them.

After breakfast, we were given the usual search. I don't know why they bothered; they never found any utensils on us. But I guess if they stopped checking, there'd be a fork attack before too long. We formed our line-up and headed for the door leading to the stairwell outside the building.

Gilda opened the door wide and had it slam back into her face. After recovering from her surprise, she again opened it by leaning her massive weight against the door. A blizzard blew in at us, stinging cold. Gilda cast her eyes upward. Come on, Gilda, it doesn't take a genius to figure out it's bad weather.

"Guess we're stayin' in today," she decided. Fine with me, too. I sat down on the couch with Gravedigger and Florence. I was seated in the middle; each friend was vying for my attention. My mind couldn't stop wandering; where would I find the strength to maim another human?

"Have a game with me," Rebecca said, walking to the shuffleboard table. I didn't know if I was in the mood to play.

"Hey! I won!" Dottie said, having defeated one of the dykes. "I get the table still. Have a game with me, Palomine."

"You've been at the table for an hour," Rebecca said. "It's my turn. Come on, Palomine," Rebecca said, trying to pull me up. I really didn't feel like playing shuffleboard.

"Girls.....," a voice came from the corner. Gilda was automatically warning us.

"Rules say I get the table!" Dottie yelled.

"Fuck the rules!" Rebecca yelled back.

"Fuck you!" Dottie screamed.

"Girls!" Gilda hollered.

"Fuck you too!" Rebecca screamed back at Dottie.

"You slut bitch," Dottie spat.

"You sissy crybaby, get away from that table!" Rebecca shouted, hauling me up onto my feet. I didn't want to play but was being treated like some kind of pawn.

"You want the table?" Dottie shrieked. "Here's the table!" With that, she fired one of the shuffleboard sliders towards us. I barely had time to duck, but Dottie's aim was true. The slider caught Rebecca directly in the mouth, and I was showered by broken teeth.

The air was silent a moment then hellfire broke out. Dottie came racing towards Rebecca and started pelting her with punches. Rebecca couldn't fight back as she was next to dead from that hit. Blood poured from where her mouth used to be. I was hurled back onto the couch, on top of Gravedigger. Gravedigger threw me off to take on Dottie. Gilda came toddling over, screaming at us.

In no time, it was over. Gilda had separated Dottie from everyone else and had her in a suffocating bear hug. She hauled her over to the intercom system and paged for extra assistance. Another guard came running up and a nurse took over supervision of the room.

I was stupefied. Dumbfounded. In shock. What was safer? Lyman's Institute for the Criminally Insane or the City of New York? I walked up to the nurse. "Excuse me, ma'am, but I'm supposed to be checking out of here about now," I said.

I chose the mean streets.

CHAPTER SIX

"I'm poor!" became my new motto. It sure felt a lot different than when I'd used my former "I'm rich" line. Matter of fact, it sucked.

I arrived at my luxury suite just hours before my eviction. They'd even gone to the trouble (at my expense) of packing my belongings. I didn't have that much, considering I'd moved into a furnished suite. I stormed into the manager's office.

"What the fuck's going on? Why's my stuff all packed?" I demanded, close to institution re-entry state.

"You have no money left!" the Chinese lady informed me.

"How would you know?" I sneered.

"Bank tell us. You ignore eviction notice. We think you leave town," the lady informed me in barely decipherable English. She was already reaching her own angry, hyper condition.

Ah, what could I do? I didn't have the rent for the place. They had me. "I'm going then," I said.

"By four o'clock!" she yelled.

"Hey!" I yelled back. "My rent is paid 'til midnight. I'll leave when I want to leave."

"Four o'clock. Bring keys."

"Learn English," I retorted and walked out.

I went up to my place and turned on the TV. Maybe an hour with Judge Judy would relax me. I discovered I no longer received Channel 18; hence my cable was probably cut off. Oh well, I'm quite sure the bank took care of them too.

With everything in boxes, I couldn't really find anything to do. I stood by my huge picture window with a view of the park and the Statue of Liberty. At least I had the view to soothe me.

Then it hit me. I didn't have it! I had nowhere to live! I needed to find a place! My functional mind broke free from my institutional mind. In the joint, your biggest brain effort went towards wondering if you'd play cribbage or crazy 8s that night. Now I had to think like a real person. I slipped back into Alice Kumplunkem, once known as Palomine.

I quickly ascertained it was a weekday; the banks would be open but only for another hour or so. Before I went house-hunting, I should know how much cashola I had left to spend. It would make the difference between Manhattan and Harlem. I donned my winter garb and ran to my bank.

They had Christmas garland up still. That red ropey-looking stuff. I waited twenty valuable minutes in line and finally approached a bank teller. She yelled "Next, please!" as I was five steps from her.

"Yes, I'd like to find out how much money I have in my account," I said.

"Your account number?" she asked.

I rattled it off by heart. Heaven knows I should've remembered it; I used to deposit so much money into the account.

"Oh, this one," the teller murmured into her computer screen. "One minute, please," she told me and went over to a Chinese woman. They consulted a moment and the Chinese lady walked over to me.

"May I see you at the counter, please?" she asked me.

"Sure," I said and walked parallel to her over to another area – the counter. "How much money do I have?" I asked again when we faced one another.

"As you know, we've been paying your bills..."

"Yes, so I found out, thank you so much. How much money do I have?" I again enquired, my patience wearing thin.

"You still have 600 dollars left," the Chinese lady reassured me.

"Oh, great!" I said. "Six hundred bucks to start a new life. Just great!" I briefly considered fleeing to Toronto but I'd still have to find a place to live there and pay my bus fare on top. No, I needed a place in the next hour. I glared at the lady. "I want my money out of my account and then I no longer wish to do business with this bank."

"Do you wish to close your account?" she asked.

"Yes! Learn English, for cryin' out loud!" OK, I was rude. But I don't recall giving the bank permission to throw my money around like they were Santa Claus. She counted out my money and placed it on the counter.

"648.27," she said. "You are a very bad customer."

I grabbed my money. "Merry Chinese Christmas," I bid her as I pulled a section of the garland down. I stormed out.

On the street, I regained my rationality. *Place to live, Alice. How much can we spend? Think of food. Think of getting your stuff out of your sweet apartment.* I didn't know where to find a place to live for...I figured...$300 a month in New York. Raunda's cockroach-filled dump cost $1200 a month.

I started at a rundown house that advertised it housed boarders. The carpets were threadbare. There was no tub in the bathroom; just a shower. The lightbulb was located in the shower stall. It was a tiny room with no windows but two radiators going full blast. Surely I could afford this! "How much?" I asked.

"$700 a month," came the reply.

The next place was worse. Heading downtown in a bit of a panic, I saw a cardboard sign taped in a store window. 'Room for Rent'. I walked into the store, which specialized in leather apparel. They had some fancy gay-men duds on display. I walked past a mannequin wearing a pair of ass-baring chaps, a studded arm band, a motorcycle cap and nothing else. "Helloo?" I called out.

"Can I help you?" the mannequin spoke. I jumped about six feet. He really did have an artificial look about him, what with the red lips and eyeliner.

"I'm wondering about that room for rent...?" I began, when a customer walked in.

"Stephen!" the proprietor greeted him. "How was the Fag Ball last night?"

"Oohh, you missed it?!" the customer, Stephen, replied. "How cooommmme?"

"Oh, Peter had an earache," the owner replied. "And I had the most divine gown! So how was it?"

"Just fabulous! I didn't stop dancing! And the drag queens there? Honey..." Stephen batted his lashes.

"Uh...that room?" I reminded them.

The owner barely glanced at me. "Go up the stairs at the back. The room's at the top." He turned back to Stephen. "So did you take anybody home, hhmmm?" I didn't want to stay and find out. I took the stairs up to the room.

At one glance, I knew I didn't want it. In one thought, I knew if the price was right, I'd have to take it. There was a single room with a cot very similar to the one I'd had in the ward. Paint was peeling off the walls. Right above the bed, on the ceiling, was a great water stain and a bulge. I suspected the roof would collapse at any moment. There was a stained sink, a fridge that needed eight years' worth of defrosting and an antique stove with the oven door missing. I couldn't find a bathroom and walked out of the room. I saw another door with a sign reading 'Reserved for Tenant and Customers Only'.

I walked back downstairs where Stephen was giving a play-by-play account of the Fag Ball. "How much?" I nervously asked.

"$600 a month," he replied. I shook my head, walked past the nipple ring display and exited.

I was sunk. I'd never find a place for $300 a month. I was in the Times Square area when I glanced up at a club. My eyes went above the marquee advertising GIRLS!GIRLS!GIRLS! to a small neon-lit sign saying 'Rooms to Rent'. Without hesitation, I walked into the lobby.

"I need a room," I said to the Chinese man seated behind the counter.

"20 dollars an hour," came his reply. 20 bucks an hour! That'd work out to about 12,000 a month for the dump!

"I wanted it for more than an hour," I informed him.

"Oh. Then 60 dollar a night," the Chinese man said.

"How much a month?" I wearily asked.

"A month?" he asked, astonished. "You want room for month?"

"Yeah, for a month," I repeated. "Is there something wrong with that?"

"Very unusual," he said. "I look for you." He flipped through some cards. "We have room with hotplate and fridge. You take that room."

"Wait!" I said. "How much is it?"

"500 dollar. You take?"

500 dollars was about the best I could hope for, so I took it. I wearily nodded and handed over the bulk of my ready cash. In return, I was handed the key to room 315.

If you could call it a room. It was more of a roomlet. My fridge was the size of a picnic cooler, my hotplate had two settings – hi and lo – the bed had an inch-thick mattress and my new view consisted of the brick building a foot away from my window. There was no sign of plumbing anywhere in the room and I suspected the latrine was down the hall. Well, it was home now. I left to go get my belongings which I was now thankful were meagre, judging by the amount of space I had in the new place.

What a stab to the heart it was, walking back to my old apartment. I saw the lovely exterior from a distance, then my beloved doorman, and finally my boxes in the lobby. I ran to the manager's office. "Now what are you doing with my stuff?!" I yelled.

"There are new tenants," she said. "It past four o'clock."

"Man, you're killing me," I sputtered. "Just leave my stuff ALONE. I'll take care of it."

"Where are your keys?" she asked, again in an angry state.

"Relax, here's your stupid keys." I threw them on the desk.

She pulled out the form I'd signed when I first rented the

apartment. "You sign here," she said.

"What's this?" I asked, picking it up. It was a declaration saying I'd left the place in good order. I was about to sign when I glanced further up the form and saw that I'd left a damage deposit when I'd paid my first month's rent – a grand total of 2000 bucks. "Hey! I should get my damage deposit back!"

"We send it to you," the Chinese manager said.

"When?" I asked.

"Two weeks," she said and gestured for me to sign the form.

"What's your rush?" I asked. She was making me suspicious so I re-read what I was about to sign. Yup, it said I'd be getting my money back, every cent of it. Right now, 2000 bucks sounded as good as 1,000,000.

"Past four o'clock! I want to go home! You sign!" the manager almost screamed at me.

I signed before she karate-chopped me. "I'll be back here in two weeks exactly for the check," I said as I handed the form back to her. "Take a ginseng."

It took three cab rides to get all my stuff over to my new address. My room was filled to overflowing. The only space I had to move was on my bed. Sitting there, I counted my money. Eighty bucks and change. Sure I could make it last two weeks. Surely.

*　*　*

I had a budget of $13 a day. At this rate, I'd be able to bank $2 at the end of two weeks. The first day, I splurged and spent the entire amount on food. I was able to find Chinese noodle packages, 3/$1. Even though I currently had a beef against Chinese people, I still appreciated their cheap food prices. After buying 24 packages of noodles, I went to a thrift store and bought a bowl, fork, pot, cup and plate. All I'd need to make my noodles.

The next day I was going to buy fruit but I got woman troubles. There went that day's budget.

The next day I was BORED. I had no TV and the view didn't offer much so I decided to buy something to read. First I purchased more groceries; my body was already demanding a change from noodles. I bought lots of rice, which is also pretty cheap. With $5 to spend, I walked into a used bookstore and bought a thick, juicy, sexy, steamy novel for $4. I wondered how I could constructively spend my last buck. If I bought a newspaper, I could read it from cover to cover and then use it to line my cupboard under the hotplate. I'd found droppings of some sort in there.

Back on my thin mattress, I started reading *Desperate for Love*. I finished it by 8 a.m. on the fourth day. It was such good reading; just chockfull of perverted sex. And now it was even an investment because I could sell it back to the bookstore for half of what I originally paid.

After a long sleep, I woke up and wondered what I should do. I was becoming extremely lethargic. I didn't care for the streets of New York and I didn't care for the hotel I was in. All day and night, I could hear the faint music coming up from the strip club below. The tenants changed by the hour. There was only one girl I saw a lot and she had a different man with her every time. I knew she was a hooker because, with ease, she climbed three flights of stairs in five-inch heels. The hallways smelled of urine and vomit and old bums. I suspected I was the only real resident. The washroom at the end of the hall was unspeakable. Often drunks were passed out on the toilet. I must confess, one night I woke up and was too scared to go down the hall to take a leak. I raised the window in my room, hung my ass out and in freezing winter temperatures, created a three-foot icicle.

Lying there, I picked up the Daily Times. I was flipping through the pages when a heading under 'The Editor's View' caught my eye. It read 'New York Rent Hikes Seem Acceptable'.

The headline alone caused me to sputter. I read the Editor's View with growing astonishment.

It seemed the editor, Mr. MacGregor, owned his own home plus a vacation home in Florida and a cottage by the lake two hours out of the city. BUT his son, an aeronautics engineer, rented an apartment in Manhattan. His rent had only gone up 30% in the last five years, while his salary had doubled in the eight years he'd been out of school. The son, Gavin, has been able to afford a Porsche and a month in St. Tropez every year. Gavin was even managing to save money. All in all, obviously Mr. MacGregor Senior thought that since his son was doing so well, it must be because he was able to afford the rent on his apartment.

Well! I didn't stop to think. I grabbed a pen and a brown paper bag that had held a dozen oranges (for $2). I started writing a letter to that editor.

How DARE he presume that everyone was as fortunate as his son! Did he stop to think that there were people whose lives had taken a turn for the worse? That a flea-infested, freezing, 5'x 8' cubicle in a flophouse costs $500 a month? Some of us don't have 12 years of university and an influential parent to help us. Some of us are downright poor and if my rent were to go up by 5%, there would go my total food budget. I congratulated him and his son on their affluence but I suggested they rather flaunted it in our faces. Perhaps their newspaper wasn't geared to the faithful two-million low-income readers after all, and I didn't think I would be buying the Daily Times anymore.

I calmed down by the end of my letter. I felt better. For fun, I re-read it. *Damn good, Alice. You stated your view with eloquence, even though you did get pretty steamed at points.* I thought about sending it. But I didn't want to attach my name to the letter. The editor would read this great missive and then see 'Yours truly, Alice Kumplunkem'. He'd say, "Oh, joke letter!" and throw it out. Also, I'd made a little bigoted statement about Chinese people taking over the real estate. I wanted to get in a dig at the Chinese because I've been in a rage against them ever since I got poor. Now they were giving me a hard time at the market and my Chinese hotel manager accused me of having men over. I wish. So now I made a remark against them – call it payback – but it made me feel better.

So what name should I sign it with? I wanted this name to reflect the state of my letter, which was frenzied, angered, carried away. Aretha Gallant? Joan D'Arc. Hhmmm, I liked the idea of an accent in my name. Let's see...the letter...it's frenzied... angered...carried away. I wracked my brain. Frenzied, angered, carried away...

Carrie D'Away! Without a second thought, I scrawled my fictional signature to the letter and went out to blow some dough on a stamp.

* * *

I became a bed-ridden hermit. I lived for the day after tomorrow, which had come to be known as Damage Deposit Day. Two thousand dollars! The first thing I was going to do was go to a dentist. I had a wicked toothache, probably brought on by stress. The second thing I was going to do was walk into a restaurant and order a huge steak and three baked potatoes and an order of fries with an all-you-can-eat salad bar. I had finally reached my desired weight (cost me a quarter to find out, but I also got a fortune saying 'A friend in need is a friend indeed') and was now plummeting beneath it. I never knew I had such shapely arms. My rump didn't split seams anymore; my panty-line was finally under control. I hadn't been this weight since I was nine.

I suppose I was quite healthy. I was subsisting on a dollar's worth of oranges a day. This wait-and-see attitude had simply descended on me. It seemed that my life could only begin after I got that damage deposit check and for now, I'd just pass the time away getting bedsores.

I was re-reading *Desperate for Love* for the third time when a knock came at my door. I froze. Who could be wanting me? I no longer had the feeling I was a criminal; the institution had cured me of that. Although I still had two weeks left on my rent, the only person who knew where I lived was the hotel manager, so what could he want? Forgetting I lived in New York City, I foolishly opened my door.

A couple of suits stood there. Both were well-groomed, well-attired men of obvious importance. I stared at them. "Alice Kumplunkem?" one asked.

"Yeaaahhh....," I cautiously replied.

"We're from the Daily Times," the same guy said.

They'd tracked me down! It wasn't possible! "How'd you find me?" I asked.

"We had the letter dusted for prints," the Daily Times guy said. The other one had only been nodding for punctuation every time his partner spoke. "Seems you're a Canadian citizen working here..."

"It's legal!" I interrupted. "I have a working visa. There's two months left to go!"

"Yes, we know," the man said, the other nodding. "We matched the prints to your visa. We hired a private investigator to locate you."

Fuck, man, they really wanted me found. I MUST have committed a crime. "Am I under arrest?" I timidly asked.

They both guffawed, so I knew the silent one wasn't a mute after all. I gave an insulted look and they immediately stopped. The speaker held out a card. "I'm Dave Galloway, an assistant editor," he said. "Let me tell you why we're here. Maybe you noticed that the Daily Times printed your letter to the editor?"

"No," I primly said. "I said I wasn't going to buy that paper anymore and I haven't."

"Well, it was printed and what an avalanche of replies we got!

You had a lot of people rooting for you and the paper's circulation, believe it or not, increased for a few days. Now we're back to normal, if not a shade lower. We had a meeting about it, and one idea brought up was that it was because the readers wanted another letter from Carrie D'Away, and there was none. We believe our readers enjoy conflict and we'd like to conduct a little experiment. Alice," Dave kindly asked, "could you write another letter to the editor?"

What a stupid thing to bother me about. "Well," I yawned, "maybe I'll pick up the Daily Times now and then and if I see something worth writing about, I will."

"We're prepared to offer you $200 for every letter we print," Dave offered as incentive.

"Really?" I asked incredulously. I was going to add that I wasn't much of a writer – that letter had just been a lucky strike – but I didn't want to jeopardize my chance at a new job.

"Yes," Dave confirmed. "We hope you'll be writing soon. There's a lot of contentious issues of importance going on right now." I nodded along with El Silento, making a mental note to look up contentious in a dictionary. "Animal welfare, abortion, U.S. military involvement in Iraq..." he suggested. Again, I intelligently nodded. Inside, I was ready to die. There went my job. I realized I knew basically nothing about everything going on in the world.

"Sure, I'll see what interests me," I think I cleverly replied.

"Just send correspondence to me, at the address on the card," Dave said. "Nice meeting you, Alice. Write soon now!" he added as a little joke. We all laughed. They left, passing Penny and her latest john coming up the stairs.

I watched them leave. What did the other guy do? Was he some kind of enforcer? What if I had turned down the job? Would I have been made to write against my will?

But write I would! Two hundred bucks a pop? I'd send them a dozen letters a day! But what should I learn to do first? Find out what's going on in the world or how to write? I was thrilled; I had a meaning to my life once more. I devised a plan – I would spend my days at a local library, reading their Daily Times the first part of the day, read how-to-write-properly-constructed-letters the second part and then rip off a few letters to the editor in the evening.

What better time to start than the present? In a delirious joy, I blew my day's budget on Toothache Tamer and headed off for some serious studying.

* * *

Damage Deposit Day! I woke up early and was at the old landlady's office before she had even arrived. *Come on, lady! I need my money! I have a toothache in desperate need of a dentist!* I had a huge wad of Toothache Tamer jammed onto that tooth and my tongue was aching from constantly stretching to caress the hurt.

After pacing in pain for a while, I decided to use my time constructively and dwell on my previous day's gathering of information. My conclusion: My God, but I'm an idiot. I really knew nothing of what was going on in New York. After the dentist, I was going back to the library. There was so much learning left to do!

The Chinese manager approached and I greeted her with, "Do you have my check?"

"Yes," she answered. "Came in last week."

"Why didn't you tell me?" I roared, then realized she had no way of contacting me. I didn't apologize. "I'm in a hurry," I informed her.

She opened her office, went to the top drawer of her desk and pulled out my old rental agreement and a check. "You sign here," she pointed to another space.

I scrawled my name and grabbed the check. Almost running, I went to the closest bank which just happened to be my old bank. My luck! No line-up! I approached the teller, handed her my check and said, "I'd like to cash this."

"Do you have an account with us?" she asked.

"I used to," I said. "It's a good check." The teller looked uncertain. "Look, your bank manager knows me," I said.

That gave her an idea. She walked over to a desk in the far corner, where the manager sat. The teller barely spoke when the manager glanced in my direction. She stood up immediately and came hurrying over, yelling all the way. "I said this bank didn't need business like you! How dare you come back here after the destruction you caused?"

"I just pulled down some Christmas decoration," I retorted. "Big deal."

"You're a troublemaker!" she yelled in my face. "Take your check and leave immediately!"

"Come on, you can cash it for me, at least," I tried. "I used to keep so much money here."

"Now you're poor!" she reminded me. "And you're crazy! Leave now or I'll call the security guard!"

"Oh, you scare me," I said sarcastically. "I'll take my business elsewhere. You have no idea how rich I'm going to be again." I walked out like a snob. This time, just before the exit door, I knocked down a sign saying 'You Can Bank on Us!' I really don't like being so violent but I prefer to think of it as an eye for an eye.

I headed for a bank down the street. The teller there also asked if I had an account with them. "No, I don't," I said.

"It's much easier to cash checks when you have an account with the bank," the teller informed me.

It didn't seem she would cash it either. I thought for a second; hhmm, I'd be rich soon and would need another bank account, so why not open one right now? "I'd like to open an account then, please," I said politely.

"Fine," she said. "We'll use this check as the initial deposit?" she enquired.

"Sure," I said. She did her business thing, I signed a few places and proffered all necessary identification, and before long I had an account with this new bank. After the teller thanked me for banking with them, I said, "You're welcome. Now I'd like to withdraw $300 from my account."

"Oh, we have to wait until the check clears," she said. "That takes a minimum of five business days."

"Five days!" I shrieked. "I need money now!"

"I'm sorry," she said.

"Five days exactly?" I whimpered.

"About a week," she sympathetically replied.

I staggered out. All I had left to spend was that $2 I'd carefully saved up. Right beside the bank, I saw a business called 'ChekCashers'. There were signs blazoned everywhere with 'Cash your check here! No ID required! Lowest charge around! Only 2% of your check!"

I turned around, darted back into the bank and ran up to my teller, who was busy with another customer. "Excuse me," I interrupted their conversation, "could I just have my check back? Let's forget I opened an account here."

"I'm sorry," the teller said. "That's against regulations."

"Can't you break a regulation, just this once?" I wailed, then realized the whole bank had heard me. I didn't think the teller would break a rule now, for all to know.

"I'm sorry," she repeated.

"Can you break two dollars into quarters?" I sadly asked. I knew I'd now have to budget for 25 cents a day. I'd still be able to bank a quarter. The teller, obviously feeling sorry for me, served me before her other customer.

What to do, what to do? I needed a dentist! I wanted to walk up to a thug and ask him to smash me in the mouth. Hopefully he'd knock that tooth out. *Oh, think logically, Alice. You need money and you know what you have to do. Write one letter and ye shall receive $200.* But wait! ... They'd probably pay me at the end of the week, and with a check too.

I used my street smarts and two days' budget to call Mr. Dave Galloway, Assistant Editor, The Daily Times. As soon as I told the secretary it was Carrie D'Away calling, I was put in touch with ol' Dave.

"Yes, Carrie!" he said and laughed, because he really knew my true name. "What's up? Have you sent a letter yet?"

"That's what I'm calling about," I said. "I have a counter-offer. I think you should give me $200 to start, as a gesture of intent to use me. Do you understand? I mean, if I see actual money, then I'll know you're serious and that'll encourage men to write."

"I thought you knew we were serious," Dave said.

"Oh, I think you are, but this would be an incentive," I said, remembering my initial soap opera contract. "But for that $200, I will hand you a letter to the editor. If you print it, you don't owe me $200."

"That sounds fair," Dave agreed. "You have a deal."

"I can come by today, by four," I said, "if you'll have 200 in cash waiting."

"Matter of fact, your timing is excellent," Dave said. "In today's paper, the editor shares his view on organized crime. I can't wait to see what you'll disagree with about that."

"Uhh...I have to write about the Editor's View?" I asked. I didn't know that.

"Yes," Dave informed me. "The same as you did the first time. A Letter to the Editor regarding his editorial."

"Of course, fine I'll see you by four," I quickly said and hung up. Well, shit! That limited the amount of letters I could write to one a day. A measly $200 a day. Then the thought occurred to me that 200 bucks would be a damn sight prettier than a quarter.

I headed off to the local library to read that day's Daily Times. I wondered on the way about the Mafia's good points. Did they have any? They'd better, or I'd be out 200 bucks.

* * *

I was late in delivering. With money riding on it, I had no idea a letter would be so difficult to write. Why was my first letter to the editor so easy?

"I didn't think you were coming, Alice," Dave Galloway said when I entered his office.

"Please," I said, "call me Carrie. I don't want anyone else knowing my real name." Especially when they saw how I had sided with the Mafia. I clutched my epistle to my chest. "Do you have my money?" I asked, as if I were holding the letter for ransom. I could barely enunciate, my tooth pained so badly.

"Right here," Dave said, handing over an envelope. It looked mighty thin and I suspiciously opened it. There were two $100 bills nestled inside. What did I expect? Quarters? "It's all there," Dave assured me.

"Great," I said. "Here's my letter to the editor." I handed it over. Dave started to read it. "Oh, please!" I cried out. "Read it when I leave."

"Alright," Dave agreed. "I hope we can use it. You'll find out in tomorrow's paper."

I couldn't decide if I should spend a tiny part of my pay on some supper. Fortunately I realized that my tooth hurt so much, chewing food would be absolute torture. I still had a few oranges that had gone soft left to eat in my frigate. I knew it was too late to see a dentist but I would get up at the crack of dawn to go see one.

I was up before dawn. I hadn't gone to sleep. The pain in my mouth became so fierce I was almost delirious. I didn't know if it was one tooth or all of them decaying anymore.

I walked all the way over to a finer part of town. My budget didn't allow for a bus fare. I lurked on the stoop of a dentist's office until I saw a lady open up the door. I waited a moment and then made like a customer.

"Hello," I said as pleasantly as I could manage. "I'd like to see the dentist."

"Do you have an appointment?" she asked. Sheesh! Accounts, appointments. *No, people, I have NOTHING in this world to my name but a toothache.*

"No, I'm sorry, I don't," I said, still pleasantly.

"Would you like to make one?" she enquired. *Yes, you dimwit!*

"Please," I replied. Oh please please please.

"We have an opening a week from today at 3:45," she said, after consulting a datebook.

I had a moment of stunned silence. I stared at her and softly, in pain, pleaded, "I need an appointment TODAY." More like yesterday, but I didn't have the strength to add that.

"I'm sorry," she oddly giggled. "The dentist is booked up."

"May I speak to him?" I asked, on the verge of tears.

She wasn't moved in the least. "I'm sorry, he's fully booked. Besides, he isn't in yet."

I left without a word but I didn't give up. Excruciating pain drove me to take a more drastic measure. I sat on a bus stop bench and waited for a dentist to appear. It didn't take long. A meek, balding man showed up in a cab, carrying a bag. If he wasn't the dentist, I'd have mistaken him for a doctor. I gave him five minutes. I gave myself strength to carry out my plan.

I stormed back into the dentist's office. The receptionist glanced up and frowned. "Did you want to make an appointment after all?" she asked uneasily.

"The dentist is here," I growled.

"Yes," she agreed.

"So yeah, I have an appointment," I said mysteriously and walked into the dentist's workspace. He was busy brushing his teeth. He glanced up and looked surprised.

The receptionist came running in behind me. "I told her you couldn't take her!" she cried. "She just barged in!"

"Helllooo?" a voice called out from the waiting room.

"See?" the receptionist accused. "There's his first patient!"

"Look, Doctor," I said as he spat out his toothpaste, "I have a very, very bad toothache. I can't stand the pain. You have to help me." I felt faint even as I said that much.

"I'm very busy with patients all day," Dr. Spalding said.

"I KNOW! I've HEARD!" I yelled. "I am going crazy with the pain! Can't you PLEASE spare five minutes to just pull the fucking tooth out of my mouth!"

"I'm sorry....," the dentist began.

I grabbed a drill and wielded it. "If I don't get help in the next minute, I'm going to stab myself right here. I MEAN IT!" And I really did mean it.

"Gina, call...," the dentist again began.

"Don't call anyone or I start drilling!" I screamed.

"Hello?" a voice timidly repeated from the waiting room.

"Doctor, listen, all I want is that tooth pulled. I also have 200 dollars you can have. I don't need anesthesia, I don't need my teeth cleaned, just get that tooth out of my mouth. I'm dying!" I felt like blacking out already.

The doctor put on a face mask. "Tell Miss Beazley to wait," he said. "I'll take care of this lady."

Grateful, I staggered into the dentist's chair. I whimpered a bit as he forced my mouth open. "What tooth is bothering you?" he asked. I couldn't tell but obviously my tongue knew. It darted immediately to the source of my pain. "Oh, my, yes, it is in bad shape," he said. "Quite the cavity. Now, normally, I could just give you a filling and that would cost you about 100 bucks. But...since you wanted it pulled for 200, here goes..."

With that, he wrenched my tooth free. I didn't see it coming; my eyes had been clenched shut. And if I thought I had known true pain before, well, this was on a much higher plateau. "YEEEOOOWWW!" I screamed. I rose four feet out of the chair but the dentist restrained me from going through the ceiling. I fell back and started crying.

"That'll teach you from trying to terrorize people!" my mild-looking dentist yelled, now wielding the drill himself. "And I'll take that 200 dollars now."

I fished it out of my pocket and handed it over. Beat by a fellow New Yorker, this one more seasoned. I spit out a load of blood. The receptionist, Gina, walked into the room. "Everything alright?" she asked.

"Hunky dory," Dr. Spalding replied. "Please make an appointment for this young lady as soon as possible."

"What?!" I yelled. "Are you nuts? You're a maniac!"

"You, young lady, have a mouthful of cavities," he sternly reprimanded me. "I don't know what you've been eating or if you've been brushing, but I counted at least nine. I told you my price – 100 bucks a cavity, plus you need your teeth cleaned. That's another 100. If you can come up with a grand, I'll clean them and fix any cavity I find."

My teeth felt loose just from his speech. "I'll see you a week from today," I said.

* * *

I went back to the strip joint...I mean, my apartment. My mouth was in agony, I was weak from hunger, but most of all I felt tired. I felt like I had been dragged through the mud. I fell into a deep sleep.

I woke up late in the evening and felt a million times better. My mouth barely ached and I felt refreshed, with a healthy appetite. I opened my tiny fridge and saw an orange and a loaf of week-old bread, bought two days before for only 25 cents. (I had never been so aware of money; I was turning into a miserly penny-pincher, literally.) Suddenly, with delight, I remembered I hadn't spent my quarter yet for the day! I donned my jacket and went to the convenience store down the street.

Wandering the aisles, my mouth savored at the TV dinners

and coils of garlic sausage. Then, looking at the quarter in my hand, I went over to the counterman. "What can I buy for a quarter?" I asked him.

"Aisle two," he suggested. I turned into aisle two and saw the section for the preschoolers. All sorts of candy. I carefully priced everything and selected two nickel caramels and a ten-cent licorice pipe. For dessert, I selected a five-cent chocolate jawbreaker. Well-balanced meal, I thought. And so what about what candy would do to my teeth. I was getting them fixed next week anyways.

I paid for my meal and then unwrapped one of the caramels. I hadn't chewed more than five times when a huge chunk lodged into the empty space my tooth had once occupied. My overworked tongue struggled to remove it. As I stood there, I happen to notice today's newspapers.

Oh yes! The Daily Times! My letter...did it get printed? I didn't have the funds to buy a newspaper and the library would be long closed by now. I pondered a moment and glanced up when a group of teenagers walked in. The clerk became instantly alert; he hawk-eyedly watched them for possible shoplifting.

And paid no attention whatsoever to me. I opened up the News and immediately went for the 'Letters to the Editor' page. OHMYGAWD!! There it was! Lead letter and with a heading to itself even! 'Reader Believes Society Has Need for Mafia'. They had printed my letter in its entirety. Upon rereading it, I cringed. It was so amateur! A high-school English exercise.

Then I realized I had better read the editor's view-of-the-day while I had the chance. It was opposite the Letters to the Editor page. Today he decried fast-food chain outlets. I was just concluding the article when a voice boomed above my head. "You gonna buy that newspaper?"

"Oh, no, thank you," I said and hurried out. I went straight back to my room. *Time's awastin', Alice. There's letters to be written, money to be made, teeth to be fixed. Fast-food outlets. That should be easy enough.*

I labored long into the night. At 8 a.m., starved and cranky, I scrawled 'Carrie D'Away' to the end of my letter. I wasn't proud of it. Of course a nice fancy dinner at a cozy restaurant is better than a gobbled meal at Burger Thing. But I had to find an opposing angle and I based my letter on the fact that you didn't have to tip at fast-food joints.

I hand-delivered it to Dave Galloway. Again, I walked the entire distance. I was bedraggled as I entered his office. "Hi, Dave," I said.

"Congratulations, Carrie D'Away!" he greeted me. "You're in print again!"

"I noticed, and here's my...uh...rebuttal to the Editor's view from yesterday," I said, handing over my rejoinder.

"Fabulous," Dave said, taking it from my hand. "You're for fast-food outlets then?"

"Sure," I said, not giving a damn one way or the other.

"Well, if it's printed, there'll be a check waiting for you here the next day," Dave said.

"Uh...couldn't we make a deal like before?" I asked. "Where you give me the money first?"

"Al...Carrie, we prefer to do it with check," Dave said sadly. "It's easier than taking it out of petty cash."

"Aw, sh... Look, Dave." I said beseechingly, "I'm really broke. Can't you just LEND me 20 bucks until I'm printed? I promise to pay you back out of my first paycheck." I felt terrible asking a next-to-total stranger for money. I never borrowed money in my life. Next thing you know, I'd be panhandling on the street.

Dave took out his walled and pulled a 20 from it. "Don't worry about it," he said. "Pay me when you have the money."

"Oh, I will," I said gratefully, snatching the 20 out of his hand. "Thank you so much! I'll see you soon!"

Thinking carefully, I decided to spend this money wisely. I went to a greasy spoon and had their breakfast special. The food was either too rich or too greasy because I felt ill afterwards. I got off the bus near a fast-food outlet and used their washroom facilities. Then, not trusting myself on a bus, I hailed a cab and scooted home.

I rushed up the stairs to the washroom on my floor. I had to poop. My pants were halfway down by the time I flung the washroom door open. Some junkie was in there, passed out on the can with a needle in his arm. For a microsecond I thought of running down to the second floor washroom, but my bowels had already started their movement. I ripped the needle out of the junkie's arm, shoved him off the toilet seat and pulled my pants down before I soiled my undies. I didn't say I made it to sitting on the seat, but most went into the bowl and not the junkie.

Quickly, before the junkie fully came around, I wet some paper towels then rushed to my apartment. There, I cleaned up a bit (myself, not the apartment).

Since I had nowhere to move but on my bed, I stretched out and knew I had more work ahead of me. I fell into another long sleep.

* * *

I was at the convenience store again. This time I marched in and paid for a Daily Times. My stomach had settled but I wasn't taking chances. I bought a can of chicken soup.

Back at my flat, I anxiously opened the newspaper. What?! No letter!? Then I realized I had only delivered it that morning; it would logically and hopefully appear in the next day's paper. I was about to turn to the Editor's View when a name caught my eye. Carrie D'Away...oh yeah! That's me! It was a heading above a letter. 'Carrie D'Away Angers Reader'. Oh oh. That's what I was afraid of! The gist of the letter was that this man had been beaten by loansharks and he was still paying off a $3000 loan that had escalated to $15,000. He thought the Mafia were scum.

But wait! There was another heading! 'But More Agree With Her...' There were three excerpts of letters; one said her husband was a Mafioso and was providing handsomely for her and their six children. Another agreed with me that a career in the Mafia reduced the unemployment situation and the third said that for a paltry $150 a week, his store never got robbed.

I wanted to write them a personal thank you note but all had 'name withheld' under their letters. I turned to the Editor's View and saw what he had to say. Today he complained why Coca Cola shouldn't be allowed to buy another film studio.

I groaned. I didn't even know they had one film studio to begin with. And I used to be in the movie business? I reread the Editor's View about fifteen times. I didn't see what difference it made if Coca Cola bought ten film studios. I worried over my dilemma for some time and decided I'd have to do some research the next day at the library.

Then since I had absolutely nothing to do in my apartment, I decided to read the Daily Times cover to cover. Amazingly, in the Entertainment Section AND the Business section, I read article upon article about Coke's latest takeover.

God love a duck, but I still didn't see what the big deal was. I fell asleep wondering about it and woke up not giving a shit about it. I tried writing letters for hours but they all ended up in the waste bin. Finally I tried a different approach. I simply wrote was on my mind. The main point I made was that Coca Cola could buy whatever they pleased; as long as they kept the prices reasonable and the service fair, why should we complain? Weren't there larger issues in the world needing our attention?

I thought it was a pretty weak letter. I used my few remaining cents to bus it over to the Daily Times building. Dave stood up when I entered the room. "Congratulations again!" he said. "Fine letter!"

"Did I make today's paper?" I gasped.

"Didn't you read it?" he asked.

"No," I replied. "I was too busy." Too busy slaving over this letter. And that reminded me that I had to pick up today's paper as soon as possible so I could start slaving over the next letter. My teeth demanded I make $1000 before the Daily Times caught on that I'm just a flash in the pan.

"You can pick up the check tomorrow," Dave informed me. "You wouldn't happen to have another letter, would you?"

"Yes, right here," I said as I reluctantly handed it over. It wasn't a $200-award winner. I stood there a moment, wondering about my next move."

"Anything else, Carrie?" Dave enquired.

"Dave, 10 more bucks!" I begged. "I'll pay it all back to you real soon. I can give it to you in a couple days even – 30 bucks – 20 from yesterday and if you can spare 10 today...," Dave stopped me from blathering any longer. He handed me a 10.

"Sure, when you can afford it is alright," Dave assured me. "I'll see you tomorrow anyways."

I picked up the Times on my way home. After cooking up some wieners, I turned to 'my' section – Page 5 and 6 of the Daily Times. I jumped to the first letter and there I was, under a minor heading, 'Fast Food Fine for Carrie D'Away'. Again, excerpts under my letter from other writers agreeing with me over past letters.

But the Editor's View today was a real wingdinger. He was talking about the American ambassador to Bulgaria and the amount of his expense bills. He listed a few and they WERE horrendous. This time I was on the editor's side of the fence.

But NO, Alice! If your view doesn't differ from his, you don't get a pearly white paycheck the next day. I labored over a letter but couldn't find an angle. I was flipping through the newspaper when I saw a tiny item about a massacre in Bulgaria. From the article's 50 words, I deduced that Bulgaria was a third-world country.

I fell asleep and dreamt of famine and barrel-bellied children.

When I awoke, my hand immediately went for pen and paper. I knew what I would write and jotted down the main idea. The actual writing of the letter took most of the day though. I ate the rest of my wieners, cleaned up and delivered my letter to Dave by five.

"And here's your check for yesterday's letter," Dave said. "I'll see you tomorrow for the check for today's letter."

"Huh?" I remarked. I was too tired to play these word games. Save them for the puzzle page.

"Your letter was printed today...didn't you know?" Dave asked.

"Oh, yes," I said. I didn't know. I kept forgetting to buy the paper. "Dave...you're not gonna believe this..."

"What?" Dave asked.

"Five bucks?"

I now owed Dave $35.

* * *

I was plain not cut out to be a writer. It has to be the most unglamorous profession, and the most difficult. I sweated over each and every word. Almost every waking minute was spent laboring over a letter. I laughed over the time I thought I'd write a dozen letters a day. Once I got enough saved for my dentist bill, I was going to take one day off from writing.

I'd just picked up a check from Dave. This was for my letter they'd printed about the ambassador to Bulgaria. I'd said that if the government were going to be sending people off to third-world countries, then they SHOULD pay through the nose for it. And besides, the government rips us off all the time; why can't someone rip them off for once?

"You're early today, Carrie," Dave said.

"Yeah, I've got some business to take care of," I replied. My dentist awaited me in less than an hour. I had only four checks accumulated – $800. I left the office and walked to my new bank. I had never prayed so hard for good luck.

God must have mistaken me for someone else because he smiled on me. "Can I withdraw money from my account?" I tentatively asked a teller as I slipped her my debit card.

She ran my number through the computer. "Sure," she replied. "How much?"

"One thousand smackers!" I whooped, then said, "Make that ten-fifty." May as well pay Dave the $35 I owed him and eat while I'm at it. She gave me my money. "Now," I said dramatically, "I'd like to DEPOSIT money." It felt like such a grand, decadent thing to do. I wish the teller saw it my way.

The next few hours weren't so pleasant. I'm sure the dentist carried fond memories of me because he only gave me enough laughing gas to last half an hour. I spent the next hour not laughing. He finally snapped off his drill and sat back. "Twelve cavities," he remarked. "I must say, you got a good deal for 1000 dollars." I figured that was my cut so I pulled the money out of my pocket. "Thank you," he said, taking it.

"Do I have even more silver in my mouth now? I asked. I was afraid of looking like some horror-film antagonist.

"No, we use white fillings these days. I fixed a lot of the old ones. Your teeth look normal," Dr. Spalding said. "Now, they could look even better for an extra 400."

"How?" I asked.

"I could put in a lovely fake tooth to replace the one you're missing," he said, as if he wasn't the cause of it missing in the first place.

"I'll make an appointment," I replied and left his torture chamber. I had a letter to write.

* * *

"Did you read the paper today?" Dave asked. He always asked.

"No," I replied, I always replied.

"Hhmmm....," he said. That was strange. Usually he said, "I'll see you tomorrow for today's letter check," or something similar to that.

I didn't pursue it. I left and immediately bought the paper. I opened it up to my page and glanced down, as usual, to the lead letter in the Letters to the Editor section. What? Who was this Mrs. Faye Darleenah? I scanned all the letters. None from Carrie D'Away. I wasn't printed! They found a letter of mine unacceptable! What letter was that...? That would have been my stand on allowing an underground parking lot under the Statue of Liberty. Yeah, that one was pretty terrible; my worst effort yet.

So I dashed to the Editor's View. My reply to that would have to be dynamite! I wanted those 200-dollar checks! My teeth were fixed, my hair was cut, but little money had been spent apart from that. I was saving to move out of that rathole. Someone had died in the room across the hall and they hadn't found the body for five days. I knew something reeked but it wasn't all that different from the usual bums' collective smell. Anyhow, I'd decided I was a step above the other residents and wished to relocate.

The next day, feeling embarrassed that I wouldn't be picking up a check, I pretended I was in a rush. I raced up to the receptionist and put the letter on her desk. "Can you give this to Dave Galloway?" I breathily asked. "It's from Carrie D'Away."

"Certainly, 'Carrie'," she said, then giggled. I gave her an affronted look; I felt bad enough not being printed and she didn't have to make a joke of it.

I kept up this routine for three days. I was working myself to death, in a panic the whole time. They still weren't printing my letters! Every day, I'd pick up the newspaper and flip to Page 5. I wouldn't read anything but the names under the letters to the editor. None from Carrie D'Away. Then I'd frightfully look at the Editor's View and see what I'd have to oppose today. Were they no longer in need of my services? Did I have to work myself into a casket before I would be told?

I became angry at them and decided to consult with Dave about the matter. I also wanted to know why the editor was making it so difficult for me. How can one disagree with the merits of recycling? I brought a poorly written letter with me to Dave's office.

"Alice!" he cried out for all to hear. "Where've you been? Your checks have been piling up."

"My checks? What checks?" I asked. "You haven't been printing me."

"Of course we have; what are you talking about?" Dave said. "You've got your own column now!"

I DID? I played dumb and said, "Just joking! Look, I've got to get going. Can I have my checks?"

He handed over a small pile of checks. My eyes gleamed. I took them with as little greed as I could muster and left his office. In the elevator, I tucked them into my brassiere. Not that I needed the extra padding but I wasn't about to go walking around New York with this much money on me. It was different from the old days, when I was making thousands a week and could afford to lose a few G's in a robbery. But this money had a purpose; to get me out of the dump I was living in.

I picked up a newspaper then decided to treat myself to supper at Ed's Eating Establishment. I was waiting for my eggs benedict when I opened up the Daily Times to my usual section. I carefully scanned Page 5. There was a cartoon and sixteen letters to the editor, none authored by me. I slowly turned to the Editor's View. Hhhmm, I would have to write why Roman Catholics should allow priests to marry. That would be fairly easy, I thought. I was wondering where my letter was. My column, I should boastfully say.

The waitress delivered my eggs Benedict and simply set them on the top of my newspaper. The bottom of Page 6 stuck out from under the plate. A new heading caught my eye – 'Carrie D'Away', with a byline – 'by Alice Kumplunkem'.

I lost my appetite. Why, those louses! They betrayed me! I was supposed to remain anonymous! I didn't want the readers to actually think ALICE KUMPLUNKEM was a bigoted, self-righteous, crass, warmongering bitch. Carrie D'Away, sure, but not me!

I went home but couldn't write. All I could think about was the Daily Times' act of stupidity. The next day I went to the local library. Looking at a back issue of the Daily Times, I saw when I first got my column. There was a little accompanying story saying that Carrie D'Away had become quite popular with the readers and continuously offered a well-thought-out differing view than the editor. Due to popular demand, Carrie D'Away was being given a column all to herself.

I felt a bit better knowing I was so popular. Looking at today's paper, I saw I was again in print. At least money was coming in too. I went over to Dave's office to pick up a check.

"Here's your money," Dave said. "Got a letter?"

"No, not today," I said. "Dave, I thought we weren't going to use my real name. What happened?"

"Alice, a couple readers clued in. They wrote and questioned the authenticity of the writer," Dave explained. "We thought the time was right to use your real name."

"You should have asked me first, you know," I said. "I don't like the idea."

"It's for the best, I think," Dave said. "Where's your letter?"

"I didn't write one," I repeated.

Dave looked stunned. "Excuse me a minute," he said and ran out. He was back in five. "Alice, according to our figures, we've gained half a million new readers since you've started writing for us. The Daily Times would like to hire you on a weekly basis; $1000 a week guaranteed, and you have to write a minimum of five letters a week. What do you think?"

I was going to ask for dental coverage too, but my teeth were all brand spanking new. "Fine," I said. "I'll have a letter for you tomorrow."

I raise their readership by half a mill and they pay me the same salary. And since I didn't write today, I had five in a row to write. I went back to my firetrap of a room, sprawled out on my dirty sheets, and wondered how I could disagree with the city's proposed spring cleanup of the streets.

* * *

I found a new place to live. It was gorgeous; a one-bedroom in a corner brownstone for only $1900 a month. The only problem was that I wouldn't be moving in for another week. Moving day coincided with the last day of my working visa. I hadn't worried about that; the Daily Times was a pretty important newspaper and I'm sure they had good connections. They would get me another extension on my visa. Sebrings did it; the Daily Times could too.

I was sort of worrying about my social life. It was non-existent. Why couldn't I just write a letter in a normal eight-hour workday span? But no, each letter seemed to take almost fifteen hours. The job still wasn't getting easier, although I didn't fret anymore if I delivered a crappy letter – they seemed to print anything I wrote. Well, the rent and damage deposit almost cleaned me out financially, but I was on my way to Dave's office for my weekly paycheck.

"Alice," Dave said, "can you stick around for a minute?"

"Sure," I replied. "Is there a problem?"

"No, no!" Dave emphatically replied. "We're all quite happy around here these days. I just wanted to call in a photographer."

Something strange zeroed in around my heart. "Why?" I asked.

"Well, it was going to be a surprise," Dave said, "but we

decided to do a little feature story on you in the Lifestyle Section. We'd like a couple photos of you." I didn't know if I liked the idea and stared at him in horror. "Oh, you don't have to thank us," Dave said. "You deserve this."

"Whaddaya want to write about me for?" I asked.

"Oh, don't be so modest, Alice!" Dave reprimanded me jokingly. "You're a celebrity!"

"I am?"

"Didn't you know?" Dave looked shocked.

"Uh…I guess I've been too busy to notice," I replied. I felt rather honored. I remembered I had already been a celebrity once, when everyone thought I murdered the original Beluga, but this was certainly a different occasion. "Do I look alright for the photographer?" I coyly asked.

The photography session was short and so sweet that I almost left without my paycheck. But I did miss the bank. No problem; I had about $30 to last until Monday. My usual weekend fund.

The next day was Saturday, my 'day off'. The Daily Times didn't publish a Saturday paper so I didn't feel the nagging urge to buy one. I slept in, managed to get ten minutes of hot water in the communal shower, polished my long nails, ate at a trendy eatery, smiled at three young men (got called a slut by one and it didn't even bother me) and waited for the Sunday Daily Times.

I was up with the morning light. I quickly donned my coat and went quietly down the gritty steps. Used condoms, but no bums. I walked past the night manager, who never said boo to me.

"Hey, you!" he called out. "You're Carrie D'Away!"

"Huh?" I said. "Carried away?"

"The newspaper lady," he remarked. "I didn't know we had some big shot living here."

"How do you know?" I dumbly asked.

He lifted up the early edition of the Daily Times. "There's a story 'bout ya in here."

"Oh, can I have that?" I asked, springing forward.

He clutched the newspaper to his chest. "Ohhh, no!" he said. "I'm gonna cut out your picture and put it in the window. I'm gonna make a big sign sayin' ya live here."

"Not for long," I said and walked out. It wasn't a very good start to my anticipated exhilaration over being featured in the paper, but now I was overly curious to read what it said.

I bought a newspaper out of the first box I saw then walked into a donut shop across the street. I chose a seat at a table and put the newspaper down. On the front page, there was a blurb above the News' logo. 'Carrie D'Away – Voice of the People. See Story Page 51.'

I turned to Page 51 and was greeted by a huge photo of yours truly. I gasped in amazement. That was me? Why, I looked a bit like a young Sigourney Weaver with boobs. I remembered the photographer taking that particular shot. He had run out of film and was reloading when I noticed my shoelace was untied. I had bent down to tie it up when I heard, "Alice." I glanced up and he snapped a picture. I remember thinking, *Boy, I'll look pretty goofy in that one. My hair fell in my eyes, my mouth is hanging open.* But wow! I looked quite sultry! I hoped the story would be equally flattering.

It was like watching the entire series of *Tomorrow Will Come* again. The reporters were pretty investigative; my whole life was splayed out before me. Why oh why would anyone be interested in that silly suicide saga? Who cares if I was a failed actress? Big fuckin' deal if I committed myself into a psycho ward? So what so what so what?????

I looked at my photo again and this time I saw a lecherous she-devil. There was only a small mention in the article that I even wrote for the Daily Times. It was too mundane an item for the rest of the story. And oh, how these writers can gloss up a life! Instead of saying, "Alice didn't have a boyfriend until she turned 21," they said, "Alice was scorned by men well into her adulthood." No, folks, Alice does NOT "prefers to live in squalid corners above a nightclub rather than a home befitting her stature." The story had a subtitle under 'Voice of the People'. It said 'The Rise, Fall and Rise again of Alice Kumplunkem.' It gleefully went into detail about my made-in-the-shade job at Sebrings (so they thought), my departure and subsequent commitment to the psychiatric institution, and my current claim to fame as the Daily Times' Carrie D'Away.

I read the article 20 times, trying to like it. All it did was depress me. The donut shop was filling up and everyone was reading a newspaper. All it took was one, "Hey, aren't you...?" to make me run out.

I didn't leave my room all day. I berated myself over that. *What are you ashamed of, Alice? Your past?* But it really wasn't as awful as those writers (of both the Daily Times and *Tomorrow Will Come*) made it out to be. I'd just get up the nerve to venture out when I'd think... BUT THE READERS DON'T KNOW THAT!!!

* * *

The first thing I did Monday morning was rip my photo out of the strip joint's window. Nobody had to know this was HOME TO CARRIE D'AWAY! The next thing I did was walk to the bank to cash my check.

I almost made it. I was walking past an alleyway when I heard a guy say, "Spare some change for a coffee?" He looked down and out and I knew I could spare a few cents.

I opened up my purse and fished two nickels out of my change pocket. My check stuck out of my handbag live a waving flag. At the same second that I became aware of the fact, I was jerked into the alley and tossed behind a garbage container. "Give me your purse!" the bum commanded.

I clutched it. "No way!"

He made a motion to kick me. I curled into a fetal position

among the spilled garbage and threw my purse at him. He whipped out my wallet, took the check, flung everything else to the ground, threw a bag of garbage on top of me, and ran off.

I laid there a moment until the smell of shrimp shells became too strong. *MY GOD* my mind kept repeating *I'VE BEEN MUGGED!* I simply couldn't believe it. *I'VE ACTUALLY BEEN MUGGED.* Then worse news hit me. *Good God in Heaven! He got my paycheck!* I was trembling. I stood up, wiped gooey yellow stuff off my clothes and, crying all the way, I went home to Carrie D'Away.

I didn't settle down after a while. I just got madder. It finally dawned on me that I should call Dave Galloway to tell him my check had been stolen. "Dave," I said on the phone, "you won't believe this! I just got mugged! The guy took my paycheck!"

"We'll put a stop-payment on it and have a new one for you in a few days," Dave calmly said. "Alice, we need a killer letter from you today, to capitalize on the feature we ran on you. So see you around four today, OK?" He hung up.

I got even madder. I'd just been brutally mugged and my boss still wanted me to calmly submit another stupid letter. Is that all he cared about? His stupid paper? I didn't even have a dollar to buy the stupid paper, so I angrily stalked off to the stupid library to read today's stupid Editor's View.

* * *

The editor strongly disagreed with the Museum of Modern Art's recent donation of three Picasso drawings to a small-time museum in Victoria, British Columbia, CANADA. Something to do with the two countries finally fulfilling a free-trade agreement.

For the first time ever, I simply ripped off a letter and decided it was good 'nuf. They printed anything anyways. I knew I didn't have the concentration for a proper letter and besides, I wasn't one single bit over my recent trauma. My God! That mugger could just as easily have KILLED me.

I went off to the Daily Times building and searched for Dave Galloway. I found him in the typesetting room, checking something over. He saw me and simply waved me out. "Just put the letter on my desk, Alice," he said. I stood there a moment and he glanced up. "Your check's not ready yet, you know."

I knew that. *But geez, I'm your celebrity, man. Don't go brushing me off like that. I'm not in a good mood today; don't push me.* "I'd like to speak to you, Dave," I said as civilly as possible. "In your office."

Dave sighed. "Back in a sec, Phil," he said. I didn't like that either. I would appreciate more than a SECOND of his time. We walked into Dave's office and he asked, "Well, what is it?"

"Here's my letter," I said and thrust it at him.

"Good one?" Dave asked and winked. "Now that we ran that story, you're gonna get a whole lot more readers."

"Yay," I sarcastically deadpanned. "Dave, you know, I got MUGGED today." I realized I really wanted a shoulder to cry on and almost began shedding tears again.

"Happens all the time in this city," Dave replied. "Your first time?"

I nodded, then said, "And I hope it's my last!"

"Don't wish for miracles," Dave cautioned me. "Anyways, you should have a replacement check in the next few days." He picked up my letter. "I'll bring this down to the typesetter."

"Dave," I added, "he got my bank card, all my ID, everything! Can you...just until I get my replacement check...lend me 50 bucks?"

Without a word, proving I was still a valued employee, he withdrew his wallet and handed me a 50.

The next day, Tuesday, was a normal day. No muggings, I bought a paper, did my usual letter-grind (why I think the national anthem should be discontinued at schools), dropped it off and spent the night alone.

Wednesday was a bit different. I was very nervous carrying around the 40 bucks I had left from Dave's 50. If I got mugged again, I'd be destitute. I went to my bank to report the loss of my debit card and to make a deposit as a gesture of good faith.

I gave the bank teller my story and even came up with the account number. "There should be no problem," the teller said. "Your name?"

"Alice Kumplunkem," I replied, then tittered. "I guess you might know me as Carrie D'Away." Might as well use my celebrity status.

The teller gave me an odd look then scurried off to the manager's office. He walked out of his room, made a transaction on the computer in front of me and handed over $8.13. "What's this?" I asked, puzzled.

"That's what remains in your account," he said.

"Keep it!" I said, pushing the money back at him. "I want to put in 30 dollars more."

"I'm sorry," the manager said, pushing the money back at me. "We're closing your account. We do not want to be known as the bank that associates with Carrie D'Away." He was being snooty as hell.

"What'd I do to you?" I questioned him.

"What haven't you done to the United States of America?" he patriotically replied. "Take your dirty money and get out of my bank!" He slammed a 'Closed' sign down. All the tellers were staring at me. I left the bank with more money than I'd come in with.

I tried to open another account with a different bank but they refused my business. Then I decided I'd better get to work. I saved my money and walked over to read the library's newspaper. What was this? The Editor's View centered on my letter of the previous day. I thought hard...what was it? I took a glance and saw my national anthem letter printed today, so it wasn't that one. I very rarely re-read my letters anymore before handing them over to Dave. I remembered I had written it when I was in that black rage and it had something to do with paintings. Finally I asked the librarian for yesterday's Daily Times. I flipped to my section and re-read the letter I'd written. With a sinking feeling, I realized maybe I should have re-read it before I submitted it. Maybe I shouldn't have even submitted it.

Dear Editor, it read. *On behalf of my fellow Canadians, I really feel I must reply to your editorial. You make it sound like such a big deal because the United States is giving Canada three Picasso paintings. But you're not really GIVING them to Canada, are you? You mention it's part of an old Free Trade Agreement, so obviously, since it's a trade, you're going to get something back. Now, I wonder, what would you think your three Picasso's are worth? What can you ask Canada for in return? I foretell that you're going to ask for Newfoundland. And what's more, you'll probably think you got the low end of the deal.*

As your feature story on me mentioned, I am a Canadian living in the United States. I didn't ask to move here; you WANTED me. I'd much rather prefer living in Oak Paw, Saskatchewan (located just above Montana, illiterate readers) than to living in New York City, New York, AMERICA. Your streets are not paved with gold; they're paved with dog poop, human bile and people who can't afford to live here but have nowhere else to go. Oak Paw has one bum and he lives as well as anyone else. In New York, the people with any money are too cheap to give it away.

Oak Paw has only one family that's of a different nationality from everyone else, and they're native Indian. New York – the States for that matter – is so greedy, they're letting in loads of people of every nationality. No one's learning the language, everyone's getting madder and the whole city is starting to resemble a zoo! The Chinese are taking everything over, blind men! They want to buy your Statue of Liberty! The Muslims are taking over your cab trade! Try getting anywhere for under $25! The white man can't get a job because all the Mexicans are willing to work for below minimum wage. I'd like to put forth a call to *the Immigration Office for an immediate massive crackdown on illegal immigrants.*

Editor, have you ever been to Canada? Classy country, let me tell you. People are a whole lot friendlier, you can still breathe fresh air and you can still drink our water. I'd like to find out what the ultimate benefit was with this free-trade thing. What? Canada surrenders itself completely to the US and in return, we get complete nuclear missile protection? But who would want to bomb Canada? We're a peace-loving nation! But read the Daily Times; the whole goddang USA is at war with each other! Grade Two kids going on a school rampage, a serial killer every six blocks... Though I must congratulate you, NYC. I read that you reached a ten-year record low last week – one day, there were only twelve murders. Bully for you.

I see creepy Americans every day in this city, everywhere I go. There's no peace from you aggravating people. You're all yelling at each other. You're all grouchy. You're all too caught up in yourselves. You all have a stick up your ass.

In conclusion, I'd like to inform all the readers that as far as this free-trade business is concerned, I don't want to be traded. I'm quite happy with my team. Sincerely, Carrie D'Away. P.S. I spit on your Picasso paintings.

I slowly put the newspaper down. Did I somehow manage to offend every single citizen of the U. S. of A.? Pretty wicked letter, Alice. Spiteful enough to cause the editor to reply to it. I went back to his view for today.

Well! Fuck him too! He calls me a white supremacist? How dare he? Perhaps I did come off sounding that way, but I'll have you know I once had a little crush on Chris Rock, so there! And he says I'm biting the hand that feeds me. Am I supposed to believe that my life has turned so wonderful since I arrived in this godforsaken country? Hey, they bit first so I'm biting back. He wonders how they could have hired such a crude, vicious racist such as I.

And that's how he ended his editorial. Oh oh. Even though I

still felt I was in the right, I figured I'd better write a remorseful letter or my job would be in some jeopardy. OK, OK, the letter was a bit much, I agree. I settled down to write an 'accept my apologies' letter.

I was having a difficult time writing it until I took a break and decided to scan a bit more of the newspaper. HOLY SHIT MOLY! Even the readers were damn pissed off at me! Every single letter to the editor, barring mine, had to do with their hateful feelings towards Carrie D'Away, otherwise known as Alice Kumplunkem. I instantly returned to my letter in progress and poured out bucketfuls of "I'm sorry"s.

So embarrassed and ashamed was I that I didn't bother going up to Dave's office. I dropped it off at the reception desk; a letter simply marked for Dave Galloway, Assistant Editor. No return address or name. Then I scurried back to my grungy room, keeping my head low. I almost didn't notice the sign in the window of my residence – 'Carrie D'Away No Longer Lives Here'. Oh, shit...trouble. *Please don't put me out on the street!* I knew it'd only be for a couple days, until I could move into my new, cushy place, but I didn't want people recognizing me.

I walked into the lobby. "What's with the sign?" I asked. "Don't I still live here?"

"Oh, yeah," the day help replied. "We just don't want any trouble, ya know? Your name is mud right now. But your money's still good and as long as you pay your rent, you can stay here."

"Thanks," I said. It wasn't the right time to give my notice.

"Shit, we had a war criminal living here five years ago," the guy went on. "A little old guy who killed…"

"I get the picture," I interjected.

"They came in the middle of the night for him! Took him out in handcuffs and chains!" he called out as I walked up the stairs. His last words stayed with me all night.

On Thursday I rose early and raced to the library. I impatiently waited fifteen minutes for three people to finish reading the three available copies of the Daily Times. As soon as a burly Italian closed his paper, I took it out of his hands. "I'm reading this now," I said.

He did a double take when he saw me. Then he spat at my feet. "I spit on you!" he said.

I was stunned. "What the fuck?! That's...that's against library rules!" I sputtered.

"Carrie D'Away, everyone!" the Italian presented me to the library crowd. Boos and hisses filled the air. Before they decided to attack me, I fled. To hell with my careful budget. I bought a newspaper from the box outside the strip club I lived above.

In the safety of my room, I opened the newspaper to my section. This time I went straight to the Letters to the Editor page. Oh God oh God oh God...where was my column? Oh shit oh shit...I wasn't printed anywhere!

I then read the editorial. Judging by the editor's words, everyone was still pretty sore at me. They had received innumerable phone calls and emails, and the general consensus what that I should be tried for treason. I settled down and wrote the teariest, most contrite letter to the editor that he will ever see.

Eight hours later, I sat back with a tired smile. This letter would do it! I'm sure the spirit of Henry Longfellow had inhabited me, as my missive was a poetic ode to forgiveness. To boot, I'd promised my firstborn child would serve time in the US Army if everyone would just forget this little incident.

Feeling stronger, I walked with my head help high into Dave Galloway's office. "Hi, Dave," I bravely said. "Here's my letter to the editor."

"What the hell do you think you're doing here?!" Dave yelled.

I immediately wilted. Holding my letter out tentatively, I repeated. "I've brought my letter to the editor."

"Do you REALIZE what you've done to us?!" Dave continued yelling. "Our circulation has reached an all-time low!"

"I'm sorry," I said, as if I hadn't said it two hundred times in yesterday's unprinted letter to the editor.

"You're sorry? You should have been sorry before you wrote that letter!" Dave said, rather stupidly, I thought. "Well, after the article we put in tomorrow's paper, our circulation should get back to normal."

"Good!" I said, showing I was happy for him.

He looked at me as though I'd won top honors at Idiot School. "Good?" he asked. "Good? That article will be informing our readers that you have been fired. As far as we're concerned, you were fired as of last Friday."

"But I wasn't!" I cried. "You printed my national anthem letter!"

"And so we'll print a retraction. That means it doesn't count."

"Does it?" I didn't quite get his logic, but I had bigger worries. "Hey, what about my check that got stolen? You still owe me money for that!"

Dave walked over to his desk and picked up a bank statement. "No, we don't. You reported your check missing too late. That mugger had cashed it already. But YOU owe ME 50 bucks still."

"I don't have it," I admitted.

"I want my money!" Dave began yelling again. "Pay me!"

"Pay me for my anthem letter!" I yelled back.

"Get outta here!" Dave screamed, red in the face. "You're fired! Fired! Get out!" A crowd had gathered to watch my lesson in humility so I took Dave's advice and split.

Friday morning, I woke up in better spirits. Last night, instead of crying the blues, I felt an urge to quell my misery in another way. I gathered up all the Daily Times' in my room, went into the back alley, and burned every page slowly, one by one. By 11 p.m. I was cold, tired and hungry, but more at peace. So I lost a job. I could always find another one. I wasn't qualified for much, but I could wash dishes.

The first thing I did when I awoke was buy myself some breakfast. I knew that this fiasco would blow over soon and I'd be a speck in everyone's memories, so I kept my head held high. I did order take-out though.

After my meal, I busied myself by packing a few things into one more carton. Today was moving day! At least my first and last month's rent was paid, all I had to concern myself with was feeding myself. As I shook a bug off my housecoat, I gleefully thought of my new place. One of the things that sold me on it was that it was cockroach-controlled.

A knock came at the door. The Daily Times, begging me to come back? Ha ha! Even my sense of humor was coming back. I opened it and saw three men standing there. All three immediately flipped badges at me. "Police?" I asked.

"Immigration," all three responded. One looked into my room. "Good," he said. "You're leaving."

"Yes," I replied. How'd they know? Did they say Immigration or CIA?

"We have to give you an escort," the same man said.

"An escort?" I repeated. "Why? I'm nobody special."

"You are Alice Kumplunkem?"

"Yes," I said. "But I don't need an escort! I'm not going far."

The three men glanced at each other and made a motion to grab their guns, just in case. "You are going back to Canada?" another one asked.

"Yes, I guess so, eventually," I said, starting to get a bit annoyed with their line of questioning. "But today, I am only going a few blocks."

"No," the guy said. "Today you're going back to Canada."

I remembered my visa was up today but decided to play it dumb. "Oh, did my visa run out? Look, on Monday, I'll go to your office and straighten it all out, alright?"

"I wouldn't bother," another officer informed me. "The US Embassy considers you an undesirable alien..."

"Fuck them too," I said. They all stiffened, the loyal peons.

"We have been instructed to put you on a bus for Toronto,

Canada; your last place of residence. Pack only what you can bring on a bus, which is three suitcases. I'm also instructed to tell you that you may not apply for citizenship again for the next 10 years, and that all customs points across the US will have your photo and statistics..." The officer went on with his litany; USA vs. Kumplunkem. In stunned silence, I packed my most precious belongings.

I was sent back to Canada in disgrace.

CHAPTER SEVEN

Upon arrival in Toronto, I gathered my suitcases out of the Greyhound Bus. Those three suitcases represented everything I owned in the world. I didn't care. I walked over to a bench in the bus terminal and sat down. Now what? What did I do with my worthless life now? And I meant NOW. I had nowhere to live but I didn't care. I had almost no money and I didn't bother to count just how much I did have because I didn't care. I really didn't give a shit about anything.

I am not a suicidal person. I may have felt extreme misery at times but I've never considered killing myself. Life was a real drag but I wouldn't choose death over it. I wondered if there was a place I could go to, just to check out of life for a while. If it would have been possible to freeze my body cryogenically for the next 100 years, I would have done it. I no longer wanted to think or make decisions anymore. I was tired of thinking. My brain had so many thoughts in it, it just overheated. Now it was a lump of sawdust in my head and I was left with an ambivalent personality.

Should I call Velda? I hadn't spoken to her since I left Toronto and she'd probably be as mad as hell at me. So what though? What's one more person mad at me? Besides, she was probably shooting some film in Paris or something.

I dialed her number. After two rings, it was picked up. "Hello?" Velda answered.

"Hello, Velda? It's Alice."

"Alice!" she shrieked. "Where are you?"

"Toronto," I replied. "I just got in."

"Where are you staying?" she asked.

"I haven't gotten a place yet," I said.

"Well, you know I have an extra bedroom," she reminded me. "Come stay with me!"

"You wouldn't mind?" I had to ask.

"Not at all!" Velda trilled. "I'd love to have you!" What a nice homecoming line!

"Thanks a lot," I said. "I really appreciate it." She didn't know how much I appreciated it.

"So grab a cab and get over here!" Velda commanded. "We have so much to catch up on! I'll see you in a few minutes."

I lugged my suitcases onto a public transit city bus. I would have loved to take a taxi but my pocket money disallowed that luxury. After getting off the bus, it took another 40 minutes to haul my suitcases the two blocks to Velda's house. First I'd take the two lighter cases and walk ahead about a hundred feet, just far enough so that my other suitcase was still in my sight. Then I'd walk back, get the heavier case, and walk ahead two hundred feet with that. It was a dumb way to do things but I didn't want anything stolen. As I said, these suitcases contained everything I owned.

I knocked on Velda's door and it was flung open. "Alice!!!" Velda laughed, throwing her arms around me. "Oh, I've missed you so much!"

"I missed you too, Velda," I said. Seeing her was an instant reminder that she was the only true friend I'd ever had.

"Let me help you with your baggage," she offered. "Your room's a bit messy but we'll take care of that later." We threw my suitcase into a room I believe served as Velda's closet. Not that it was tiny; it wasn't. It was just strewn with all types of clothing.

She led me back into the living room and pulled out a bottle of wine. "I've been saving this for a special occasion," she said, displaying a bottle of France's finest, "and this is a very special occasion. Welcome back!" She poured two glasses full and toasted me.

"So what've you been up to, Velda?" I asked.

"Me!?" Velda replied, astounded. "I want to hear what's been happening to you since you left Toronto!"

"Oh, this and that, you know," I lacklusterly said. "Nothing much."

"Nothing much! Come on! You were working for one of the best soaps!" Velda countered, all wonderstruck.

"Yeah, but I quit," I noted.

"So what? People quit jobs all the time," Velda reassured me. "And besides, I read you got all sorts of offers to work for other soaps and YOU turned THEM down."

"You say what? You read?" I shook my head in confusion.

"Oh, yeah!" Velda affirmed. "You're big news here! I wish I could have talked to you but I felt sort of shy."

"Shy? Why in the world would you feel shy?"

"Oh, because you had this big job and I just felt so small-time compared to you. I didn't want to bug you," Velda, my bosom buddy, said. "And I knew you were way too busy to get in touch with me."

"That's not exactly how it was," I admitted. "And you were thinking stupid."

"Oh, it's so nice of you to say that!" Velda cried, giving me another hug. "We're still friends, aren't we?"

"Of course," I said. "Hey, Velda, where did you read about me?"

"All the papers...the entertainment magazines...everywhere," Velda said.

"They wrote about me?" I asked.

"Sure!" Velda replied. "Why not? You had an important job in the United States of America! Canadian Girl Does Well!"

"Hhmm. My life didn't go too well after that job though," I bitterly added.

"How can you say that?!" Velda asked, her eyes wide. "Then you ONLY got a job as a FEATURED columnist on New York's BIGGEST newspaper."

"Yeah, but I got fired," I again admitted.

"In a blaze of Canadian patriotism!" Velda fairly saluted.

"You know about that too?" I asked, myself now bug-eyed.

"After you got that second job, everyone was talking about how well you were doing," Velda told me. "But then a few people were getting envious. Then you wrote that letter! You became our nation's hero! You rank up there with Terry Fox."

"Please, Velda, don't make such a big deal outta it," I said. "I was pretty mad at something else when I wrote that letter. I took my aggression out on a lot of the wrong people."

"Oh, you were always so modest," Velda chided me. "I'm surprised there wasn't a big crowd waiting for you at the airport."

"I don't think anyone knew I was coming," I said, neglecting to add I took the bus.

"You got deported Friday, didn't you?" Velda asked.

She was blowing me away! "How the hell did you know that?!" I asked.

"Alice, I told you!" Velda huffed, as if she needed to repeat it again. "You're in the news!"

"Since I left Toronto?"

"Here and there," Velda nodded. "After you got that column, news on you calmed down. Then when the trouble started, you became headline material. They printed your letter to that editor and everybody here flipped. They want to nominate you for premier of Ontario even."

"Oh God!" I laughed. "Come to think of it, why not? I haven't been qualified for any other of my jobs so far. Why not a politician?"

"Are you serious?" Velda enquired.

"No!" I firmly stated. "Vel, all I want to do right now is stay OUT of the spotlight. I don't want any more high-profile jobs and I never want to see my name in the newspaper ever again."

"I can't believe it," Velda said. "Everybody wants that."

"Not me," I held my stand. "Maybe you, being an actress, wants that, but I'd be happy to toil my little life away as a chimney sweep from now on."

"If you say so..." Velda said disbelievingly.

"So enough about me," I changed the subject. "What have you been up to? Working a lot?"

"Let's see...you've been gone about a year...oh, by the way, Alice," Velda said, "I must say, you've changed 100 per cent."

"Yeah," I agreed. "Older, but wiser."

"You look five years younger!" Velda exclaimed. "And so thin! Your hair looks like you just got out of a salon."

"Really?" I asked. *Tell me more.*

"You look amazing," Velda decided. "I barely recognized you."

"I didn't realize I'd changed so much," I admitted. "Anyways, tell me what you've been up to all year?"

"Let's see...I did that Stewardessess of the Americas, but it got cancelled right away. They only showed four episodes. Then I got a couple commercials...four, actually." Yet Velda looked wistful. "Then this big European director came to Toronto and wanted me for this great role – a lead! Finally, a lead role! But my agent got greedy and demanded I get this and I get that. I told him, 'Don't blow my chances!' but sure enough, he did. They started shooting already and ended up hiring my biggest competition in this town."

"Aww, that's a shame," I said.

"Yeah," Velda agreed. "My agent and I have been kind of scrapping for weeks now. What's worse, I haven't worked in weeks!"

"Oh, oh...so you're broke too?" I asked.

"Oh, no!" Velda laughed at the idea. "But you are?"

"Yeah. I didn't want to tell you."

"Don't worry about it!" Velda said. "Stay here for as long as you like. I'll give you a few hundred for play money. I'm honored to have a guest like you staying here."

Funny how life works out. I used to be so honored just having

Velda as a friend and she's honored that I'll be soiling her bedsheets. "Just one more favor, Vel," I said. "Please don't tell anyone I'm staying here. I just want to be left alone."

I could see where Garbo was coming from.

* * *

It was a full two weeks before I started feeling normal again. My ambivalence had left me and I was actually starting to feel bored. Velda wasn't pushing me to find employment or to help her with the bills, but I didn't feel right sponging off her. It was time to get a job.

My room-mate came home from an audition. She was trying out for a sitcom to be filmed in Toronto. Velda slammed the front door closed and stormed over toward the couch. "How'd it go?" I asked.

"Another blonde-bimbo part!" she griped. "I can't figure out why Scott keeps sending me to them. Sure, I did a few to get my career started but my agent KNOWS I can play other characters. I'm so sick of doing the wide-eyed, breathy, booby parts."

"Just like I got so sick of playing the ugly duckling roles," I commiserated, then made a suggestion. "Talk to him."

"I HAVE been! We must have discussed this a dozen times this year already. And guess what else I discovered!" Velda asked. "The casting director left his desk for a minute and I wanted to see what kind of Polaroid I'd taken. So I go over to his desk quick and I see it – it was fine – and then I see this list. It's got all the actresses names on it who are trying out for this part, and the amount their agents want them to be paid, right? Well, there's good ol' Shirley Bloom's name, my main competition, and her agent has her down for double scale. I think to myself, Shirley's moving up in this biz, her agent is asking for double pay. Then I see my name and I see TRIPLE scale! I TOLD Scott not to axe me out of the running by insane salary demands. I'm not a big star yet! And you know what, Alice?" she asked tearfully.

"What?"

"Shirley Bloom is gonna pass me by. Why wouldn't the producers hire someone just as talented as I for half the price? I would." Velda had a problem alright.

The phone rang. I didn't pick it up, as I hadn't been for the two weeks since I'd arrived. I left the answering machine to its business when Velda wasn't around. "Hello?" Velda said, then listened. "They made their choice already? Can't you get back to them and say we'll go down...? Fine...I don't agree, you know, but you're the agent...Right...Sure...Bye." She looked at me then yelled, "SHIT!"

I have to admit I was shocked. Velda was so well brought-up. "Wow, you swore!" I gasped. "Must be bad news."

"Oh, just another part I didn't get and Shirley Bloom did," Velda replied. "You know I never let it bother me when I don't get a part, but this is different. This goes deeper than not getting a part."

"Dump him, Velda," I suggested. "He's ruining your career."

"But he's the best agent in Toronto!" she cried. "It's quite prestigious to belong to that agency. I just wish they didn't think they knew everything and actors know nothing."

The phone rang again. Velda looked at it for precisely two rings and then picked it up. "Hello...oh, hi, Rafael! ... I found out already; I didn't get it... Oh well... So what time are you picking me up? ...What? ...Oh, no! I was looking forward to it... Can you? ... Maybe I'll still go... Thanks. See you." She hung up.

"Bad news again?" I hated to ask.

"Remember that opening I was going to tonight?" Velda asked. "That big play at the Royal Alex Theatre?"

"Yeah, *Guys and Dolls*," I said knowingly.

"Right. Rafael can't make it. He had an invite to the opening AND to the party afterwards." She looked at me as if she needn't say more.

"You wanted to go to the party?" I asked.

"Of course!" Velda said. "Those are the places to be seen!"

I would rather have gone to see the play. My high school had done a production of it and although I wasn't cast in it, I still went to see it. To my surprise, I thoroughly enjoyed the show. I hinted at Velda, "I'd like to see *Guys and Dolls* again."

"You want to leave the house?" she asked.

"I've been cooped up long enough," I confessed. "I don't know if I'm into a party though."

"Rafael said he'd drop the tickets off anyways, just in case I wanted to go still," Velda said. "Let's go together!"

It was fun getting ready to go. Old Girls Club. Giggling, trying on each other's clothes. I ended up wearing a smart black dress that belonged to Velda and she ended up wearing something of her own too. I never thought I'd live to see the day that I would fit into Velda's clothes. She even gave me a few helpful make-up hints, such as 'limit blue eye-shadow to just the eyelid' and how to fill in over-plucked eyebrows.

The play was even better the second time. And surprise, surprise! My old boyfriend Joe was in the cast, playing a second-banana gangster. He excelled in his role and I knew I was foolish to deny his apparent talent.

The play left us in exuberant spirits. "I'd love to be in a show like that! It must be fun!" Velda exclaimed. "I've never been in a play. Just film."

"I was lucky I got to do both," I said. Time obscures memories. "The good 'ol days."

"C'mon, Ali," Velda said. "Let's go to the party." That was one more reason Velda was cementedly endearing herself to me. She'd found a nickname for me that I actually liked. Ali. Ali. Actually, I loved it.

"Aw, I don't know," I whined a bit.

"Come on!" Velda pleaded. "Just for a few minutes? I promise I won't introduce you to anybody."

Sounded like a fair shake. Besides, I was dressed to kill. Why hide it in a dark theatre? We walked over to the bar and Velda immediately started chatting up a storm with a well-dressed man. I ordered two white wines. Just as the bartender handed them to me, Velda grabbed my elbow. "Let's go to the food table," she directed.

"But weren't you talking to someone?" I asked.

"He's the father of one of the actors," Velda informed me. "Nice guy, but not the director, you know?" Sometimes I got the feeling Velda could be cold-hearted but she never gave you more than a fleeting doubt. Even as she said that last line, she laughed girlishly. And I guess she WAS at this party for a purpose.

The food table was laden with all sorts of delicacies as well as my favorite – desserts. There was quite a crowd of people surrounding the table and Velda surveyed them for a quick moment. She motioned me to follow her over to the other side where she then squeezed us in between two gentlemen. Helping herself to some pate (just the end of the table I didn't want to be at), she struck up a conversation. "Wasn't the show fabulous!" she gushed.

Control the fireworks, Velda, I thought, but one of the men beamed. "I'm glad to hear you say that!"

"Why?" Velda innocently asked. "Do you have something to do with this production?"

"I was one of the investors," the portly man preened. "Floyd Wortman. And this is my friend, Ron Base."

"Don't you write an entertainment column?" Velda coyly asked.

"A few," Ron replied. "Pleased to meet you."

"My pleasure!" Velda stroked their egos. "I'm Velda Springfield and this is my friend, Al…" she was pointing directly at me when she remembered our deal. "Ali," she concluded.

"Hi," they both said to me and resumed conversing with Velda. Just the fact that she was still talking to them confirmed that they were 'important people'. I had had enough pate and excused myself to wander down to the cheesecake section. I was debating over the double chocolate or raspberry-topped when I became conscious of a very attractive woman standing next to me. A little too much make-up though, I thought. *Why, her eyeliner is extended far too much, you can tell she's wearing pancake make-up and the four-inch eyelashes have to be fake.* She looked like one of the hustlers in the play I'd just seen.

"Are...are you an actress?" I asked.

"Yeah, I was in the show," she beamed, then waited for my compliments to tumble forth. Instead I rushed back to Velda. She was still in deep conversation with both men. She hadn't even touched one bite of her pate.

"Vel...Velda," I whispered, trying to get her attention. She kept on talking so I bopped up next to her, waiting my turn. She finally responded to my tugging on her skirt and turned to look at me. "Vel, actors are coming to this party," I gravely reported.

"Well, they have a right, don't you think?" Velda replied. "Why, what's the matter?"

"JOE! He'll probably be here," I said in a panic.

"Probably," Velda agreed, then changed her mind. "Oh, but probably not. You remember Joe! He's so intense. He hates parties."

"That's right!" I remembered and relaxed. How could I forget Joe's behavior? Our cozy nights at home, watching Francis Ford Coppola films for the umpteenth time. And he WAS intense. I remember watching *Rumblefish* and almost choking on an acrid odor. I finally said to Joe, "Joe, honey, your socks stink." He responded by jumping up and throwing my bookshelf to the floor. "I'm going back for cheesecake," I told Velda and turned around.

I was staring directly into Joe's face. He looked at me blankly for a moment until realization came into his eyes. "Well, if it isn't Alice Kumplunkem," he drawled, just loud enough for Velda's companions to hear.

The investor, Floyd, whipped me around. "You're Alice Kumplunkem?" he asked. I could only nod in fear. "Do I have a sweet deal to offer you! Listen to this! I've got the money to put into a film and I think the film should be based on your life story. Ron here can write the screenplay and you..." here he stopped a brief second and took a hard look at me, "...your friend here can play you. Whaddaya say?" He spoke so quickly.

"That's a great idea!" Velda chimed in.

"Uh...no, thanks," I stammered. "It wouldn't be a very good movie."

"With the right director and a great script..." Ron began.

"She'll get back to you," Joe said, taking my arm and steering me away from them. Obviously he remembered my old behavior because he walked me over to the dessert section.

"They're going to tell everybody I'm here!" I worried aloud. "I don't want to talk to anyone."

Joe looked over toward Velda and the men. "Not for a while yet," he deduced. "They're going to try and get to you through Velda, so they'll be talking to her for a while longer."

"Hi, Joe," I said.

"Hi, Alice, Little Miss Show-Us-All," he said jokingly. "How've you been?"

"Oh," I laughed weakly. "I've had my ups and downs. Hey, what are you doing at this party?"

"I'm in the show," he said.

"I know, I saw it," I told him. "You just were never the party type."

"I'm still not," Joe declared. "I hate all the schmoozing that goes on. I'm hungry though. I'll eat a plate of food and then split." He started helping himself to the buffet. "Will you join me for a bite?" he asked like a gentleman.

"Sure," I replied. We filled plates and walked over to a secluded portion of the room. We talked idly, sort of just checking to see where we stood with each other. I found I wasn't mad at him anymore and I guess he found me bearable again. And Joe, never given to flattery, remarked that I really fixed up my looks.

We finished our meal and left the plates on a table. "Look at your friend," Joe said, pointing to Velda. "That's the director she's talking to now. She's good."

"Yes, she is," I agreed. "Can you excuse me a minute, Joe? I have to use the washroom."

"Sure," he replied.

I walked into the washroom behind two cutesy young types, obviously actresses. I was still occupying my stall when they finished their tinkle. "How'd your audition go today?" one asked the other.

"Oh, I'm so mad at that director!" the second exclaimed. "The first thing she said when I walked into the audition was 'You're not the right type!' Couldn't she tell from my photo what type I was?"

"Shit. I'm the same type as you and my audition is for tomorrow," the first said, a bit unsettled.

"Well, I don't know what to tell you. The role called for a farm girl. I wore jeans, put a bandana in my back pocket, a checkered shirt, everything. What else do they want?" the second girl said bitterly.

"Hey, did you hear who's here?" the first asked. "Alice Kumplunkem!"

I had been about to exit my cubicle but held back. "Really?" the second girl asked. "How do you know?"

"Someone told me," the first said, "but I haven't seen her yet. She's in a black dress."

"We're all in black dresses," the second said. "Is she pretty?"

"Not as pretty as us," the first stated. "Let's go look for her."

They left the washroom and I came out feeling ill. Now what the hell did people want to look at me for? This was what I'd feared. I slunk out of the ladies' room and scurried over to Joe. He stood up. "I've had enough of this party," he informed me. "I'm gonna split. What are you up to?"

I looked over at Velda. Now she was speaking to one of the actors in the show. I didn't want to tell Joe I'd probably just hang out in a washroom stall until Velda was ready to leave. "Nothing," I replied.

"Wanna come with?" he offered. "Let's grab a coffee downtown."

It was the perfect offer. I looked back at Velda, now stepping onto the dance floor with the actor. She'd make it home alright without me. Then I noticed someone pointing directly at me. How rude! Didn't their mothers tell them it was impolite to point? "Yeah, let's go," I said to Joe.

He always had impeccable timing.

* * *

The next morning, Velda and I awoke late. I stretched contentedly. I felt good. Even though I realized I wasn't able to relax in public yet, I'd had a nice time with Joe. Nothing romantic happened although I'd have screwed him if he'd asked, but it was comfortable just talking to him. He brought me up to date on his life since I'd last heard of him. His career was flourishing; he rarely had to audition for anything anymore and never in Canada. He didn't exactly approve of my working on a soap opera (beneath him) but he did admire the fact that I'd switched to being a writer. And him and Beulah were splitsville. I felt inner satisfaction at hearing that. *Maybe you should've stuck with me after all, Joe!* He was going to be in town for another month and promised to call.

Velda and I made coffee and sat around rehashing the previous night. I told her about Joe and she displayed all the business cards she'd received. It was a wonderful night for both of us.

"I still can't get over how great that show was," Velda repeated. "I feel so jealous of the actresses in that play."

"So why don't you do one?" I asked.

"Scott doesn't send me to any auditions," Velda answered.

"Oh, speaking of auditions, I heard of one last night," I remembered, trying to recall more details.

"For what play?" Velda asked.

"I only heard about the character," I said. "A farm girl. THAT'S what you should be playing, Velda. Something totally different from the actual Velda Springfield. Now that would show off your acting abilities!"

"Yeah, you're right!" Velda said, considering it. "I'm gonna phone my agent and see if he knows what play it is." She placed the call and it was brief. "Hello, Scott? Do you know what theatre in town is casting a farm-girl role? ... Thank you. Bye."

"He didn't know?" I asked rather incredulously.

"No," she said dejectedly. "Oh, well."

"Hell, I bet with a few phone calls, he could find out," I said, none-too-impressed with this Scott.

"Should I call him back and ask him?" she asked uncertainly.

"Of course," I said, then, "Aw shit, I could do it myself." With that, I picked up the phone and the yellow pages. After seven calls, we found out Nightwood Theatre was doing *My Favorite Field* and the farm-girl role was nothing else but the lead.

"Ohhh!" Velda exclaimed. "That would be the perfect part for me!"

"So call Scott," I now directed her. "With his connections, he should be able to get you an audition."

Velda dialed again and spoke to Scott. "Scott? I found out about that farm-girl role. Nightwood Theatre is doing it and Scott, it's a great part! It would break the stereotype I'm stuck in...but... Yeah, but... Can't you get... Scott, I...FINE, THEN." She hung up. "I hate him!" she screamed.

"What'd he say?" I asked.

"He doesn't want me doing theatre! There's no money in it!" she retorted. It was an argument I'd heard before. "But he may have an audition for me tomorrow. A commercial. Marilyn Monroe types." Even though Velda usually got those jobs, she didn't seem to be too pleased.

"You really wanted to audition for a theatre job, didn't you?" I asked. She simply nodded and began applying red nail polish in anticipation of tomorrow's audition. I thought for a moment. "Hang on with that nail polish a sec, Velda," I said. "I'm gonna phone Nightwood Theatre."

Don't ask me what I was doing. I just didn't want to see my buddy so down and out. I managed to speak to the secretary handling the auditions. "Yes," I said, "I'd like to know if you have any openings left for the farm-girl role."

"I'm sorry," the secretary said. "We're booked up."

Velda was hovering at my elbow. I whispered they were full and she threw herself dramatically onto the kitchen chair. I returned to my call. "Oh, too bad! Because Velda Springfield just got back from a six-month tour of the States. She heard of the part and really wanted to audition for it. But don't worry, she'll just take the...the Neil Simon play then."

Velda was staring at me, horrified, but the secretary was invisibly impressed. "I don't know if the director can see her, but if she'd like to come down any time before 4:30, maybe we can squeeze her in. Who is this?" the secretary asked me.

"Uh...," I didn't want to blow Velda's chances by saying her room-mate, so I said, "her agent."

"Fine," she bought it. "I'll pencil her in." We hung up.

Velda pounced. "Ali! You told two barefaced lies!"

I laughed and snatched the nail polish out of her hand. "Red nails won't cut it, Vel!"

* * *

I was waiting with such bated breath for Velda's return that I almost became faint. It was murder getting her out the door.

"No, Velda!" I yelled as she plugged in her hair straightener. "No plucking!" I groaned as she pulled out her tweezers. "You're not gonna wear make-up!" I wailed as she lugged her cosmetics case out. I was more nervous than she was.

"No make-up?!" Velda howled. "How can I go to an audition with no make-up? I don't even leave the house without putting it on."

"Vel, we have to think carefully here," I cautioned. "Farm girl. Think of the image that comes to your mind."

Velda thought then said, "Ugh."

"Exactly!" I congratulated her. "Now look like that."

She looked at herself in the mirror. I was seeing the real Velda. The morning Velda – in her natural state. Her mussed-up hair was held in a loose ponytail, her clean-scrubbed face sans make-up, a scrubby pair of sweatpants and a baggy oversized t-shirt. "Shit!" she complained. "I may as well go looking like this."

That was a hell of a good idea! "Velda, yeah!" I exclaimed.

"What?!" she said, aghast at the idea. "Show up at an audition like this? You're crazy!"

"Listen," I commanded, "you don't want to go looking like your usual self because then you fit that Marilyn Monroe look, and not a farm girl. BUT, you don't want to go looking like a stereotype of a farm girl either." I was remembering that other girl's get-up. "You follow?" Velda looked undecided so I took the plunge. "Take my advice. Look like you look right now."

Velda looked at herself in the mirror again then sighed. "Alright," she said, "but I'm taking a cab."

I was staring at the front door two hours later; the anticipation was killing me. The phone rang and I jumped like a startled cat. I grabbed it, thinking it was Velda. "Hello??"

"Velda?" a voice asked.

"She's not home," I said. "Can I take a message?"

"This is her agent. When do you expect her back?"

"I have no idea," I said. "Do you want to leave a message?" I wish I'd left the impersonal answering machine on. I didn't want Scott pressing me for any more details.

"I have an audition for her tomorrow," Scott said. He proceeded to give me the information.

I had just hung up when Velda danced in. "Ali!" she hollered for me. "I got a callback!"

I came running into the entrance, proud mother hen. "A callback!" I was thrilled. "Congratulations!" She may as well have won the Tony award.

Velda proceeded to tell me how her audition went. "They were quite nice! I got there and to tell you the truth, I was nervous 'cuz all the other girls were in jeans and checkered shirts and I'm looking like a slob...I was thinking of those holey designer jeans I have... Anyways, they let me have time to read my lines over...Ali, the best scene in the world! I'm fighting with this farm hand 'cuz he's cheating my daddy; he's feeding his family with our chickens! So I fight with him and then I storm off to this unused field and then I had a monologue! About how I want to leave the farm and go to the city and...get this...be a waitress! So the whole audition went quite smoothly and at the end, they asked me where my photo and resume were. Ali, we forgot them!"

I quickly saw the benefit in that and told her. "Good thing too, Velda. Your photo makes you look like a Barbie doll."

"No way!" Velda strongly contested.

"I'm kidding, but it is a very glamorous picture of you," I told her. "And your resume just screams film, film, film, no theatre, all over it."

"Yeah, you're right," she conceded. "So they asked me who my agent was and I don't want Scott knowing about this and I remember on the phone you said you were my agent, so I gave them your name..."

"Me?!" I gasped.

"I said 'Ali Kumplunkem', if that's any consolation," Velda said. "And I was NOT going to say I didn't have an agent. Let me have a little dignity!"

"Well, it's OK, I guess," I said. "So then what happened?"

"So they write your name down and then they say, 'Can you be here tomorrow at 11 a.m., for a callback?' And look!" she said, displaying a script. "The director gave me a copy of the play to read!"

"Oh, that reminds me, your agent called. You have another audition tomorrow, at 2 p.m.," I recalled, giving her the rest of the information. She briefly glanced at it and said disdainfully, "Same ol', same ol'."

"Wanna read the play together?" I asked.

"You're such a big help, Ali. Ali, my theatre agent!" Velda laughed, then naively added. "Ok, I'll read the farm-girl part."

* * *

The next morning, I was up at dawn with Velda. She was re-reading the play and I was trying to make a decision. Finally I told Velda, "You know, I think they're gonna make you do that dream scene." There was a scene in which the farm girl dreams she has that dream job in the big city. A quick set and costume change, the other actors double as city folks in a restaurant, and the farm girl is the waitress. In her dream, the job would be wonderful all the time, a far cry from reality.

"I was thinking they'd make me do the monologue again," Velda figured.

"No, they saw you do that already," I thought aloud. "They're going to want to see something different."

"The director said I should be prepared to do two scenes," Velda recalled. "Maybe it'll be the monologue and the dream scene."

"No, if there's a second scene, it'll be the one with her and her daddy at the end," I declared. That was where her father tells her she's old enough to get a job during the winter months, when farming was slow, and he'd arranged for a waitressing job at the local tavern in town.

"You think?" Velda asked quizzically.

I nodded, satisfied with my choices. Then, for some dopey reason, I said in a solemn tone, "Take my advice."

"Alright," she said, "then what shall I wear today?"

She was already wearing a long paisley skirt. It was rather nice but Velda thought it too quaint, and only wore it around the house when she felt cool. Over that she wore a heavy wool sweater. "That," I said.

"Again? With just the clothes I threw on for the day??" she groaned. I nodded. Velda kept her clothes on.

The door opened at noon, signaling Velda's return from her callback audition. I sensed it didn't go too well. I'd been lying in bed, trying to quell my nerves. I jumped up to check on Velda.

I could tell she'd been crying. "Ali, I bombed!" she wailed.

"Why? What happened?"

"I was doing that scene with my dad…the one you said they'd make me do? I'm cooking supper over this stove prop when my dad comes home from town, right? … And I'm about to deliver my lines…and I start coughing. I just got this tickle."

"Did you have to stop?" I asked.

"No, I got through it," Velda said. "And the dream scene, when I'm rushing around trying to serve customers? Well, I trip over my skirt and I'm embarrassed, so I just spring right back up and I'm laughing and I keep on going like a fool…"

"Do you think the director liked your work?" I asked.

"Not like yesterday," Velda stated. "After I finished the last scene, they said they'd be contacting everyone's agents by this afternoon to let people know one way or the other, and that was it. I left."

"Well, don't let this audition bother you," I told her. "Remember, you said you don't let them get you down."

"This was different!" Velda groaned.

"Don't forget the other one...your commercial audition this afternoon," I reminded her.

"Oh, yes, right," Velda recalled. "Get to see Shirley Bloom again. You know, for once, at this theatre audition, Ms. Bloom wasn't my competition."

Even though Velda was in a bitchy mood, she still managed to leave the house looking like Christie Brinkley's sister. I could see her heart wasn't into this audition and I wanted to tell her to cheer up, but I felt bad for her too. Poor girl; only getting called in for roles that require someone beautiful.

I was reading the Help Wanteds in the newspaper and had made a few calls regarding employment. The phone rang and thinking it was the TraveLodge calling me back about the housekeeping position, I answered.

"Ali Kumplunkem?" a woman asked.

"Speaking," I said, wondering if I'd mistakenly given personnel my new nickname.

"This is Margaret McKay," she announced. "I'm the artistic director at Nightwood Theatre. I'm calling in regard to Velda Springfield's audition today." I was about to say Velda wasn't home but I remembered I was supposed to be her agent, so kept quiet. "I must say, she quite impressed us." Now if she were talking about an audition of mine, this is where the "but" would come in. I waited for it. "Very, very natural on stage." I waited some more. "A sense of honesty, sensitivity and naivety that would perfectly suit the role of the farm girl." BUT...? "She's really the one to play that part."

I wanted her to get to the point. "Yes?"

"Yes," she said. "Would she be available for the next six weeks?"

How did I know? Velda was a busy girl. I know she really

wanted the part but did my little cadet know that a play lasted six weeks at the minimum? I wasn't about to make any major decisions on her behalf. "Could I get back to you on that?" I asked. "I'll have to speak to Velda."

She encouraged me. "I called Equity, the stage union, and found out Velda didn't belong to the theatre union. As well as being able to get her union card, we'd also pay her scale and a half."

"I'll mention that to her," I said. "Look, I'll be in touch by the end of the day."

I hung up then whooped. Velda got the job! And somehow I felt like I had also gotten the job. I was exhilarated. Moments later, Velda came home.

"Hey, Vel," I greeted her, feeling smug. I had a secret! "How'd it go?"

"Fine," she said apathetically. "Blue jeans commercial. I stare at my boyfriend's rear end as he walks away, turn to the camera and whisper, 'He's so fine'. How can you blow that?"

"Was Shirley Bloom there?"

"Of course. I'm starting to wonder if we don't have the same agent," Velda pouted.

"Think you got it?" I idly required.

"I don't know," Velda replied. "I don't care. That's not the part I wanted."

"Oh, you wanted the theatre job?" I tried to lift my eyebrow. "Don't worry about that. You got it."

I was too blasé. Velda didn't get my drift. She gave me a weak look and said, "Ah, you're just trying to cheer me up."

I sprang to life. "No, Velda! You got the play! They just called! You got it!" We spun in circles and squealed and cried. Then I had to calm her down. "Listen, Vel, I told them we'd get back to them this afternoon about it. I didn't want to say yes without talking to you first."

"Call them!" Velda said, pushing the phone at me. "Book me

before they get somebody else!"

"Oh, they want you, there's no doubt," I said. "They're gonna give you your Equity union card AND pay you scale and a half." Velda's face clouded over for a moment. "Hey, I didn't ask for it. They offered it!"

"Scale and a half on my first theatre gig?" Velda was amazed. "You should have just said yes right when they called."

"Velda," I said sternly, "do you know that they want you for six weeks? That means you can't just drop them if a movie comes along. You can't leave them in a bind. And the money isn't as good as film work either."

Velda also knew the value of a stern voice. "Alice, you know how badly I want this part. I thought about what you said, about breaking this image I have, and a better opportunity couldn't have presented itself. And I know what I'm committing to – six weeks of real work."

"So I'll call already," I said, Jewish all of a sudden. "What I do for ten puhcent." I was efficient once I was speaking to Nightwood Theatre's director though.

"Hello, Ali Kumplunkem here. Velda Springfield will be able to do *My Favorite Field*... Your terms were agreeable, yes... You'd like her to start when?" I looked at Velda, who whispered she'd start today if they wanted. "...Tomorrow will be fine... Yes, just send the contract to me." I gave her my address and we had a deal.

"I'm very impressed, Ali," Velda informed me. "You really are a pro."

"Ahhh, I'm just helping you out, Vel," I shucked and shawed.

"Well, you deserve every cent of that commission," she replied.

"No, no!" I protested. "My saying I was your agent was just a scam to get them to see you. You don't owe me anything."

"Listen," she flatly stated. "I'm a professional too. You got me the audition and you handled my contract. In my books, you are automatically entitled to a commission. Besides, you were there for me emotionally and spiritually and helped me prepare myself. That was more than my real agent ever did for me."

* * *

Velda's real agent was extremely angry at her. Freaking, shrieking, roaring mad at her. They were speaking together over the phone and Scott was so thunderously peeved that I heard every word he boomed out.

Scott had phoned earlier and left a message with me. Velda was to contact him immediately. I did not want to say that Velda was at rehearsal because he wasn't supposed to know about the play. I don't know how Velda planned to pull it off. Sooner or later he would find out. Scott didn't leave any more details with me but later I imagine he tried to, because the phone rang more often than usual. The answering machine took over.

Velda waltzed in. I could see she wanted to enthuse a bit but I stopped her. "Your agent called. He wants you to call back immediately."

"Yeah, I didn't charge my cell phone, so I didn't get my messages today. When did he call?" she asked.

"About six hours ago," I said.

"Yikes," she replied and started dialing the phone.

"WHERE WERE YOU??" an earsplitting voice came over the line. "I've been leaving messages all day!"

"I was busy," Velda began, "I..."

"You know damn well you're supposed to keep in constant touch with me!" Scott roared. Since I couldn't help but overhear, I couldn't resist giving a haughty snoot to this remark. Velda glanced at me and nodded.

"Scott, I do not HAVE to do anything," she replied firmly. "Maybe I wanted a day off or something."

"Then tell me, Velda!" Scott yelled. "Anyhow, you got the

Rodeo Blue Jeans commercial." I didn't quite catch the last part so I leaned forward a bit.

Velda cupped the receiver and whispered to me, "I got the commercial!" She then returned to Scott. "Does it shoot on the weekend?" she asked.

"Of course not," Scott retorted. "Next Monday. I'll get back to you with more info later."

By now Velda and I were both listening on the same earpiece. "I'm sorry, Scott," Velda said, "I'm working on Monday."

"No, you're not," Scott informed her. "I have your schedule right in front of me."

"I...uh...I'm in a play," Velda actually came out and told him. "It's an amazing part, Scott! It'll..."

"A PLAY!?" Scott screamed. "Get OUTTA it! Now!"

"I can't," Velda said. "I signed a contract."

"Bring the contract to my office," Scott commanded. "I'll get you out of it."

"I don't WANT to get out of it!" Velda shouted back. "Scott, I know what's good for me, and this play is very important to my career."

Scott was fuming. "Rodeo Jeans is very important to your career!" he yelled. "They might even get you to do a poster!"

"Jeez, Scott, I don't want to be a pin-up girl," Velda bewailed to her agent. "I want to be a REAL actress."

"Real actresses don't make any money, honey," Scott said patronizingly. "Rodeo is prepared to pay double scale right across the board. Is your little play going to pay anything near that much? You're not even Equity! Don't tell me you're doing AMATEUR theatre?"

I couldn't stand listening to Scott rant on like he was such a smarty-pants. I reeled to the couch and flung myself down. Velda was mad too. "Listen, Scott, I'll have you know I now belong to Equity! I am also being paid top dollar. And I ALSO happen to be enjoying my new job very much. So you know where that leaves

Rodeo Jeans?"

"If you take a play, you can't do anything else for weeks!" Scott let her know.

"I know that," Velda replied. "I'll let you know when I'm available for work again, alright?" She was trying to get off the phone on a good note.

"Listen, Velda, you're not a big star yet," Scott said. I could smell a threat. "If you don't drop this silly play, then you can kiss our association good-bye."

Velda gave me a look. It wasn't one of fear; it was more impish. She then blew a loud kiss into the phone. Covering the receiver again, she giggled. "I wonder if he got my point?"

"Velda, does that mean what I think it means?" Scott screamed. "Answer me, you bimbo!"

Oohhh, never call Velda a bimbo. She may look like one and even act like one sometimes, but she is definitely not a bimbo. She gathered herself together and in the most dignified Boston-bred accent, she spoke. "Scott, the association between myself and your tasteless turd-licking agency is OVER." With that, she severed the connection.

She looked triumphant. I looked worried. "Velda, he was the best..." I warned her. "Maybe you should call him back."

"Are you serious?" Velda laughed. "Oh, I feel so good about it! What a weight off my shoulders! I've been oh-so-wanting to do that for ages!"

"But, Vel," I tried to get her back on track, "what are you going to do for an agent?"

"You're my agent for everything now," she calmly informed me.

I saw a challenge.

* * *

Being Velda's agent was pretty simple the first few weeks. She was busy, so I didn't need to find her a job. Basically I'd serve as her sounding board at the end of rehearsals. Some days she was euphoric. "Ali," she softly said, "I reached deep inside myself today to conquer a scene. I pictured my puppy Rosalita when it died in my arms. And I used that sadness in a field scene, when a fire has just destroyed three of our henhouses. I actually cried." Other days she was near hysteria. "My father and I aren't connecting! I don't feel a deep paternal love for him. It doesn't help that he eats Greek food every day for lunch!" All in all though, I could see that this play was enriching Velda, if only for the fact that she finally had to really work for her pay.

I still hadn't found another line of work. Every time I mentioned to Velda that I should start carpet cleaning or delivering flyers, she acted as if I were making a joke. "Right! Ali Kumplunkem doing menial work!" She still had me up on some kind of pedestal. "Don't worry, Ali," she said. "Soon I'll be making big money again and you'll be rich once more." My pride didn't allow me to say I WANTED a lowly job. In the meanwhile, I spent some time wondering how agents went about getting their clients work.

Out of the blue, Joe called me. He wanted to get together that night. I spent the entire afternoon bathing, primping, styling and dressing myself. I looked even more stunning than on the night I'd last seen him. He took me to a movie house that showed second-run films, where we viewed both *The Godfather* and *The Godfather II*. I was physically fighting off sleep when the films finally ended. "Coffee?" Joe asked.

"Sure," I replied. It was going to take three cups of espresso to rejuvenate me.

Once we were seated, Joe went into a speech about how important this guy Coppola was. He was the director of the films we'd just seen. "He really knows how to bring out the best in his actors," Joe declared. "Man! I'd love to work with him!"

"Get your agent to arrange an audition," I suggested.

"Right!" Joe said sarcastically. "That's like asking to have an audience with the Pope. My agents wouldn't even THINK of approaching a guy of that caliber."

"Guess what?" I asked. "I'm Velda's agent now."

"No kidding?" he replied. "You're in the agent business now?"

"Sorta just fell into it," I answered. "But I got Velda work already. A play."

"Good for her. Good for you," Joe, the master of eloquence, said. "Hey, didja like how Al Pacino stayed so cool when he had to kill those guys? Just his eyes showed..." He went on about those damn films. It was like watching a third movie. Thank God I had coffee to sustain me this time.

Things hadn't changed much with Joe. But then again...they had in a couple ways. Joe got a bit more classy – he sent me home in a cab. Yet, unlike the old days, he didn't give me a good-bye kiss. I don't know why I wanted one. He didn't exactly turn me on. I just felt comfortable with him and thought the night would end nicely with a kiss. I guess he wanted to be friends.

And knowing now just how important friends are, I guessed I could settle for that.

* * *

Joe was my invited guest to the opening of *My Favorite Field*. It was Velda's big night and my greatest task so far as an agent was getting her to the theatre.

She had fallen to pieces so much, I almost had to sweep her up and carry her there in a sack. It was even touch and go for a while whether I should call the theatre and inform the stage manager that Velda Springfield would be unable to make it for tonight's performance. I promised Velda that I would be third row center. I'd left my jacket over two chairs for a week now, to ensure I had those seats. Velda wanted to know exactly where I'd be sitting so she could "play" to me.

After escorting her to the dressing room, I quickly made an exit. I ran to a nearby coffee shop and drank a cup slowly. I was intent on saying my Hail Mary's three dozen times. I'm not big on religion but I wanted God with me on this score. If Velda did well, we'd all be happy. If she bombed, I had a feeling I was responsible for a lot of the blame. Big Mouth, Know-It-All Kumplunkem.

Joe met me at the theatre. He looked like he had just gotten out of bed. Two days' growth of beard, jeans with holes in them and a baggy suit jacket worn over a lime-green t-shirt. I was wearing a backless dress. I guess I wanted to flaunt my back in front of Joe, now that my acne scars had disappeared. Instead, I just felt overdressed.

"New dress?" Joe asked. Of course it was. When I'd last seen him, over a year ago, I'd have been lucky to get a leg through the hole in the back. But at least he'd noticed. "Hey," Joe hesitated to add, "I hope you don't want to go to the party after?"

"I kind of have to. For a while, anyways," I grimaced back. "This is the play I got for Velda."

"We'll see," Joe decided.

Joe didn't mind claiming our seats early. He wasn't one for socializing. We thumbed through the program. "Holy shit," Joe remarked. "Velda will flip when she sees her photo."

I searched it out. It was a shot of a plainer Velda, still lovely, but looking more like Miss Red River Valley. Her smile only showed six teeth and her hair was left unstyled. "No," I corrected Joe. "She knows about it." She'd brought a copy of the photo home and studied it for four solid hours. I had also been expecting a flip-out, but none came.

The theatre became packed. There wasn't an empty seat in the house. Joe recognized a couple faces in the audience – theatre critics from the city's biggest newspapers. The lights were just about to go up when a loud crash was heard. The lights went back down and a giggle went up from the crowd. My heart sank. *Don't let this be a forewarning!*

An interminable time later, at least three minutes, the stage lights came up again. There sat Velda, my morning Velda, staring out of a farmhouse window. Joe leaned forward in his seat, stared hard, then whispered to me, "That's not Velda, is it?" I nodded and he shook his head in amazement.

The play went from swell to downright magnificent. When it ended, I wished I'd grown up on a farm in New Brunswick. I yearned to go home and put on a flannel nightgown and make a stew. There was curtain call after curtain call and finally, a standing ovation. Tears were streaming down my cheeks and for the first time, Velda looked right at me. She started crying too and blew me a kiss.

When the applause died down, I turned to Joe. "Guess we should go to the party for a bit," I said negatively.

"Yeah, sure," Joe said. He seemed to be lost in thought.

Joe bought me a beer and we just stood around. I could sense he wasn't in the mood for conversation but I didn't blame him. That play really had an effect on us! I was waiting for Velda's arrival but she was taking her time. Joe finally spoke up. "You got her that play, huh?"

"Yup," I simply said. As if it was a run-of-the-mill occurrence. "Oh, there's Velda!" We moved to greet her but about thirty people got in front of us. Velda looked ravishing. She wore a gingham dress, but it was low-cut and off the shoulder. Her make-up was on in full force. She really was a smart cookie. Let the people see you plain but never let them think you ARE plain. Here she was showing that she could also play in the Hugh Hefner story. She assaulted the senses.

It was impossible to get to her. She saw us, waved and shrugged her shoulders. "She knows we're here," Joe said. "Let's go. I wanna talk to you." He said this so gravely, I wondered what I did wrong.

"What's the matter, Joe?" I asked as we walked along.

"I'm just trying to decide something," he said then paused. "OK, I've decided. You're my new agent."

That stopped me right in my tracks. "WHAT?" I shrieked like a fishwife.

He opened the door for me at some eatery. I didn't read the sign; I was too busy studying Joe's face for signs of a joke. He chose a seat for us then told me more. "I just want you for my agent."

"But what's wrong with your agent?" I continued nagging. "He's done so much for you!"

"Yeah, in the beginning," Joe said, which was all of two years ago. "Now he just takes the phone calls. He's not pushing for me."

"Not when they're offering you work on a platter," I scoffed. "Joe, you're one of the busiest actors in this country! No agent can do more for you." It really sounded like I was trying to talk myself out of a job.

"You're probably right," Joe agreed. "But I like to take chances. I'm bored with my guy and wanna switch. So what's the big deal? Or don't you want to take me on?"

"Joe, I'll take you on...," I began. What was I saying? "...but I have to tell you, I'm new at this. I'm real green. And I have a confession. Velda's play? Pure fluke. We just lucked onto it. You better think about this some more."

"Nah," Joe settled it. "You're my agent. Cappucino?"

* * *

It was pretty easy being Velda and Joe's agents. They were both working. Velda was raking in accolades for her role as the farm girl and Joe was leaving the next day for Texas, where he was playing some desert terrorist role. As a matter of fact, Joe had scheduled a 'meeting' with me. We were going to get together at my 'office'. I was in my pink housecoat and fuzzy slippers when a knock came at the door. "It's open!" I yelled. Yeah, yeah, I know...stupid of me. But hey, I was in Toronto now, not NYC.

Joe popped into the kitchen. "Hi," he said. "Coffee still hot?"

"I'm just putting it on," I replied. "Velda's not even up yet." The saintly farm girl was living it up post-performance, allowing herself to be squired around town on the arms of various noteworthy men. I just slept in because I had nothing else to do.

Joe reached into a large brown paper bag. "I brought us some bagels."

"From that shop..." I began, then stopped. I was going to bring up a romantic aspect of the past. You know how they have 'our song' or 'our table'? Well, we had our 'bagel bakery'; a shop where a tiny pair of overworked Chinese men served the best bagels in all of Toronto.

Joe nodded. I served coffee while Joe got the plates. We were munching when I prodded him. "So?" I asked. "What's the meeting for?"

"Oh, I just thought I'd drop by before I left," Joe said. Oh, really? "Anyways, I completely cleared things up with my old agent. This job is the last one with them. I have no bookings after. I wish I didn't have to do this one as it is."

"Joe, you don't have to do it," I said. "Well, at least, you didn't have to, but then you signed that contract."

"That's what I'm going to like about you, Alice..."

"'Ali', during business hours, thank you."

"I feel like you're gonna stand behind my decisions," Joe stated. "You were an actress once too, so you know this end of the business."

"If I were an actress still," I told him, "I wouldn't pass up a chance to work with Vin Diesel."

Joe looked crestfallen. "You like them beefy types?"

"No! Of course not!" I laughed. "But he's a big star. A lot of people go see his films."

"I don't care," he groused. "I'd be happy doing a role I really liked on a stage in front of 11 people. Or working with someone I really admired, like..."

"I know, I know," I interjected. "Coppola, Pacino..." There were a couple more but those two were his favorites. "Joe, did you remember to bring me that stuff?" I asked. I'd been asking every day for photos and his demo tapes and he kept forgetting them.

He reached inside the paper bag again. "Here's about twenty photos. I've only got a couple demo tapes left too." He gave them to me. "My resume is on the back of the photo," he showed me. I didn't know you could do that with your resume.

"Well, Joe, I'll see what I can do for you," I told him. At that moment, I didn't have a clue.

"Something will come up. It usually does," he calmly said. "And if not, I guess we starve." We laughed. "Well, I should get going. I thought I'd do my laundry before I pack."

I stood up. "Have a good trip. Say hi to Vinnie for me."

We both stood looking at one another. It was an awkward moment. Joe yet again reached into that worn paper bag and this time he withdrew a box of chocolates. "Uh...these are for you," he said.

A box of candy? It may have been the thing to do at one time, but absolutely no one bought candy for the lady anymore. It was an old-fashioned move and that's why I loved it and that's why the awkward moment became even more awkward. "What for?" I breathlessly asked and looked up into his deep brown eyes.

"Ah, you know," he said loudly. "For being my agent, I guess. Well, I'll see you in a few weeks."

A couple days later, I sat musing at the kitchen table. I'd just finished watching one of Joe's demo tapes seven times and that started me thinking fondly of Joe. I even chuckled over his pet desire – to work with Coppola. For a lark, for something to do and knowing I was at least making an effort, I started making phone calls. My target was a mailing address for Francis Ford Coppola. I got a kick out of talking to all those people. *So what if I'm asking dumb questions? You don't know who I am.* Not entirely true, since I was introducing myself as Jane Poundoff. And usually I got a great answer to a stupid question.

Eight phone calls later, I had an address for the man. Then I wrote a short but to the point letter to him. *Hey, Frank! This guy is big-time in Canada, he's crazy for you, he wants to work for you, he's a superb actor but I'll let his demo CD do the talking. Call me sometime, Ali.* No, really, I was a little more formal but that was the gist of it. Funny, I didn't have a difficult time writing the letter. It seems easier to write about something you actually believe in.

Throwing the tape, photo and CD into an envelope, I decided to send it by Priority Post. Might as well try to impress someone along the way, and there was less chance of it getting lost in the rest of Coppola's mail. Didn't cost much more than a hamburger, so I went without lunch.

Go ahead. Call it a shot in the dark. I was.

* * *

Someone finally called me! Not me, plain Alice, but me, Ali the Agent. "Am I speaking to Velda Springfield's agent?" a voice asked over the phone.

"Yes, you are," I replied, my heart a-racing. What was I booking her for? A mini-series? *Gossip Girl*? A role opposite Tom Cruise? "Can I help you?" I asked.

"My name is Guenther Schomberg. I work for the Fashion Section of the Star newspaper. We have a photo spread of Lula Kola's clothing coming up," he informed me. "You probably know her stuff?" *Refresh my memory.* "All cowboy chic and farm fashionable. Lula saw *My Favorite Field* and thought Velda would make a wonderful model. I spoke to the theatre already; they wouldn't mind the publicity. What do you think?"

I wanted to know if this was a freebie. It felt like it. But what the heck – may as well put on the tough act and see where that leads. "What's the pay?" I asked, praying he wouldn't answer "exposure!"

"Six hundred, and it shouldn't take more than four hours, three tops. We'll supply a hair and make-up artist. Thing is, I'd like to do it this afternoon. Is she busy?"

"Hang on a sec, I'll wa..." I was going to say 'wake her up', but I didn't want people thinking we had anything more than a working relationship. "Waaa...wait, I'll check her schedule." I was still going to wake her up and see if she felt like doing this shoot, but I stopped. *Hell with that! I know she isn't working until later tonight and if she made a lunch date, well, toots, you gotta break it. I need to make money so you gotta work. Too bad you didn't get home until three a.m. Put on some cowboy cheek and make me sixty bucks.* "Yeah, Guenther? Be there at two, OK?" I said. "You can have her until five at the latest."

Thankfully, Velda really was a professional. I woke her up, told her the news and she launched out of bed. "Oh, boy!" she cheered. "Exposure!" She never stopped yammering while she bathed and refreshed her appearance. "Do you think I've gotten fatter? Are my teeth still white-white? Oh, Ali, you're such a good agent for getting me this job!"

That's what kind of bothered me. I didn't get her the job. The job came to her. I had a feeling jobs would be coming for Joe as well. But wasn't I expected to find GOOD roles for them? If I could find just one, maybe I'd prove worthy of the title 'Agent'.

Guenther was right on time. His assistant started setting up lights in the living room. They'd asked for permission to shoot Velda at home and I'd agreed. I figured Velda's beauty would overshadow the messy background.

The make-up artist sighed when Velda came out of her bedroom. "Ohhh, you are such a natural beauty!"

"That better not mean you're not going to make me look even better," Velda wisecracked. It was the beginning of an enjoyable shoot. A lot of bantering, joking and tomfoolery. The outfits Velda was modeling were hilarious; even Guenther thought so. Even so, Velda did a marvelous job of looking comfortable and at home in them.

The only unsettling thing was that Guenther kept giving me the occasional look. Make that stare. I didn't sense any romantic interest in me and I don't think we'd ever met before, so I wondered what the attention was about.

As they were packing up to leave, Guenther asked me, "What was your last name again, Ali?"

Instantly on guard, "Why? Is this for the photo spread?"

He laughed. "Can't a person ask for someone's last name?"

"It's Kumplunkem," I said, waiting for the usual guffaw.

He nodded. "I thought so," and that was it. They left and Velda showed me the cards she'd received from the make-up artist, hair stylist and photographer.

Two days later, a knock came at the door. I opened it and there stood Guenther and another man. Guenther looked startled. "Ali? I thought Velda lived here."

"Uh...she does," I replied. "I'm visiting. Do you want to see her?" That meant I would have to wake her up.

"As a matter of fact," Guenther said, "you're the one we want to see."

My warning antennae bristled. "Why?"

"This is Bud Whilt," Guenther said. "He's a reporter for the Star." I felt a dead faint spiraling on. "I figured it was you – Alice Kumplunkem, the Canadian girl wonder in the USA."

"The Star would like to do a story on you," Bud informed me. "You've kept quite a low profile since your return to Canada."

"I'd like to keep that low profile," I said. "I'm sorry to be rude, but no. No story on me." I shut the door politely in their faces, walked to the couch, sat down and started shaking. What kind of dastardly turn would my life take now? Why did adverse publicity stalk me? Why couldn't people leave my life alone? Why did some people choose water while others chose concrete when they leapt from high altitudes?

A few days later, I had gotten over that newspaper-guy fear and was now dwelling on bigger problems. Velda's play would be over soon. Joe would be home in a few days. No one had phoned me with any job offers. I didn't know what the hell to do, so I drank my fourth cup of coffee. Velda woke up just before I finished the pot.

"You look miserable, Ali," Velda observed. "Cheer up! What's the matter?"

Obviously I didn't want to tell her. I wanted her to continue thinking I was SuperAgent. "Nothing," I replied. "Just down."

"Then come to my play tonight!" she insisted. "I'll leave a comp at the door for you." She knew how good her play left me feeling. I had seen it five times already.

"Yeah, I'd love to see it again," I said. "Thanks. I'll wait backstage for you after the show." With all her other admirers.

"No, that's silly!" Velda said. "You're my agent, dummy. Come to the dressing room."

The phone rang and Velda picked it up. "Hello? ... This is Velda...my agent's number? ...Uh, well, she's right here, as a matter of fact. Do you want to speak to her?" She handed me the phone. My heart held out rays of hope. Work for Velda?

"Hello?" I answered. "This is Ali Kumplunkem," I corrected the man who'd asked if he was speaking to 'Alice'.

"This is Bud Whilt, from the Star. Do you remember me?"

"Yes, I do," I replied in an icy voice.

"Look, Alice...Ali," he said. "The Star is going to do a story on you regardless of what you want. Now I thought I'd give you the chance to represent yourself. That way, at least you've given us your side of the story. Our article will be fair to you."

WHY ME???? Where could I run to now? Cuba? But if they

absolutely had to do a story on me, then Bud was right. At least let me get my two cents in.

"When do you want to see me?" I asked glumly.

"Oh, you set the time and place!" Bud said.

I looked at my empty datebook. I needed a few days to prepare for this. "Monday, four o'clock, 150 Brunswick Avenue." He thanked me and hung up.

I told Velda and she was thrilled for me. I tried to impress on her that my life was the shits in America, but she pooh-poohed me. "Oh, just because you spent a few days in some dinky little institution." Then she again raved about the wonderful jobs I'd held. There was just no getting through to her. In her eyes, my steady gig on a soap opera was only second in importance to being President of the United States. Even though Velda was extremely positive about the upcoming interview, I was a negative Nellie.

I really needed a dose of *My Favorite Field*.

* * *

Aaahhh, it was only intermission and already I was feeling that familiar feeling – a mournful yearning for life on a pacific farm, where your biggest concern was a bunch of chickens and getting supper on the table in time. A simple but honorable life. *My Favorite Field* was really a very powerful play, and Act II, still to come, was even better.

I was ordering a Diet Coke when I picked up on a conversation two couples away from me. A tanned lady was spouting off to her companion. They both looked like tourists because they were dressed better than anyone else in the room. "Sue, my husband should see this play!" the more attractive woman commented. "Every actor in this play should get a part in Sam's show. I've never seen such good theatre." She even had some kind of accent.

"And to think we weren't even going to come!" Sue exclaimed. "The boys should have come here instead of going to the casino. Of course Sam should see this show because that's his job, but Roy hates the theatre, you know. Oh, don't tell Sam I told you that! But I think Roy should see this too. He grew up on a farm!"

"Tomorrow night," Sam's wife decided, "we make the boys come see this play."

"Tell Sam it's his job," Sue insisted. Wives' talk.

Their conversation stuck with me and during Act II, I came up with a plan. I hadn't planned on making a plan, but ideas began hurtling themselves at me. I absentmindedly applauded at the end of the show and unthinkingly joined the standing ovation. I decided I was gonna try something.

I was the first one to exit the theatre. I stood by the exit and waited for Sue and Sam's wife to appear. I hoped Velda wouldn't miss me backstage because I wasn't going to be there. I was going with these ladies, although they weren't to be made aware of it. I was going to tail them.

The first thing one said when they left the theatre was, "Where can we find a taxi?" Oh shit! How was I going to follow them by cab? I don't think I had more than five bucks on me.

Fortunately, Sue asked Mrs. Sam and not some fellow Torontonian. I dropped my Sam Spade impersonation and jumped right into their conversation.

"Oh, do you need a cab?" I innocently asked. "I'm going to catch one too. I can show you where to get one."

"Why, thank you!" Mrs. Sam cooed. "That's very nice of you!"

We began walking down the street. Cabs usually drove by the front of the theatre every couple minutes, so I didn't waste time. "I figured you were from out of town," I remarked. "You have some sort of accent."

"We think you have an accent!" Sue said and laughed. Yup, they definitely sounded Southern.

Hurry, Alice. "Where you from?" I asked, then decided I was wasting time on trivial matters. "Where you staying in Toronto?"

"The Four Seasons," Mrs. Sam replied. "Lovely hotel."

"Did you like the show?" I enquired.

That set them both off; they'd been subconsciously searching for a third party to pile more kudos on. I nodded and agreed everywhere, even adding a few praises of my own. Out of the corner of my eye, I saw an empty cab driving up.

Go for it, Ali. Just be nosy and pushy then say you're an agent and that'll excuse your behavior. "Look," I began, "I represent one of the actors in the show. If you'd like to see the play again, I could get you complimentary tickets."

They looked at each other in delight. Then Mrs. Sam turned to me. "We'd love to bring our husbands. Can you arrange for four tickets? Is that too much to ask?"

"No problem," I said, hoping it wouldn't be. Then I went for broke. "My name's Ali Kumplunkem. Why don't you save some time after the show tomorrow? I'd like to take the four of you out to dinner." That way they'd be sure to come see the show.

"You Canadians are so nice!" Mrs. Sam declared. "Oh, here's a cab! You take it!"

"No, go ahead," I offered.

"No, you," she insisted. "You've already been so kind to us strangers. Oh, I'm Iris Platnum and this is my friend, Susan King. Now you go ahead and take this cab. We'll see you at the theatre tomorrow." I stalled. "Go on! We're fine! We'll flag down the next one."

"Alright, thank you," I said, getting into the taxi. "See you tomorrow."

"Where to?" the squinty-eyed driver asked me.

I didn't think he was going to like me. "Around the corner," I ordered. He swore a bit, and even more when I discovered I didn't even have enough money for that. To compensate for it, I suggested he go back and pick up the two rich ladies I was with.

The next morning, I asked Velda for four comps to her show.

She didn't know if she could swing that many and asked why.

"Uh...I've invited some people to see your show before it closes...," I began.

"Which is tomorrow night," Velda added, dejected. She wasn't sad because she didn't have another job lined up, but because she was thoroughly enjoying this theatre experience.

"They'll be coming tonight," I said.

"What kind of people?" Velda asked.

"Uhhh...producers?" I gamely said.

"Oh, Ali!" Velda shrieked and went into her 'good agent!' speech. I asked her to meet us after the show. "Sure! Where?" she asked.

"Ed's Foodhouse," I'd decided. It was the most gaudy restaurant I could think of and the one that would most appeal to showbiz people.

That day I made a few calls around town, trying to find out who Sam Platnum was. I was beginning to love that anonymous phone. However, I had no luck with my calls. No one in Canadian theatre had heard of the guy. I hoped I wouldn't be dishing out $300 treating some nogoodniks to a fancy meal. I decided to go with my instincts though.

I met the foursome at the theatre. Iris and Sue had noticeably had their hair frosted. Roy and Sam were two well-fed jovial types. Both wore suspenders they liked to tug on. These men looked more like good ol' boys wearing suits than artistic directors of theatre. "I'm sorry," I said. "I won't be sitting with you. Why don't we meet in the lobby after the show? We'll go to dinner from here." I thought it a good idea to let them have their space so they wouldn't feel pressured into liking the show just because I had some actor in it. I wanted them to have a natural reaction.

"I could go to dinner right now!" Roy declared, patting his ample belly. "Ah'm starved!"

"Oh, Roy!" Sue chided him. "You'll love this show. At least

watch the first act! Come on, let's go get our seats."

I had neglected to get myself a ticket so I waited in the lobby until the show let out. I had been worried that Velda would have an off-night but by the sounds of it, she was terrific as usual.

I was happy to see my foursome approach me after the show. I took them over to Ed's Foodhouse, anxious to discuss business. As we took our seat, I asked how they liked the show.

"Well, Ali, I know show business, and I'd say this play will be held over for at least another six months," Sam prophesized.

"It closes tomorrow," I informed him. "Another show was booked for the theatre. It's already been held over for three weeks."

"Ali represents one of the actors in the show, Sam," Iris told her husband. "Don't you, Ali? Which one?"

"Velda Springfield, the one who played the farm girl," I proudly stated and got the expected response. Both couples went into spasms on her acting ability.

"Oh, are you directing a show?" I asked him. I really wanted to know what this guy did for a living.

"I own a string of theatres in the South," Sam said. "Right now I'm putting together a big show that'll tour all my places."

"He starts casting on Monday," Iris told me. "Sue and I managed to talk him into taking us on a lil' holiday before he really gets going with this show."

"Velda will be available for work as of Monday," I pushed. "Her last show is tomorrow night."

"Honey, I'll tell you, that Velda is about the best actress I've seen in ages!" Sam said. "I wouldn't even bother auditioning her if only I had a role for her. Now that guy who played her daddy...him I could probably use. He was pretty good. Whaddaya think, Roy?"

"He reminded me of my father," Roy replied.

I tried. But if there were no roles for her, then that was it. I couldn't do anymore. They were probably producing some war drama. "What kind of play is it?" I asked dully.

"Something the Southern audiences will just eat up," Sam said. "A remake of *Frankie and Johnny*. You know that story? We have the perfect Nellie Blye. Meg Ryan promised she'd dye her hair red for the role."

I tried to recall the story. *Frankie and Johnny*? Sounded like a song I'd heard...then I remembered the Michelle Pfeiffer film. "Who's playing Frankie?" I enquired.

Sam shrugged. "We'll find out Monday. That's when casting begins."

I persisted. "Would you consider looking at Velda?"

"Honey, Velda's a wonderful actress, I don't have to repeat that, but she's too plain for Frankie...too earthy," Sam said regretfully. "We want to cast a real siren for Frankie."

"Fine," I simply said and waited for Velda's arrival. She was late, and we were about to order when I saw Sam and Roy's jaws drop. Every man was staring at something and I turned around to see what it could be. A luscious blonde vision in a clinging red dress, hair cascading around her shoulders, made her way across the room. I turned around again and watched the amazement in Sam's face when this bigger-than-life creature walked right up to our table.

"Everyone," I smugly announced, "this is Velda Springfield."

* * *

It was Monday afternoon, only a couple hours to go before my interview with the Star. I didn't know where I'd gone wrong. Velda had charmed the pants off Sam and, perhaps more importantly, his wife. As we parted company at the restaurant, all buddy buddy, I gave them my phone number. I was sure Sam would call before the weekend was over. I guess Velda wasn't right after all. Obviously she wasn't bothered. She was too busy studying a photo of herself that had appeared in today's gossip section of the National Post.

I was readying myself for the newspaper interview. My matte-finished face was ready for any photos to be taken and I had a speech prepared defending every move I'd ever made. Velda had abandoned trying to pep me up for this interview. "Just believe in yourself, Ali!" she insisted. "Do you want me to leave when they get here?"

"NOOO!" I wailed. "I need moral support!"

The phone rang. "Please let that be the Star cancelling," I prayed aloud and picked up the receiver. "Hello?"

"Ali!" a voice boomed over the phone. "It's Sam!"

Sam? Sam Putnam!! "Hi, Sam! How was the trip back?" I brilliantly asked, as if that were my uppermost concern.

"Splendid," he replied. "Well, today's Monday, casting day! I was wondering if we could use Velda for the Frankie role?"

Could he?! Don't ask me why, but I played it cool. "What's the deal?" I asked. I listened to his proposition and then made my decision. "We'll take it."

"I just faxed Meg Ryan's contract to her agent," Sam said. "What's your fax number?"

"Uhh...I just moved into a new office and don't have my fax machine set up yet," I said. "Just...uh...express it to me?"

"It's going in the package now," Sam said. "Been great doing business with you, Ali. Look, do me a favor, would ya? Swing a deal with that actor who played the daddy in that farm play. It's a minor role but I can discuss that with his agent."

I saw a quick way to make another five per cent. I was sure I could get that from Daddy's agent. Velda wouldn't mind working with him again; she'd grown to admire him. They were almost friends now.

"I'll look into that and get him to call you," I said. "Good luck with the show, Sam. Velda will see you in a week."

I hung up. I was flushed from top to bottom. Damn if I didn't do it! I got Velda a job! I walked into her bedroom, where she was pasting the Post article into her *My Favorite Field* scrapbook. It was already bulging with clippings.

"Vel, how does this sound to you? Three months in Alabama, Georgia, Mississippi and Louisiana, six grand a week, all expenses paid, in the lead role of a play?"

She smothered me in her thankfulness. After ungluing myself from her embrace, Velda began talking excitedly. "I'll be working in the USA!" she said, her eyes taking on a faraway look. "Down south! You know I'm really a Southern girl at heart. I can do the accent perfectly!" She began talking that way and it was pretty good. "Twenty-four thousand American dollars a month!" she exclaimed. Wow, she was right! We really were in the money. "And in another play! I was feeling so depressed already because this one was over and here you found me another one! And such an exotic one! Oh, Ali, my career has gone fabulous since you took me on."

For a moment there, I almost believed I did take Velda on as a client. Then I remembered she basically took me on, as did Joe. I was lucky to have such clients. "We'll go out and celebrate after my interview," I said. My impending interview didn't even worry me anymore; I was in too good a mood.

That reminded me. I had agent work to do. Velda gave me the name of Bill Dudley's agent and I went to phone her. Five minutes later, I was five per cent richer. Yeah, I was getting to like this job.

The phone rang again. With assurance radiating from my voice, I answered it. "Ali Kumplunkem?" a voice asked.

"Speaking," I said businesslike.

"Francis Ford Coppola."

I actually clutched the table. This couldn't be happening. My breath wouldn't come. Surely, surely, this man would not be calling me. "Ali?" Lord Coppola asked.

"Yes?" I gasped.

"I received the demo tape you sent me for Joe Smith."

"Yes," I gasped again.

"I like it," he simply said. "You sent it just in time. I was almost done casting *The Godfather IV*."

"Oh?" I squeaked. I hadn't realized he was casting anything.

"All the leads have been cast for months," he said. "I have a small role I'd like Joe to play. It's only about a dozen lines but if he works out, who knows? I always rehire actors I like."

"He'll take it," I managed to stammer out.

"Great. I'll put you through to the production coordinator and you two can hammer out a deal," Francis said. "Thanks again for sending me that tape."

"You're welcome," I said, but he'd already connected me to another guy. I was glad to be finished with Francis; he was too much for my sensibilities. I was put on hold and sat there, numb for a moment. Then, with building force, a realization hit me. *MY GOD! Ali Kumplunkem, you've reached the pinnacle of your current career already!* I would never be able to top this. I was glad to be taken off hold because the production coordinator brought me down to earth. I turned back into SuperAgent. "That sounds fine, sir," I said to the financial deal. "Do you think we can swing something else? Keep him around set for another week and if you need him, he's yours for nothing." That was readily agreed to. It may sound like an odd business arrangement but I knew Joe would appreciate being in the company of Coppola.

The doorbell sounded as I hung up. My former defensive attitude had left me. It was replaced by a cocky Ali Kumplunkem. I was ready for the interview.

To my surprise, I wasn't ready for it. They weren't the vultures I'd expected. Instead they were gracious, considerate and very attentive to everything I had to say. I told them they were the first to hear my big news and proceeded to tell them of Velda and Joe's good fortune.

"So you're a talent agent now?" Bud Whilt asked.

"That's right," I replied.

"How many clients do you have?"

"Only two so far," I answered, "but I've just opened my business."

"And look how well you've done already!" Bud said, scribbling some notes down. "How does it feel to be back in Canada?"

I praised this country. I didn't say I had friends in this country, a roof over my head and plenty of food to eat. He would have thought I'd spent the last year in Ethiopia. Instead, I complimented the beauty of Canada and its people.

"Do you think you'll ever go back to the States?" he asked.

"No," I answered. Not on your life.

"Not even if Fox TV or the New York Times wanted you?" Bud asked disbelievingly.

"I'm very happy to be HOME," I stated. "I love my new job and hope to succeed at it."

Bud made more notes then stood up. "Thank you, Ali," he said. "You've been very cooperative."

"Uh...when is this story coming out?" I asked.

"Most likely tomorrow," Bud said. "Thanks again." He left.

They were just too darn nice. The reporter didn't ask any embarrassing questions. The photographer took 200 digital photos of me, just to make sure one would turn out decent. Both treated me as if I were the First Lady of Canada.

I knew I was in for a set-up.

* * *

The next day, Velda was up early. She was going to a library to research her role. "I'm going to stay home and wait for that package from Sam Putnam," I said. "Can you pick up the Star on your way back?" In reality, I didn't want to leave the house. I pictured repercussions of the last time a feature story was done on me.

The package came and I was curiously studying the contract.

It all looked too wonderful to be true. Velda would be paid for this, for that and for everything left over. I didn't need a lawyer to tell me we had a legal, binding, lovely deal. My Grade Twelve education was enough. I signed for Velda, just as she walked in the front door.

"Did you get the paper?" I asked, running into the entrance. She was carrying an armful of Stars. I grabbed one off the top of the pile. "Did you read it yet?" I asked her.

"At the library," Velda said. "Ali, you're gonna love it!"

She turned to the story and there was my photo. I can't say I looked real pretty but I did look like I meant business. I quickly read the article and then went back to savor it. I was astounded. The reporter made me out to be some kind of world-class figure. I ranked in smarts with Henry Kissinger.

Then it finally hit me. I should have realized it sooner from all of Velda's chatter, but it took this article for it to hit home. Canada, my beloved country, approved and accepted me.

Why was that? Because I had worked in the U.S. of A. Sure, I'd bombed, but the big thing was that I made it to the States. Now I actually WAS somebody. At least in my country, which is all that mattered to me.

Velda started clipping one of the artless and singing, "More publicity, yeah, more publicity for me." The Star had included pictures of my two star clients and the local update on their careers. Then I remembered! Joe was flying in that day! I didn't want him getting the good news about his new job from some newspaper; and I knew he wasn't travelling with a cellphone. I prayed I could have the golden opportunity to tell him myself, perhaps to brag a bit.

I grabbed my datebook and glanced at one of the few entries. I saw the arrival of Joe's flight and figured, if I left immediately, I should just catch him.

The phone rang. "I'm not here!" I yelled at Velda. "I'm going to the airport to meet Joe!"

"Take my car," Velda said as she answered the phone. She cupped her hand over the receiver and said, "It's for you."

"Take a message," I said. I thought I heard Velda say, "Donald Sutherland?" but I was already flying out the door.

I arrived at the airport just as the American Airlines flight from Houston landed. For a couple minutes I felt uncomfortable. *How will it look when Joe sees me waiting for him? He'll get a weird vibe.* But then I told myself that, as an agent, I had a legitimate reason for being there.

I saw Joe emerge from customs. He walked past me, not seeing me. I didn't say anything; just studied him a moment. He was concentrating so hard, it was no wonder he didn't see me. "Joe," I simply said. His head shot up in amazement, but he didn't look around. "Joe!" I repeated.

He finally looked at me. "Alice!" he exclaimed. "I was just thinking about you."

"Really?" I asked like a giddy schoolgirl.

"What are you doing here?" he asked back.

"I thought I'd pick you up," I said. "Besides, I have some news."

"Yeah, me too," Joe said. "I need to talk to you, Alice."

"About the film?" I asked, concerned. "Was it that awful?"

"Oh, no," he replied. "It was OK."

"Well, I have to talk to you about something, too," I said, building up to the big surprise.

"I want to go first," Joe said solemnly. "Is that OK?"

"Sure," I said. My news could wait a while.

We got into Velda's car and I started driving him home. He didn't say a word. After ahem-ing a couple times, I finally had to come out and remind him. "Joe? You wanted to talk to me about something?"

"Yeah," he said, and nothing else. I knew I would just to have to wait until he was ready. I had to bite my tongue to withhold from spilling my good tidings.

Joe didn't have much baggage to take in. I stayed in the driver's seat, wondering if I should go in the house with him. He got his duffel bag out of the trunk, walked halfway up his sidewalk and then looked back at me. "Come in," he commanded.

I sat at his kitchen table and marveled a bit at the kind of fellow Joe was. There were 40 pieces of mail that he didn't even glance at. His answering machine was chockfull of messages but he didn't even bother to check them. He dropped his duffel in his room and came to sit at the table with me. We just looked at one another. It was beginning to get uncomfortable again. I was about to scream, "WHAAAT?" when Joe started talking.

"I was thinking about you a lot in Texas," he said. I waited for more but nothing came.

"I thought about you a lot, too," I said, feeling goofy afterwards.

"Were you dating while I was away?" he asked next.

My face gave my thoughts away. Why in the world was he asking me that? Why did he care? I just gawked at him then said, "No!" You would have thought he'd asked if I slept with a different man every night. "Why do you ask?" I really was curious.

"We used to have a pretty good thing together," Joe reminisced. I don't know if I'd say 'pretty good' but it was pretty alright. I nodded again. He thought some more then suddenly rushed his sentences. "Well, I was feelin' like I missed ya, and I started remembering the nights we'd spend at your place, and I know it was all my fault that we busted up. You didn't do a thing. And you know, Alice, you and me get along pretty good too. I've changed a lot and so have you. Do you think that maybe we can start...sort of...well, dating, although I hate that word. Can we just start being together again? Do you want to try it?" He finished and sat there like a frightened child.

The uncomfortable feeling I usually had around Joe

dissolved. It actually felt like I was washed free, cleansed, a murky yellow puddle settling at my feet. The feeling was replaced by a rosy glow.

I opened my mouth to speak. I hadn't realized what I was going to say but the simple truth spilled out. "Oh, Joe, I've missed you..."

AND WE KISSED! Delicious lips I'd never forgotten. The skinny frame my encircling arms knew so well. Our long kiss ended and we looked directly into each other's eyes. Without saying a word, we both got up and went into his bedroom.

Sex was spectacular. Of course, we were both trying and I knew that within a month we'd probably be down to twice a week, but it was good times right now. I noticed a change in myself. Before with Joe, I'd like to keep my pajama top on when we did it. I was ashamed of my big belly. I didn't mind when he didn't caress me. Now, I threw my body at him. He seemed appreciative of my new svelte figure and aggressive style. For the first time ever, we did it twice.

We were lying in each other's arms and I guess we both fell asleep. I woke up and looked at the clock. "Holy shit!" I yelled. "Midnight!"

Joe woke up. "Might as well stay here," Joe suggested.

"I've got Velda's car," I explained. "Shit, we've been asleep over six hours!"

"Did you have somewhere to go?" Joe asked.

"No, but Velda must be wondering what's up. Do you think it's too late to call?" I asked, then shook my head. "No, I'll just go home." Joe looked crestfallen. "I can stay over another night, Joe," I added reassuringly.

"'Night, Ali," he said, giving me a tender kiss.

"'Night, Joe," I said and started walking out the door when it hit me. "JOE! MY NEWS!"

"Oh, yeah," he remembered. "What is it?"

"I got you another film," I began.

Joe perked up maybe a smidgen. "Oh, good," he said. "What's it called?"

"*Godfather IV*," I said. His eyes did a weird dance; I could read them. *Godfather? As in de Niro and Pacino? She serious? Nah, must be a copycat film.*

"You sure it's called *Godfather IV*?" Joe asked questioningly.

"Yeah," I replied, then dropped the bomb. "The Francis Ford Coppola film."

Joe outdid himself the third time.

* * *

I snuck into the house around 3 a.m. There was a note waiting for me from Velda. *I don't know where you are,* the note said, *but WAKE ME UP the minute you get in. V.* Oh, oh, she was pissed off. I didn't exactly feel like catching hell at three in the morning and besides, I was too full of love and the smell of sex. I'd talk to her in the morning.

At 9 a.m. the next day, I was shaken awake. As soon as I saw it was Velda, I started sleepily explaining. "Sorry 'bout the car, Vel, but see, Joe and I decided we were in love..."

"I don't care about the car!" Velda yelled. "I wanted to talk to you last night! You're busy today! I've got three auditions, count them, three! And Joe's got a meeting with some director in town and your mother called to say she's coming down for a visit and..."

"What's going on?!" I yelled, sitting bolt upright in my bed.

"Oh, man, the second you left yesterday, the phone started ringing off the hook! All sorts of people..." Velda was interrupted by the doorbell.

I grabbed a housecoat and followed her out of the room. She let in a postman who had a Special Delivery letter for me. He passed a courier on his way out who had a package for me. A UPS van pulled up and a man walked up the sidewalk with a big bag. "You Ali Kumplunkem?" he asked. I was handed an armful of brown 8 x 10" envelopes. I recognized them. Photos, resumes, demo tapes.

At 9:02 precisely, the phone started ringing. "Are you taking on new clients?" consisted of 80% of the calls. Most of the mail dealt with people wondering the same thing.

Velda looked frazzled. I was dazzled. I took the phone off the hook and told Velda to sit down. "Velda," I soothed her, "have no fear. As of next week, I'll be in my own office." I smiled at the thought. "With a secretary." I was grinning now. "Three phone lines...a fax machine..." and suddenly I was sniffling. "Oh, Velda, can you believe this?"

"Are you happy?" Velda asked softly. Maybe she did realize what I'd been through.

"Happy?" I repeated. "Yes. Happy, scared, excited and looking forward to my next 50 years." I pulled out a photo from one of the envelopes. "I think I'm going to call Mr. Jamie Carlson in for an interview."

Yes, I was happy. I loved my country. My claim to fame was shame, but hey – I was given a second chance. God Save the Prime Minister.

- T H E E N D -

At Roundfire we publish great stories. We lean towards the spiritual and thought-provoking. But whether it's literary or popular, a gentle tale or a pulsating thriller, the connecting theme in all Roundfire fiction titles is that once you pick them up you won't want to put them down.